Jane de La Vaudère

Three Flowers
and
The King of Siam's Amazon

Translated and with an Introduction by

Brian Stableford

THIS IS A SNUGGLY BOOK

ISBN: 978-1-64525-018-0

Three Flowers
and
The King of Siam's Amazon

JANE DE LA VAUDÈRE was baptized Jeanne Scrive and was married to Camille Gaston Crapez, who began styling himself Crapez de La Vaudère after inheriting the Château de La Vaudère from his mother. Her prolific literary work is very various but she was assimilated to the Decadent Movement firstly because of two scandalously scabrous Parisian novels, *Les Demi-Sexes* (1897) and *Les Androgynes* (1903), and, more pertinently, because of a series of accounts of *moeurs antiques*, some of which—notably *Le Mystère de Kama* (1901)—set new standards of excess in their exotic eroticism and fascination with torture.

BRIAN STABLEFORD'S scholarly work includes *New Atlantis: A Narrative History of Scientific Romance* (Wildside Press, 2016), *The Plurality of Imaginary Worlds: The Evolution of French roman scientifique* (Black Coat Press, 2017) and *Tales of Enchantment and Disenchantment: A History of Faerie* (Black Coat Press, 2019). In support of the latter projects he has translated more than a hundred volumes of *roman scientifique* and more than twenty volumes of *contes de fées* into English. He has edited *Decadence and Symbolism: A Showcase Anthology* (Snuggly Books, 2018), and is busy translating more Symbolist and Decadent fiction.

His recent fiction, in the genre of metaphysical fantasy, includes a trilogy of novels set in West Wales, consisting of *Spirits of the Vasty Deep* (2018), *The Insubstantial Pageant* (2018) and *The Truths of Darkness* (2019), published by Snuggly Books, and a trilogy set in Paris and the south of France, consisting of *The Painter of Spirits*, *The Quiet Dead* and *Living with the Dead*, all published by Black Coat Press in 2019.

CONTENTS

Introduction / *vii*

Three Flowers of Sensuality / 3
The King of Siam's Amazon / 151

INTRODUCTION

This is the fourth of six projected volumes translating fiction by Jane de La Vaudère (15 April 1857-26 July 1908). Five of those volumes each contain two of her short novels, while the second in the series, *The Double Star and Other Occult Fantasies*, contains a selection of her short fiction. The first volume, *The Demi-Sexes and The Androgynes*, contains translations of *Les Demi-Sexes*, originally published by Paul Ollendorff in 1897, and *Les Androgynes, roman passionel*, originally published by Albert Méricant in 1903. The third volume contains translations of *Le Mystère de Kama, roman magique indou* (Ernest Flammarion, 1901) and *Les Courtisanes de Brahma* (Flammarion, 1903). The present volume contains translations of *Trois fleurs de volupté, roman javanais* (Flammarion, 1900) and *L'Amazone du roi de Siam* (Flammarion, 1902). The fifth volume, *Syta's Harem and Pharaoh's Lover*, contains translations of *Le Harem de Syta, roman passionel* (Méricant, 1904) and *L'Amante du Pharaon, moeurs antiques* (Jules Tallandier, 1905). The sixth volume, *The Witch of Ecbatana and The Virgin of Israel*, contains translations *of La Sorcière d'Ecbatane, roman fantastique* (Flammarion, 1906) and *La Vierge d'Israel, roman de moeurs antiques* (Méricant, 1906).

Jane de La Vaudère was baptized Jeanne Scrive; both her parents died when she was still a child, and in the social class to which her family belonged, which might be described as the "upper bourgeoisie," the standard practice when a young girl was orphaned at an early age was to put her in a convent, where she would be educated until her teens, and then marry her off as soon as possible. That appears to be what happened to Jeanne Scrive and her elder sister Marie. It is necessary to say "appears" because almost nothing is known for sure about Jane de La Vaudère's personal life and death, all of it covered by an obscurity that remains virtually impenetrable today, save for the recorded statements she made in a few newspaper interviews and a few other objectively determinable facts.

In one such interview La Vaudère said that while she was in the convent of Notre-Dame de Sion she seriously considered remaining there permanently, the idea of living as a nun having a certain romantic attraction, but she soon abandoned the idea. In fact, shortly after leaving the institution—when she apparently went to stay for a while with Marie, by then married to a military surgeon—she was married to Camille Gaston Crapez (1848-1912), who inherited the Château de La Vaudère in Parigné-l'Évêque in the Sarthe from his mother and styled himself thereafter Crapez de La Vaudère. The name with which she signed her books was not, as many sources report, a pseudonym, although she deleted the Crapez and anglicized her forename.

The Crapez de La Vaudères had one child, a son named Fernand, who apparently stayed with his father when his mother went to live in Paris, where she seems to have lived alone. Although she was never divorced, and her body was taken back to Parigné-l'Éveque for burial after her death in Paris, the separation appears to have been complete, no newspaper reports of her appearances at social events or interviews conducted at her home ever mention the presence of her husband. Nothing was reported about the circumstances of her death, and neither her husband nor her son appear to have been with her at the time; the unusual brevity of the death notices and the conspicuous absence of the customary post-mortem eulogies suggest a diplomatic silence, but we can only speculate as to what it was that was deliberately not being said about her sudden death at a relatively young age.

The circumstances of Jane de La Vaudère's early life evidently had a profound impact on her literary work, to which she turned a trifle late in her career. She initially attempted to make a career as an artist, and exhibited at the Paris Salon; when she decided that her real vocation was literary, she first began writing poetry, and then wrote for the stage. Her first collection of poetry, *Les Heures perdues* [The Lost Hours] (1889) appeared in the same year as the production of her one-act comedy *Le Modèle* [The Model]. Her verse is Romantic and might have seemed a trifle old-fashioned at the time of its publication; she was certainly not unaware of contemporary trends in Symbolist poetry, for she was a very voracious reader and her influences were eclectic. *Le Modèle* was the first of many frothy one-act comedies, usually written in verse and often performed with musical accompaniment—fifteen of them were collected in *Pour le Flirt! Saynètes modernes* [approximately, Just For Fun, modern satirettes] (1905)—but she also wrote a few longer comedies and dramas.

She continued to write poetry and plays alongside her prose fiction, but there are very striking differences between her work in the three genres, and her prose work also shows sharp generic divisions. It is not unusual for writers to manifest seemingly different world-views in their prose fiction and their work for the stage, especially if the latter mostly consists of vaudevilles written as pure entertainment while the former is more earnest and intense, but in La Vaudère's case the difference is extreme. Even in her contemporary Paris-set novels, which often feature female characters not unlike those routinely featured in her stage comedies—young socialites, actresses and artists' models—the stories are much more acerbic, but the remarkable series of exotic novels set in far-flung places and times that make up the last four volumes of the present series of translations are very different indeed in their attitude and intensity.

La Vaudère's first novel, *Mortelle étreinte* [Mortal Embrace] (1891) is the story of a young orphan brought up in a convent who then goes to live with a relative, where she continues to live in virtual seclusion, in the psychological environment of her vivid imagination and the books she reads in abundance. She knows nothing about the real world and is utterly unready to cope with her own hectic emotions when she is first attracted to a man—a man who is also greatly attracted to her, but is, from every other viewpoint, quite unsuitable and incapable of providing her with the existential anchorage and security that she needs and desires.

The basic features of that story-line were to recur again and again in the author's work, even in the most bizarre décor. Its melodramatic intensity is inevitably restrained in *Mortelle étreinte* by the conventions of the society in which it is set, but when it is removed to ancient India or ancient Babylon, in the author's accounts of *moeurs antiques*, such shackles no longer apply and the pitch of that intensity is turned up to a level unequaled in the work of any other writer of the era. The sensation of having been brought up in an artificial environment, with little or no parental guidance, and then thrust into a world equipped with hopes and expectations that are bound to be betrayed, is developed in story after story, in variants that are extraordinarily wide-ranging, often wildly exaggerated, and almost always brutally tragic.

Following the publication of her second novel, *Rien qu'amante* [Only a Lover] (1893), La Vaudère devoted her principal effort to novels, although she contributed weekly articles to *La Presse* between 1897 and 1901 and then went on to supply a long sequence of unreprinted short stories to the weekly supplement of the daily newspaper *La Lanterne* in 1901-3. She published a good deal of poetry in the same newspaper, and several further poetry collections. As well as her solo work for the theater she adapted a short story by Émile Zola for the Grand Guignol and collaborated with a number of other writers on theatrical work, including Félicien Champsaur and Aurélian Scholl.

Once begun, her literary production rapidly became unusually prolific, and she published more than twenty novels between 1894 and her death in 1908. Seven more appeared posthumously under her name. It is unclear why she wrote in such profusion, and even if she needed the money, that was surely not the only reason. She certainly seems to have been avid for success, however, trying out several popular formulae in her varied fiction, as well as deliberately plowing new literary ground in order to fish for something sensational.

The direction that La Vaudère's later work took seems to have been largely defined by the success of her first best-seller, the controversial *Les Demi-Sexes*, whose *succès de scandale* she tried hard to repeat in one of the strands of her subsequent work, to considerable effect. Equally important, however, was the evident inspiration she took from the novel that was the great best-seller of the era, Pierre Louÿs; *Aphrodite, moeurs antiques* (1896), which sold three hundred thousand copies and, inevitably, launched a bandwagon chased by many Parisian publishers, including Ernest Flammarion and especially Albert Méricant, who became La Vaudère's second major publisher in the last few years of her life, and was the publisher of most of the posthumous works signed with her name.

La Vaudère's first venture into exotic erotica, the Java-set *Trois fleurs de volupté* (1900; tr. as "Three Flowers of Sensuality") is not set in the distant past, and it owes something to the fiction produced in celebration of the symbolically important French notion of an existentially-enlightening "voyage to the Orient." La Vaudère was presumably aware of the stories set in Java by the Romantic writer Joseph Méry, including the novella "Le Diamant aux mille facettes," in *Nuits d'Orient* (1854) and the three-volume novel *Les Damnés de Java* (1855), and the novel is as much a celebration of exoticism as it is of eroticism. It foregrounds one of La Vaudère's recurrent fascinations with regard to exotic mores—dancing girls kept and raised in closed religious communities dedicated to the celebration of female deities. Of all the fanciful images of that kind of community contained in her works, the one featured in *Trois fleurs de volupté* is the one that suggests most strongly that their imaginative bedrock is the author's own experience of having spent her childhood and early adolescence in a convent. Although the "duennas" in charge of the bedayas' training are not a straightforward substitute for Catholic nuns, and "the enchantress Kidoul" is certainly not a simple clone of the Virgin Mary, the echoes are sufficiently sonorous to make the connection, and the imagery of the novel thus provides an imaginative bridge of sorts to the description of the closed society of the temple dancers of *Le Mystère de Kama*.

It is possible, of course, that La Vaudère's frequent depiction of very young girls obsessed with sex is completely imaginary, as is her frequent allegation (but not depiction) of the brutal sexual exploitation of those same young girls by priests; nothing like those depictions features in her novels of contemporary French life, in spite of her occasional ventures in pushing the envelope of the conventionally-unmentionable. On the other hand, it would perhaps be surprising if such imaginations did not have psychological roots of some kind, and in the attempt to determine what those roots might be, *Trois Fleurs de volupté* probably provides more clues than the later novels; it is, at any rate, the only one that is a sentimental love story rather than an account of brutal exploitation, although the hyper-sensitized modern eye might not be able to appreciate that difference fully, or even at all. Although Soakia is no younger that Shakespeare's Juliet or Bernardin de Saint-Pierre's Virginie in *Paul et Virginie* (1788), Stéphane is a good deal older than Romeo or Paul, and that necessarily changes the aspect of her great romance, though perhaps not as much as the strange avidity with which she involves her sisters in it. There are, however, no prizes for decoding the sexual symbolism of the volcano and its climactic eruption, and the effects of that eruption, including the final ironic plot-twist, which are telling.

Trois fleurs de volupté is not the most bizarre of La Vaudère's exotic novels, and hence not the most dreamlike in terms of its weird imagery, but it might be the one in which the author's own sexual fantasies are transfigured in the most interesting and revealing way. She was over forty when she wrote it (although she lied about her age and might only have represented herself as thirty-nine at the time) but she certainly retained a sharp memory of the days when she had been utterly innocent, free from all the corruptions that, in her own expressed estimation, made her a typical product of "extreme civilizations." If the plots of her books can be taken as evidence, she seems to have been convinced that ideal amour—the only thing that could possibly make life worth living—was absolutely impossible for anyone thus corrupted, and could only be achieved by the innocent, whose age, in the eyes of French society, disqualified them from looking for it, let alone finding it . . . although, she was free to imagine, that things might conceivably be different in Java.

In the order of publication of La Vaudère's works, *Trois fleurs de volupté* was followed by *Les Mystères de Kama*, but that was not necessary the work she wrote, or at least planned to write, immediately thereafter. In the works recorded in *Trois fleurs de volupté* as "en preparation," *Les Amours d'un fakir*, which was presumably the working title of *Le Mystère de Kama*, is listed second, after *L'Amazone du roi de Siam* (1902), which might, therefore, have been written earlier, or perhaps simultaneously. Either way, however, there was a gigantic imaginative leap between the exotic eroticism featured in *Trois fleurs de volupté* and its successor. Although there is a passing mention of a "*jardin des supplices*" in the earlier novel, nothing of that sort is actually featured therein, but *L'Amazone du roi de Siam* features an actual torture garden of gruesome atrocity, and that novel, *Le Mystère de Kama* and *Les Courtisanes de Brahma*, all feature physical violence and torture on an extraordinarily abundant scale, replicated in at least three of the further novels in the series.

At first glance, the fascination with torture displayed in La Vaudère's erotic fantasies might seem odder than the fascination with childhood sexuality, on the part of a small, seemingly frail, upper-class woman in her forties. To some of her contemporaries, at least, both fascinations seemed shockingly indecent, strangely perverse and frankly sadistic, although the politeness with which her novels were reviewed by the daily newspapers of the day, almost always in gushingly complimentary terms, also seems a trifle odd to the modern eye. It seems probable, in retrospect, that *L'Amazone du roi de Siam was* partly a reaction to another notorious Decadent novel of the era, which, although it did not sell as well as *Aphrodite*, certainly attracted a lot of attention: Octave Mirbeau's *Le Jardin des supplices* (1899; tr. as *Torture Garden*). In *L'Amazone du roi de Siam*, La Vaudère seems to have deliberately set out to describe a torture garden that would make Mirbeau's look tame.

Like the heroines of *Trois fleurs de volupté*, Kali-Yana inhabits and has been brought up within a secluded all-female society. Her age is not specified, but she is certainly nubile, albeit recently arrived at puberty. However, she has had to take a vow of chastity, like a nun, even though her vocation is military rather than religious—a vow whose restriction, accepted during innocence, becomes awkward when her hormones start stirring. She is offered a way out of that dilemma, but it does not appeal to her, even though she has been frankly warned, at the very outset of the novel, that disaster will follow if she does not take it. Like a moth to a flame, she is inexorably drawn by fatal temptation, so powerfully that none of the horrors she experiences in consequence—which proceed in crescendo to an atrocious extreme—can deflect her from her obsession.

The novel also presents the first of La Vaudère's several depictions of Decadent dictators corrupted absolutely by absolute power, in the sadistic Phaja-Tak, the King of Siam, who became the prototype of Shah Jahan in *Les Courtisanes de Brahma*, Darius in *La Sorcière d'Ecbatane* and Belsharuzur in *La Vierge d'Israel*—although all four are effectively clones of Diodorus Siculus' Sardanapalus, the imaginary last king of Assyria, who became a symbolic exemplar of the ultimate effects of cultural and moral Decadence, especially in the eyes of the *fin-de-siècle* Symbolists. The characterization of such figures by La Vaudère is interestingly ambiguous, in that all of them appear to be internally conflicted in a fashion not dissimilar to many of La Vaudère's male characters who are far less powerful, including Mappy in *Trois fleurs de volupté*; Phaja-Tak, in particular, seems to be representative for La Vaudère of an inescapable male existential dilemma complementary to the inescapable female existential dilemma in which Soakia and Kali-Yana find themselves trapped.

Exploring the possible psychological roots of such strange imaginings is always a speculative and problematic business, in which certainty is far out of reach and even plausibility is difficult to obtain, but that does not reduce the temptation. There is an inevitable temptation to charge writers describing scenes of gruesome torture as "sadistic," and it is necessarily the case that they credit sadistic motives to the characters responsible for the described torture, but that sets aside the crucial question of whether the author is inviting the reader to identify with the torturer or the victim. Invariably, in La Vaudére's case, her narrative voice shares the distress of the victims and witnesses of torture, especially when they are her heroines, and offers the same facility to her readers.

La Vaudère's most extreme deployment of atrocious imagery—the repeated torture of Kali-Yana in *L'Amazone du roi de Siam*—is certainly a compassionate nightmare, not a sadistic one, and the same is true of the ordeals to which many of her other heroines are subject, which frequently feature extravagant and exotic mental torment even when no blood is shed. Significantly, the few who avoid mental torment entirely—most conspicuously, Soakia and her sisters in *Trois fleurs de volupté*—still end up dead, although La Vaudère always keeps in reserve the possibility that the pain of dying, and even the pain of prolonged torture, might be completely anesthetized by the effects of boundless amour, and she always remains aware that the fact of dying young is bound to spare novice lovers from inevitable disappointments and agonies to come.

There is no cause for surprise in the fact that almost all of La Vaudère's literary work focuses intently on the literary mythos of amour—the idea and the ideal of an exclusive, omnipotent and all-consuming passion—because that had been common-place in the work of female writers since the pioneering days of Mademoiselle de Scudéry. La Vaudère's work, however, represents that ideal with an intensity, extremism and perversity that might be difficult of achievement for someone not brought up in remote isolation from the real world in an ambience of assertive religious pretence. For La Vaudère, perhaps to a greater extent than any other writer, the idea of extreme amour embodies both the idea of Paradise and the idea of the Inferno; it is simultaneously the most sublime exaltation and the ultimate torment, the only really worthwhile desire there is, but an essentially self-destructive desire, opening a gateway to damnation and eternal, inextinguishable, volcanic fire.

The two novels contained in the present volume display that idea at its purest, in two different, but equally striking ways; although remarkable individually, they are even more remarkable in juxtaposition, especially as the author seems to have moved from the composition of one to the composition of the other almost without psychological transition. Both remain fascinating, although the one that the author and her contemporary readers presumably regarded as the more shocking of the two, *L'Amazone du roi de Siam*, is likely to seem less disturbing today than its companion, given the manner in which moral sensitivities have shifted in the interim.

The translation of *Trois fleurs de volupté* was made from a copy of the Flammarion edition. The translation of *L'Amazone du roi de Siam* was made from the copy of the Flammarion edition reproduced in the International Archive Digital Library at *archive. org*.

—Brian Stableford

Three Flowers of Sensuality

PART ONE

I
Nostalgia

In the shadow of varigniers, teaks and tamarinds, near strange flowers with heavy and delicious scents, three Javanese dolls are walking, dancers of the Susuhunan, "the beseeched," the master of Surakarta. Those bedayas are adorable in finesse and grace, with their onyx irises mounted in the blue-tinted nacre of the eye, beneath long eyelids that one might think edged with feathers, their minuscule mouths always serious and the amber skin of their slender bodies. They advance slowly, holding one another by the waist and whispering trivia in a soft voice. The wind agitates the silver lotuses that they wear in their hair, wound in large ebony spirals and cut in front in such a fashion as to form seven gilded or crimson triangles over the edge of the forehead.

Behind their necks float clusters of little white and blue bells, and their faces are tinted with yellow boreh, which is the imperial color. They are sisters, and their names are Soakia, Wakiem and Taminah.[1] Soakia, the eldest, is twelve years old; she is the most reasonable of the three and the most elaborately adorned. Large golden flowers with hearts of precious stones bloom on her incarnadine velvet bodice, which leaves her arms free. Her waist is tightened by a belt of plaques, alternately mat and shiny, sealed by an emerald clasp. A white silk sarong embroidered the fabulous animals and flamboyant red corollas falls all the way to her ankles, circled with bracelets studded with cabochons.

---

1 These were the names of three Javanese dancing girls who performed with a troupe at the Paris Exposition of 1889 and became briefly famous; the names had been borrowed by other writers, including Maurice Vaucaire, in the nouvelle "Monsieur Tabouret" (1889) and Catulle Mendès.

Wakiem is clad in somber blue and Taminah in yellow.

They leave in their passage a mild odor of melati, which is the jasmine of that region, and that perfume, in the mystery of things, seems to be their little soul, which flies toward calices.

"Wakiem," sighs Soakia, "I'm bored today! Our life is sad."

But Taminah protests. "What do you lack, then? You're the most fêted of the Susuhunan's dancers, and none of us has received as many gifts. Look, the bracelets of your ankles are worth a fortune, and I'd give all my jewels for that emerald!"

In a nostalgic voice, Soakia goes on: "Warm gusts heavier than the vapors of a volcano are exhaled from the depths of my being. Breaths brush me with a dolorous caress that envelops me continually. Don't you sense anything similar, my sisters?"

"No," said the little girls, fixing their anxious and curious gazes on the bedaya.

"Are you happy with our lot?"

"Perhaps . . . we don't know."

Insouciantly, they have collected scarcely fleshy lotuses from the edge of a pond, with which they have surrounded their shoulders and their slender hips, pausing sometimes to follow the sustained flight of a migratory bird in the turquoise sky. In the distance, a herdsman is modulating the tune of an ancient gending on his flute, of which he does not know the meaning, but which he repeats religiously; and the little dancers listen, charmed, to the plaintive notes, which resemble the amorous appeal of a turtle-dove.

The enervating heat weighs more heavily, causing the invisible beasts that populate the bushes to swoon, along with all the wide-open calices by the roadside, the bees and the dragonflies that settle, quivering, at the hazard of the kiss.

"I would like," says Soakia, "to wander in the sleepy countryside, further away, ever further away . . . to know unexperienced caresses and embraces, to inspire a tender and powerful amour. I would like, with a man, to penetrate the mystery of woods, and profound solitudes, and, in order to be loved forever, to visit Borobudur, who grants the wishes of virgins."

"Borobudur, the supreme Buddha, no longer protects us. Allah alone is great!"

"Personally," affirms Wakiem, "I believe in the legends of spirits and benevolent gods. I have often prayed to the enchantress Kidoul to emerge from her coral palace guarded by djinn, to bring me pearls and those pretty red seashells that go so well with my dark hair."

But Taminah, the skeptic, laughing, ripostes: "And Kidoul has never come! She's asleep in the seaweed, and doesn't care about adorning the little dancers of the Susuhunan."

Without replying, Wakiem has opened her blue silk sarong, embroidered with chimeras, over her breast, and has shown her companions a bizarre stone with reflections of opals and aquamarines, sustained by a thin golden chain.

Soakia lets the jewel slide through her slender fingers, covered in gems, and exclaims, laughing: "Oh, what a strange thing! Is it a sacred scarab with a metallic carapace, a moonstone found in the pale reeds haunted by malaria, or a seashell from the distant isles?"

Taminah waxes ecstatic in her turn. "Is it a cerulean apple of beryl, or a ball of amaldine, olivine or chrysoprase? Tell us what it is, Wakiem."

"It's a fetish that the enchantress Kidoul brought me, while I was asleep near the pond of pink lotuses. I found it on my knees when I woke up."

The brown bedayas consider Wakiem respectfully, remaining thoughtful.

"Since the enchantress wishes you well, it's necessary to ask her to favor our escape."

"Oh, Soakia! We'd be captured and condemned to death."

"In what tortures!"

"Burned alive or crucified . . ."

"Or sealed in a goatskin with a snake and a cat . . ."

"You can't think that!"

"Why run away? We have sarongs of all colors, necklaces, jeweled pins and clasps. Our master doesn't refuse us anything."

But Soakia raises her little head proudly.

"He's a master, and a master that we can't cherish! Believe me, nothing is worth as much as liberty."

"Liberty is poverty."

"Bah! We'll dance along the roads, like the public rong'geng; we'll eat fruits, we'll sleep in barns or ditches full of moss."

"There are reptiles in the ditches . . . green snakes and striped spiders."

"They won't do us any harm. Are we not sacred bedayas, protected by a charm?"

"I'm afraid!"

"I'm afraid!"

"Don't you have the gift of the enchantress Kidoul, which will bring us good luck?"

"But how will we escape?"

"Once out of the Kraton, we won't know which way to go."

"We've never left this palace!"

Putting her arms round the necks of the little dancers, Soakia brings their heads closer to her own, and whispers; "Have you never seen a troop of public dancers led by a thin, sad figure passing by, from the edge of the terraces?"

"Yes, only yesterday . . ."

"Well, that's Mappy, who has stopped more than once to exchange a few words with me. I've told him about my ennui . . . and he's consented to take us into his wandering troupe."

"What! You've dared to talk to that man!"

"You aren't afraid of his black magic, reckless little sister?"

"It's said that the rong'geng, with their leader, evoke evil spirits and cast spells on those who listen to them!"

"All that is folly," Soakia continues, shaking her delicate willful head. "Mappy only wishes us good, and he'll treat us in accordance with our rank. In any case, we can't travel the country on our own, and the dancers of the highways will be precious guides."

"Then everything's already arranged for our flight?"

"Yes, at the first signal Mappy will wait for us at the door to the garden."

"May Kidoul watch over us, and may the enchantress guide us!"

"I want to dance for her."

On the velvet grass, Soakia has taken off her thin sandals, and has started gliding lightly, her naked feet laden with rings and the bracelets of her ankles, linked with little chains, clinking: a phantom of hieratic and passionate amour, a frail idol descended from her niche . . . Ardent breaths agitate the silver lotuses in her hair, the odor of melati is exhaled more forcefully from her saffron body. On her forehead, the seven gilded triangles are displayed, fatefully; her eyes semi-revulsed, plunge beneath her voluptuously weary eyelids, and the magnified arch of her eyebrows remains motionless.

Wakiem and Taminah have each taken their rebab—a kind of viol in the form of a calabash, whose long ivory stem is twisted in the decorative style of Indo-Chinese temples—and they make the two yellow copper strings vibrate with a bow coated with resin.

Adorable beneath the trees in flower, which let petals of snow and blood fall upon them, they turn and turn in the soft chant of the voluptuous gending, going back and forth in a gradual movement, pausing momentarily, and resembling then, in their brilliant garments, butterflies asleep in the calices of roses, butterflies whose folded wings will open at the slightest contact, and float into the azure in pursuit of the eternal dream.

II
Projects of Flight

Two old ladies in brown sarongs have come to look for the little dancers in order to take them back into the Campong. Everything is calm. Only the melancholy plaint of the toads pierces the profound silence, with a kind of double note. The three bedayas traverse the deserted rooms of the pendoppo, and reach their private apartment, where other frail and decorated creatures similar to them are crouched, cross-legged, on cushions or mats, with filigree caskets in front of them containing betel leaves, catechu and tobacco. Some, mechanically, are making the strings of their rebabs vibrate, others are eating flower preserves or carefully combing one another's hair, enlarging their eyes over the yellow boreh that already coats their faces, or retouching the gold of the seven triangles on their foreheads or the cracking rouge on their lips.

Two very fragile bedayas, barely eight years old, have painted the minuscule nipples of their breasts red, and have put so many necklaces on their bare shoulders that they seem to be buckling under the burden. Laughing, they rattle their heavy pendants and pull one another's hair with the gestures of loose-limbed monkeys, as charming and unreal and hashish visions. One child on all fours imitates a panther, uttering muted roars, and advances menacingly toward another, with pale bronze skin, who is playing dead, her arms dangling and her eyes closed.

The old women go from one to another, silently, straightening them up and rebuking them.

"You're free this evening," they say. "The master is resting."

"Is the master ill?" Soakia asks.

"The master is sad; he prefers solitude."

"We aren't going to dance for him?"

"You won't be dancing. But it's necessary to rehearse the steps of the pantomime that you'll be performing tomorrow."

"Work? You said, duennas, that we were free?"

"Free to chat and laugh, free to retain your daytime sarongs and to sleep, like little animals drunk on light and perfumes, but the time hasn't yet come. On your feet, let's go!"

The girls stretch themselves, yawn, stick out their meager breasts and tighten the metal girdles around their curved waists. The strings of the rebabs grate dolorously under the bow, and, in an adagio movement, the theme of the gending that will serve as the symphony for the mime becomes precise. Adapting their gestures to the slow rhythm, the bedayas, becoming melancholy and proud little idols again, advance two by two, almost without lifting their bare feet, constellated with rubies and sapphires.

While they disappear under the curtains that separate their apartment from the rehearsal room, Soakia draws Wakiem and Taminah into a redoubt illuminated from above by a multicolored rose-window, and which is garnished with soft fabrics and cushions indurated with precious embroideries.

"Here, darlings, we can talk."

"I'm trembling," says Wakiem.

"Let's speak in low voices," Soakia recommends. "It's necessary that no one hears even the murmur of our words; we'd be betrayed."

"What do you intend to do?" interrogates Taminah, whose burned topaz eyes are gleaming like those of felines.

"I want to run away tomorrow, with you," Soakia affirms, "if your courage can support us. Mappy has been alerted. Just now I wrapped a paper ribbon around one of my golden pins and threw it to the foot of the terrace"

"*Run away* is easy to say . . . but the Campong is well guarded and we'll never get over the walls of the alun-alun."

"It's necessary to put old Sukuta to sleep, who has the keys of the little door. Mappy has given me a sprig of the herb that procures pleasant dreams. Look . . ."

Soakia takes a handful of gray herbs from beneath her sarong, which emit an odor of bitter almonds.

"That's true—but we won't do any harm to old Sukuta?"

Wakiem bursts into pretty laughter. "We'll procure her dreams woven in gold and silk. It will doubtless be the first time in her life that she'll think that she's loved . . ."

"Loved all the way?"

"To the kiss on the lips of infinite ecstasy!"

"Lucky Sukuta!"

"Which of us will prepare the beverage?"

"Me," says Soakia, bravely, "and the old woman won't leave a drop, because I'll mix it with the sugared wine of the blue lotus, which she prefers to any other liquor. And we'll amuse ourselves at her expense before we leave."

"She's so funny when she's drunk."

"Ssh! Here she comes . . . Tomorrow, after the fête . . ."

Sukuta, the wisps of her gray hair wrapped in a sort of head-dress embroidered with pearls, the flaps of which, like the ears of a bat, spread out to either side of her face, finally comes to look for the three bedayas. With the tip of her bony finger she shows them the door, while a hurried flood of insults falls from her toothless mouth.

The cavernous rumble of gongs and the shrill clamor of tom-toms arrives from outside, while the little dancers flutter around to a livelier rhythm, rehearsing the sacred pantomime. Then their infantile voices rise up, holding the same note in unison, indefi-nitely; their hands have strange palpitations, like the wing-beats of dragonflies rocked by light breezes.

Silky scarves float over their shoulders, and their torsos undu-late with a sway so regular that it seems as if there is only a single mime reflected in a series of mirrors.

Soakia, more learned than the others, has regulated the dance, a flower-woman and woman-flower, with unforgettable metamorphoses.

For a long time the girls move their bare feet with rosy toe-nails over the pink marble where they glide smoothly; then they prostrate themselves in order to honor Allah, perhaps with regret for the old divinities, whose grim beauty their nostalgic little souls understand better. Secretly, they address prayers not only to Borobudur but to Shiva, and even to the monstrous Durga, who have survived in spite of the new religions. A strange confu-sion of notions and symbols reigns within them, a mixture of Brahmanism, Buddhism and Mohammedanism, which exalts without appeasing their anxious sensibility.

After the frugal evening meal, the bedayas have lain down on immaculate mats, among sumptuous cushions, and, under the gauze mosquito-nets, they resemble shiny scarabs, insects of sapphire and emerald caught in collectors' nets.

To help them go to sleep the duennas imitate on quivering angklungs the tremolos of the wind in the foliage, while, outside, the amorous plaint of the toads still resounds.

III
Preparations

Soakia gets up first. She summons her companions.

"It's this evening."

"This evening, after the fête . . ."

"Be ready."

"We'll make a packet of our scarves, our jewels and all the most precious things we have."

"Don't forget your rebabs, for it will be necessary for us to dance on the roads to earn our living, with the vagabond rong'geng."

"We'll only dance when we're far enough away from the Kraton, for someone might recognize us and send us back to the Susuhunan."

"That mustn't happen; it would mean death."

"Or eternal reclusion."

"This evening, then, at the little door of the alun-alun. Our bare feet won't make any noise in the sand."

"In the darkness," says Soakia, "I'll take you by the hand . . ."

"We'll wait for you immediately after the sacred pantomime. Be exact . . ."

Sukuta, the old woman, looks at them suspiciously, and they turn away in order to laugh at her surly face.

"Did you see the witch?"

"The red bat!"

"The horned viper!"

"She'll be humbler tomorrow!"

"Why are you putting on parade sarongs in the morning?" Sukuta demanded. "They'll be dirty for the fête. And that triple row of black pearls with the cabochons of pink coral? For whose benefit is so much magnificence?"

"For yours, Sukuta!" exclaims Wakiem, whose joy is escaping in silvery cascades.

The old woman shakes the plushy wings of her headdress, and goes away mumbling; the three bedayas kiss one another on the lips in an ardent desire for deliverance.

The bleak hours of the day drag on in the habitual occupations of the Kraton. Outside, corteges of rong'geng, the public dancers, pass by, accompanied by their musicians. At times, a scrap of harmony is audible, and the roll of buffalo-hide drums, which the vagabonds strike in cadence with their hands. Shrill voices offer conserves, dried fish and rice cakes; the little bells of oxen rattle in the distance, accompanied by the guttural cries of the pastors leading the herds.

The bedayas have prayed, chatted, and coated themselves with rare essences that surround them, so to speak, with a halo of aromas. Over a first layer of bitter-scented myrrh they have placed a pure and sweet cedar oil, heightened with the red emanations of oliban. They have passed a brush steeped in yellow boreh over their bright bronze shoulders, have gilded their lips and the seven triangles of their forehead, caressed their eyelashes with a little brush covered in black powder, and have elongated their eyes toward their temples with streaks of lilac paint. Their virginal teeth have not yet been turned brown by the habit of chewing tobacco, nor deformed by filing; they are as bright as fresh almonds in the painted pulp of the mouth. But those little mouths are almost always serious, and the gaze of the admirably onyx irises, speckled with tawny sparks, is melancholy.

Upright in their simarres patterned with blue flames, steeped in effluvia, their arms tucked behind the back, they remain motionless while slaves enliven their beauty. At times, however, frissons pass over them, and the gems of their robes suddenly sparkle, stirred by the emotion of their breasts.

A few bedayas—a strange whim—have hair discolored by salts and tinted artificially with pink or mauve reflections. All of them are small, scarcely developed, almost boyish, seeming by turns perverse and mystical little girls. Very slim, but nevertheless slightly plump, they have the faces of kittens drinking milk, their eyes half-closed in temporary ecstasy, and passing the sharp tips of their tongues over their quivering lips.

"Be careful, Sukuta, you're tickling my ear with your brush!"

"You're pulling my hair . . ."

"These flowers are too white . . . I look like a corpse!"

"You're hurting my nipples! Is it really necessary to gild the tips?"

"All these essences are intoxicating us frightfully! We're like bees at dusk!"

"You've forgotten my earrings, Kroum!"

"This belt is bruising my hips, Schaoul!"

"I want my chrysoprase clasp."

"I want my peridot bracelets."

"That buckle is too low down."

"That lotus on my neck . . . oh, I'm going mad!"

A thousand cries and a thousand complaints overlap. The little dancers want to be obeyed, and become irritated to the extent of striking their slaves when their desires are not satisfied immediately.

The day dies slowly, and Surakarta wakes up for the fête. The gongs vibrate in the campong, interrupted by shrill tom-toms and the sobbing notes of viols or flutes. Other metal instruments, under the percussion of hammers and sticks, carillon like bells. It is a barbaric and picturesque symphony, a savage transposition of European music that no description can render.

The crowd is beginning to assemble, turbulent and impatient. The Susuhunan, or sultan, is about to give an audience and produce his sacred mimes—a hundred and fifty frail bedayas who never leave the Kraton and are only seen on days of solemnities, so ornamented and painted that they seem to be disquieting apparitions of an unknown world, creatures of mildness or malediction.

The sultan is the most important of the kings of Java. He has been obliged to accept the conditions of the Dutch, who, in exchange for that obedience, pay him an annual income of four million florins. But the dynastic fanaticism of the Javanese would make our more ardent monarchs pale. It is with idolatry that they carry out their master's will, and no monarch, in spite of his apparent submission to a foreign power, was ever more respected. Apart from the income that the Dutch guarantee him, the sultan is the proprietor of considerable agricultural wealth and maintains at his expense in the Kraton a population of ten thousand indigenes, soldiers, officers, aristocrats and personnel of every sort.

The service in the palace is performed exclusively by women; it occupies more than three thousand of them.

Soakia has reason to fear, for the palace is guarded night and day, and flight seems very reckless . . .

IV
The Fête

Night is falling. In the Kraton, the mirror of the fish-ponds reflects the low buildings shaded by clove-trees and bamboos. Further away, the brick chimneys of factories of aromatics are smoking, and those of merchants of every sort, who see subtle spices, delicate glassware as elegant as the calices of flowers, objects carved from odorous wood, gems mounted in copper or silver, plant essences, pastes of powdered stone for polishing the skin, Asiatic rosellas with aquamarine plumage, ready-charmed snakes, bitter mandrake liquor, and large metal mirrors surrounded by precious arabesques.

Near the doors, the helmets of the sultan's militia are reddening. On both sides of the central avenue the crowd advances, composed of semi-naked individuals, a legion of heaven and hell, ardent and silent before the orchestras disposed at regular intervals, whose musicians play impassively, clad in bright pink, lilac and blue.

The odor of bodies rubbed with oil makes the atmosphere heavy.

Here and there, lighted fires indicate the dwellings of prostitutes or seeresses. Svelte in their violet simarres, brown virgins with silver clasps fixed to their breasts and hips are stimulating flaming embers for the altars of perfumes. Others are carrying cakes and flowery branches. Saffron-painted dwarfs are leaning against the arches of vestibules in their yellow robes, jostling one another and laughing.

Here come the mandarins, dignitaries and army officers armed with pikes and terrible krises, coiffed in tall helmets and clad in red, who greet one another solemnly.

Sheaves of halberds loom up at intervals outside, in front of the palace surrounded by high walls that flank white minarets. Only four doors give access to it, and the curious, ever more numerous, are densely packed in order to see the agents and the princes pass who traverse the interior courtyards and florid terraces illuminated by myriads of torches. Each portico is guarded by a bellicose picket of soldiers, lances in hand and black and gold turbans on their heads.

Idols taken from the temple of Borobudur open eyes devoid of gazes over all that magnificence. The great Buddhas are crouching, as in the niches, but they no longer have their attributes or their aureoles and, sadly, their lotus flower is devoid of petals in the emptiness of so many religious enemies.

The standard, ornamented with a fantastic bird decorated with old and precious stones, is lowered before each dignitary who enters into the principal courtyard, surrounded by a colonnade of pink and green marble. In the center rises the pendoppo, an open pavilion whose base is porphyry and its roof sandalwood. The interior is charged with a thousand sculpted arabesques, and the exterior presents the svelte curves and contorted stages of a Chinese temple. The black or white tiaras made of rice straw that rajahs wear can be seen.

In the alun-alun an absolute silence reigns. Officers arranged to either side of the perron that gives access to the pendoppo are silent, respectfully awaiting the arrival of the Susuhunan, whose fête is being celebrated.

He cannot be long delayed. With sabbatical gestures, young women laden with rings and jade bracelets, kneeling in the midst of cushions, are burning powders of myrrh and red sandalwood and grains of olibanum in cassolettes enameled with sardonyxes and opals, or agitating ostrich flabella at the end of long golden reeds.

But here comes the sultan, decorated with precious stones. With a sun of diamonds on his breast and a spray of emeralds on his forehead, he is resplendent and disconcerting. In his desiccated visage, a strange, feverish, enigmatic gaze is shining. His lips are contracted in a sad smile, which causes the extremities of his long moustaches to stand up, and he makes his way to his throne slowly, in the midst of members of his family, who crouch down as he passes, their folded legs dissimulated under the broad pleats of sarongs.

When everyone has taken his place, slaves circulate with flowers and fruits, pannags, unctuous herbs, peacocks ornamented with all their feathers, cedrats, insects pickled in honey and vinegar, Liberian black coffee, birds with ruby and topaz reflections on a pineapple puree, flagons of viscous wines and filigree caskets containing betel leaves, areca nuts and tobacco mingled with catechu and calcium carbonate.

Although the pendoppo is luxuriously illuminated, a mysterious half-light reigns there, and in the shadowy corners one divines the undulations of bodies, like the supple slithering of reptiles. They are kneeling maids of honor, covered in metallic veils, who are agitating bizarre emblems announcing the sacred pantomime.

Suddenly, from a door opening to a part of the Kraton, a frail being who seems frosted with moonlight and stardust, so brilliant are her simarre and her jewels, advances smoothly. It is Soakia, leading the tremulous dream-like farandole. Another bedaya appears behind her, also gliding without any appreciable movements of her limbs, and then a third, and then ten, and then twenty, and then a hundred. The charming apparitions drift like a swarm of dragonflies, with iridescent corselets between open wings, toward the center of the hall, borne by the breeze of flabella or the passionate breath of the gamelan.

They are, at first, the musiciennes of forbidden songs, objuratrices of amour,[1] who allow their tresses of darkness, mingled with tuberose, to hang down, and dance to the sound of timbals and cymbals. Then, here come the charmers of the kiss, who offer their breasts and their loins, and ring the little silver bells that fringe their syndones, sacred courtesans clad in crimson, daughters of delights, living flowers of burning solitudes in which the mouths of volcanoes open. They twirl, agitating spangled veils, green serpents and garlands of pink and yellow lantanas.

A scarcely perceptible murmur is produced in the crowd, like the plaint of waves on shingle. It swells, and then calms down, augments and decreases again, and becomes a precise rumor of profound voices, holding the same note in unison.

Four old women, one of whom is Sukuta, drag themselves on their knees as far as the throne. Their attitude of prostra-

---

1 This unusual seven-word phrase is borrowed from "L'Annonciateur" (tr. as "The Annunciator") one of Villiers de l'Isle Adam's *Contes cruels* (1883), which describes a fête given by King Solomon; understandably, La Vaudère often looked for inspiration to writers associated with the Decadent Movement and its precursors.

17

tion, the profound humility panted on their faces, furrowed and winkled like road maps, contrasts with the richness of their black costumes, florid with vervain, and their scintillating loincloths, whose ends they have tucked in. The choir falls silent suddenly, and they intone, in a single broken voice, a sort of chant announcing new figures of the dance.

"The enchantress Kidoul and her nymphs have emerged from the waves to charm mortals and challenge evil spells. They shake their flowering palms at the horrors of war, delivering prisoners. But the enemy is powerful, they return against them in order to recover their booty. Then they cause arms and reptiles to spring forth from the ground, interlacing the flashes of their javelins, making their necklaces of serpents hiss, and whirling their bucklers. The torches cast reflections of blood over tresses, cries of amour and joyful hymns resound toward the wounded, who get up, and finally, each goddess gives herself to the lover of her choice. After the battle comes the sensuality, after the threats, the babble of an infinite sweetness, a hectic ecstasy."

Then the choir, in spite of the new religions, intones a hymn to Brahma, taken from the Hindu poem by Kalidasa, in which the gods are seen, with Vishnu and Shiva at the head, coming to render homage to the supreme creator.

"Adoration to you, god of three forms, soul who existed alone before the creation! Because you cast a fecund seed into the bosom of the waters. from which all mobile and immobile beings were born, you are the god of amour and sensuality.

"Ineffable androgyne, you give and you receive. You have divided your form by virtue of the desire to create. You are the father and the mother of the universe, and only you can fecundate yourself.

"You are liquid, you are solid by the adhesion of parts; you are thick, you are thin, you are heavy, you are fleeting, you are visible and mysterious, and nothing hinders your superhuman will.

"Glory to you, god of supreme delights."

The seduction of the pantomime, which is often varied, is exercised on the spectators. Its style is pure, of a chaste, supra-terrestrial sensuality, each bedaya seeming, in reality, a nymph emerged from the fog of some distant sea with eternally soothing waves.

Soakia, leading the different parts of the ballet, has inclined again before the Master, raising her hands, held flat against one another, toward her face.

The Susuhunan's eyes have gleamed with a brief flame, and he has made a sign that the girl has understood, for her entire body has started to tremble.

"Soakia," whispers Wakiem, who brushes her shoulder, "the master desires you."

"Never! Never! Be ready, as I've told you."

They have resumed their impassive expressions. The dilated pupils are fixed beneath the slender arch of the eyebrows, the lips mute.

The plaint of the choir has stopped, leaving uncovered the voice of the rebab, whose copper strings are grinding frenetically under the bow. It enunciates, in a livelier movement, the theme of the gending that will serve as the basis for the new symphony. For the combat of the nymphs, the play of the horizontal timbals resonates, and metal plates struck by buffalo-horn hammers; the battery of gongs, kempuls and ketuks punctuate the bellicose phrases.

The gamelan then simulates the rage of tigers, while they attack one another between hedges of pikemen, and the hissing of serpents; then it calms down, in order to allow the sourak to speak, which expresses the tenderness of enlaced couples, long caresses, sighs and kisses.

The little dancers have finished, and, still mute, slowly gliding over the marble like sylphs, they vanish to the depths of the gynaeceum.

But the sultan, with a further imperceptible sign, has stopped Soakia, who fixes a fearful gaze upon him and remains motionless. Sukuta, who has not missed any of the master's movements, prostrates herself before him and, in response to a further order, leads the trembling girl away.

V
The Toilette

While the fête continues, Soakia collapses on the paving stones, and remains there, her arms extended between her knees, with a frisson of all her limbs, like a victim at the feet of the executioner, awaiting the *coup de grâce*. Her temples are throbbing; she is weeping and imploring.

"No, no, Sukuta, I beg you!"

"Such an honor!"

"I'd rather die!"

"You're mad! Get up!"

"No!"

But the old woman was firm. Seizing the dancer's slender wrists in her large hands, she dragged her into the secret chamber where the duennas prepare the virgins for amour. Crouching on an onyx step on the edge of a basin, she drew back her broad sleeves behind her shoulders and commenced the ablutions, methodically, in accordance with the sacred rites. Through the high window the moon was shining and the faint sounds of the gamelan arrived like voluptuous sighs

Sukuta unfastened the necklaces, the bracelets and the parade sarong. She loosened the coils of her tresses over the girl's brown shoulders, and for a few minutes, shook them like a mantle of darkness. Soakia, her entire body swaying, intoned prayers, and her garments, one after another, fell around her. She no longer resisted when the old woman passed layers of balm over her breasts and her loins, with subtle and fresh essences. Perfumes floated round her, like an aureole, and evaporated from her flesh in gusts, sometimes agile and sometimes heavy.

She was naked, supple and frail, her breasts scarcely emerged, circling the nipple with a golden line. Her hips rounded softly over tapering legs like colonnettes of pale bronze.

20

Sukuta then tinted the insides of her hands with vermilion, passed antimony over the edges of her eyelids and further elongated her eyes with a mixture of gum, musk and ebony.

The virgin thought about the beverage that she had prepared in an amethyst phial, and searched for a means of making the old woman take it.

"Aren't you thirsty, Sukuta?"

"No, mistress."

"The air is so hot this evening."

"No more so than yesterday."

"I have a fever. Let's drink to my health. Go fetch the cups."

But the duenna shook her head. "You ought not to drink or eat at present. Later . . ." And, smiling with the grimace of an old monkey: "Don't worry, you won't lack anything."

"Go quickly, then."

Sukuta resumes her task while the girl squeezes the liberating phial in her hand.

At present, she is wearing a white silk gauze, merely wrapped around her loins, another gauze of pink silk embroidered with hummingbird feathers, and a belt of broad golden scales, which covers her abdomen and descends to her knees. Her feet and ankles, studded with a profusion of gems, attached by little chains, remain bare.

The old woman is no longer talking, and her victim is still clutching the slender amethyst bottle that contains the juice of the herb of pleasant dreams. A sudden idea causes her to raise her head.

"Take me to the Master's apartment," she says. "I'm ready."

"You're finally docile, then?"

"Yes, I'm grateful for the favor with which I'm being honored. Take me to the chamber of amour, I tell you."

The moon was no longer shining, hidden by thick clouds, and the monkeys, frightened by the noises of the fête, were uttering shrill cries outside while pursuing one another through the trees.

They emerged from the secret room and traversed the court-yard that led to the Susuhunan's private apartment.

The oblong flames of torches trembled over the ground. Between the colonnettes, the table of the feast was perceptible. The guests were lying on cushions around large trays, feasting on birds stuffed with mangosteen, snails in cumin, cicadas with pisang raja bananas and dormice swimming in saffron. Pyramids of fruits were rising over honey cakes: mangoes, grapefruit, saumanillas, kapulasans, pisang-masas, salaks, langseps and rose-apples, some fresh and others preserved. The thicker smoke of meats rose toward the ceiling, along with the chords of gamelans, now playing quietly in order not to disturb the conversations.

Sickened, Soakia looked toward the garden. Lines of pink and white flowers described long parabolas, like starry rockets, over the earth bathed with pale light, and shady clumps of bushes stood out in honeyed and peppery tufts.

She thought about the liberty, the pleasure there would be in fleeing into perfumed night, in wandering along roads bordered by trees in flower, and all the magnificence that surrounded her added to her chagrin

With Sukuta she traversed the gilded rooms ornamented with mats, cushions and low beds with decorated and painted backs. In the corners there were wooden spiral staircases and high-perched loggias on which cassolettes of perfumes were burning.

Now she was in the Master's chamber, mysteriously close. Sukuta had closed the door on her, but without going away, and she could be heard walking heavily over the sonorous paving stones. The girl's thin nostrils were palpitating. She twisted her slender fingers, separated by the bezels of rings, and bruised her heels on her ankle-chains, which were trailing on the ground. Her ear, applied to the wall, could no longer perceive any echo of the feast, which must have ended. The hour of sacrifice was about to sound for her.

Spotting an amphora three-quarters full of crimson wine on an ivory stool, she took the risk of pouring the contents of the little amethyst phial into it; then, feeling a little calmer, she crouched on the cushions and waited. The ringlets of her hair spread out around her, Sukuta only having maintained the unruly locks around the ears by means of bunches of formosa. Her veils, parted over her bosom, covered one leg, leaving the other bare, folded in a charming pose, and her toenails, painted and polished, shone like amaldines.

A lamp in the form of a ship was burning, suspended from the ceiling, and the indecisive radiance that escaped from its golden hull trembled over the walls, covered in red paint with black arabesques. At the back of the room, a low divan stretched, lost in the shadow.

Feverish footsteps, an abrupt entry, followed by a joyful exclamation: it was Him.

VI
The Master

The young woman got to her feet slowly, extended her arms, and bowed three times, murmuring words of tenderness and prayer.

The sultan looked at his feet, lost in a dream, in a melancholy of regret or desire, perhaps weary of the futility of his power and the inaccessible aspirations to which it gave birth.

Motionless under his scintillating garments, the sun on his breast standing out like a monstrous diamond flower, he no longer seemed to be paying attention to the little dancer that he had coveted. In his eyes, clouded like a low, rainy sky, nothing could any longer be read but an immense ennui.

Soakia moved toward the door. Then the Master seemed to wake up, approached her, seized her metal belt with both hands, and tore away the gauze sarong; the virgin sprang forth completely naked, as delicate and gilded as a bronze statuette.

Shivering, she knelt down, and tears rolled down her cheeks. Confused, she dared not make a movement before the secret examination of the man who was studying her, scrutinizing her with an appreciative slowness, as delighted as a collector before an expensive trinket. Her revolt changed into sighs of distress, in anguish at the imminent violation to which he was about to subject her.

The fear of the inevitable embrace, ill-treating her delicate flesh, unsealing the closed ciborium of her loins, caused her to feel faint even before the possession.

"Get up," he said, in a changed voice that astonished her.

"What do you want of me, Master?"

"Your body, this evening. Afterwards we'll see . . ."

"Have pity . . ."

He frowned, accustomed to submission.

"You refuse?"

"Have pity," she repeated. "Others are prettier than me, more worthy of such favor."

"It's you that I want."

"No, no!"

"It's you."

He moved closer to her, burning her face with his breath, and his hand strayed all along her body. At that touch, the virgin felt a languor invade her; she closed her eyes and drew in her shoulders. Seizing her by the wrists, he pulled her toward him abruptly and sat down on the divan, while she remained standing. Then, for a minute, he looked at her from bottom to top, holding her between his knees in order that she could not escape.

"Are you afraid of me, then? Your companions would be proud . . ."

She could no longer find the strength to reply; she smiled mechanically, devoid of voice and thought.

"I'll give you turquoises and rubies, more jewels than any bedaya has ever had. And you'll burn rare perfumes in hollow pearls. Every morning, tuberoses will embalm your couch. Your slightest desires will be orders. I'm gentle, you see, I'm offering you presents when I would only have to take you, like a little thing that I own."

"Certainly . . ."

"Then you'll love me, as if I weren't your master?"

"I can't love . . ."

"No man has come to you until now . . . why are you refusing?"

"I'm not refusing, it's amour that is refusing."

"Insensate!"

He was crushing her wrists now, and she collapsed beside him, uttering a cry.

Her nudity made her ashamed; she struggled in the embrace, her mouth imprisoned by his ardent lips, in a profound caress.

Sukuta, her ear stick to the door, could no longer perceive anything but the friction of their bodies among the cushions in disarray. However, the virgin, supple and feline, was still refusing herself. The man's desire was making her suffer, and that malaise increased in such a sharp fashion that her eyes glittered wildly.

"You can kill me," she said.

He laughed scornfully. "Kill you? The struggle is making you more beautiful, and I admire you for daring to resist me."

Again he held her against him, and she turned her head to avoid his lips, but he was persistent, enervating himself and exhausting himself in wanting to take her, full of impotent rage.

The flames of the lamp flickered under gusts of warm air. Through the high window, broad lightning flashed, in the dull rumble of thunder. It was one of those overwhelming nights that cause the senses to heat up in a dolorous slackness of energy.

Sweat was running over the Susuhunan's face, and tremors shook his sides and his arms, where blue veins intersected. He ran to the decanter and, tipping back his head, he drained half its contents, while Soakia, with a mysterious smile, propped herself up on her elbow.

The Master, now pale, his fists clenched, was quivering like a harp suspended in a squall.

"Come and sit next to me, then," she said, laughing. "I belong to you . . ."

"Yes, you love me . . ."

"I love you."

A happy smile distended his lips; he let himself fall upon her, rolled his forehead over her breast, and fell asleep.

Then, disengaging herself gently, she put her feet on the floor and started to reflect.

Her reclusive life, her companions, the sacred pantomimes, and a thousand memories, whirled in her head in tumultuous and distant visions. It seemed to her that she was no longer the little girl of old, that a barrier was rising slowly between the past and the present, that everything was about to change, in her heart as in her life.

The storm was growling outside; large raindrops were falling without interruption, immediately absorbed by the hot soil; monkeys were screeching in the trees, as if at the approach of a danger.

The Susuhunan was sleeping heavily, like a drunken man, half lying on the cushions, with one arm dangling, touching the floor. A happy expression parted his teeth, which were as shiny as his necklaces, and his pupils were fleeing beneath his half-closed eyelids toward the infinity of dreams.

Soakia thought about her project, but there was Sukuta, who was on watch, perhaps anxious about the singular silence. Time was pressing . . . what should she do?

Carefully, she put on her veils, and even enveloped herself in one of the gold-embroidered wall-hangings. At the foot of the bed lay one of the Master's daggers, enriched with precious stones. The sight of that gleaming blade excited sanguinary thoughts in the young woman. Rapidly, she seized the weapon by the hilt, bounded to the door, which she opened, knocking over the duenna, who was crouching against the batten, and hissed: "Give me the keys!"

The other looked at her uncomprehendingly.

"Your keys," Soakia repeated.

"My keys? What do you want to do with them?"

"Your keys! Your keys!"

The weapon, extended toward the old woman, glinted in the darkness. Sukuta was afraid, and handed over her bunch of keys.

But it was late. Wakiem and Taminah, tired of waiting, had gone back to the gyneaceum. Soakia, marching in the darkness, did not encounter anyone. She turned into the alun-alun, opened a small door, and found herself in the exterior garden. Bounding into the flowers, leaping over the trellises and ditches, in the pouring rain, she reached another door, which she opened without difficulty, and found herself outside.

VII
The Escape

An indecisive rumor reached her ears. It was coming from the palace, and torches were being agitated in the garden, which the squall was extinguishing. Doubtless the duenna had talked. Mappy drew the young woman away, and they ran straight ahead, scarcely seeing the obstacles and stumbling over stones. Full of uncertainly and terror, Soakia could hear the precipitate beating of her heart, hammering tumultuously, and she felt the warm raindrops of the downpour falling incessantly on her shoulders. The clouds had suddenly condensed into a solid, impenetrable mass, illuminated at intervals by the fulguration of blue and white lightning flashes, which pursued one another across the sky like snakes.

People were now running behind them, trying to overtake them, to take her back to the sultan, who would be pitiless. Perhaps, in the darkness, they had not perceived their shadows on the road.

Mappy made an abrupt detour, leapt over a hedge, took his companion in his arms, and carried her into a clump of flowering hibiscus, which closed over them. The men had stopped in order to light lanterns; seeing night watchmen coming, they asked them whether they had encountered the fugitive, and then continued their route. Only then did the leader speak.

"How late you are."

"Oh, I thought I'd never be able to get out of that accursed palace."

"Your hands are burning, your body too . . . What happened, then?"

Modesty retained Soakia, who merely replied that the duenna had locked her up far away from her companions, and that she had lost a lot of time searching for Wakiem and Taminah.

"I'll never see them again," she said weeping.

But he consoled her, humbly. "You know that you'll be the queen among us, and that, if you wish, we'll come back one evening to abduct your sisters."

"And the rong'geng?" the young woman asked. "What has become of them?"

"We'll join them soon. I wanted to act alone, and sent them on ahead."

"What's going to become of us, Mappy, if we come out of this hiding place?"

"It's necessary to spend the night here. Sleep on these clothes I've brought, and I'll watch over you. Have no fear."

"Oh, I'm so tired."

"Sleep, little queen."

He lay silk scarves down on the flowers, picked a hundred corollas at random, of which he made a soft pillow for the little girl, and while she closed her long somber eyelids, with his krise in his teeth, he watched.

All night long torches shone around them, carried by men from the palace searching for the fugitive.

On awakening, the sultan had almost felt amour for the imprudent girl who had resisted his desire, and his senses were ardent in the expectation of a chimerical possession.

Under the violently perfumed corollas, Soakia's head felt heavy. A pool not far away resembled a great fallen mirror in which Victoria regias were smiling, with their monstrous calices and their flat green trays more than a meter in diameter. Around her, trees reigned, covered in creepers and hectic vegetation, the smallest fissure in the bark giving shelter to seeds that sprouted there, bursting forth in light rockets, plumes, smokes and dusts of flowers of an infinite delicacy. Four or five hundred stems, covered in multicolored leaflets, shed petals scented with almond and vanilla incessantly, an entire bouquet of vegetal artifice.

Vanquished by fatigue, Soakia was drowsy, forgetful of the reptiles that brushed her in the grass, mingling their pale bellies with blue and yellow blotches and their glaucous backs with somber stripes with the warm colors of the vegetation. Green snakes let themselves fall from the bamboos, reanimated by the warm rain, and there was a viscous swarming around the young girl, who was dreaming pleasantly in the black plumage of her hair.

She had been brought up in the campong with Wakiem and Taminah, her younger sisters, trained since infancy to mime all tender, warlike and voluptuous sentiments to the sacred rhythms of ancient gendings. The severe duennas had rendered her limbs supple and impregnated her flesh with perfumes, teaching her to be submissive, silent and beautiful, like the other girls in the gynaeceum. Nothing had been very marked in her monotonous and mild life, exempt from great joys and great pains. She burned aromatic herbs, painted her fingernails and eyelids, made flower preserves, and played vague and melancholy tunes on her rebab with the long ivory shaft . . .

Sometimes, too, with Wakiem and Taminah, whom she loved tenderly, she amused herself in the depths of the great garden throwing stones into the water to make ripples or chasing dragonflies. In a vast railed enclosure there were royal tigers that came running in response to her voice, orangutans, leopards and black panthers. In the ponds there were large fish of singular forms, silvery, red or blue, and, to either side of the pathways, Hindu idols taken from the temple of Borobudur warmed their two thousand years in the sunlight. The three virgins took one another by the waist, forgetting themselves in infantile caresses, until the moment when Sukuta, who kept a special watch on them, came to search for them to take them back to the campong.

During the last year of claustration, Soakia had been sad, rolling projects of flight around in her brain, more imperious every day. The tenderness of her sisters was no longer sufficient for her, her heart was dilated by obscure desires that made her tremble like a leaf in a warm downpour. She struggled in an incurable nostalgia, and attained the plenitude of her spleen. An unreflective need to flee, to run straight ahead without looking back, often gripped her, and she wept on the shoulders of her two confidantes, who, more docile in humor, nevertheless ended up understanding her pain.

They multiplied their excursions under the trees in flower, in the shade of formosas, kenangyas and Victoria regias with ardent corollas, which intoxicated them mildly. In the distance, the sun skimmed the summits of volcanoes, the jagged crests of which were radiant, like molten metal, with violet flames. Gleams snaked along the peaks, in the center of which, the cone of Merapi seethed, terrible, opening a maw of multicolored fire, grinding the teeth of its furnace, perhaps roaring with muted menace.

At their feet, a vast lawn extended, seething with the bubbles of corollas, so densely packed that the grass was hardly visible. Large leaves, serrated or bristling with sword-blades, opened up high above, and the branches of the florid trees disappeared in their turn beneath the light network of creepers or the garden yellow vegetation of an accumulation of moss. Circling above the pool were large birds with metallic reflections, quicksilver breasts lustrous with celadon green, and pink velvet throats with silver scales, with glimmers of punch, auroras and ashes.

VIII
At Hazard

Soakia has woken up. It is broad daylight and she thinks about all the things that she has just left behind while stretching herself in the flowers.

Her first glance is for Mappy, who has been watching over her without making a movement, in order not to trouble her repose.

"Good day, Mappy."

"May Buddha protect you, little queen."

Mappy belongs to a race of vagabonds who have continued the practices of a strange religion, equal divided between Buddhism and Brahmanism, on the slopes and around the craters of the Tengger mountains. He prays before idols and springs, charms serpents, and wards off bad luck. He is generous or redoubtable, depending on the occasion. His thin, bony, desiccated face is animated by a disquieting gaze with an extraordinary gleam; his limbs have a marvelous agility and flexibility.

"Have you rested well?" he asks, showing his sharp teeth, blackened by the usage of betel.

"Yes, I feel better."

"I've kept the scorpions and the greedy insects away that wanted to mar your beauty."

"You're good, Mappy."

"I'm only good to you."

"What have I done for you to be so devoted?"

"You haven't done anything, and I have no merit in sacrificing myself for you. That which one accomplishes with joy is its own recompense. Would you ask me why the sky is blue today and the sun beneficent? They doubtless take pleasure in being thus, and we don't owe them any gratitude . . ."

Emotionally, Soakia contemplates all the new things that charm her, filling her eyes. Before her, a landscape of dream is deployed again. Here there is a crazy garden, an ascension of trees climbing dementedly into the sky. There is no symmetry, the terrain has been abandoned and nature has reclaimed her rights. Yellow and white tjempakas, some dead and others full of sap, seem to be shading tombs lost in the grass, as in cemeteries— presumably the sites of ancient huts toppled by some earthquake. Here and there, in those squares, gardenias are growing wild, spreading a tenacious and violent perfume, along with clumps of blood-red dwarf plants and the plumes of grass, shaking off an odorous hail of golden particles at the slightest wind.

Under the flamboyant trees, splendid with immense bouquets, the feet sink into an elastic mauve and orange moss. Pepper-trees with rugged trunks, wounds dressed with lichens, mingle their branches with the crippled heads of Victoria regias, and there are bizarre shrubs with gussets and gummed taffetas containing violet balls, and others riddled with damp nutmegs from which little simian fingers emerge with pink nails.

Soakia adjusted her light garments, made sure that no one could see her, and emerged with Mappy from the enclosure where they had spent the night. Her veils had dried on her; the soil was already hot. They had undoubtedly surpassed the Kraton, because the houses were becoming increasingly scarce.

To either side of the road there was a profusion of extraordinary vegetation. They traversed rice-fields, fields of coffee bushes, coconut palms and nutmeg-trees. Some swung fragile bells, others necklaces of little beads of amber and coral, and yet others cascades of blue buds, under an intense azure sky, as profound and velvety as a rich woolen carpet. They advanced slowly, stepping over clumps of grass, collecting fruits along the hedges to refresh their lips.

She had departed barefoot, and was walking with difficulty, not being accustomed to long excursions. Her flesh was bleeding even in the dust of the road; she searched in the profound and bushy ravines bordered by daturas, yellow eglantines and wild hibiscus, intersecting like brambles, for a watercourse in order to bathe in it. Suddenly, between the various summits, vast fissures allowed her to see the two northern and southern coasts of Java, the Indian sea and the Chinese sea, separated by the immense chain of volcanic cones, flaming under the turquoise sky. In the distance, plumes of smoke were swaying softly, and she closed her eyes, dazzled by such a spectacle. Where was she? How long had she been walking? All she knew was that her strength was about to betray her, and that she would have given her most precious rings for a little water.

Mappy guided her to a small stream whose banks were carpeted by flint pebbles torn by torrents from the flanks of mountains. Young girls were walking cautiously over the sharp stones and plunging into the muddy water. They had taken off their sarongs and twisted their long thick hair above their heads, like long black snakes.

Soakia joined them, glad to excite their admiration with the rings on her arms and her ankles, and the necklaces that hung over her meager bosom, sometimes catching on the gilded nipples of her breasts.

"Where do you come from, you who seem an empress in our midst?"

"Who gave you so many jewels?"

"It's a fortune that you're carrying on your person . . ."

The bedaya smiled, and allowed herself to be caressed by the bathers, who examined both the exquisite workmanship of her adornments and the delicacy of her skin.

"You certainly haven't worked in the fields!"

"And you're wearing the sacred triangles on your forehead!"

"Your teeth are pure, with no trace of filing or betel."

"Would you like some mangoes, or rambutans? See how beautiful their shiny red flesh is!"

"Yes," said Soakia. "I'm thirsty and hungry."

The girls emerged from the water, shook themselves momentarily, already dried by the fiery sun, and looked for the baskets that they were taking to the town. In the delicate moss and betel leaves, coquettishly arranged, they showed her bananas, sau-manillas, green peppers, mangoes, pineapples and other fruits, among which the little dancer made her choice, while Mappy, some distance away, contemplated her, smiling. All the bathers were now sitting down in the flowers of the bank, golden corollas among the snowy corollas, under the tall mimosas, chirping competitively.

"What do you do, chatterbox in the yellow sarong?"

"I work in the coffee plantation you can see over there." With her extended hand she indicated an entire forest of bright green bushes with dense and shiny foliage. The branches bore both flowers and fruits, which were picked every year. A voluptuous perfume arrived therefrom, peppered with tuberose.

"And my plantation is the most beautiful, you know," said the child.

She crushed a coffee-cherry between her fingers and showed her the nucleus formed of two juxtaposed lobes.

"I carry cut flowers in my vegetable-fiber basket," said another.

"I hunt for striped spiders and green snakes."

"I embroider ceremonial sarongs."

"I don't do anything yet, I'm too young. My big sister sometimes brings me to help fill her baskets."

The last, scarcely eight years old, only retained as a garment for her gleaming bronze body a scarf knotted around her slender loins.

"Is life pleasant for you?" asked Soakia.

"Oh, we'd much rather dance in the Kraton like the sacred bedayas."

"All they do is adorn themselves, sleep and eat preserves, the sultan's dancers!"

"What!" said Soakia, opening her eyes wide. "You wouldn't prefer liberty?"

"What do you call liberty? It's necessary to work all day long, and sometimes get beaten."

"You can go where you want, in accordance with your fantasy."

"Our fantasy is to stay in a beautiful garden full of cool shade and mime the famous legends of old before the Master!"

The bedaya sighed. What was liberty, then and why did those who possessed it testify so much scorn for it?

IX
Anxiety

Soakia and Mappy have set forth again, after having offered the young girls a few gold beads in order to thank them. They are traversing a vast terrain covered with mounds, already partly disappeared under the vegetation. It is an old Chinese cemetery, and here and there, bones emerge from the ground like the roots of a fallen tree. The road resumes, bordered by flowery hedges, with plantations of sugar cane to either side, or rice-fields, dotted, in the distance, by men and women in work sarongs, like fragile toys, and pink buffaloes hauling plows.

Under the golden clusters of the mimosas rise campongs, agglomerations of huts made of bamboo and banana leaves, which constitute hamlets and villages. On the thresholds, women with long hair, lustrous with coconut oil, sit motionless, sheathed in brightly-colored scarves, with, occasionally, the gaiety of a necklace of coral or superimposed metal plaques over the bosom. The men wear loincloths of leather or blue wool, garnished with seashells and glass pendants. By their side, or along their spine, shines the terrible krise that every good Javanese possesses, in spite of his even and pacific temperament.

But the day is beginning to decline, and the cicadas are intoning their strident concert, punctuated by the intermittent sob of an owl or the call of a green tokai in the branches. Here are rice-fields, still completely inundated by the previous day's rain, with low levees in red clay, which retain the water. Teams of large buffaloes are returning to their lodgings, conducted by semi-naked children.

Soakia, intoxicated by desires and liberty, has reached the foot of the great volcano, Merapi. Night has fallen, one of those equatorial nights that are an enchantment for the mind and the eyes. On the road, in the bushes and in all the foliage that rises up gloriously toward the stars, myriads of luminous flies are scintillating, the buzzing rockets, comets' tails and galaxies of that marvelous land.

The terrestrial constellations shift, forming complicated signs, and sometimes, a winged firefly settles on the calyx of a flower and sticks there like an electric pistil. In the splendor of that strange vision, it seems to the fugitive that she is agitating beneath a stellar downpour, a hurricane of fire that passes over her, singing, caressing her hair, her lips and her entire body, extended for kisses.

Now, sitting in the moss, she gleans corollas, an entire charming flora, which the mysterious light that is spread around her frosts with lunar reflections. Hedges of squat trees protect her: tulip-trees, mimosas and dragon-trees speckled with metallic green leaves, beneath golden tears like drops of sulfur. Everything is enchanting in this journey through the unknown. She knows only too well the ennui of the idleness that trails in the luxury of gynaecea, with fragments of landscapes glimpsed through a small window, a breach open to an infinity of ambitions that can never be satisfied.

She was in a period of torpor, the lassitude that blunts sensibility, bathes the soul in sensations of twilight and the unreal, as at the emergence from the tumultuous shock of passions. She watched the luminous insects flying, phosphorescent bees drinking nectar from the dormant heart of tuberoses; then, a shadow slid through the branches, seemed to rise from the earth, drowning the wings, condensing the thickets, winding around the trunks of the trees with the gigantic lianas, coagulated like the tentacles of monstrous cephalopods. And the holes in the lacy vegetation were filled in, confounded in a single mass of darkness. The golden dragonflies had fled; only the pale gazes of the stars were muted in the violet sky.

Mappy sang softly:

"Your tresses are somber wings that palpitate in the light, and your lips are dipped in the fire of volcanoes.

"Your eyes are mysterious and changing moonstones that speak of sidereal splendors and do not allow themselves to be penetrated.

"Your ear is a pink shell in which the amours of the waves murmur; I would like to put my tongue therein, like a coral pistil.

"You breasts are twin cups in which a ruby mounted in gold trembles.

"Your loins are a jade buckler that no weapon has violated, and the secret of your divine body is like a hive of honey lost in the flowers.

"I want to drink from the cups of your breasts, I want to know the honey of your lips. I am the pigeon that sighs and the bee returning to its nest. I want . . ."

"Go to sleep," said Soakia. "The ruby of my breasts and the nectar of my mouth are not for you."

"You can't love?"

"The man I shall love has not yet made himself known."

"Who will he be?"

"I don't know. However, I'm certain that he will be different from those who surround me, and that I will belong to him entirely."

"Then you're refusing me?"

"Yes, the moment has not yet come."

Resigned, Mappy lay down beside the little queen, after having collected fruits for her along the hedges, and having brought water for her in magnolia corollas.

He was happy to gaze at her, to respire her breath and intoxicate himself on the voluptuous perfume of her charming body.

Suddenly, Soakia felt the weakness of the entire body that the vertigo of the eyes and the imagination brings in its wake. Her solitude, the immensity of the menacing beyond, the azure ocean rolling over her head, the debris of unknown shipwrecks and warrior fleets of stars battling for who knew what formidable conquest, left her almost tremulous, overwhelmed by the desolate sensation of emptiness before which the soul suddenly takes fright.

She remained breathless, stunned, experiencing a sort of anguish in her side that flowed all the way to her legs, which had become limp and unsteady. Lying down gracefully, with one arm folded beneath her proud little head, helmed in darkness, she closed her eyes to all those menacing splendors, ignoring the moon that suddenly surged forth above a colossal pale trunk, like the raised head of some terrifying reptile.

X
The Rong'geng

Music reigns in Java; all popular active and sentimental life is spontaneously expressed by that means. Although it distracts people from long labor under the oppressive sun on the fiery land, it also contains their sense of beauty and mystery.

The humble herdsman trying to play on his primitive flute an ancient gending that he has heard in a distant festival evokes for himself and for those who follow him the memory of divine poems.

Soakia suddenly woke up to the sounds of a light chant, and sat up, curiously.

Mappy's rong'geng were arriving along the road to the sound of angklungs, imitating the tremolos of the wind and the languid plaint of waves. In front of them, their "leaders" were striking light buffalo-skin drums rhythmically.

The bare feet of the pauperesses were bleeding slightly, the make-up was cracking on their fatigued faces, whipped by the rude locks of their hair, and the withered garlands of flowers with which they had girdled their slender loins were hanging down to their knees.

Seeing Soakia, they extended their hands to her, and wished her welcome; then, taking her by the waist, they executed a few weary dance-steps.

"Where are you going?" asked the girl,

"To Djokjakarta, but we're lost."

"The chief ought to take us to the ruins of Tjambi-Seou, because we want to worship the gods."

"Oh," said Soakia, her eyes shining with joy. "I'll go with you. I can mime with you on the roads in order to make some money. Look."

The sacred bedaya began to twirl, supple and slow, her body upright, her arms agitated as if by indivisible waves, undulating and vibrant, her gaze lost in the infinity of dream. Then, with a quiver of her entire being, she threw back over her shoulder the silky scarf that veiled her nudity.

Before the hieratic attitude, the nobility of the movements and the infinite artistry of each figure, the rong'geng were silently admiring, and it was Mappy, the chief, who spoke.

"Come with us, since you're our queen."

"Our queen!" repeated the girls, prostrating themselves in the dust.

"Yes," said Soakia, "but I'll be free to follow my caprice and go my own way, if my pleasure summons me elsewhere?"

"Free," said Mappy, with a shadow of sadness on his thin yellow face, furrowed by numerous scars.

"Let's go, then, toward the unknown."

"You'll be weary before the end of the day. Your little feet are unused to long marches. They've only brushed fine mats and precious carpets. There's still a little gold on the nacre of their toenails."

"Bah! Fatigue won't put me off. I'll do as the others do, who are thinner and more languid than me."

Going around the volcano, the troupe of rong'geng set forth, gaily abusing the semi-naked women who were carrying leather bottles of coconut oil, or pink earthenware urns full of perfumes or indigo, on their heads, supported by a rounded arm circled by bracelets of glass beads. Little boys splashing around in the rice-fields ran to give them an escort; others, more laborious, after an indifferent glance, continued collecting, one by one, the gilded and hairy ears that formed sheaves, carefully sorted for decortication.

When Soakia stopped, Mappy put an arm around her waist and supported her, with a thousand unaccustomed attentions. Slightly confused, she stiffened herself and, without daring to reject the chief's solicitudes, tried nevertheless to avoid them with an attitude of determination and bravery that was belied by her dark-ringed eyes and pallid lips.

They arrived at the ruins of Tjambi-Seou—which means "thousand temples"—and decided to spend the night there, after having made a meal of honey and fruits collected haphazardly along the road.

Around them rose heaps of sculpted stones, guarded by huge statues, which the moon frosted with fantastic gleams. They were terrible Buddhas, crouching or standing, grimacing or beneficent. They attained seven or eight times human height, and the aureoles that surrounded their heads seemed to emerge from the azure vault, detached therefrom like little dead stars from all the stars wandering in the heavens.

While the rong'geng, prostrate in the dust, worshiped Shiva, Buddha and Durga randomly—for the bohemians conserved and mingled the old religions—Soakia explored the temple, curiously. Shiva, in particular, was represented there in his eight forms. He was the bearer of the heavy club, of the sonorous shell, of the resplendent disk, or, as a Brahmin sacrificer, he held the pilgrim's gourd in his hand.

XI
Terror

On the terraces of Solo, the bedaya had already seen images of the god, but in that solitude, in that landscape of dream, he took on a menacing and magnificent power.

Often, a single statue, charged with several attributes, evoked a complex being endowed with multiple powers. But only rarely was the white god to be seen next to the black Vishnu, and the only time that he figured in the Brahmanic trinity, he occupied the sovereign place there. Soakia went up the disjointed steps to a sort of bell-tower in which every stone threatened ruin. In the bosom of profound niches, the guardian of the place, a venerable Buddhist with a long white beard, and amulets clinking on his emaciated torso, illuminated with the flickering light of his lamp groups of idols with four arms, extended in menacing gestures, with the heads of goats or elephants, twisted and terrifying. Bats entered through the windows; the wind stirred the shadows accumulated under the vaults and enormous cobwebs hung like sacks from every angle.

Soakia became feverish in that solitude, an unexpected fear, a fear of the unknown, a terror of the nerves, exasperated by noises, disquieting in that nest of darkness, clawed her. She tried to reason with herself, to make fun of that weakness, drawing away slightly from her guide, but whatever she did, her disturbance intensified. A dull growl now resounded above her head and she looked up.

In the air, something enormous filled the vault, and the old man's lamp, as if shaken by a squall, inclined its flame, darting acrid jets of smoke, scarcely giving any light, and finally went out. With the roaring breath of a forge, a mass threw itself upon her, and two jets of phosphor punctured the darkness . . .

As she recoiled, screaming, an arm close to her, lashed out at the turbulent mass, pricking with an agile krise the two fiery dots, which were extinguished.

The guardian had lit his lamp again, and the trembling girl gazed, at her feet, at the cadaver of a gigantic owl, whose clenched claws were striping the ground with bloody droplets.

Wiping his red-striped hands, Mappy laughed silently.

"Oh!" she said, astonished to see him there. "You saved me . . ."

But the old guardian, discontented, protested.

"They're the Buddha's birds, they're not malevolent, and they watch over the gods. It's necessary not to do them any harm."

To console him, she gave him a gold fetish with an emerald eye, which she wore between her breasts, and he pushed the inanimate body of the bird against the wall.

"Come," said Mappy. "I know all the secrets of the temple. With me, you won't be afraid."

In a mausoleum turned toward the Southern Cross he showed her a statue of a strangely beautiful woman with wide-open eyes, looming over a profound well hollowed out at her feet. On the north side, a death's-head reposed on the head of an elephant, but he was unable to explain the significance of that mysterious emblem to her.

In front of them, the jagged crest of Merapi, the great volcano that they had circled, stood out in crimson arabesques, ablaze in long streaks, and swarms of luminous insects were flying over the rice-fields.

Exhausted, she let herself fall on to a shawl that Mappy laid on the ground, and he held her against him, burning her face with his ardent breath.

As she had next to the sultan, she felt a languor invade her, and closed her eyes delectably, allowing herself to be soothed by an unknown force.

XII
Mappy

Leaning over the little sacred dancer, Mappy caressed lightly, with his lips, the seven triangles on her forehead, her closed eyelids, as soft as silk, the perfumed skin of her cheeks, her delicate and willful chin, and her frail breasts, circled around the nipple with a thin line of gold. Then he descended to the published pubis, also shielded with a golden flower, the legs tapering like jade colonnettes, and the sacred jewels of her slender feet, which he wiped with lotus corollas.

"Soakia," he said in a low voice, "I am no longer the chief, and you will command for me. I want to put between your frail hands my male power, my soul and my heart. I will drag myself over the ground kissing the traces of your footfalls and your slightest desires will be orders. You can give yourself to me, become my wife among all, or refuse yourself; you can enable me to die of joy or languish in suffering. You will be everything for me, for you are the most beautiful and the most adored."

Again his lips strayed over the feverish body of the dancer, making her a sarong of kisses softer than silk and velvet. Plaintive, she allowed herself to be explored avidly, and it seemed to her that a new blood was circulating in her veins, burning and fresh by turns. Her sensibility was displaced, following Mappy's mouth, ardent between her breasts, in the hollows of her raised arms, the undulating ambiguities of her torso to the ridges of her hips, crawling over the curve of her loins and running in jets of fire along her trembling legs.

And as he paused, panting, she uttered a profound sigh and weakened . . .

"Do you want to?" he asked, pleading.

In a sudden resurgence of pride, however, she refused herself.

"No, no, not that . . ."

"Why? Do I displease you?"

"No, no, let me sleep . . ."

"Tomorrow, then?"

"Tomorrow . . . yes, perhaps . . ."

He lay down, and put the girl's head on his breast; then, in order to soothe her, he chanted in a plaintive and tender voice:

"At the source of all life, I have slaked my thirst.

"I have tasted the honey of your smile. Your breath is more perfumed than the melati at the approach of evening. It glides over me like a voluptuous wave, and all my flesh is in joy.

"Your body is a closed calyx that no one is worthy to unseal. It is doubtless a god who will be the first to fathom your depths.

"At the living wound of your corolla, let me then intoxicate myself, and enlarge it with all the force of my desire.

"At the source of all life, I have slaked my thirst.

"Soakia, it is raining kisses in the sky and on the earth. Woman gives herself to man, it is the eternal law. The gods have wanted amour, amour has vanquished the gods, and everything that exists only exists by means of amour.

"At the source of all life, I have slaked my thirst . . ."

Soakia, confident, sleeps on the somber curls of the hair that Mappy keeps, over his wrists and arms, like a warm caress, and the little rong'geng, a little further away, also sing in order to soothe their nostalgic dream, summoning the slumber that comes so slowly in these lands of fever and desire.

Around them, the mountains, like stages of petrified granite waves, rise toward the stars, and the fireflies of the earth shine like little fallen stars, sprinkling the bushes and the moss with a phosphorescent galactic snow.

Sigete and Mana'í, the two seeresses of the band, have collected the fireflies and fastened them in their hair; with two green snakes fallen from the bamboos they have made supple necklaces, which undulate over their brown skin, and they have whistled in a certain fashion in order to summon the owls and the bats wandering in the ruins.

"Sigete, send him one of the children, the chief is amorous."

"He's neglected them to sleep next to the flower of Solo."

44

"She's so pretty!"

"Well worthy, in fact, of that preference."

"She'll marry Mappy."

"And we'll obey her. Do you want that, Sigete?"

"Certainly, Mana'i, I want it, as you do."

"And then, a sacred bedaya! No one can dance like her! She'll be given precious stones and perfumes, which she'll share with us, for she's good. Let's try to sleep. All our companions are asleep, and it will be necessary to leave at daybreak."

XIII
The Seeresses

"You who know the will of Vishnu, Mana'i, can you see the destiny of the little queen?"

Sigete has tried in vain to close her eyelids; an anxiety has been gripping her for some time.

"The destiny of the little queen?" said Mana'i. "To know that I'd need a drop of her blood."

"Do you have your dagger?"

"Would you dare?"

"Certainly. I can no longer hear Mappy's voice. He must have fallen asleep too. Let's slip through the long grass next to Soakia."

The rong'geng have crawled over the moss, in the grass with silvery tufts, and have stopped some distance from the enlaced couple, curious. Mappy and Soakia are asleep on an uncovered mound, and the moonlight is illuminating them.

"Oh! Look, Sigete!"

"Yes, a bad omen."

Soakia's hand is resting on her heart, and a mysterious shadow is extending to her left, like a tombstone.

"A sign of death!"

"We might be mistaken. Let's consult the gods . . ."

Mana'i has taken a crimson droplet from the little dancer's breast, which she has extended over a leaf of the pink lotus, and she has lain down very quickly in the long grass, which hides her from view. In any case, Soakia has only shivered slightly, and her eyelids have scarcely parted.

The rong'geng, who know all the secrets of the ruins, traverse diagonally the terrain where the bas-reliefs representing the Aryan pantheon are. Niches are distributed along the galleries, containing aureoled Buddhas, sitting or standing. Further away are the images of gods, including Indra and Brahma, prostrate before prince Cakya, who is astride Vishnu's eagle.

The young women move cautiously over the fallen stones, which earthquakes displace continually. The sculpted frames of the niches are broken, and many of the statues lie in the dust, deprived of their heads and arms. An odor of sulfur still floats, retained in the large stone corridors.

Mana'i reached the black idol, ignited a few pinches of aromatic herbs that she kept in a silk bag, and raised a reed flute to her lips, imitating the buzzing of bees and the rippling of streams over pebbles.

Then Sigete sang, in a plaintive voice:

"On the blue mountain of Kailasa lives the god Shiva, whose magnificent image we venerate. He reigns on a golden throne scintillating with vermilion gems that crown the sacred lotus.

"Above is the triangle, the origin and source of all things. From that triangle emerges the Lingam, the eternal god who makes his dwelling there, and radiates in twelve branches of light. Brahma, Vishnu and Shiva, adorable trinity, tree, corolla and pistil, we humiliate ourselves before you.

"The shadows of death have folded like the night before the stars. By the hidden symbols, by the sound of sweet angklungs, by the murmur of the dormant earth and the rumble of angry volcanoes, by the eternal silence and the eternal destruction, dominator of the unknown world, we salute you!"

She swayed her body to a rhythm livelier than that of the little flute, and then threw herself face down in the dust, her arms extended. Then Mana'i raised her head to contemplate the idol, and went on, offering it the lotus stained with blood:

"Omnipotent and terrible god, it is by you that acts of amour and hatred are accomplished, it is by you that that fearful dreams and voluptuous phantoms blossom. You can do good and evil, for you know all the secrets of life. What do you want of your servant?"

The divinities around her seemed to grimace. They raised their hideous, elongated or squat heads, showing enormous bellies or flattened breasts, opening menacing mouths, spreading their arms, their hands holding forks, cannonballs or javelins.

Mana'i prostrated herself in her turn and remained motionless, seemingly listening to mysterious words. Then, her lips trembling, her gaze vacillating, she got up and covered her face with her hair as a gesture of desolation.

"The gods have spoken! The gods have spoken!"

"Yes, woe betide us!"

"Should we warn the chief?"

Sigete reflected for a moment, then replied: "What's the point? What must happen will happen, by the will of the gods. Mappy is happy; let him live in his error."

By the dazzling glare of a flash of lightning crawling across the vault, they perceived against the wall an infinity of fantastic beasts, emaciated, breathless, bristling their claws and darting out their tongues. Serpents had feet, bulls had wings, gigantic fish with human heads were holding apples in their mouths, elephants were raising their trunks, crowned with flowers, and crocodiles were devouring tigers. All the strangest forms, creations of delirious brains, nightmare and terror, were accumulated there, mutilated or still standing, in the profound niches. Paws, skulls, eyes sprung out of their lids, terrible and obscene symbols, lay everywhere, impeding progress, and the two rong'geng, jostling one another in the long gallery, returned toward the starlight at a run . . .

XIV
Djokjakarta

When daylight appeared, the little troupe set forth again, the chief opening the march with Soakia leaning on his shoulder, and the young women followed them, singing to the caressant leitmotiv of angklungs. As they approached the city, the country was ornamented by marvelous roads in the shade of varigniers and tamarinds, lined with bamboo campongs, and lawns so crowded with flowers that not a single blade of grass pierced the carpet of corollas. The jagged crest of Merapi was still designed on the horizon in colors of fire, and Soakia manifested regret at not having visited the mouth of the volcano.

"We'll see other furnaces, little queen," said the chief. "We'll see things that you can't imagine: lakes of flames and mountains of lava moving like gigantic veils falling from the heavens agitated by the tempest . . . and the very ground will dance under our feet, with the bushes, the rocks and the tall trees with the arrogant crowns . . ."

"Oh," she said, "I'll be afraid . . ."

"No, because I'll take you in my arms and I'll be strong, in order to conserve your life. Not one flower in your hair will be disturbed."

With her slender hand she brushed Mappy's cheek; he closed his eyes in a delectable ecstasy.

Soon, they would cross the threshold of the ancient city of Djokjakarta. There, as in Solo, the representatives of twenty different races rubbed shoulders: Arabs with white burnooses, proudly draped: Hindus in green and red tunics, decorated with complicated designs and wearing turbans in the form of enormous dahlias on their heads; Chinese, waddling in blue silk trousers, their torsos smooth under thin cabails; Javanese and Malays clad in open sarongs, in pastel shades, walking with a light and supple step.

The sky is an ardent vivid turquoise blue striped with gold; intoxicating gusts of perfume are disengaged from the greasy earth, in which trenches display a russet brown with silver and copper glints.

The imperial Kraton of the city resembles that of Solo, but it contains five thousand more worshipers.

In front of the palace, the pagodas, the terraces and the pendoppos, Mappy and his rong'geng perform their strange dances; then Soakia, adorned with all her jewels, her loins girdled by a bright pink scarf that the chief has just bought her, initiates the passers-by into the mysteries of the enchantress Kidoul, and makes gold and silver coins rain down in the wooden bowl that Sigete holds on her knees.

In the gardens, pomegranate trees, magnolias and tamarinds overlap their metallic leaves under the bold jet of coconut palms, causing a red-brown shadow to float over their aerial plumes.

Under the tents disseminated along the streets, Malays with amber and coral necklaces are selling depilatory pastes, arachnean ceremonial sarongs embroidered with chimerical birds, cakes shaped like the moon, and images of the sultan.

The road, paved with pink and white stones, broadens out before the imperial palace, which is deployed over a cleared area. First of all one perceives two long porticos, whose architraves repose on thickset pillars. They flank a sort of armed minaret with a golden crescent on its platform. On the corners, vases full of ignited aromatics stand, maintained by young women naked to the waist, and covered in necklaces of glass beads with little tinkling bells. Pomegranates and colocynths charge the capitals; traceries of diamond shapes and garlands ornament the walls and the steps of the sandalwood staircase that descends to the vestibule.

In the square, however, bewildered women and children are contemplating a young man with a pale face who is working at an easel.

Curious, Soakia has approached, and the painter, on seeing her, has let an admiring exclamation escape.

In pure Javanese, while Mappy frowns and puts his hand to his poisoned krise, he asks her: "Where have you come from, pretty little enchantress?"

"From Solo," she says, simply.

"What do you do?"

"I dance with the rong'geng, my companions."

And the art-lover studies her, having not yet seen in the land such a fragile and charming doll of amour.

XV
Stéphane Gautier

Under the charmed gaze of the young man, Soakia feels infinitely troubled. It is as if a flood of flame were circulating in her veins, and she is frightened by that strangely unexpected emotion. Stéphane is handsome, with his delicate face, accentuated by a silky blond moustache, his tall, elegantly formed stature, and his blue eyes with a playful and seductive expression.

"What is your name?" he asks the dainty dancer.

"Soakia, and I was a bedaya of the Susuhunan of Solo." Suddenly, she experiences a need to magnify herself, to give him an advantageous opinion of her.

"A dancer of the Susuhunan! That's very good! But how old are you, then?"

"Almost thirteen."

"And still new?"

He has posed that question with a slightly skeptical smile, to which the girl replies, bravely: "Yes, a virgin."

Meanwhile, Mappy is becoming increasingly anxious.

"What do you want with her, and who are you?"

"Who are you?"

"The chief, as she is the queen."

"Indeed, you seem to be of a very different origin. But if she's your queen, she's free in her person?"

"Certainly," says Soakia, with an urgency that strikes poor Mappy dolorously.

"And if you're free, you can go with me?"

"I can."

The chief has prostrated himself in the dust and has struck the ground three times with his forehead, as a sign of desolation.

"You wouldn't do that! You won't do that! I'll summon the malediction of the gods upon you if you abandon us."

Mana'i and Sigete speak in their turn. "We've interrogated the sacred Trinity, male and female, and it has replied to us that a misfortune is hanging over you, Soakia."

"A misfortune hanging over me? What have I done to the gods then?"

"They haven't told us, but the oracle is formal."

Stéphane was suffocating in the hot atmosphere that the walls of the palace were projecting back upon him. The perfumes, the radiations and exhalations were augmenting the fever that had been consuming him since his arrival in that land of fire. Through an ardent dazzle he contemplated the little dancer, with the desire to slake his thirst on her fresh lips. She was confounded with the foliage, the flowers and the whiteness of marble; she was a beautiful flavorsome fruit that his hand would have liked to pick.

The irritated rong'geng, like bees whose hive is coveted, surrounded their queen. They agitated, and their bodies, greasy with unguents and make-up, exhaled an odor of spices and extinct cassolettes.

"You can choose between them," said Mappy. "I'll let you have them . . . but Soakia is sacred."

The young man looked at the girls without desire. They were pretty, however, with their slender forms, and their rounded and firm breasts, sparkling with amulets of jade or coral.

But they seemed the servants of the bedaya; their eyelids were tucked up, and their lips were too thick.

"No," he said, "keep your property . . ."

And with a weary expression, he drew away, after having made a sign to two domestics who were with him to carry the easel, the canvas and the brushes.

XVI
The Tigers

Soakia mimed the adventures of the enchantress Kidoul for two more days in the public squares, the streets and the crossroads, but her soul was sad.

At night she slept, her cheek in her left hand and her other arm unfolded, which is a sign of anguish. Mappy, beside her, attempted timid caresses, and sometimes slept on the ringlets of her hair, which resembled a nest of black feathers. With his lips he refreshed her feverish palms and her little bruised feet. The chaplet of his kisses glided all along the adored body, and the girl sighed feebly, unconscious and nostalgic, but in her sleep, however.

"Go away, Mappy!"

But the chief's kisses traveled more devotedly; he did not hear, or did not want to hear. The light of the stars was like the splendor of her skin, something divine that only belonged to her. The polish of her nails continued the smoothness of the gems that covered her fingers, and the nipples of her breasts resembled two pink shells blooming on the golden sand of her flesh.

As soon as she woke up, she thought about Stéphane's soft voice and his blue gaze. He was the most charming of the children of men, and she would have liked to give him the first fruits of her body. Why had he not come back?

Mappy was preparing for a grand performance the following day, which was a day of rejoicing in Djokjakarta. Tigers enclosed in an immense cage had been reserved for the festival combats. They were launching themselves from one end of their prison to the other and clawing the wooden spikes that kept them captive. Their eyes were darting sparks, their tails beating their nervous flanks frenetically. It was in the most spacious of the courtyards of the palace that the combat was to take place. Six princes, known as the "six brave men before the sun," coiffed in golden helmets, naked to the waist, were to provoke the beasts and measure themselves against them.

The people flocked to enjoy the spectacle. Blue and white veils agitated on the terraces; they were the sultan's dancers, who, half-hidden, were gazing between the garlands of flowers hanging from the balustrades. They struck tambourines from time to time, caused rebabs to groan, or shook castanets; then, when the instruments fell silent, they imitated with their mouths the stridulation of insects or the plaint of waves. A few, plaintive—as Soakia had once been—remained crouching with their chin in their palm, and, as motionless as sphinxes, and gazed somberly at the multitude.

At the bottom of the wall, Mappy's rong'geng went by, with gardenias and tuberoses in their hair, their torsos and arms bare. While awaiting the performance, the people fêted them, and they spun indefatigably under the disdainful eyes of the captive bedayas.

In shops covered with tarpaulins, set up in haste, Chinamen and Arabs offered embroidered fabrics, caskets encrusted with nacre and ivory, bronze perfume-burners, brown and gilt lacquer and flower pastes. Malays sold mangoes, bananas and mangosteen pomegranates, whose interior is like solid pink snow, balms and amulets. In large baskets watched over by negresses there were also hyacinth robes, poisoned arrows, daggers with jade and onyx hilts, tortoiseshell pins, sponges, scrapers, brushes and antimony stamps for painting the eyebrows and the eyelids, pickling salt and fish in honey.

In order not to lose their places, men and women were eating fruits bought at the hazard of the excursion standing up. Children, stark naked, smeared with indigo and vermilion, resembled marble statuettes painted blue and red.

A wedding party passed over the main square, preceded by two gigantic mannequins coiffed in feathers and clad in bright sarongs. They reached the roofs of the houses, resembling a carnival exhibition of delirious students. Then came the musicians, and then, mounted on ponies caparisoned in scarlet velvet, the gaudily costumed guests, and, finally, the bride, so covered in necklaces, clasps, pendants and amulets that one could scarcely perceive a few narrow strips of her saffron-tinted skin. She appeared in an ornate litter with bouquets of ostrich feathers at the corners. Chains of crystal and pearl beat the velvet curtains, and gray horses ridden by the nearest relatives followed, sounding little bells suspended over their breasts. Young women offered loaves of bread sprinkled with anise, tilting bulging wine-skins and jars full of lotus syrup over metal cups.

But the gamelan resounded and the six princes, coiffed in golden helmets, entered the arena in order to fight the beasts. Bravely, they cut the ropes that retained the door of the cage and backed away before the bounding animals while executing a bizarre dance punctuated with shrill cries and appeals. The tigers braced themselves and launched themselves forward, causing their somber fur to undulate, lacerating themselves on the human wall bristling with spears, and ended up collapsing in the middle of pools of blood. The fighters stopped then, and placed their feet on the vanquished enemy, and the pelog gamelan intoned the brutal hymn of triumph.

The sounds burst forth like claps of thunder, uniting in an immense symphonic rumor, a tumble of arpeggios punctuated by the flashes of gongs.

Six tigers were put to death; then new characters entered the scene. Their coiffure was a silver garuda with wings spread over their temples, somewhat reminiscent of large bats. With no other weapons than their slender muscular arms they gripped one another, disengaged, stepped back and then came to grips again, uttering savage clamors at every new effort. Then deformed dwarfs sketched rapid dances with simianesque contortions, alternating with the mimes of the bedayas, as frail and pale as phantoms gliding through the mystery of nights.

Soakia, confounded among the spectators, watched those things with an indifferent expression, habituated since infancy to similar enjoyments. Agile and supple, she had slid into the closely-pressed ranks, leaving Mappy and her companions behind.

Suddenly, an arm touched hers, and a soft voice murmured in her ear:

"I've been looking for you."

XVII
Further Encounter

"You were looking for me?"

"Yes, for two days I haven't been thinking about anything but you."

All a-tremble, she did not reply. Then he put his hand on her shoulder as a sign of possession.

"Come on, follow me."

Dejected, she said: "I can't. I promised . . ."

"Are you not the mistress of your body and your thought?"

"I'm attached to Mappy by gratitude."

"What has he done for you, then?"

"He's protected my flight and had pity on my weakness."

"Say, rather, that he's exploited you. Have you not mimed for him and the pauperesses he trails in his wake? They all have new scarves and necklaces of glass beads. It's doubtless to you that they owe being so well-clad?"

"At any rate," said Soakia, suddenly rebelling, "I know where they come from and where they're going, whereas I don't know you."

"That's true," said Stéphane smiling. "You have the right to be suspicious of me. I'm French and I'm traveling for my pleasure."

"Alone?"

"With two Malays, who carry my easel and my canvases. I don't have any great talent, but I'd like to keep a few souvenirs of this beautiful country. Come with me, child; I'm rich . . . very rich; you won't lack anything."

"Oh," she said, disdainfully, "I don't care about money."

"I also love you . . ."

"How do you love me? Do you have other wives?"

"I'll only have you."

"And we'll travel?"

"We'll go wherever our caprice takes us."

"Listen," she said. "Mappy is jealous. He might kill you if he knew your designs. Stay with us . . ."

They were jostled by the crowd which was going away, the spectacle having ended.

"Let's flee. We won't find a better opportunity."

The stars were lighting up one by one; whiteness was shining almost everywhere; the angle of a wall, suspended rags, a pearl necklace on the bosom of a god. He took her hand and drew her away.

They went past the ditch where the wild beasts had been enclosed. Half-eaten carcasses of dogs and sheep still remained there, poisoning the surroundings. With difficulty they reached the extremity of the Kraton, but they had to pause in order to let the cortege pass of a prince accompanied by his scarlet-clad dragoons, his green lancers in long loose skirts and a squadron of white cavaliers with gold braid, mounted on isabelline horses. They were brandishing long forks ornamented with sharks' teeth, ebony clubs and ironwood maces. The people prostrated themselves in the dust and the fugitives resigned themselves to waiting.

The moon now spread its light over the gardens and the smoking mountains, which resembled, in the distance, the motionless waves of an ocean of metal. Behind them, the Kraton was asleep, with its buildings of stone, planks, lava and pressed earth, its palace with its columns and light capitals, its bronze cupolas, its marble architraves, its minarets pointing into the sky: enormous candelabra, each candle bearing a star.

Soakia uttered a cry. Mappy, surging forth beside her, looked at her silently.

"Don't think I wanted to run away," she said, in a tremulous voice. "Only I was lost . . ."

"Really?" he said, sadly.

"Really . . . ask him."

She indicated Stéphane, who seemed to be challenging the chief. The gazes of the two men met, charged with hatred, and Mappy put his hand to his dagger.

"Oh!" said Soakia, who saw the movement. "I want you to like one another, and for you both to stay with me."

"You want?" groaned Mappy. "But you don't know anything about this man!"

Indignantly, she straightened up. "I know that he's my friend. Am I not the queen?"

"You are the queen."

"Then I order you to obey him, as you do me!"

XVIII
Borobudur

"Yes, I have two companions, two sisters that I left in Solo."

"We'll go to fetch them."

"How good you are, and how I love you!"

"But before then, you'll be mine . . . you promise me!"

"You'll do with me what you wish . . ."

"Tonight?"

"Tonight . . . if we find a safe hiding-place. The chief is watching . . ."

Mappy and his rong'geng want to make their devotions at Borobudur, and Stéphane has hired ponies for the band, which are snorting and prancing. It is nine o'clock in the morning; not a breath of wind is stirring the ardent plumage of the rhododen-drons and the rounded heads of the pink and blue azaleas. The flowering tulip-trees are hanging sadly over the plantations of quinine, coffee, cinnamon, clove, tea and vanilla, which incense the travelers with a tenacious and peppery perfume.

The princely lands that the rong'geng have just traversed are like independent islets that rise above a sea submissive to Holland. How many secrets, ambitious embraces and mysterious and impotent intrigues there are in those islets, each of a thousand men, volcanic lands where the subterranean ire of nature and the fires stirred by the spirit of conquest rumble simultaneously, the last oases where the ancient race of dominators of Malaysia have taken refuge! A little cannon-fire would suffice to annihilate the vestiges of Javanese nobility; but gratuitous consideration for two princes assures the gratitude and servility of twenty million indigenes.

Kadu, which the little troop is traversing, is an uneven country, with impenetrable virgin forests on its rounded summits. Here is the "Nail of Java," a mountain of bizarre form, which resembles an immense florid cone plunging into the molten sky.

After a light meal at Magelang, Mappy takes his dancers to the temple of Borobudur, where the nomadic tribes that have served the old religions come to make their devotions.

The monument rises on a symmetrical hill in the middle of a large circular valley, which forms a girdle for it studded with the gems of all the wealth of Javanese flora. In the distance, on the horizon, like the crenellations of a natural fortress, the crests of extinct volcanoes dominate it. And here there is the triumph of Buddha! He reigns, from the foot to the summit of the immense pyramid; he grows, he multiples, he is everywhere and always, radiating over the world!

On the parapets of five superimposed galleries there are more than six hundred Buddhas of heraldic grandeur, in preciously ex-cavated open niches, which resemble the decorative pleats of an expensive lace—for there is not a stone that is not sculpted, accommodating subjects in bas-reliefs of admirable workmanship.

Right away, Mappy prostrated himself three times, touching the ground with his forehead, murmuring words of adoration and submission, which Mana'i and Sigete repeated. Soakia remained standing next to Stéphane, and surreptitiously put her little hand in his.

"Tonight!" breathed the young man, in an ungraspable voice, which only the pretty dancer could hear.

"Tonight."

The chief continued his incantations before a statue larger than the others, issuing from a tall lotus flower. Birds were nailed to the walls of the niche, wings spread. Blood, trickling through the feathers, had formed stalactites on the edge of tails ocellated with shades of red. They were enormous owls, which other travelers of the road had sacrificed to Cakyamouni. A few had been dead for a long time, and nothing any longer remained against the stone ridges but the debris of their skeletons; others, less eroded, still seemed to be darting phosphorescent gleams through the enlarged holes of their orbits.

Green and blue flies were fluttering around, as well as tiny birds that scintillated like living gems.

Soakia turned her head away in disgust, and looked behind her at the roseate plain bordered by mountains. Here and there, a coconut palm inclined over a hill of sand, and in the distance, a rainstorm hung from the sky over the fuming head of a volcano, like a long gauze scarf speckled with silver. Rumbles of thunder rolled above them, sometimes muffled, sometimes urgent and vehement.

Through the opening that someone had had the curiosity to carve out in the Dagob, one can perceive the recumbent effigy of a human being, scarcely emerged from a block of stone. It is the image of the supreme Organizer of the world, which has remained unfinished, because the hand of man ought not to pretend to the real reproduction of divine features.

"Everything here speaks of amour," said Stéphane. "The mountains have ardent mouths and also seem to show the bosoms of women with their breasts swollen."

"Everything loves," sighed Soakia.

"In order for Buddha to be favorable to me," said Mappy, "I shall spend the night in prayer . . . and Soakia will stay with me."

"Oh, Mappy, I'm so tired! And in any case, your beliefs aren't mine."

"That true," replied the chief, sadly, "but I thought that you had pity for my pain."

"Your pain?"

"Yes. I've observed the movement of snakes in the grass, I've breathed on the ashes of the dead, and pricked my breast with my curved krise in order to ward off ill fortune. Alas, the gods are against us."

"Against us? What have we done?"

"I don't know, but I only see somber presages."

Mappy does not say that he wants to keep the little queen beside him because he is jealous of the handsome young man with the white skin, and that a murderous obsession has gripped him since he prayed to the great Buddha to be propitious to him.

After a furtive signal from Stéphane, Soakia resigns herself to obeying, or making a semblance of doing so. Behind the hastening chief she reaches one of the platforms of the temple, where the marvelous tableau of the life of Prince Cakya unfurls.

"We'll stay here," he said, and continues, with a malevolent laugh: "and the traveler can make his choice among the rong'geng, who will keep him company. He will have nothing of which to complain; Sigete and Mana'i are charming."

Soakia holds back her tears and does not reply. All the gratitude she had for the chief is suddenly annihilated; it is almost hatred that he inspires in her now.

XIX
Jealousy

Sigete and Mana'i are charming . . . ? Will Stéphane be unfaithful already, before the possession?

The little dancer knows nothing of life, but her soul is in anguish; it seems to her that an ardent beast is devouring her heart. Scarcely has she known amour than she already knows suffering. To love is to live, and to live is to lose every day a scrap of the precious veil that, for very young girls, masks harsh reality.

For the little girl, an anxious sadness has replaced the astonishment of the first days. The solitude of her thought frightens her, for she cannot confide in anyone. It will require the tenderness of amour to give her the calm that she can no longer find, and Mappy always surges forth between her and her desire.

Without any right, and although still very submissive, he is manifestly jealous of her preoccupations, her smiles and her tears. He understands that a new hope is shining in her life and he is suffering cruelly in consequence. She seems tormented by some secret attraction, and she is struggling against some occult power that is soliciting her.

Why is Soakia not a doll like the others, with eyes of indifferent enamel and a breast stuffed with bran? The gods that have given her a soul have been needlessly cruel, for the torture of a pauperess can add nothing to her glory.

She leans over the terrace, trying to perceive the rong'geng who have remained at the foot of the monument with the two seeresses. She cannot see anything, but she can hear bursts of laughter and something like a sound of kisses.

"Mappy," she says, resolutely, "I don't want to stay with you; I can't worship your god, who isn't mine."

The chief, who has divined her secret anxieties, is also suffering from jealousy and desire. He replies, almost brutally: "Cakyamouni will give you peace; he will lead you to Nirvana, which is the goal of all wisdom."

"Your god is an impostor; I'm not yet at the age of renunciation. In order to renounce the joys of this world, it's necessary to know them . . ."

"There is no joy down here: nothing but a temporary intoxication, of which the memory is often bitter. Stay in this place of meditation, little queen . . . the two of us will pray together."

Soakia is a woman; although very ignorant, she nevertheless knows that it is necessary not to oppose the caprice of men overtly, and that cunning achieves more than the best arguments. She lies down on the rugs that Mappy has prepared for her and closes her eyes, while the chief sings plaintively, as he has the custom of doing, in order to lull her to sleep. She has never stirred his being thus; he digs his fingernails into his flesh in order to resist the desire to take her completely, to stifle her cries of revolt with his kisses.

The jagged crests of the volcanoes irradiate white flames around them, like molten metal. Gleams crawling along the peaks raise menacing tongues toward the sky, and in the hollows of the mountains, an entire mysterious revolt is swarming, betrayed by muffled baying. Further away, a petrified sea shows waves of coagulated lava, immobile torrents, a tempestuous exasperation, anesthetized as if by a miracle.

What is happening in that strange land where everything is fluid and igneous, in constant incandescence, with enormous rocks, heavy, inert masses of minerals and metals, which are bones, a skeleton, the hard form that maintains an expansive soul and prevents it from rising toward the light?

Many a time, leaning over the burning, boiling mud, the chief had witnessed the efforts of that delirious soul to emerge from itself, to launch toward infinity; and he had said to himself, in his naïve fatalism, that it would be good to die in a convulsion of the world, in a sudden upheaval of the elements. Of his torn, burned, consumed body, nothing would remain but a light ash, which, in better days, would settle in the calices of flowers with fecundating pollen; and that would be an admirable annihilation!

But the craters, this evening, seem to be sighing without anger. Long trails of mauve vapor extend, at times, over the passes; here and there, moonlight frosts some nearer hill with silver, glittering like a pigeon's throat. Other rumps, bizarrely twisted, seem to be making graces like some figure sketched by a lascivious dancer. Although it is night, light is streaming from that mountainous ocean, resembling a golden liquid that is throwing a phosphorescent spangled foam over every obstacle.

Mappy was panting now, droplets of sweat descending over his hollow cheeks, in his frantic desire, exasperated by the musky odor that Soakia's young and supple body exhaled. He uncovered her, placed his lips on her flesh, but he was ashamed of what he was about to do, and, getting up abruptly, he resumed praying before the image of Cakyamouni.

Through her lowered eyelashes, the young woman was spying on the chief's every gesture. A temptation even came to her to pick up the weapons that he had deposited beside her and to threaten him with them if he did not let her leave. But she thought that he was brave, that he did not fear death. Doubtless he would be glad to be struck by her, would offer her his breast, and the sight of blood would make her weak . . .

For a long time she waited, watching slender snakes undulating in the fissures in the stone, appearing and disappearing. The monument, one of the parts of which she could see, obliquely, was as tawny as the pelt of a lion by virtue of the reflection of the mountains. The Buddhas, in their niches, also inspired some terror in her; she was gnawed by impatience.

Finally, Mappy collapsed on his heels, and then, falling on his side, remained motionless.

With infinite precaution, the girl got up, enveloped herself in her veils and went down the steps of the terrace. Fear held her back, at every moment she extended her ears in the direction of the sleeper, thinking that she could hear him getting to his feet and launching himself in her pursuit.

XX
Possession

At the bottom of the staircase, the rong'geng were asleep. Stéphane was not with them. Soakia breathed deeply, and, walking on tiptoe in order not to wake the children, she explored the surroundings. After a quarter of an hour of anxious searching, she found the young man in contemplation before a black snake with yellow spots, as dazzling as precious stones, which was writhing in the grass.

"Don't do it any harm," she said. "It brings good luck. It's a benevolent spirit that has placed it in our path."

"Dear Soakia!"

Already he had clasped her to his heart, seeking her lips.

Soakia, who had always repelled the desire of men, savored that new caress delightedly.

"Let's find a shelter," he said.

Without resistance, she followed him through the long grass, which thousands of fireflies illuminated with a sparkling galactic frost.

When they were well hidden, he held her against him again, and kissed her hair, her forehead, her somber gold-flecked eyes and her little ears, slowly, as one savors a treat long coveted. Without really knowing what he was saying, he murmured words of naïve tenderness, for he only spoke her language imperfectly. His ardor increased, causing his temples to throb, and if he refrained from possessing her brutally, it was in order to refine his pleasure, augmented by the terror of a surprise.

She listened to him without interrupting him, charmed to sense herself loved other than she had been thus far, for the sentiment that she inspired in him was neither the scornful caprice of a master nor the tremulous ambition of a slave. She felt that she was the equal of the man who was soliciting her, and the consciousness of her reconquered dignity rendered her more loving. Stéphane was the grave and passionate lover that all women desire, the lover skillful enough never to make the disdainful pride of his triumph felt.

He held her against his breast, sensing her shoulders trembling. The warmth of her body, rubbed with aromatics, invaded him, exasperating his desire to take her, to make her his irresistibly, and he took off her necklaces, removed the scarf that veiled her loins, his fingers trembling madly, irritated by the obstacles.

The girl had allowed herself to fall in the grass, languid and feverish, all her fears having vanished in the passionate expectation that delivered her, defenseless, desirous of sensuality.

He admired, marveling, bewildered by new sensations, the meager breasts, already erect and turgid, inverted amber cups, in which a topaz dew remained like a drop of generous wine. The girl's firm flesh rebounded under his lips; they ran over all of it, surprised by that perfection of forms, dazed by an ardent joy, hungry for brown amour.

Soakia had closed her eyes upon the intoxication of the dream, allowing her nectar to be drunk here and there, like a great flower blossoming for the felicity of butterflies. She abandoned herself, glad of the violation of her fragile corolla, glad of the supreme and penetrating adoration that made her a woman, a mistress and a sovereign of sensuality.

Stéphane raised himself up suddenly, feeling something cold sliding between his shoulders. With a weak hand, Mappy was still holding the weapon with which he had tried to strike.

"This girl is mine," he said. "Go away."

Stéphane looked at the chief scornfully.

"Soakia has given herself freely," he said. "She belongs to me henceforth."

"She is of our race, not yours; she cannot deny it."

"Choose," said the young man, turning to the dancer.

Without hesitation, she put her hand on the foreigner's shoulder. "It's you that I've chosen."

"You see, it's me that she prefers."

Mappy, dazed by rage, raised his weapon in order to strike for a second time. But Stéphane, drawing a revolver from his belt, took rapid aim and fired. The chief uttered a dull moan and fell.

While the reng'gong lamented, brought at a run by the noise, tearing their hair, and performed a kind of bizarre dance around the master, in which cries and imprecations were mingled, the lovers unhitched two of the ponies that had brought them, and drew away at a fast gallop.

PART TWO

I
Honeymoon

They had returned to Solo, where Stéphane wanted, for a few weeks, to shelter his amours and liberate the two younger sisters of his mistress. In the palace in which they lived, there were no banal ornaments on the stucco walls, garnished to the height of the wainscot with curiously carved cedar paneling. The ground disappeared under an immense carpet made of royal tiger skins, and between the colonnades of pink marble, the gaze was only arrested by harmoniously shaded clumps of tropical vegetation.

Profound basins, in which jets of water were singing, spread a mild gaiety everywhere, and women were asleep on white mats at the doors of cells, ready to come running at the slightest signal. Their bodies, slick with unguents, exhaled an odor of spices and musk, which mingled with the other aromas of the soil and the plants.

Stéphane was suffocating slightly in the hot atmosphere that the vaults and the foliage beat down upon him. The perfumes, radiations and breaths intoxicated him like a heady wine. In the dazzle of this new life, he never wearied of slaking his thirst on his lover's lips. She was confounded with the enchantment of the dream-like décor, and his amour was released more ardently, blooming like the great pink lotuses that flowered on the motionless mirrors of the pools.

"Doesn't it seem to you, little golden dragonfly, that everything is metamorphosing in accordance with the dispositions of our soul? I was suffering in this beautiful land before knowing you, but now, it's certain that it's heaven on earth. Where were my eyes, in order not to enjoy such splendors?"

"Before encountering you, my beloved, I was a fragile plant that grew at hazard, without joy and without pain. My sensitive heart only opened next to you. We shall never be separated again, and if you can't stay here, you'll take me to France?"

"Yes, my love."

"You'll take me, and also my sisters Wakiem and Taminah? They will love you as I do."

"You won't be jealous?"

"Why would I be jealous? I wasn't jealous of the rong'geng, who were not of my rank."

"Then you'll permit me to have other lovers?"

"My religion doesn't forbid it. My sisters and I will render you happy."

The young man remained thoughtful, slightly alarmed by that conception of amour, so different from the one that people have elsewhere, but he did not protest, curious to know the Susuhunan's dainty bedayas.

The ardent sun reddened the marble around them, giving the stone amber and micaceous tints, dressing the minarets in a sheath of crimson and gold. On the columns and the stairways, the arabesques seemed suspended in droplets of gems.

When her friend was absent Soakia leaned on the corner of the terrace and gazed on the city in which she had lived, in which she did not know anyone, where she was more unknown than a migratory bird passing over like a winged flower to go who knows where, to live or to die; and that solitude pleased her.

She was agitating in a tale of enchantment, and, when she closed her eyes, she imagined a thousand phantasmagorias in the land of France, which she desired to see with her friend: palaces descended from the clouds with towers, colors of crenellations, domes resembling crushed fruits, and sheaves of slender obelisks like golden pistils. The bas-reliefs, in the light of colored glass, oozed gems of amaldine and chrysoprase, a dew of blood and honey. Everywhere, vine-stocks of flames climbed; everywhere, clusters of emerald and amethysts flowed; the ground seemed to be moistened by a flood of stars.

But when she told him about her dreams, Stéphane smiled gently.

"My poor Soakia, my homeland isn't as beautiful as you suppose. It's cold there, and everything there seems drowned in mist."

"Will we be leaving soon?"

"Why leave? The flowers of sensuality fade in the northern fog."

Impressions came to her that she had never sensed before. It seemed to her that she had undergone a transformation, that her childish melancholy had disappeared, in order to give way to an enthusiastic ardor that she had not suspected. Then a fear came to her of being abandoned by the man who was now her reason for living; she threw herself into his arms, begging him to love her forever, to guide her, already wheedling like the inexperienced little girl that she still was.

With further transports, he embraced her, proving to her that she was still desired as ardently; and, indeed, he cherished her for her bizarre beauty, the pepper of her feverish kisses, the shocks that she imprinted upon the slightly torpid nerves of a blasé Parisian. She truly was a corolla of sensuality, a bird of light with delectable plumage, whom he never wearied of caressing, and to whom he never wearied of listening.

"Oh," she sighed, rubbing her supple and perfumed young body against him, "I feel that I have an entirely new soul, a soul that sighs and sings like an amorous rebab. Have I existed until now? I no longer remember . . ."

He thought he was disentangling a new self in her babbling, in the singing freshness of her little girl's voice, in which the notes of true passion were weeping.

II
A Pleasant Game

"How can we alert your sisters?"

"I don't know. It will be necessary to see Sukuta."

"The duenna who guards them?"

"Yes, and give her money."

"Might she not betray us?"

"Not if the sum is large enough."

"I'll think about it. But tell me, is Wakiem as pretty as you?"

"Much prettier, certainly, and she's only ten years old."

"And Taminah?"

"Taminah is eleven. She resembles me a little."

Smiling, Soakia advanced toward a large mirror, and threw off her veils. First her breasts appeared, crowned with warmer flowers, with a pistil circled by a line of gold, and the belly haloing a navel similarly iced with gold, the tapering legs, charming, with the delicacy of a precious statuette, and the dainty feet, ringed like the hands.

With a finger she indicated her bosom and her groin.

"Wakiem is even thinner, Tamiah plumper . . . And then here . . . and then there . . ."

He placed his lips in the spot that she indicated . . . and she swooned under his hectic kisses.

After the game, he wanted to dress her again, to make her a puerile and magnificent idol. Over a sarong of narrow mesh, made of translucent blue and white operas, he slid an arachnean scarf, which allowed the sight of the upper part of her svelte body, adorned with a triple row of turquoises and opals. He composed a bizarre hairstyle for her, retained by long tortoiseshell pins, dotted with sapphires, or allowed her heavy tresses to fall all the way to her heels like a mantle of darkness. For a moment, elbows tight to the body and knees together, she remained very straight, in a hieratic attitude; then, suddenly, she raised her arms, glided softly on her bare feet, and mimed in order to please him with the most lascivious poems of amour.

"Now sing," he said.

And he collected her song from her mouth, note by note, bead by bead, like a crystal rosary.

She huddled against him in their nest of tenderness. She was sure of him, and she imagined that she had known him for years, forever . . .

After the game, they fell silent, narrowly enlaced, watching the shadows descend gradually, the garden metamorphosing, preparing itself for nocturnal caresses. In the profound blue, almost black sky, the mysterious gleam of the stars was muted. There were pale waves, fixed in places, while others were ardent, more active, flowing in infinite space toward some unknown goal.

The immensity of that prodigious sea, illuminated by fever-inducing gleams, left them almost tremulous in one another's arms; Soakia sighed softly, like a wounded turtle-dove, and tipped her head back on her friend's shoulder, who rocked her then like a little child.

III
A Luminous Idea

"I've found it! I've found it!"

Soakia clapped her little hands, sparkling with jewels, joyfully.

"You've found it?"

"Yes. I know a means of liberating my sisters."

"What?"

"You'll disguise yourself as an Arab merchant, an old merchant of pastes and perfumes, and you'll go to offer your products to Sukuta."

"What an idea!"

"Sellers of unguents and treats enter the palace freely, for the bedayas love extracts of roses and preserves tasting of acacia. You'll see the duenna, and you'll offer her a lot of money to bring Wakiem and Taminah."

"And if she refuses?"

"You'll kill her and take her keys . . . but she'll consent."

"In spite of the punishment that awaits her?"

"Bah! It's easy to replace two little dancers, and the Susuhunan won't even notice the substitution."

"So everything here can be bought, as it can at home?"

"It's doubtless only the color of the face that changes."

"You're right, darling Soakia; the human soul is the same everywhere."

"Then you want to do it?"

"I want to do it."

"Oh, how kind you are!"

And the child gave him the kiss behind the ear that he loved, which immediately changed the course of the conversation.

After the bath in the basin with the singing waves, where they delivered themselves to a thousand games—as they did in the garden, as they did on the terrace, as they did everywhere, since they had known one another—Soakia drew away from her lover slightly, suddenly adopting a severe attitude.

"It's necessary not to exhaust ourselves, you know."

"Why?"

"Because it's today."

"Right away, just like that?"

"Certainly, since I have the means."

"I'll need the costume of an old Arab."

"That's easy! You'll see."

Completely naked, except for two gardenias inclined over her ears, she runs outside and claps her hands to summon the sellers of seraglio pastilles and rose preserves, who never cease hawking their merchandise.

72

An old man with a long white burnoose is walking past, with his small inventory before him. In two minutes the bargain is concluded, and Sidi ben Amed, as naked as Job, draws away hastily in order to hide his . . . confusion.

"It's no more difficult than that," says the scamp, bursting into laughter. "Come here, my handsome Stéphane."

Stéphane lends himself to the metamorphosis, allowing himself to be swathed and to pass to red and to black; his eyes are blurred with antimony, his eyebrows elongated with a mixture of gum and crushed flies' legs; he is superb and terrible.

"But I don't know any Arabic," he says, anguished.

"Nor does Sukuta. You'll speak Javanese."

"With a French accent?"

"That doesn't matter . . . anyway, here's the irresistible argument."

She takes a handful of gold from a casket, which she drops in a cascade into her friend's hand.

"Come on, I'll take you to the bedayas' little door, passing through the alun-alun."

"You'll be recognized."

"Look."

She puts a white scarf over her face, which, passing over her forehead and her mouth, only allows her intense red-speckled eyes to be seen; and she winds around her slender body a silky yellow sheet that trails in the dust lightly on one side, and is lifted up graciously on the other by a golden scarab.

"Let's go!"

They traversed the Kraton, went alongside the shops covered in canvas, where women crouching in front of displays watched them pass with a vague gaze; others were hawking their merchandise: fruits, dried fish, honey-cakes and rice-cakes, fabrics with flamboyant floral patterns, silver and coral jewelry of a barbaric richness, little bells for the necks of great pink oxen with a nonchalant stride, and krises with poisoned blades . . .

The streets are narrow and tortuous and the most beautiful boutiques are made of bamboo. A Chinese clockmaker, his pigtail braided and his upper body uncovered, is fitting fragile cylinders into a watch, which he is turning back and forth in his expert hands. A Malay is selling monkeys, the tameness of which he praises, and which are frolicking at liberty, flinging a mango or a banana back and forth. Brown adolescents are walking with snakes spotted with ocher and vermilion, which are coiled round their necks or their arms. A soft whistle causes them to raise their head and dart their forked tongue. There are even young crocodiles in vats, which serve to amuse children and resemble playthings of articulated wood.

Soakia marches gravely, pulling up the pleats of her veil and examining enviously the barbaric adornments with pendants of copper and coral, silver rings and belt buckles with enormous glass cabochons.

"They're not worthy of you. I'll buy you jewels with finely worked and sculpted gold, and strings of pearls to sheathe your tiny feet. You'll be ornamented like a legendary princess."

But she forces him to stop in order to buy a light dagger with a jade hilt encrusted with silver.

"It's fortunate, though, that the chief didn't stab you; his blade was steeped in the juice of herbs that cause death."

"Poor Mappy wasn't so lucky."

"Bah! Perhaps he got away with it, and that would be so much the worse for us. These road-runners have tough skins."

"I didn't want to do him any harm."

"You're good, Stéphane. He, too, was good, but it's you that I love . . . Now I'm scared . . ."

"Shh! Let's not give ourselves away. It seems to me that people are smiling as we go past."

They maintained silence as they approached the palace.

There was doubtless a rehearsal of a sacred pantomime in the bedayas' quarters, for the cavernous voice of gongs was audible, punctuated by shrill tom-toms, and then the sighs of the rebab and the suling, the joyful sounds of bonangs and gambangs—

horizontal arrays of metal plates struck by sticks wrapped in cloth—and the harmonious arpeggios of the celempung, the strings of which are plucked with the two thumbnails, the other fingers remaining free to stifle the sound.

Black men were crouched on the steps of the vestibule, holding pikes before them. Their saffron-colored robes were extended over the marble, and they rolled their white eyes without speaking. Young women providing sweat-baths were emerging from the women's apartments. They had coral necklaces and squares of scarlet cloth covering their loins, attached in front by clasps of glass beads. Others, their tunics tucked up by garlands of foliage, were throwing away withered flowers and milky water mingled with vehement perfumes.

Soakia went along the small garden and stopped before a little door to the pendoppo, where there were only two guards, half-asleep.

"Go in there," she said.

"You think they'll let me through?"

"Yes, it's rehearsal hour."

"I feel very nervous. What if I compromise everything by some imprudence?"

"No, I've given you the lesson. Have no fear."

"And you'll wait for me here?"

"Yes, behind that wall. Go on, then!"

"And I ask . . ."

"You ask for Sukuta. Don't forget my instructions."

IV
The Rehearsal

"Sukuta will come, but if the talismans of beauty and balms are as inferior as those she bought last week from another fake Arab, she won't want them."

"My talismans are infallible. Here are oil of cedar, and oliban, kohl, rose pastilles and delicacies."

"That's good. Wait here."

Schaoul, a third class duenna, has taken Stéphane into a long room closed by a curtain, and Kroum, another unimportant duenna, examines the make-up and the essences.

"We know these unguents," she says. "They're worthless, and as for your pastes, they smell rancid at fifteen paces."

"You don't know anything about them!"

"What are you daring to say? I'm the one who presides over the bedayas' ablutions, and it's me who rubs their bodies with perfumed oil after the bath. I know all the secrets of sensuality."

"There are, however, some you don't know." ripostes Stéphane, sardonically.

"Which, if you please?"

"I'd prefer not to talk about them, for I sense that I'm incapable of instructing you."

"Get out, insolent fellow! Out! Out!"

"Why all the noise?" demands Sukuta, lifting the curtain and showing half of a simian visage.

"For nothing," said Kroum, scornfully. "For an Arab selling polluted drugs . . . look what he's offering us!"

The young man prostrates himself and, in a humble posture, solicits an audience.

"I have a few words to say to you, noble Sukuta, only a few words; you won't have the cruelty to send me away thus? And then, I have precious essences on me that I'll allow you to respire when we're alone."

"Essences?"

"Unknown extracts of a marvelous potency and suavity."

"Truly?"

"Send this woman away and you'll see."

"Kroum, we're rehearsing the pantomime of the hero Pangdi, and it isn't working at all. Wakiem and Taminah are particularly unruly. I've taken away their sarongs and necklaces to punish them. They're as naked as poor rong'geng from the arid mountains, which hasn't diminished their impertinence at all. Perhaps the two of us will be able to reckon with them."

The duennas disappear behind the curtain, and the young man, moving the silky fabric aside slightly, perceives the dancers, who are gliding over the marble harmoniously, almost without lifting their delicate feet: puerile and charming phantoms, a fragile procession of indifferent idols. No frisson disturbs the expert disposition of their hair, florid with little white bells, and the seven fateful gold triangles shine on their foreheads. They are holding their infantile heads very straight, their eyelids extended toward the temples by lilac-tinted dashes, with painted lips contrasting with the amber hue of the complexion. They are wearing similar robes, decorated with blue flames and mandrakes, with gold-embossed girdles, and moving their fingers as if to seize dream butterflies . . .

Their attitudes express grave, almost dolorous things, and one cannot tell whether they are mourning a god or pleading for amour. But now two bedayas have separated from the group, and are pursuing one another, laughing. They thumb their noses at the duennas, with lively gestures, and the bounds of playful kittens.

"Sukuta, we're mocking you!"

"Try to catch us Sukuta!"

"Oh, the nasty old woman!"

"Oh, the nasty old witch!"

"Hou! Hou!"

The little rebels are devoid of all clothing, and Stéphane, by means of certain particularities of their slender bodies, recognizes Soakia's sisters. His heart beats more rapidly, for he thinks that they will soon be his, and that he will string kisses everywhere over their new flesh.

"You say that we can't dance?" says Wakiem. "Watch this!"

Her feet pass in front of one another swiftly, she whirls like a bee, like an intrepid and vagabond fire follet. Then, her eyelids half-closed, she twists her figure, swaying her belly with bizarre undulations, evocative of the lasciviousness of Islam—which extracts indignant cries from Sukuta.

"Such a dance! Here! It's a horror! What indecency!"

"Look! Look!"

Taminah now sways like a flower caressed by the breeze; she bends gently over her hips, straightens up, and spins frenetically around the old woman; then, throwing herself on to her hands, with her heels in the air, she remains motionless, with an air of comical bravado. She resembles a little gray grasshopper, ready to leap.

"You won't mime tomorrow before the Susuhunan's guests!"

"So much the better!"

"You'll be deprived of your adornments."

"Too bad!"

"And you'll work for a week in the closed room on gala sarongs, like seamstresses."

"We'd rather work than see your surly face!"

"Enough!" says Sukuta, in a dignified manner. "We're going to recommence the pantomime of the hero Pangdi, and Schaoul will read you the poetic introduction in order for you to grasp the sentiment of the sublime drama fully."

The little bedayas sit down on the floor, their legs crossed, while Schaoul, in the voice of a hoarse parrot, intones the lines of the sacred song. She is supported by a melody executed in unison, with closed mouths at first, and then, with increasing emphasis, until the expansion of an immense crescendo.

"You're celebrating," Kroum says, "the beauty of the hero's women, and your enthusiasm no longer has any bounds. Salute now, and go put on your warrior helmets."

The dancers get up, all together, and salute a fictitious person—doubtless the Master—by putting their hands to their faces, held flat against one another.

Wakiem and Tamimah, hoisted into a kind of loggia fitted into the wall, let their naked legs dangle, and mime some burlesque parody, pulling aggressive faces and striking their heels against the sonorous woodwork.

Through the narrow opening in the curtain, Stéphane sends them a cluster of kisses from his fingertips, which scatter en route and settle at random on their thin, amorously mischievous bodies.

V

The Irresistible Argument

"Let's see these rare essences? These creams and cosmetics?"

Sukuta, having returned to Stéphane, examines his meager display of coarse products suspiciously.

"Lotus of the enchanted lakes," he says graciously, "I haven't come to sell you seraglio pastilles. I'm not offering you my merchandise, but I intend, on the contrary, to buy yours."

The old woman opens her eyes wide, and folds over her meager bosom a veil with a gold floral pattern, which her struggle with the unruly bedayas has disturbed.

"What is this joke?"

"I'm speaking seriously, noble duenna. And here's the proof."

He makes a purse bulging with joyful coins clink, and Sukuta, with broad laughter, displays sharp teeth all blackened by betel.

"You've robbed a nabob then, Sire Arab?"

"I've done better, lady of my heart."

"A murder!"

"Better still."

"Several murders?"

"Truly, for such a distinguished person, you lack intuition. I haven't stolen anything or killed anyone, venerable Sukuta."

"What then?"

"I simply found a large sum in my crib when I came into the world. I don't have the cunning of a thief, nor the breadth of a murderer. Let's be modest."

"Why this paltry accoutrement?"

"In order to reach you, since only merchants of youth and beauty are admitted into this gynaeceum."

The old woman moves the curtain aside in order to watch the bedayas, who are slowly miming the sacred poem, with the gestures of automata.

"Faster! Faster!" she says, nervously clapping her stiff hands. "We're not representing the sadness of a faint-hearted lover but the triumph of an adventurous prince! Mussuga, your helmet is titled and your garuda with outspread wings wasn't sufficiently buffed this morning—it's full of verdigris! What are you thinking, Kroum? Such negligence is unpardonable!"

"We buffed them! We buffed them! Make way for the Susuhunan's little dolls!"

Wakiem and Taminah have put on bizarre clothes that hang oddly around them, and immense paper headdresses over their hair, simulating donkeys' heads. They come in, gesticulating, and stop, confused, in front of Stéphane, who smiles.

"The darling creatures! Would you like to sell them to me?"

"Oh!" says Sukuta, trembling with anger. "May the evil spirits rid me of them! But it's not for me to dispose of their fate."

The children have tears in their eyes before the foreigner who is looking at them so passionately. They try to slip away, but Stéphane takes them by the hand.

"Wakiem and Taminah," he says, "would you be content to be with me?"

Without transition, they start laughing.

"Oh! Yes!"

"Oh! Yes!"

They are laughing because they are thinking about the possibility of seeing Soakia again, and because the stranger definitely has a very soft voice.

"But how do you know our names?" says Taminah.

"Can it be," says Wakiem, "that you know our sister?"

"She's begging on the roads, poor sister!"

"Quickly, give us news of her."

"Soakia is happy and sent me to you. If you want to come with me, I'll love all three of you."

"All three! What joy!"

Like Soakia, they find sharing quite natural, and rejoice in belonging to the same man. That would be a very virtuous existence.

"We'll have necklaces?"

"Rare flowers?"

"Bracelets for the legs and arms?"

"Gold-embossed belts and gold-embroidered sarongs?"

"Perfumes and fans?"

"I wouldn't refuse you anything."

"Let's go! Let's go!"

Meanwhile, Sukuta has recovered somewhat from her surprise, and puts her thin fingers on the girls' shoulders, like tentacles.

"These bedayas belong to the sultan."

"I'll buy them."

"The master might find out; it would cost my life."

"Bah! There's no shortage of rong'geng to replace the fugitives. I'll send you two of them this evening, well trained and of facile humor."

The old woman makes the gold coins clink, and her owl-like eyes seem lined with a leaf of the metal themselves, so brightly are they shining with covetousness.

"In addition," says Wakiem, "I'll leave you all my jewels."

"Me too," says Taminah.

"I'll only take the fetish of the enchantress Kidoul, which is of no value to you."

Sukuta still hesitates, torn between the love of gain and the fear of reprisals.

"Can't you add something more, noble stranger? See how supple and well-turned the little ones are. I can guarantee that they're brand new."

Now, with comical tenderness, she caresses the dancers, lifting their garments to show off the firmness of their flesh and the perfection of their slender limbs.

"They are, in fact, charming."

"Say that they're accomplished. You won't find their like, and I've raised them especially for the master's pleasure. Truly, I'm making a fool's bargain . . ."

So close to reaching his goal, Stéphane does not know what else to offer, having no jewels on him.

"Take my stock," he says. "I don't have anything else."

"Give."

"And I can take them away?"

"So be it. Not that way, by the secret door. Come."

The children are clinging to him like the pleats of his burnoose, and, holding them tightly enlaced, he leaves the palace thus, guided by Sukuta, who is glad to get rid of the importunate pair.

VI
Caresses

Soakia, weary of the long wait, was beginning to get impatient, and to doubt the skill of her friend. But now they are reunited, under the flowering tree that allows its red corollas to rain down incessantly, perfumed with honey and almond.

"Soakia!"

"My sisters!"

What embraces! The frail creatures jump for joy, give one another a thousand caresses, which the young man contemplates with tenderness and curiosity. Like goat-kids, they have taken the lead in order to find shelter more rapidly and to confide to one another their fears, their troubles and the long dolors of their separation.

Now, in the love-nest, huddling together, they are all talking at the same time, but understanding one another anyway, so similar are their thoughts.

He lay down at their feet, kissed them randomly, and they laughed, falling over backwards under the sweetness of those kisses.

"Take them," said Soakia.

But he preferred to wait longer.

"I don't want to take them. It's necessary that they give themselves, when they love me a little."

"They love you already. Don't you. Taminah, and you, Wakiem, want to be his?"

The little ones tilted their heads with seductive expressions.

"We'd like that."

"See how handsome he is."

They looked at him, mischievous and confused, their eyelids half-lowered, and passed their greedy tongues over their painted lips.

Then they laughed, and laughed again, without knowing why, doubtless because it is good to laugh when one is ten years old, eleven or thirteen. He dreamed of uniting in a single canvas the three gracious movements of woman: one standing, one kneeling, the third lying down. He would also paint them dancing in the pleats of their veils, with lantana flowers in their dark hair. He would paint them in a hundred different ways, in order to carry away a little of them when he returned to France, in order to retain a durable memory of their tender and puerile grace.

"Give them the kiss on the lips that you know."

Soakia is absolutely intent on initiating her sisters to the intoxications of possession; she is impatient to know that they are her equals in voluptuous science.

"Oh, the surprises that you'll have! Truly, in the harem, they don't know the secrets of amour. Stéphane will teach you thing of which you'd never have dared to dream! He'll play with the golden buds of your breasts, the warm cups of your armpits and the hairs on the nape of your neck. He'll bend your body over his arm like a reed, and you'll feel yourself dying under the penetrating passion of his mouth. Oh, his kisses . . . !"

Stéphane thinks that in the first canvas, he will put them in translucent blue scarves dotted with opals and beryls, lunar jewels, mysteriously illuminated on their brown skin, and he will not forget the helmets with deployed wings, the seven triangles of the forehead, and, under the transparency of the veils, yet another triangle with cleverly blurred shadows. Thus their beauty will be distinguished as if through limpid water.

"Give them the kiss on the lips that you know!"

Nervously, Soakia has pushed Taminah into Stéphane's arms, because she is older than Wakiem, and she has the right to more consideration.

Stéphane leans over, obediently. His mouth has taken Taminah's mouth. They intoxicate one another at length. At close range he sees the child's black pupils dilate, vacillate momentarily, and then become clouded under the almost dolorous ecstasy, while her eyebrows, ebony darts, draw closer together in the lascivious effort. Slowly, expertly, he darts supple and ingenious sensuality, accelerates, slows down, and recommences.

It is the turn of Wakiem, who, impatient to know the singular ecstasy, offers of her own accord the flower of her gilded lips, the corolla of which he parts profoundly. There are frictions, caresses, which he varies, which point or turn, which are fixed momentarily, and are then animated with all his desire and all his passionate fantasy.

VII
Harvest of Flowers

But he stops . . . he does not want any more . . . Why exhaust all his pleasure in one go? The sheaf of amour and youth is there, under his hand; he can, without haste, plunge his lips thereinto, intoxicate himself with the perfume of April calices, which excessively ardent rays have not yet caused to bloom.

84

Stéphane, at thirty, had tasted many joys, without conserving anything of them but a little ennui and disdain. Seduced by the rumor of his wealth, his success and his talent, many women had desired to know him better, with the consequence that, having never suffered in anticipation, he had only ever experienced the banal sensualities of the flesh, caprices too easily realized. He had become insupportable to his best friends, by virtue of too much amorous glory, and, not knowing how to avoid so many homages, he had fled, one morning, to sunlit lands where the fruits and the women have a different flavor.

Now, he had resumed living delectably. There was no longer any question in his soul of calculations or projects; he abandoned himself frankly to the charm of that adventure, so delicately spiced. While the children, very weary, slept on his heart, he gazed at the broad leaves that were quivering over the terrace, reminiscent of the umbrellas of giants kneeling in the grass. Fluttering wings and frissons ran like a breath through the embalmed countryside. Before the sun, a curtain made of a thousand hermetically enlaced branches fell gently, and the glaucous daylight, nuanced with the entire gamut of greens, enveloped him with the mysterious tint of a precious stone.

He laid the three bedayas across the bed. They slept, offering the treasures of their brown nudity. They were similar, with their slim waists, their infantile upper bodies, florid with the double golden calyx, scarcely emerged, their narrow hips, which they had surrounded, before repose with clusters of melati, the pink and blue garlands of which undulated all the way to the ankles.

Lightly, Stéphane kissed their naked feet and went out into the garden. What was he going to do with his three lovers?

To keep them with him, so close to the Susuhunan's palace, might be imprudent. It would be better to take them into the interior, in order to lead, far from habitations, a charming existence of labor and amour.

The sun was going down, bringing sparse perfumes of a more acute ardor. There was the incense of aromatics, the honey of herbs, the odor of the earth and shady woods, warm plants and swooning corollas, an entire powerful bouquet that intoxicated him to the extent of vertigo. The verdure was drowned in the blood of the sky, steeped in a rosy and mauve glow. The water had luminous smiles, and seemed to be carrying topazes; there was an apotheosis that burst forth over the distant volcanoes in a dazzling firework display.

He went back under the vault of foliage. At the slightest breath of wind, the path rolled crimson quoits at his feet, and strung a chaplet of rubies and emeralds over his forehead. Many little paths hollowed out verdant cul-de-sacs, where the lianas remained suspended, extending the flaps of a flying tent from one tree to another, and nothing could any longer be seen, between those veils, but microscopic violet pinpricks, cut out like an expensive lace, a fine sieve from which a fine dust of light descended.

He collected flowers, and more flowers, unknown, eccentric, feverish flowers, as disquieting and excessively beautiful girls, of a beauty suffering by dint of having bloomed. They were hairy, or as silky as tentacles, as light as feathers, or as curly as locks of hair. Some had the hue of dead leaves and autumn dreams, of copper, of blood or rust. Erect on their long stems or lost in the moss, they danced sarabands, forming mad rounds, in which all the colors vibrated. These had the fluffy collarets of pert little girls, tapering strawberries of precious guipure, allowing a glimpse of a pale velvet heart. Those, in their white cotyledon, resembled nuns at prayer, and held their virginal lobe chastely closed. Others, immodest, threw their mossy ballerina skirts to all the winds, displaying, all the way to the depths, their brown stamens, so wide-open that the hands shredded them merely by brushing them. And all of them, with the voice of perfumes, sang recklessly passionate canticles that troubled the young man and made him pale with desire.

Finally, he went back in, his arms full of corollas, and threw his embalmed harvest on to the sleepers. Laughing, they woke up.

"Oh, the naughty man!"

"The dear friend!"

"The beloved lover!"

With the supple branches, they played a thousand charming games, to which they lent themselves, quivering and sighing when the caresses became too direct; then, he leapt into their midst, separated them, and, in the flowers, respired the calices of their fresh lips.

VIII
Again

That kiss never ended. With tears, cries, sobs and happy stammers, the children gave birth to unrivaled joys.

There was an exquisite transfiguration.

By turns, braced or indolent, they offered themselves or asked for mercy. Their drowned eyes went astray in the shadow of the long lashes and the vertigo of their gaze; their small breasts, flowering like lotuses, inflated their frail gold-starred cups.

Stéphane went from one to another, drowning his face in the blue-tinted waves of their hair, and, at times, no longer seeing them, so similar were they, with their thin astonished faces and their harmonious gestures, in spite of the feverish transports of which he was the direct cause, which he excited or repressed in accordance with his whim.

He taught them to love and to love one another. Docile, they listened to him, understood him, and imitated him, creatures of sensuality made for all caresses. And under that beautiful sky, in that nature intrepid with passion, the union of those young and beautiful beings, made for the kiss, seemed lovable and natural.

Then he knelt before the couch and, from below, watched them die and be reborn, exalting one another to the point of the supreme swoon.

"Stéphane, I'm yours."

"I'm yours."

"Yours."

They were not jealous, not pained, in belonging to the same man and, through him, knowing the same joys at the same time. He was the friend, the lover, the unique, and they united fraternally to please him. So true is it that sentiments and morality change in accordance with countries, religions and climates, with the consequence that nothing can be perfectly good or perfectly bad.

As they were tired, they had a snack of mangoes, bananas and rice. With the tips of her gilded fingers Soakia prepared a salad of bamboo and chutney in order to renew their strength.

"Little Wakiem, I want to teach you a new manner of eating these fruits," Stéphane said.

Taminah opened her eyes wide, and laughed like a madwoman, although all of her flesh was still dolorous from too much happiness.

"Show me too."

"Again! Again!"

"They didn't teach us anything like that in the Sususuhan's house."

"Are they French games?"

"They're lovers' games."

"Here, you see, we don't know how to love. We're considered as dolls without a heart and soul. When we've served the master's brutal pleasure, he rejects us immediately. However, we know that the man who disposed of our beauty and our youth is a man like any other."

"You aren't scornful, and yet, you're handsome, you're rich, and you have everything necessary to charm."

But Wakiem seemed chagrined. "Why," she said, "don't you want to taste this grasshopper confit? I assure you that it's very good."

"I'm no longer hungry, little Wakiem. Give me again, on your lips, that pale pink wine with the exquisite taste. In passing through your mouth, it's much better and doubly intoxicating."

And on all their mouths he drank three sorts of wines, and then fell asleep, thinking about the roses of France, whose perfume is so listless.

IX
Fireflies

The following day, at dusk, he took his beloveds for an excursion in a bizarre carriage hitched to ponies from the isle of Timor, with bald heads and soft intelligent eyes. They knew nothing about the city, having been raised in the gynaeceum for the master's pleasure, and everything there was a subject of puerile surprise for them. In order not to be recognized in case of pursuit, they had slid long veils over their faces, which draped in light pleats over their white sarongs starred with silver, delicately embroidered with pink monsters, and over the bright langoutis tightened at the waist. Their eyes wearied by the joys of the night, they allowed themselves to be carried away at the gallop of the little horses, becoming suddenly animated and clapping their hands at every unexpected spectacle.

They went along the thin red-tinted watercourses bordered by pale lotuses, gardens and buildings ornamented with arcades, verandas, and terraces over with climbing plants falling back in flowery cascades. At intervals, houses rose up by the roadside; they were the residences of suppliers and merchants, often devoid of upper stories, with adorned women on the thresholds offering their merchandise. The evening was warm, stifling and intoxicating for Stéphane, who felt faint in the midst of that exuberant nature, drowned in a languid atmosphere of tuberose.

"Are you suffering?" Soakia asked.

"Yes, I'd like to sleep for an hour on the edge of the ravine."

"Let's get down from the carriage here. You can tether the ponies to those coconut palms."

"Look," said Wakiem. "Here's a charming spot. We'll watch over you."

"We'll fan you gently."

"We'll drive away the crawling creatures and the nocturnal birds."

The young man lay down delightfully on the edge of the abyss, with his head on Taminah's knees, and his arms round the waists of the other darlings.

In the depths of the ravine ran a torrential stream with phosphorescent waves, and on both banks, as far as the eye could see, a magical vegetation flourished, with corollas of dream and murder. From time to time, the ululation of owls rose up, and the brief calls of chameleons; luminous flies were buzzing, forming complicated lacy arabesques in the air, whose mesh was cleverly studded with precious stones. Then there was a galactic sash, a seed-bed of insects, so tiny that they formed a single sheet of light undulating over the pale guipure, clinging to the asperities of the slope, tumbling into the abyss like a silent cascade of gold dust.

The girls were haloed in light, reminiscent of the sisters of the goddess Kidoul in the palace of amber and topaz guarded by djinn. They were as gentle and light as moonbeams in their simarres, which hung down, open, around their bodies, and in order to affirm their fragile royalty they had put glaucous crowns of glow-worms into their hair. Their velvet eyes retained the magic reflection of their dreams; they were thinking about the ecstasies of the night, only living for further sensuality.

Gradually, the tunics embroidered with monsters slid over the folded legs. They seemed to be emerging from the sacred lotus, charming divinities offered to the cult of amour. With a promising smile at the corners of their lips, they lowered their gazes upon the sleeping lover, and contemplated him with an infinite tenderness.

Above them, giant plants reigned, the dimensions of which were disconcerting. The colossi sculpted menacing gestures over the sky, fixed in the azure, and from their branches the rain of fire still fell, the buzzing rain of ephemeral existences that sought one another, united with one another and exhausted one another in a few hours of lust.

In that apotheosis the three beloveds leaned over and placed their ardent mouths on Stéphane's face.

"Yes," he said.

And, without opening his eyes, he savored their caresses.

X
Alert

The svelte ponies of the isle of Timor had wings. For a week there were charming excursions in the unknown quarters of the city and the surrounding areas. In the evening, the lovers reposed in some solitary place where they were only troubled by the inoffensive slithering of green snakes under the bamboo leaves. They especially liked the coolness of pools shaded by Victoria regias with immense flowers leaning like the pale faces of naiads over the mirror of the water. Around the trees, roots intersected with rebellious upsurges that the damp earth was impotent to contain.

Thick rounded branches emerged from hectic vegetation knotted in silky belts; the smallest fissures in the bark gave shelter to fugitive seeds that sprouted here in fans of tender florets, sheaves of diaphanous grasses, smoke, swirls and flames of thin corollas as soft as smiles. Life was overflowing everywhere, from the gigantic trunk to the blade of grass. Sonorous bumble-bees with ruby and emerald bodies flew from perfume to perfume, along with dragonflies that seemed to be rowing in the air with sapphire and nacre oars, horned moths larger than bats with plushy blood-red wings, dotted and mottled.

They traversed diambalangs, light bridges thrown over rivers with banks carpeted with fragments of flint extracted by torrents from the flanks of mountains. In the morning, the roads were furrowed by merchants in brightly-colored langoutis carrying poles on their shoulders bending under the weight of baskets of fruits—pisang radja bananas, mangoes, pineapples, shiny coral-red rambutans, saumanillas, sirkajas, or cinnamon-apples, and kapulans—ardent peppers—and coquettishly arranged betel leaves.

They bought the beautiful juicy fruits and made incredible meals in the long ferns, from which they emerged with shining eyes and feverish hands.

One day, Soakia, who had gone to draw water from a nearby spring, came back shivering.

"Oh, Stéphane, do you know what I've seen?"

"Tell me, quickly?"

"Mappy."

"Recovered from his wound?"

"Barely. He's camped not far from here with his rong'geng."

"They didn't see you?"

"I don't think so. They're thin and covered in rags."

"Let's run away!" murmured the little ones, trembling for the life of the beloved.

But Stéphane is very brave. "Bah! That bandit wouldn't dare attack me."

"You don't know Mappy," says Soakia. "He's doubtless searching for us, and his vengeance will be terrible. Let's go."

"Dear lover!" Wakiem and Taminah are weeping.

They wrap their supple arms around him to protect him from any danger, and roll their foreheads over his breast seductively, desirous of dying if he does.

XI
Opium

Two days later, Stéphane encountered the chief in the opium smokers' quarter. He had wanted to see the terrible vice that gives sensuality and leads to madness, the dispenser of dreams and lies, the ironically cruel magician that charms its victims in order to strike them harder.

Alone, desirous of new emotions, the young man had penetrated a bamboo cabin illuminated by the yellow light of a large quantity of small lanterns filled with coconut oil.

Malays and Chinese lying on their backs, hands open, were sleeping feverishly or profoundly, agitated by epileptic tremors or fixed in a cadaverous immobility. Others, newcomers, as soon as they had crossed the threshold, hastily bought small pastilles of green-tinted opium displayed on a pewter tray and installed themselves for the fiction of amour, forgetfulness or annihilation.

Warming a long needle in the flame of the lamp, they smeared it with the paste, which they fixed to it in a pellet the size of a pea, and introduced it into their bamboo pipe. The ignited opium grilled slowly, sending clouds of acrid smoke up to the ceiling, in which the shadows of the dream evoked were designed.

The hallucinated eyes opened slightly or died, only showing the whites, suddenly convulsed, and sighs occasionally escaped from panting throats. Fleshless chests swelled like the bellows of forges and then collapsed, lamentably, showing the sharp relief of the ribs. Those human rags, scarcely-thinking larvae, seemed creatures of nightmare, the exhausted participants in some *danse macabre* reposing in the shadow of tombs. Visages appeared behind the extended bodies, like severed heads, posed on the edges of beds. They were the smokers who had rolled off their couches and no longer had enough strength to climb back into them.

The flames of the lamps vacillated in gusts of warm air, and Stéphane, pale with disgust, groped beneath the blue flickers;

then, as the obscurity deepened, he no longer saw anything but bewitched eyes shining like embers in the darkness.

He was about to leave, sickened by all that misery, when a wan figure loomed up in front of him, barring his passage.

"What do you want with me?"

"Nothing," said Mappy. "I've forgiven you."

"Can I do something for you?"

"Perhaps. Listen—I'm not fortunate."

"Accept some money."

"No, with my dancers I could earn it, if I wished. I've come here to forget, to stun myself. And then, I knew that I'd find you again; the oracles told me so."

"Then . . . I don't understand."

"Come into this corner, where we'll be left tranquil."

"Let's go outside instead."

"I'm not solid enough to stand up. This poison is terrible. You don't know what it can do. Look!"

A possessed man tore off the rags that covered his body. Ulcers appeared, almost touching. All the way to the bone his flesh was eaten away by a terrible disease, and the man was digging his fingers into the wounds, enlarging them, while tears ran down the hollows of his cheeks.

"It's necessary to stop him," said Stéphane, terrified.

"No, he's doomed."

The other had seized one of the long needles reddened by fire, and had perforated his abdomen, turning it furiously in the sizzling skin. Blood fell, slowly, in large black drops, along the buckling thighs. But, death not arriving quickly enough, the desperate man seized a dagger. Motionless, the spectators watched, accustomed to suicides that no one seeks to prevent, so indifferent is the idea of death to those hallucinates.

The agonizing man got up, and fell back, making with his lips the sound that infants make when shivering with intense cold; then there was a furious tremor that shook him like a dry branch; he collapsed, and did not move again.

Another smoker got up, tottering, cleaved the breast of the cadaver and then pricked the heart with a needle, and attempted to draw it out. But the master of the establishment drove him away with a kick, and had the corpse picked up.

Further enthusiasts came in, searching for a place, walking through the red pool without paying any heed to it.

The smoke became thicker and more blinding.

"Hurry up," said Stéphane. "I can't support the odor of this room much longer."

"Oh, I only have a few words to say to you. Keep me with you. I'll be your domestic, it doesn't matter to me."

"What about the dancers?"

"They'll find another chief, don't worry. Or, if you prefer, they'll be your maidservants."

"But why are you asking me to keep you?"

"In order to have a shelter . . . don't ask me any more . . . If you continue your travels I'll be very useful, for I know the country thoroughly."

"Is it truly to rest that you want to live with me?"

"It's to have a shelter, I repeat. The métier I've had is too tiring. I'm exhausted, you see, and if I come here, it's only to suffer."

Without suspicion, Stéphane shook the chief's hand.

"Tomorrow," he said, "our house will be open to you."

XII
The Wolf in the Sheepfold

Next to his companions, he kept silent at first, confused by having made such a rapid decision.

As he expected, Soakia was very worried when she learned the strange news.

"It's necessary not to consent."

"I took pity on the poor fellow."

"Send him away."

"Is that possible? I've promised."

"He'll do us harm."

But she did not have the time to continue her desolation, for Mappy, accompanied by the rong'geng Sigete and Mana'i, knocked on the door.

"Here I am," he said, "and I've brought my two seeresses, who will assist you, like me."

Wahiem and Taminah laughed, unconsciously,

"They're pretty . . . but you won't possess them, Stéphane?"

"No, darling."

"You'll stay with us?"

"Always."

"We love you so much!"

And they extended their ardent lips, hoisting themselves up for his kiss. When it was Soakia's turn, Mappy shuddered and turned away. The lovers were too lost in their ecstasy to notice that movement, but Sigete and Mana'i looked at one another silently.

Since the chief had almost died, they had not quit him, caring for him night and day with an unfailing devotion. He scarcely saw them, remaining in the smoky catacombs of dream. He felt a sort of continual vertigo, the daze of a drunken man, which robbed him of all memory. Adroitly, Mana'i had extracted the bullet lodged between two ribs, and then had rubbed the wound with aromatic herbs, and the fever had passed. But Mappy cured was more terrible than Mappy in danger of death. Mappy cured was gripped again by the obsession that tortured him.

What is the good of so many efforts, troubles and struggles, if a man suddenly ceases to belong to himself, and is no longer the master of his thoughts and actions? *Why this futile martyrdom,* the chief said to himself, *which leads to nothing and only has for an excuse the sunlit lure of a distant amour?* Soakia was lost to him, Soakia, whom he had desired uniquely, and who, alone, could soften his incoherent and vagabond existence slightly. When he had abducted the little dancer, he had dreamed of living with her in one of those magical palaces that emerge from the ground to lodge our illusions. His ears had heard new melodies, his lips had quivered in the breath of infinite kisses and even in his sleep, next to the dainty queen, his heart had been delectably stirred.

Scornfully, he laughed today at the pleasure he had found in lulling himself with so many puerile chimeras, in putting his fate in the hands of a woman, a creature of ignorance, vice and lies! If he was still alive, it was in order to avenge himself in a terrible fashion. He did not know how he would attain that goal, but he knew that he would surely reach it, since he had the will that leads to anything.

He made himself supple and affectionate with regard to the bedayas, and tried to gain Stéphane's good graces with a thousand singular stories capable of capturing the enthusiastic imagination of an artist. He took him to see the amusing quarters of the city, the shady dens kept by old Chinamen who sell rice cakes and honey, spiced wine of lotus and jujube, and undertake another, more mysterious, commerce.

In a back room of a shop, on white mats, sit half a dozen yellow figurines with tucked-up enamel eyes and painted lips, so infantile that their sex can barely be determined. At a signal, they get up, throw off the gauze scarf that covers them, and mime desire and amour by means of lascivious poses and slow but precise gestures. They glide, pursue one another, simulate fear, enlace one another and embrace one another, sighing, seem to flee and to appeal for a more direct caress. Their loins quiver, their hands sway, shifting their bosom, clenching their buttocks, and then they lie down, exhausted, offering themselves amid the mutilated flowers of their hair. An odor of naked women spreads, mingled with the exasperated perfume of wines and dying corollas.

Then the men make their choice and disappear into boxes closed by a curtain, or simply couple in the common room.

With his obliging guide, Stéphane learned all the prostitutions and all the caprices of that hot land—those that are admitted, and those that are hidden. He believed that his opium nightmare often continued in the songs and gasps and the regular rhythm of enlaced bodies, but he refused the possession of perverse dolls, keeping himself for his little friends.

XIII
Monkeys and Snakes

"This evening, I want to show you something you've never seen."

"No, Mappy, I'm tired."

"When you know, you'll come with me."

"I don't want to know."

"You're wrong."

"What is it, then?"

"The game of monkeys and snakes."

"No, no, enough anguishing visions."

"Oh, it's not what you think."

"Really?"

"I assure you that you'll laugh."

Devoid of energy, Stéphane followed the chief, who took him to a bamboo hut where young women were stretching themselves nervously on cushions beside large black monkeys, enchained . . .

The quadrumanes with fiery eyes had silver collars and bracelets; they agitated against the wall, uttering irritated or dolorous hoarse sounds at times . . .

Two little boys struck gongs, and a third made a rebab groan, spinning slowly in the confined space.

Newcomers were offered metal cups containing elements for chewing: betel leaves, areca nuts, catechu, tobacco and calcium carbonate.

But Stéphane felt faint, so insupportable was the odor of the place.

"Let's go," he said. "I have a headache."

"You'll get used to it. Wait."

"What more is there to see?"

"But you haven't seen anything yet. It's very amusing."

"These women are no better than anywhere else."

"You can't judge them. It's the turn of the snakes."

"Oh."

"The seeress over there will tell you your destiny."

"My destiny . . ."

Mappy makes a sign to a creature crouching in a corner, who has a long brown reptile with orange stripes around her loins. The monster undulates feebly, swaying its flat head and darting its sharp tongue.

Houramis, the charmer, gets up and comes toward the visitors. She has a sad and feverish appearance; her tawny body seems to be consumed by a morbid ardor, always throbbing, and her long blue eyelids are half-lowered over a crazed gaze in which the pupil shines, enormous and round.

"I was working just now," she says. "I can't do any more."

"You misunderstand, Houramis; it's your science we want to know."

"Oh, so much the better. Mascaro and I are resting."

"You love him, your snake?"

"Yes, he obeys all my caprices. You wouldn't believe how demanding the men who come here are. It's sometimes necessary to recommence twenty times in one night."

"You don't seem to be rich, though. Your jewels are badly cut and their stones devoid of glare."

"People pay so poorly."

"This foreigner is generous, Houramis; reveal the future to him."

"Interrogate me . . . no, there's no need; I can see clearly that nothing unfortunate will happen to him."

Mappy frowned, and his hands trembled.

"You're not infallible . . ."

"No one knows the will of the gods exactly; in any case, with a little blood and a lock of hair, I can inform you more precisely."

No," said Stéphane. "Thank you."

He gives her a gold coin and gets up, while the young women, to the accompaniment of an enervating and monotonous cadence, detach the monkeys . . .

XIV
The Fire

That night, as Stéphane was asleep next to his brown mistresses, the house caught fire. The conflagration reached the frail partition walls swiftly, and long white spirals rose toward the window, hiding the stars.

Soakia, the first to awake, gave the alarm. All around the house, bamboo huts were burning, and the hollow stems were exploding in the smoke, twisting, and flying into smithereens like fireworks.

Taminah and Wakiem, terrified, ran around the room lamenting. Stéphane took them in his arms, and with one bound, traversed the column of flame. Soakia, as nimble as a kid, was already outside, calling for help.

It really was a fine spectacle. On the horizon, now entirely red, black shadows were running in confusion; walls were collapsing with the rapidity of houses of cards that a breath is sufficient to topple. Then roofs of thin wood, rose up, were deformed, and flew into the air; minarets, domes and flamboyant triumphal arches, still metamorphosing, crackled madly and fell back in luminous cascades. The trees, illuminated from the side, agitated topaz braches and emerald leaves, which soon withered in the heat, curled up, and then, completely desiccated, flew away like thin bats.

In the burning air, conflagrations burst forth like lightning flashes and only stopped for lack of aliments.

Stéphane, with his darlings clinging to him, watched the voluptuous nest burn, where he had lived hours of true happiness.

Soakia was weeping, gripped by a bleak presentiment, and he wiped away her tears with his lips, hugging her forcefully to his bosom.

"We'll go further on," he said. "We'll be happy regardless."

"What about everything we've lost? Our clothes, our jewelry . . ."

"I'll give you others."

"Your canvases, your paints? Our portraits, in which we were so pretty!"

"I'll begin them again, since the models belong to me."

Wakiem and Taminah, already consoled, watched the furnace extend into the distance, illuminating the slopes of the volcanoes, which opened their rosy mouths under a rain of tawny light, a phosphorescent foam of spangles, clinging on to all the protrusions.

The vegetation took on magical hues; all the treetops became lilac, a dazzling flowery lilac, while the bases had splendors of agate, ruby and aventurine. The terrace was a lake of flames, and the cries of the multitude agitating in the streets resembled, at a distance, the song of waves dying on a shore, the song of wavelets with pizzicati of foam, iridescent crests, murmuring, palpitating and caressing, while the bass notes rumbled and large cellos uttered their profound plaint untiringly.

Now, everything seemed to dissolve in a dream of glory for the smile of the dying monster. The ground shuddered under its bites, covered with an incomparable cope of fulgurate gems sown in profusion, overlapping and entangled, twisted in menacing reptiles, woven in garlands of roses, here scarcely flesh-colored, there as crimson as a garden of tortures . . .

When it was all over, Mappy emerged from a bush.

"I was looking for you," he said. "I ran through all the rooms of your house to bring you help."

"In fact, your hair is singed and your hands are covered with burns."

"I wanted to be certain. What a joy to find you again."

"And the reng'gong, Sigete and Mana'i?"

"They're in a safe place."

The chief was smiling, but his gaze was evasive, and his fingers were clenched on his dagger.

XV
En Route

"We'll find a solitary place where we can shelter our amour before returning to France."

"You'll take us with you?"

"Yes."

"What joy!"

Soakia and her sisters formed a hundred projects for the sunlit future that awaited them. Paris! Paris . . . ! They would see Paris, about which people talked in low voices as a place of charming delights, disquieting and perverse.

They would be fashionable enchantresses, with silk dresses fitted to their flexible figure, and plumed hats. What a prospect!

"When will we leave?"

"In a month or two."

"That's a long time!"

"Before returning there, I want to see your beautiful country, your blue forests and the angry magnificence of your mountains."

Mappy, when consulted, opined that it was necessary to go to Garut, one of the regions of Java that contains the most volcanic craters.

"It's there that I grew up," he said, "with vagabonds who camped at the foot of the craters; I'll serve as your guide. And then, the climate is delightful; exhausted Europeans go there in search of health."

As everything had been burned, the preparations for the departure did not take long, Sigete and Mana'i took charge of buying clothes for Stéphane and sarongs and diaphanous veils for the dancers.

They traversed Djokjakarta again at the gallop of their little ponies, stayed overnight at Djoka in order to renew their devotions at Borobudur, saluted the colossal tomb of the god at the summit of the edifice and the five hundred statues of lesser importance staged on the steps in the depths of open cupolas carved in the granite.

Stéphane was thoughtful, struck by the somber beauty of the temple.

"This is where you wounded me," said Mappy, drawing away, "but I don't hold a grudge. Buddha protects you and Soakia loves you. You have become sacred to me."

Sigete and Mana'i prostrated themselves in the dust, singing softly to appease the evil spirits.

The following evening they reached Tasikmalaya, and then went along the coast of the Indian Ocean as far as Tjilatjap, a city situated facing the island of Nusa Kambangan, one of the most insalubrious and marshiest places in Java. The heat was stifling on the muddy or fissured ground, strewn with rocks, with lava flows in the midst of stratified craters and dead volcanoes. In the distance, mountain peaks were profiled, barbed and jagged, with shades of verdigris. The blistered crust of former marshes gave way under the feet of the horses, which got bogged down continually.

"Wasn't there another road?" asked the young man.

Mappy shook his head silently.

They threw themselves further into the furnace, feeling an impression of distress that increased by the hour. The little dancers with wiry bodies did not suffer much, but Stéphane sensed the blood congealing in his veins and an inextinguishable thirst drying out his tongue. The atmosphere was now charged with heavy perfumes mingled with corruption, and the sun was shining with more ardor.

"Isn't this the fatherland of malaria?"

"Yes," said the chief, tranquilly. "It's the region of murderous beaches where one falls asleep in the great slumber that consoles everything."

On sandy strips sown with pale vegetation, the milky green of jade, a few watercourses designed arabesques of dead turquoise. On the banks, fragile huts crouched in the reeds. Stéphane wanted to call a halt, feeling exhausted by illness, and Mappy took him by the shoulders and laid him down gently in the grass while the girls searched for a shelter.

XVI
Malaria

The sun skimmed the summits, the jagged crests of which were radiant with white flames, like molten metal. Glimmers swarmed along the blue and great crests, seeming to devour the sparse vegetation that still persisted, and the craters ground their fiery teeth, roaring dully in the distance. In the depths of a bamboo cabin raised a meter above the ground, the invalid reposed, surrounded by his three lovers. Weakly, he squeezed their little hands, not always able to recognize them, for delirium had arrived with the hallucinations of the fever.

Removed from the sentiment of the present life, his troubled vision entered into union with the images of his imagination. He felt, in an anxious pleasure, transported distantly, among the roses and the mosses of the land of France, and while his thoughts fled madly he remained immobile, his eyes devoid of a gaze. Sometimes he became livid, as if all his blood had quit him, and in a supreme exhaustion, fell back as if into death.

Then, Soakia approached a pinch of herbs with a vehement scent to his nostrils, and a hint of carmine returned to his cheeks. At the end of the day, however, his face, mortally weary and drawn, the agony of his features, his gaze, hollow and almost inverted, testified to the progress of the poison.

The terrified dancers often heard the voice of their lover become sobbing, stifled, moaning childishly, break and fall silent after a cry of anguish; then his bloodless face convulsed, tending toward something that they could not divine.

He remained thus for a long time, in a dolorous disorder, invaded by the sentiment of a physical change in his entire being, having the illusion of a force that lifted him from his burning couch and bore him toward infantile sensations.

His eyeballs fixed, and his eyelids, striated with brown bruises, no longer having any movement or flutter, a sudden blindness filled his gaze; his hands, veined with blue, rose up to seize the wings of his chimera, and fell back again, discouraged.

"Oh, don't die!" the children wept. "What do you expect to become of us, if you abandon us?"

Soakia rebelled. "It's necessary to take him away, Mappy. You can see that he's getting even weaker."

But the chief shrugged his shoulders. "Take him away? The slightest movement would be fatal."

After a few hours of distraction, Stéphane returned to himself with a great tremor of his entire body. After an initial stupor, he searched around him to see if anyone was there, for he was confused, almost ashamed of have dreamed so many follies. And, reassured, only finding his beloved there, he went to sleep, a profound slumber this time, even more terrifying for them.

Thus the fever, which ate him away, diminished him and intoxicated him. The extenuating continuity of the exaltation, the deregulated effervescence of his mind and the tension of his nerves, painfully contracted, brought him rapidly to a state of complete exhaustion.

Wakiem had an idea.

"My sisters," she said, "you know that this is the dwelling of the enchantress Kidoul? She lives in a palace of precious stones, and she sometimes deigns to listen to the prayers of bedayas. Let's ask her to cure the Beloved."

"Yes, yes, let's implore her!"

"*O enchantress of the profound solitudes, benevolent and tender enchantress, O enchantress of Amour . . .*"

Their voices trailed in a plaintive and seductive fashion, swelling or becoming lighter than a thread of spider-silk.

"Goddess of the moon and the waves, goddess of the moving sands and the majestic mountain . . ."

Wakiem went on, alone, confidentially.

"By the hidden symbols, by the resonant gendings, by the eternal silence and the eternal harmony, by the adoration of all that surrounds you, O queen of the humid lands, come to our aid!"

They swayed gently, murmuring more vague incantations, and then threw themselves face down in the dust.

A cloud obscured the sky, the turbulent leaves took flight madly under the squall; the reds curbed with a sound of tearing silk. In the green-tinted daylight in the depths of the cabin, Stéphane seemed even paler, with his hollow cheeks, his pinched nose and his lips parted by hoarse breath.

No longer doubting, they fell on to the couch uttering groans and cries of anguish. Then dusk descended upon them, and, of all the vibrations of life, they only perceived any longer the intermittent and lugubrious plaint of their hearts.

Finally, the night enveloped them: a dismal, dense night, as implacable as the sepulcher.

XVII
The Enchantress Kidoul

It was not rain but a deluge that fell from the black clouds passing in a fantastic charge through a phosphorescent sky. The stunted trees twisted with muffled plaints and creaks, sweeping the ground with their weeping crowns, like tresses. Innumerable reptiles and nameless larvae were crawling in the soft sand.

Wakiem, her eyes fixed on the desolate landscape, had a vision: from waves rising up in foaming turbulence sprang a form as light and mild as a moonbeam, which rose up very precisely, clad in a sea-blue simarre, which was retained at the shoulder by medusae of beryls, and in front by a pink octopus that gripped the breasts with its supple tentacles and descended lower like a voluptuously stretched string of opals. The enchantress was slender, all white, with fluffy hair and large green velvet eyes.

"O enchantress, lovely enchantress, have you come to save the beloved?"

"You will save him yourself," said Kidoul, smiling.

"How?"

"By means of caresses . . ."

"But we no longer dare . . ."

"Amour cures everything."

"Then it's necessary . . . ?"

"As much as you wish."

"And Stéphane will be returned to us?"

"Try . . ."

The apparition sank into the waves, under a spurt of wavelets crested with foam, and a clap of thunder, as strident as a blast of monstrous tom-toms, split the air.

Wakiem went back into the hut, her heart confident.

Outside, the sky calmed down; the waves, after the storm, resembled baskets of corollas and fireflies, a rolling mosaic of unknown gems, a carpet dotted with nebulae, fresh cotton wool, a down of dead leaves, a massacre of stars! It was an incomparable spectacle of grandeur and beauty. In the delicacy of the atmosphere, the waves sang more loudly. All the voices melted into an infinite chant, all the voices of desire and passion celebrating the return of the Sun God.

XVIII
A Cure of Kisses

"My sisters, I know a means."

"A means of curing Stéphane?"

"Yes; Kidoul has spoken."

"Oh, tell us, quickly!"

"Shh! Watch!"

She placed her lips on the invalid's lips.

"What are you doing?"

"Imitate me."

"Oh!"

"Yes, yes."

They leaned over, in turn, and the warmth of the body invaded them, exasperating the desire that all three of them had, recklessly.

He felt the firm roundness of their small erect breasts molding itself to his breast. As if in a dream, he ran his groping hands over their flesh, all his suffering vanishing in the passionate desire that invaded him in his turn.

He plucked the somber flowers of their eyes, the animated corollas of their mouths, and descended to pluck amber flowers even sweeter.

The air was now full of light flakes, vagabond seeds, impalpable pollen heading toward the mysterious nests of kisses. It was like a cottony flock, a warm turtle-dove down, a glittering dust wandering in the light.

And still, Stéphane's thirsty lips paused on the plump hollows and fresh roundnesses of the amorous girls.

He went to sleep, and woke up for new joys, without seeing the silhouette of Mappy, which sometimes loomed up in the doorway of the hut, a menacing and dolorous apparition.

The putrid odor of the marsh, which the avalanche had swept away, was no longer sensible. Only the sea breeze still brought a few feverish gusts exhaled by the wood of mangroves and poisonous trees that extended their porous roots, swollen by the ebb-tide, in the distance.

The King Star dipped his radiant tresses in the waves, which he also caressed with agile lips while awaiting the ultimate possession. He descended in a blaze of topazes and rubies; he seemed to emerge through a door of flames open to a sidereal furnace, a sky in the fusion of an unsustainable splendor.

Sheaves of blue light sprang from the magical conflagration, rising up in a flamboyance of hyacinth, onyx and sardonyx, while the orchestra of the waves swelled, burst and unleashed a formidable gasp of amour. It was the intoxication, the delirium, of violins sighing over the sharp chanterelle, in the fanfare of brass recklessly sounding the eternal hymn of sensuality!

XIX
The Continuation of the Journey

The next day, Stéphane got up and wanted to leave. Kidoul had told the truth, and a miracle had been accomplished under the caresses of the three little dancers with sincere hearts.

Mappy protested furiously.

"Leave, when you were dying yesterday?"

"I'm in a state to continue my journey, you see . . ."

With a firm step he marched into the hut.

"It's insane! Sigete and Mana'i think as I do."

The rong'geng, submissive to their chief, raised their hands to the level of their foreheads.

"By Brahma, Shiva and Vishnu, you won't get better."

But Wakiem became annoyed. "I swear by Kidoul that he's out of danger."

"That's not true!"

"I saw the enchantress emerge from the waves, I tell you. She informed me of the remedy that cures all ills."

"And what is it?" said Mappy, scornfully.

"You'll never know it," replied Wakiem, angrily. "If you're in doubt, you only have to consult a mirror."

Soakia and Taminah laughed, rolling at the feet of the beloved like teasing cats.

"Make the preparations," Stéphane ordered. "I want it."

Tamed, Mappy gave in, but a double flash sprang from his tawny pupils.

A few hours later they ate breakfast in Maos, slightly blinded by the thick smoke and scoria of Sumatran palm oil. In the evening they arrived in Tasikmalaya, where they took lodgings for the night.

The temperature was already much cooler; the young man was respiring with delight, feeling revived, his body and soul filled with a new ardor.

He lay down on immaculate mats with his three darlings.

"Sleep today, it's necessary to be sage."

Soakia put an arm around his neck, tenderly

"Tell us, Stéphane, when we're in France, will we have a house where only the four of us will live, and a garden full of flowers?"

"Yes, flowers that you don't know, frail calices like the embroideries of your sarongs."

The idea of that claustration with his young friends did not frighten him, for he was fatigued by the noisy life and the facile pleasures that his large fortune offered him. When he had encountered Soakia he had been in a period of distinct lassitude, in spite of his work and the variety of the voyage he was undertaking. He had delighted in his sadness, incapable of any effort, weary of living. He had wanted to be one of the privileged individuals who pass through events without seeing anything except what was shown to him, and who did not worry about the unknown. A feverish sensibility, a continual shock of impressions, had made Stéphane Gautier a victim of melancholy.

However, he loved his art, and he had devoted himself to it with ardor, and at certain moments had thrown into it his passions, the fire of his ardent nature, which a simulated coldness hid from the indifferent.

The little brown dancer had interested him immediately by her prettiness and what he divined of naïve tenderness in her childish soul. She was the submissive and sincere girl for whom he had always searched without ever encountering her; she was the incarnation of the dream of possession and jealous domination that he rediscovered intact in a corner of his brain.

He divined that, in the little amorous animal, the flower blooming for the kiss of one alone, the emotions of the heart and the senses were prolonged with a rare intensity, that she forgot herself therein by virtue of experiencing them.

Conventional ideas of morality and chastity were, however, veiled from her understanding. The faith of a certain number of men in hypocritical laws, conventions and mores would have been a subject of astonishment for her. So, recognizing that the world was foreign to her, she had isolated herself in her adoration for her lover, after having offered him, with a touching ingenuousness, two other flowers of amour, who were her sisters, Wakiem and Taminah.

The young man, before the three darlings, had felt strangely troubled and grateful, attracted by an irresistible sympathy. They were different, worse or better than all the women he had known. He did not love them yet, but they interested him because he understood their nature of amorous savages.

Thus far, he had only had a relative condescension for womankind, and had never suffered seriously in consequence of one of them. Now, at the age of thirty, somewhat blasé and disdainful, he felt himself being drawn toward something unexpected, which occupied him and charmed him.

In reposing in the arms of the three adored creatures, he had something akin to a convalescence of the soul, and when he arrived at the goal of the journey, he was no longer the same man.

PART THREE

I
Garut

Garut, at an altitude of 710 meters, is one of the regions of Java in which earthquakes and volcanic eruptions have caused the greatest upheavals. Its climate, however, is delightful, and many Europeans honor it with their preference.

Bizarre summits crowned with flowers rise up everywhere, and, dominating them with a fantastic plume of lava and smoke, are volcanoes of six, eight or even ten thousand feet.

In the midst of an excessive vegetation, whose colors are infinitely varied, passing, on the flanks of distant mountains from bright pink to the rosy hue of pigeons' throats and from ash green to emerald green, those terrible convulsions of nature present a terrible spectacle.

In a pleasantly shady location, for which he searched for a long time, Mappy rented a discreet habitation with superposed terraces covered in climbing plants. It was a paradise, after crossing the fetid marshes under an intense sky, an implacable sky of living turquoise, in the midst of the baked facades of cracked buildings with shuttered windows.

By closing their eyes they could still see, as if in a nightmare, the gray mangroves elevating their spongy roots at the water's edge, the soft pale arms of sweating stunted trees, the spatulate leaves of fleshy, morbid, poisonous plants preceding plains with a putrid reek.

They took possession of their enchanted domain, wandering a little further every day in the cool forests. Stéphane put a shawl at the foot of a tree, and the dear ones sat down with him, nestling in his arms, and went to sleep after excessively profound caresses.

He remained thoughtful, gazing at them for hours, the lashes lowered over their large irises like birds' wings over the infinity of the skies. He respired their breath, brushed the dark curls of their hair with his lips, and would have liked to die thus.

At the slightest breath of wind the path was aurified by a rain of radiance that sparkled at the tips of lanceolate ferns and in the depths of corollas as large as human faces.

He had never been as happy as during the first days of their arrival in Garut. They laughed as soon as he came to join them, their shining eyes proving to him that they had sensed that he was really theirs, for entire days.

"How was I able to live without you?" said Soakia, caressing his mouth with her agile mouth.

"I no longer recall the past," added Taminah, her head tipped back on her beloved's shoulder.

And Wakiem concluded: "It's singular; nothing exists any longer but this exquisite moment. We don't wake up."

"I'm entirely yours, my dears. Let's love one another well."

They traveled roads of dream, with extraordinary plants with penetrating perfumes, and possessed one another adorably. Then, enlacing, united, mute, charmed to be no longer anything but one and the same kiss, they became torpid in the memory.

Around them, the orchids and the tuberoses jostled one another for a little light. There was a crazy, lascivious, reckless blossoming of frissons. The living flowers retained them, gripped them, and blew the breath of desire into their faces. They watched, intoxicated by tenderness, the wedding celebrations of the odorous wood, leading the virginity of calices to ardent fecundities.

Under the deployed tent of branches, all smiles shone and expanded. All the passion of nature overflowing with sap was singing in the immensity.

They remained thus all day long, contemplating the prestigious woods and contemplating one another, in order to engrave within them the sunlit quality of things around the sunlit quality of their own being.

Then the sun went down, a coppery dust of light fell from the giant lianas, and the flowers, blurring their wild gleams, were no longer anything but the last radiance of a beautiful dream.

II
The Mountain of Fire

"It's necessary to visit the volcano."

"We're not in any hurry, Mappy."

The chief smiled mysteriously.

"Tomorrow doesn't belong to us."

"We can see the crater from here. It's very frightening, and our forest is so pleasant."

They could, indeed, perceive Papandayan, the smoke of which rose straight and white into the furnace blue sky.

In the peace of things, they experienced a strange sensation before that sinister flame, which loomed up relentlessly, like an obstinate threat of destruction and death.

But Wakiem, who was curious, became interested.

"Let's go see the volcano, Stéphane."

Taminah trembled delectably. "It must be terrible."

"There are lakes of fire, mountains of red embers and stars of sulfur brighter than constellations."

"And one can hear the thunder rumbling under the ground!"

"And everything dances as if in an immense vertigo!"

The children, excited, begged Stéphane. Only Soakia remained silent, her mind anxious.

Astonished by that reserve, the young man interrogated her. "And you, darling, why aren't you saying anything?"

She turned her head away under Mappy's fixed gaze.

"I don't have anything to say. Decide by yourselves."

"Think how beautiful it must be," said Wakiem.

"Certainly."

"I want to know these ardent mountains, finally, that I've only ever seen from afar."

"If you're afraid," said Taminah, supportively, "we'll go alone."

But Soakia suddenly made a decision.

"I'll go with you everywhere."

In two hours by carriage, in the midst of an infinite vegetation, they arrived at Onadana, a modest campong, where travelers stop before commencing the ascension of the mountain. They set forth into the virgin forest along a winding path, with unexpected, slightly anguishing views. The children, mounted on their ponies, gave proof of a great ardor.

Sometimes, however, it was necessary for them to dismount in order to scale clay steps or a slippery mossy rock face. Then there were falls and bursts of laughter that ran, from echo to echo, like a shower of pearls over a crystal staircase. They skirted woody precipices, sheer ravines, thickets of daturas, wild hibiscus, rhododendrons and red mint. They passed through tunnels of arborescent ferns, under which the light was decanted in violet and mauve of an infinite softness. Vast fissures often allowed them to see both the north and south coasts of Java, the Indian sea and the Chinese sea, separated by the immense chain of volcanic cones. Then there was the chaos of landslides, cascades and rocks, in streaks of insensate vegetation, under the amorous mesh of lianas that covered everything with their royal cope.

Gradually, an odor of sulfur mingled with the perfumes of herbs and flowers, and ended up dominating them. The glorious foliage paled and became etiolated. Further on, ferns raised up fans of old russet guipure, screens and parasols of copper and gold; a dry moss that crackled underfoot felted the ground. Only denuded branches subsisted now: no longer a single leaf, not a bird, nor a snake.

They reached the crest, the entrance of the crater.

That entrance was an enormous breach hollowed out by the interior fire in its cone of eruption. It was there that the bomb had exploded, revealing the eternal anarchy of everything that exists, everything that, one day or another, will return to nothingness in order to make way for other antagonisms and other combats.

It is a somber world, which, at first glance, seems disinherited, empty, a realm of death.

On the contrary, however, life generally triumphs there.

The two souls of the globe, the magnetic and the electric, have their fête every night in the solitudes of the blazing mountains. The aerial currents and the currents of the sea are their vehicles.

First of all, an ashy curtain rises, a curtain of mists torn into yellow guipure, which allows the stars to shine through. Lower down, the glow of a conflagration extends, a luminous peak, its foot posed on the black mountain. The peak grows, oscillates, straightens, and attains the sky in a glory of radiance. Then other columns of flame rise and undulate. There is a flux and reflux of light, a golden drapery that comes and goes, folding up again and again.

The undulating jets play, tearing apart. One might think them a quiver of captive souls, with profound palpitations.

The earth is unquiet.

Which of those errant forces will vanquish, which will prevail?

In a precious necklace of islands, on the sea embalmed by roses and tuberoses, amour and death have their burning combat. The fiery summits of Java smoke, like an immense silver perfume-burner: cruel, fecund, delicious Java! It has as many fiery mouths as the entirety of America. It is necessary to add its liquid volcano, its vein of amethyst—the Japanese call it the "black river"—which runs to the north pole, warming the seas, as bitter and alive as human blood.

Warm waves, torrid sun, sniggering or moaning volcanoes, volcanoes of joy or terror, which the storms caress—frightful on the "blue mountains"—everything there is ablaze, everything metamorphoses, passes and dies with an incredible rapidity. In

116

torrents, electric rains, which intoxicate the virgin forests, also make the senses delirious. Calices fume under the sun, resembling cassolettes of dazzling gems.

The forests are sometimes inaccessible in the most abrupt places, so dense and so dark that torches are required there at midday. Nature creates monsters and masterpieces there, for herself alone, some infinitely small, of an arachnean delicacy, and others redoubtable colossi. Flowers embrace one another, swoon and pour death from their poisonous corollas. Rhizanthes devoid of stems take possession of the foot of a tree, gorge themselves on sap until the complete exhaustion of the trunk that has given them shelter. Their splendor in the night of the forest is prestigious. They are cups of iridescent crystal, precious vases of sapphire and emerald, which radiate a mysterious gleam. Set so low, in the warm and greasy breath of the soil, those daughters of darkness resemble dreams of lust and desire.

Java has two faces. To the south it is already Oceania, a pure breath, with rocks, polyps, madrepores and coral islands. To the north it is still India, in everything it has of the most morbid: a brown alluvial soil ferments and decomposes there in feverish miasmas, and superb Batavia is still a triumphant cemetery there. Animals of the ancient world, forgotten there, show themselves in the close night like funereal spirits. There are enormous bats, hairy and viscous, which float over the heads of passers-by, and other beasts, hideous nightmarish larvae that cling, crawl and swarm, eternal menaces of eternal fear.

Over those low-level terrors soars and triumphs the sublime terror of the volcanoes. They are the angry gods that the ancients came to implore in temples now in ruins. Those formidable powers had altars on which perfumes were burned and which the blood of sacrifices inundated. They still have distinct and savage names like the heroes of the Ramayana. The Gurung Tengger has a monstrous gaping crater ninety thousand feet across, from which four Etnas surge forth fuming. Another sees daylight in a desert of plaster inflated by tubercles and blistered by cysts, scorified and frosted. A third traverses a forest of crystallized ferns, whose fibers and edges shine likes furrows of quicksilver; a fourth punctures the dislocated crust of lava, erects poles of stucco, columns of alabaster crowned with flowers of amber and topaz, which sparkle so brightly that the firmament seems black. It is a Sahara of congealed whitewash, glittering with shiny dots, on a crest of crazy snow. The volcanoes are monstrous lilies with pistils of gold and fire reaching recklessly for the sky.

The Arjuna and the Rao roll with the smoke in acrid waves, seething.

The Ijen, awakening one morning, pours out a river.

Sometimes, when a peak lights up, another also catches fire a long way away.

If there is an earthquake, one crater might be extinguished, like a lamp in a current of air.

Although brothers, they are different and capricious, mocking one another, calling to one another and responding to one another in a confidential or sonorous voice, in accordance with their eccentric humor.

III
The Descent

"Stéphane, the soil is burning me!"

"Stéphane, I can scarcely breathe . . ."

"It's beautiful, though."

"I'd like to descend into the gulf!"

Their gazes plunge into the interior of the volcano, interrogating it fearfully. It is a vast solfatara eight hundred meters in diameter and about six hundred deep. The walls are ash. At the bottom there is a lake that fumes and seethes. On the edges, huge vegetations of sulfur are burning, emitting capricious columns of vapor that rise toward the crest like enormous serpents.

Stéphane holds the darlings against his bosom, clutching them jealously, while Mappy improvises a sort of altar with the two rong'geng, on to which he throws pink lotuses, which dry out rapidly, along with sticks of incense whose perfume is lost in the acrid reek of sulfuric acid. Mana'i is singing . . .

"Oh, beloved, let's go down!" says the smallest.

"I assure you, Wakiem, that it's dangerous."

"No, we'll sustain you."

"The four of us will be strong."

Their descent is nothing but a slide over the warm ash, which envelops them everywhere, and the girls are extremely amused by that new game.

Without too much trouble, they reach the shore of the lake, which forms a terrace edged by yellow crystal, whose edges light up like the points of diamonds. They lean over the edge, still enlaced, in order to contemplate the furious water, which attracts them. Here, there are whirlpools hollowed out in fantastic spirals, there sheets of pink foam, convulsive Niagaras overhanging abysses with the hoarse roars of chained wild beasts.

Mute, they admire the effort of that tormented ground spitting fire, breathing tornados and rearing up in indescribable spasms. From what frightful seeds, then, are these prodigious mountains of nightmarish vegetation the issue? What deluges of flame, what explosions of lightning have violated the cold calyx of the earth in order to mount these monstrous pistils of fire?

The sky above the gulf resembles a lid of pewter placed on the points of the summits, only awaiting a titanic effort to sink down and close the infernal box forever.

Soakia speaks in a small, indecisive voice. "Look, my love, at these trees, which are like specters with their twisted arms."

"Look, they turn to dust when one touches them!"

"I can't see any more. Shall we go back up?"

"Oh! My necklaces and rings are all black."

"The bracelets on my ankles are burning me!"

"Hold on to me tightly, my darlings, and don't be afraid."

Stéphane tries to take a few steps toward deliverance, but a further slide draws him toward a great fissure, from which the dull roar of a steamer heating up escapes. Hot mud and large splashes of yellow ocher spring forth from it on to his garments and the sarongs of his two companions. Nearby is a screen embroidered and filigreed with sulfur flowers of charming delicacy, which a gust pulverizes in an instant, and carries away in golden rockets. At the place where they were standing before, the ground blisters, cracks and slits. A red stream has emerged in a jet of water several feet high, and inundates them.

Taminah is annoyed.

"I want to go!"

Wakiem wails like a baby: "The odor is choking me. My hair is singed. I can't stand up any longer."

Soakia is triumphant.

"I told you so! I told you so!"

They exhaust themselves in vain attempts to regain the exterior edge of the crater—but Mappy throws them a long rope, and thanks to his aid, they emerge from the furnace safe and sound.

IV
Dancing on the Volcano

Sigete and Mana'i, prostrate, are imploring the gods and the spirits. They have formed garlands with sulfur crystals and red stones similar to coral flowers. Their hair and breasts are also ornamented with strange efflorescence. At this distance the heat is supportable and hardly anything can be heard except a sinister warning hiss.

A few streams are still running over bizarre green and violet rocks, very friable, which have been penetrated, saturated and oxidized by age-old projections of acidic gas.

Gathered on the summit of Papandayan, Stéphane and his companions are now contemplating the Indian Ocean and examining the mysterious depths of Preanger, a still-uncontested refuge of wild beasts and large crocodiles.

Again, the joy of the children bursts forth in crystalline notes, tinkling in the chaos.

"Oh, Stéphane, how frightened I was"

"It's odd to shiver thus."

"Without Mappy we'd never have been able to climb up again."

"Good Mappy!"

Soakia interrogates the chief, whose head is bowed, with a troubled gaze.

"Thank you," she says, simply. "I won't forget what you've done."

And Mappy murmurs, in such a fashion as to be heard by her alone: "It was for you that I did it."

With a tacit understanding, they have taken one another by the hand in a mad dance on the fuming sand, a dance of the damned who have escaped from the blue- and green-tinted depths of vagabond flames. In that fantastic flight there is no longer anything of the solemn mime of bedayas in the noble attitudes of idols, the grave gestures of warriors in golden helmets. It is a tremor of bacchantes drunk on perfumes and amour.

They have picked up pink stones and are clicking them like castanets; their feet are agitating incessantly, their torsos undulating in an increasingly lively movement, their long dark hair whirling, spreading out and inflating over their heads like an ebony umbrella; their knees apart, their thighs bent, they kiss one another and straighten up again, rattling their coral stones more forcefully.

Then they bound, lightly, pivoting on the tip of one foot, beating the air with a wiry leg, and resume their surge to settle further away. After the bounds, and the supple and feline attitudes, they pause, moving their breasts and hips in voluptuous frissons, and reach out to catch a dream-butterfly, which their slender fingers seize by the translucent wings, their backs arched, their rumps prominent, launching their winged desire to the heavens . . .

Their dilated pupils follow it into the azure, the corolla of the mouth parted for a kiss, and they stay there, arms raised, displaying the warm softness of their young bodies . . .

A cry, a burst of laughter, and they are off again, gliding like dragonflies, their singed scarves agitating behind them like smoky wings.

They dare all attitudes: those that Stéphane has taught them, and others that they imagine. They pursue one another and enlace, kissing one another and swooning, fleeing and recapturing one another, lips to lips, their breasts taut and mingled. A fine sweat makes their amber bodies gleam, tired and enervated by the caresses.

Finally, they lie down, their limbs spread, the secret flower of their flesh offered to the beloved. They call to him, they laugh, and they weep; their voices become coaxing and sobbing, moist with desire . . .

Mappy has drawn away, grimly, and Stéphane approaches the little dancers . . .

V
Return to the Forest

"Oh, what a vision!" said Soakia, after a sigh; and with an effort of will, she sat up.

"Are you suffering again?" Stéphane asked.

"A little."

"What's the matter, then?"

The young woman had suddenly lost consciousness in his arms. In response to the appeals of Wakiem and Taminah, the rong'geng, who had gone back down into the wood, came back, their arms laden with aromatic herbs, with which they rubbed the nostrils and lips of the invalid gently.

Then Soakia begged Stéphane to take her away.

"But you were so joyful just now."

"Don't interrogate me," she stammered. "Talking about evil influences attracts them."

"What influences?"

"I've seen . . . I've seen . . ."

"Tell us what you've seen."

"You desire that absolutely, my beloved?"

"Yes."

"I've seen the volcano vomiting a torrent of fire, the woods calcined . . . the dead, the dead everywhere! Then I felt a great tearing of my being, and I fainted."

The seeresses, interrogated, remained perplexed.

"It's possible that it was an occult warning," pronounced Sigite.

"Does one ever know with these furious monsters, who are always growling?" said Mana'i, supportively.

But the young man was incredulous.

"The country has been calm for a long time, in spite of the eternal menace of the flaming mountains. It's the heat that is making you feel ill, Soakia; let's go back down."

They set forth, and the ragged plume of the crater disappeared behind the giant foliage of the virgin forest. The silent file moved through the chaos of persistent landslides, cascades of rocks and irresistible surges of vegetation. The impalpable powder of ash gave way underfoot again, and they advanced with difficulty, throats dry, lungs panting.

The rumor of the gigantic furnace diminished, and then ceased completely, giving way to the thousand sounds of inviolate woods: the clamors of birds of prey, the moans of turtle-doves, and the buzz of monstrous insects with nacreous and velvet wings. There were also strange, scarcely suspected species: fabulous basilisks with fiery eyes; gigantic toads and chameleons with bronze bodies, pustulated with bright yellow and green; blue spiders extending thick webs from tree to tree like a canvas of flossy silk; moist amber slugs with triple crests; milky larvae; animals as round as gourds, as flat as blades and toothed like saws; and then, high in the branches, the winged flora of birds.

Sometimes, phyllia leaves were detached, pale green vegetal strands of closely-woven tissue with serrated edges and foliar fibers of an infinite delicacy—and those leaves started to run with an inconceivable agility, followed by other phyllias of similar appearance.[1] Flowers contracted on their fleshy stems, offering a sticky balm to insects, which held them captive, and then, with an effort of their voracious calyx, engulfed them. There were bushy crowns of poisonous trees, of which a single fruit, or even a droplet of sap, might have been fatal. Those trees, particularly pretty, agitated pearly sprays and moist necklaces of pink berries, little bells of amber and coral, tresses or helmets of jade, milky and furry shells, and fleshy cupels with pale buds, reminiscent of the breasts of virgins. Sometimes heavy velvety cryptogams clung to the rugged trunks like glaucous jellyfish or cephalopods greedy for ink and blood.

They passed under the perforated arcades of lianas allowing coppery foliage to dangle, in harmony with the warm ash tint of the soil, through fields of ferns, undulating in russet and blond waves; it was a debauchery of life preceding arid mounds collapsed by desiccation, bare, rugged hills, stripped to the bones, the beds of stony streams, with, at intervals, flanks ripped by ravines of chalk and tuff, a few plants hanging down like ropes.

Night was approaching rapidly. The less elevated mountains were extinguished first; the fearful radiance bounded from one summit to another, paused momentarily, and then, opening golden wings, disappeared into the immensity.

They were in the forest again, a violet forest, so profound was it. The plants affected fantastic forms of chimeras and dragons;

---

1 These animate leaves are mythical, but they are described in Ludovic de Beauvoir's *Voyage autour de monde* (1867; tr. as *A Voyage round the world*), from which La Vaudère also took some information about Siam for *L'Amazone du roi de Siam*. *Phyllia* is actually a genus of insects.

unfamiliar poisonous corollas darted their stamens like bewitching eyes, opening pink mouths in the depths of their calices, armed with a needle as fleshy as a tongue. Others, radiating a pale light, were phosphorescent or translucent. Stems resembled serpents, and serpents slackly coiled lianas. Tentacles clung on to the branches, medusal green and blue flowers swelled in hollows in the bark of trees.

They had increasing difficulty in walking, parting the undergrowth and stepping over clumps. Soon, the path became impracticable; ropes of lianas ran and doubled back beneath their feet, tangled shoots leapt from tree to tree, clinging to anything that formed an obstacle, and then, having reached an objective agitating gigantic clusters of ardent fruits therefrom. Here and there, colossi died of old age or struck by lightning inclined all far as the ground, serving as a support for more parasites, crested with a fine dust of flowers or crowned by tender white-felted balls. There were silky webs tightened by curls and dotted with cabochons, which hung down like nets of green mesh, sheltering a disquieting swarm of insects and larvae.

Suddenly, Soakia uttered a scream and pointed at her ankle, around which was coiled a slender yellow-striped snake of the most dangerous species. With a brief tap on the head, Mappy caused it to drop off, but a small triangular wound was pink on the brown flesh, and the girl stood stock still, her eyes dilated by fear.

"It's nothing," said the chief, and, kneeling down, he sucked the wound ardently.

His action had been so prompt that Stéphane had not had time to intervene.

"You've saved my life twice today," said Soakia, moved. "How can I repay you?"

Mappy had stood up, wiping his lips.

"Don't thank me, little queen; you have given me a great joy."

VI
New Danger

They had been installed near Garut in their pretty nest of verdure for a month. Stéphane liked hunting, and departed in pursuit of birds or wild beasts in the company of the chiefs of neighboring tribes who came to look for him.

They set forth early in the morning, and often did not return from the jungle until nightfall, harassed and covered in sweat.

One day, while Soakia, alone in the house, was reassembling the coral beads of a necklace whose thread had broken, Mappy came in silently, and seized her abruptly by the shoulders. She turned round swiftly, with a great frisson.

"Oh! You frightened me."

"Why? You knew that I was there."

"I didn't hear you come in."

She had drawn away from him fearfully, considering him mistrustfully.

"You aren't cured of your amour, then?"

"I'll never be cured."

"You seemed reasonable, entirely submissive."

"It was a pretence."

"What are you hoping for, then?"

"To have you."

As she shrugged her shoulders disdainfully, he went on, in a hiss: "And I, you know, would only have a single woman . . . a woman that I'd cherish above everything."

"You're free to choose between Sigete and Mana'i."

"It's you that I choose."

Impatiently, she replied: "I belong to Stéphane."

"Are you not humiliated by having two rivals"

"No, If I'd stayed with the sultan, I'd have had many more."

"Yes, but you wouldn't have loved the sultan, and you love your lover."

"I love him for himself . . . to render him happy. I'm not egotistical. A man can have all the women he desires, on condition of taking them in accordance with his rank. My religion tells me that."

"Your religion is mad."

"That's not for me, or for you, to judge. All that I can say is that I've given myself freely to the man I adore; I won't have any other master."

"Soakia!"

There was so much sadness in the chief's voice that the girl was moved. She took his hand affectionately.

"It's necessary not to think about that any longer."

"You don't know, then, what I've suffered for you?"

"Yes, I know that I owe you a great deal. Twice you've saved my life, and you must love me very profoundly, in fact, to lower yourself to the role that you're playing."

"I've sacrificed my pride and, even more, my liberty."

"It's necessary to recover both. Go away, assemble a new troupe to travel the roads, and try to forget me."

But he was not listening. Transported once again by the flavorsome and delicate beauty of the girl whom amour haloed with its charming fire, he could not weary of contemplating her. The power of fascination that she had always exercised on him gripped him with a greater ardor. Far from her eyes with golden gleams he had been able to struggle momentarily—futilely, in any case—but now he felt newly bound within the net of his dementia by invisible knots. It was as extraordinary as it was irresistible; all his ignited blood precipitated from his heart to his temples; he was dazzled.

Without speaking, he slid his arm around the waist of the beloved, and thought he was dissolving in the indescribable sensuality caused by her warm soft flesh.

He recalled that he had been the first to receive her smile of liberty. Every day, then, he had sat down beside her and talked to her about her new life, and her future. She had fixed her bright gaze upon him, and listened to him with a great effort of attention.

At times, her lips had parted, a sudden clarity traversed her, she had expressed her gratitude tenderly, and had seemed to consent to a complete abandonment of her being. In the midst of the scatterbrained and buzzing rong'geng she had sought out the chief, waited for him with a sort of impatience, only appearing content when he was there. Gradually, she had drawn closer to him, leaning her head on his shoulder or allowing herself to be lulled for hours by his songs and his kisses.

Why, he said to himself, *is she no longer now what she was then? Do I not have the right to take her back, like stolen goods diverted criminally from their destination?*

Since he had been following Stéphane and his little mistresses in their peregrinations across the ardent island, he had been preoccupied by the sole thought of his act of justice, and unformulated hopes had sprung forth within him. In his memories of vagabondage, in his dead life, in the shadow of his youth, he marched and prowled, listening, and seeing everything as a presage, sometimes good and sometimes bad. Whatever he did, his thoughts collided with one another around a permanently fixed desire, and he trembled in an indescribable impatience. For hours, he remained idle, gnawing himself like a lion in a cage. He spent his nights in a feverish agitation, stirring a thousand projects that he abandoned subsequently with discouragement.

Finally, the opportunity so long awaited had arrived. He was alone in the dwelling with Soakia, the rong'geng, on his orders, having taken Wakiem and Taminah to collect prestigious herbs that give strength and beauty.

"Soakia," he said, "all resistance is vain; I shall possess you."

"No, you wouldn't dare!"

She tried to flee, but again he caught her by the shoulders, tore away the thin sarong that enveloped her, and, approaching his contracted face to hers, sought her mouth.

Disdainful and icy, she felt Mappy's hand seize her and violate her delicate flesh. Then, suddenly, the earth shuddered beneath them in a convulsive fashion, the furniture tumbled, and the walls made muffled creaks audible.

Mappy got to his feet.

"The volcano!"

But as she launched herself toward the door he retained her, already reassured.

"Don't be afraid, it's a simple quake. There's no danger today."

"Today . . . but tomorrow?"

He had a singular smile. "Earthquakes are frequent in this region; they only cause minor damage. You see, everything is tranquil, as before."

"I'm trembling for my sisters."

"No, you're trembling for Him."

"And when will it be?"

"I hate him, that man, who is neither of your race nor mine. You'll repent of having encountered him."

"I've made him the sacrifice of my life. What does the future matter? I'm happy at this moment; all the rest fades away . . ." A little pity came to her for Mappy, whose suffering she observed, thoughtfully. "If you were reasonable, you'd succeed in mastering yourself."

"No, even wounded, dying, I never ceased to think about you . . . you understand that it isn't going to change now."

"Listen—I'm going to leave soon . . . perhaps tomorrow."

"Leave?"

"Yes, for France."

"When will you come back?"

"Never."

"Never!" He laughed nervously, and threw himself upon her.

She struggled, but he was robust and muscular; like a tamed infant he soon held her in his arms, tight against him, and, rudely, he rubbed her skin with his, crushing the delicate cups of her breasts and all the firm roundness of her body.

With his bony knee, he parted her legs, and devoured her lips with greedy kisses.

Escaping that grip momentarily, unconsciously, in her distress, she called out to her beloved: "Stéphane!"

"I'm here," replied the young man, who had just come in; and, shouldering his rifle and taking aim at Mappy, he added: "This time, you won't come back."

The chief drew his dagger, but Soakia threw herself between her lover and him.

"Let him go, Stéphane. Let's forget him, and let him forget us."

"He'll do us more harm. Why not finish it?"

"No, let him go."

"You want that?"

"I beg you to do it."

At the dancer's voice, Mappy had dropped his weapon. She picked it up and handed it to him.

"Go away," she said.

"Go away," Stéphane repeated.

Then, straightening his meager torso, his eyes glittering with hatred, the chief went out slowly.

VII
Projects of Vengeance

Mappy was now drawing away with great strides under the burning sun. He was no longer aware of his surroundings. The connective chain between him and reality had suddenly broken, and he had slipped into the inertia that follows great emotions.

Within him, the muted work of existence went on, supplementing the hallucinatory return of the chaos of sensations and sentiments. There were periodic returns in his soul of distant things, however, recoils and terrors.

Then his unconscious will, invaded by despair, yielded to the attraction of murder.

He experienced surges, instinctive appeals to vengeance, and his eyes searched around him for whatever might serve him most surely. He started to listen, his head tilted, to the mysterious voice of Evil, which spoke to him about punishment, suffering and death.

The temptations that teach the revolutionary the fastest means of destruction solicited him with an irresistible eloquence.

He returned to the volcano, in the burning lands where he had grown up, where he had lived his singular life, without caring about human beings. He knew the monster's secrets, and for several days he had heard it growling dully, casting its grim menace to the skies.

When he reached the summit, he lay down, placed his ear against the convulsive ground and listened to the interior sound of disaggregation that he knew well, and which had never deceived him.

"Patience," he said, rising to his feet. "The gods are for me."

He returned to the forest and hid himself there with the reptiles and the wild beasts. Dolorously, in the midst of his solitude, he sensed the nullity of all things.

One unique regret, an immense desolation, extended in his soul. Why had he had the courage to continue to live, when all joy was henceforth impossible?

Then his ideas became confused. He saw Soakia again; he heard her; he put his arms around her, and the heartbeats that struck him in his chest like the blows of a battering ram accelerated and became sonorous, filling the wood.

He paraded his gaze over the somber vegetation, as tormented as him, searching it for a distraction or a danger. No ray of light filtered through the dense branches; it was dark, the darkness populated by ghosts and phantoms, the terrible darkness that troubles the strongest.

The thought returned to Mappy of his flight with Soakia, of his first words, into which he had put caresses and sobs; he relived his torture in waiting for the encouragement that never arrived.

Oh, what a fall! What a frightful disappointment! Never, never had she loved him, never had she responded with a sincere word to his delirium of amour. Her embraces, her protestations and her kisses had been lavished on another.

She had repeated, with him, a scene that all women learned, as banal as the one that he had taught her. Poor fool! With what scorn had she not flagellated him? In spite of his suffering, the chief's bitterness in regard to evil destiny was mingled with a sort of involuntary pleasure in imagining the future, because he knew now that his triumph was not far off.

But the delirium returned, and the present vanished before the evocation of nights of tenderness in the luminous plain. He remembered how Soakia had conquered him, with certain words, certain gazes that the daughter of amour found, as bees find the blood of roses. He saw once again the temple of Borobudur where he had embraced her, found once again the warm terrace still impregnated with her perfume. Their two enlaced shadows were reborn in the shadow of foliage; they rolled, fainted, almost confounded, delectably.

"Soakia! Soakia! Little queen of amour!"

In a dolorous voice he appealed to his dream, demanded of it the furious spasm in which everything dissolves and is annihilated.

"Soakia! Soakia! Little queen of amour!"

VIII
The Faithful Guardians

"You, here!"

"Yes, we followed you."

"What should we do?"

"Order us."

"We'll obey you."

Sigete and Mana'i, very humble, interrogated the chief.

Their hair, disturbed by the rapidity of the journey, floated over their shoulders, and they were only wearing, over their brown skin, heavy silver necklaces with amethyst beads and pink topazes.

"Master," said Sigete, "we'll avenge you."

And Mana'i, extending her arms in a gesture of submission, added: "We won't recoil before any crime."

"A crime?" Mappy shook his head and pointed at the ground. "Tomorrow, I'll be avenged."

"Tomorrow?"

"Yes, can't you hear it?"

Thy knelt down and listened.

"We can hear it . . ."

"It's like a moan, and then a tearing."

"One might think it were the anger of a subterranean sea."

"And the creaking of ships in distress."

"And the growl of waves against rocks."

"It's an ocean of fire," Mappy said, "which is flowing and rising upwards."

The rong'geng shuddered.

"But if we stay here, it's certain death."

"It's necessary not to stay. Your place is elsewhere."

"What about you?"

"I know the volcano; it rocked me when I was small; have no fear . . ."

"Then you want . . . ?"

"I want you to return to the Frenchman and reassure him, if he intends to flee. But he won't flee; he's unaware of the peril."

With a vivacity that she could not conceal, Mana'i said: "You desire, then, that he'll die with those he loves?"

"I desire that he'll die alone. You'll save Soakia and bring her to me in Tasikmalaya. Go, go quickly . . . the rest is up to me."

The rong'geng took a few steps, and turned round.

"You swear that you won't die?"

"I swear it."

"May the gods watch over you."

Rapidly, they drew away, collecting here and there the flowers that procure sleep, because it was necessary to keep the little queen in the house.

While sliding through the tangled plants, they exchanged light words.

"Do you remember, Mana'i, our visit to the ruins of Tjambi-Seou?"

"Yes, and our terrifying invocation."

"And Shiva's response?"

"Oh, Sigete, destiny is against us!"

"You saw, when Soakia and Mappy lay down, enlaced, on the terrace of the temple, a tumulary shadow extended to their left . . ."

"Everything will be futile!"

"Let's try anyway."

"We'll spend the night in adoration before the images."

"Perhaps the gods will allow themselves to be swayed."

Mana'i looked at Sigete, a flame in her gaze. "If we were alone with the chief, he'd doubtless caress us? We're young and pretty, Sigete."

"It's necessary not to think of those things, Mana'i."

"Why not, if the spirits are for us?"

"The future doesn't belong to us. Let's do our duty as faithful servants."

IX
Vain Caresses

Stéphane was lying on a fine mat, his head lifted up by cushions embroidered with chimerical birds. Like an indolent cat, Wakiem was purring between his knees; Taminah was fanning him gently with a sprig of melati, and Soakia, her fingers quivering over the strings of her rebab, was singing to send the beloved to sleep.

"Sleep, the water is turning blue, the sky turning red, the forest is nothing but a soul of amour. Sleep in the peace of the world, sleep in the joy of the heavens.

"Sleep, we are watching over your precious life. We are the dreams and the kisses. We are the joys that pass and the memories that remain.

"Sleep, everything is drowsy and everything is fading away. The dead days make new days. Sleep in the peace of the world, sleep in the joy of the heavens."

Sigete and Mana'i came in silently and lit perfumes in bonze cassolettes. But they reeked of herbs and damp earth.

Stéphane, vaguely anxious, opened his eyes.

"Where have you come from?" he asked. "I sent your chief away."

"We know," they replied.

"And you haven't followed him?"

"No," said Mana'i. "We'd prefer to stay with you."

"All right. However, I thought you were submissive to Mappy. You were happier and freer with him. Like him, you were brought up in the mountains; you're little wild flowers that wither in the plain . . . And then, I want to return to France."

"Well, until then, let us live with the little queen."

The young man fell back on his cushions, wearily. His head was aching, the atmosphere was heavy. He experienced a dolorous nervous excitation whose cause remained unknown to him; his hands were burning with fever. Soakia was suffering too, and her voice became weaker. Only Wakiem and Taminah remained as joyful as little amorous animals, frivolous buzzing bees intoxicated by sunlight. Insatiably, they extended their greedy mouths and attempted frictions.

"If you want," said Wakiem, "we'll be wild beasts, like the other evening."

They ran around the room on all fours, and Stéphane tried to catch them. He succeeded, with difficulty, so supple and mobile were they. But when he had seized one of them, there was mad laughter and greedy kisses. Shivering, he held her beneath him, triumphantly, and hurt her slightly with the brutality of his caress, to punish her.

The other two made demands in their turn, and the game recommenced, more refined and more voluptuous.

Sometimes, they rubbed themselves with an odorous oil that rendered them ungraspable, and intoxicated the young man in the manner of an excessively heady wine. Then he asked for mercy, and lay down as a sign of submission, and they sharpened his desire with improvisations that charmed him.

That evening, seeing that he was sad, they had the idea of dressing themselves with flowers. With a marvelous skill they wove belts, scarves and necklaces, which made them resemble the nymphs of the enchantress Kidoul.

Soakia, covered in white gardenias, offered the living bouquet of her body, with mingled effluvia. Wakiem, sheathed in pink lotuses, allowed clusters of pale orchids dotted with fire to dangle between her legs. Taminah was nothing but a sheaf of metali, with three tuberoses in the middle, the stems hidden in brown moss.

They knelt down, extending their arms in an imploring and lascivious gesture, stirring their corollas slowly, in order to make dust fall from the stamens, make the pistils stand up, and the partly-open calices exhale their exquisite perfumes more forcefully. They swayed harmoniously, chanting soft litanies in unison to a plaintive rhythm. They resembled branches agitated by the wind, an entire pure flower-bed, flowers and women of amour, made to blossom by the desire of a god.

Without getting up, they continued their singular dances, sometimes sitting on their heels, sometimes lying down, undulating and crawling. With their lips they imitated the buzzing of insects, laughed at the touch of invisible butterflies, and, with their arms raised, agitated with a flutter of wings.

They separated capriciously, and then came together again fearfully, to battle an unknown monster, which their feverish hands drove away.

But the monster knew caresses, and they smiled, eyes closed, abandoning themselves like sylvan florets to the penetrating sting of hornets. Their flesh no longer experienced anything but voluptuous spasms, and they delivered themselves until the supreme frisson, and the murmur of their voices died away in a sigh.

"Stéphane!" they said, as they got up again.

But Stéphane was asleep.

X
Prayer to Shiva

In the next room, Sigete and Mana'i were burning poisonous herbs before a figurine of Shiva, gilded and studded with gems. Clouds of acrid smoke swirled around the small brown heads of the seeresses, and their dilated pupils seemed to be seeing terrible images.

An enormous bat came to redden its wings in the flames of the fateful tripods, and flew away heavily after describing two concentric circles around the divinity, which was a sign of misfortune.

Nocturnal birds driven by some unknown terror traversed the room madly, with hoarse cries, and distant roars were audible.

"Shiva," moaned Sigete, prostrating herself, "august god, bearer of the heavy club, the sonorous conch and the resplendent disk, have pity on us."

"Shiva," Mana'i continued, "on the blue mountain where you dwell, deign for a moment to listen to our prayer. We venerate you, we admire you, we fear you!"

"Brahma, Vishu and Shiva, adorable trinity, tree, corolla and pistil, we humble ourselves before you!"

A kind of dull rumble was audible, and the little lamps that were illuminating the idol went out, sizzling. Sigete went out on to the terrace, and uttered a cry.

"Oh! Mana'i, come and see . . ."

At the top of the highest mountain, a sort of gigantic Chimera with bloody scales rose up, twisting, into the clouds, which incessantly let red droplets fall around it, a burning murderous rain. It seemed to the rong'geng that the ground was undulating slightly under their feet at each of the monster's somersaults.

"We're doomed!" moaned Sigete.

"No, I've seen the crater catch fire like that before."

"As long as the Frenchman doesn't wake up!"

Furtively, they lifted the curtain that separated the two rooms, and saw Stéphane motionless, with his little mistresses graciously nestled against him. Tuberoses and lotuses were shedding their petals around them; the charming group seemed to be emerging from a downy nest of corollas. In the gleam of lightning flashes, the gems of their necklaces and bracelets lit up momentarily, putting multicolored fires over the brown skin.

"They're asleep."

"They're no longer caressing one another in the flowers and the harmonies."

"It's a pity!"

"Why didn't the chief choose us?"

"He would have been happier, since Soakia has already been subjected to the bewitchment of amour."

Mana'i, her eyes troubled, seized Sigete's arm. "What if we were to warn the voyager?"

Palpitating under the temptation, Sigete reflected.

"Perhaps that would be better."

"We'd have Stéphane and Mappy."

"The Frenchman would flee with his dancers."

"The chief would forget."

"Stéphane would return to France."

"Let's talk to him, there's still time."

"You speak to him first."

"I daren't . . ."

"Think, then, that we might make ourselves loved by Mappy, that he might render justice to our fidelity, our devotion . . . that all three of us might be happy . . ."

"No, that would be bad. Let's do our duty."

"Our duty? What is it? Is it necessary to obey our chief or our conscience?"

"Let's interrogate Shiva."

They let the curtain fall back on the sleeping lovers, and prostrated themselves again before the mysterious idol, while, in the distance, agile and eccentric flames danced in the black sky, twirling like monstrous ballerinas in flying skirts of luminous gauze.

XI
The Rain of Fire

The morning was calm, the sun ardent, with an unaccustomed ardor. Stéphane was still asleep when an indigene brought him a message inviting him to a tiger hunt that day. A male and a female had been seen in the jungle below the virgin forest, and the chiefs of a few neighboring tribes were going to meet at a place the guide knew.

Although still feverish and worn out, his temples seemingly caught in a dolorous vice, the young man got dressed rapidly.

"You're leaving us?" asked Soakia, anxiously?

"Not for long, darling. I haven't yet hunted tigers and I'd like to."

Wakiem and Tamiah clung to him. "Take us! Take us!"

He pushed them away gently.

"It's necessary not to think of that; it's not an amusement for little girls. Wait here for me patiently."

"Oh, bad man!"

They were almost weeping, but he consoled them with an irresistible cajolery, and left.

With the man who had brought him the letter he arrived at the meeting place: a sort of platform overlooking an almost impenetrable ravine overflowing with a tangle of plants, ferns and giant reeds, where swarms of metallic insects were flying. Apart from a few narrow trails it was only by breaking a thousand stems, aiding oneself with one's arms and knees, that one could move in the dense network.

A few trackers were waiting for them, armed with flintlock rifles, primarily intended to make noise, and more dangerous at first use to the hunters than the wild beasts.

"Be patient," said the guide to Stéphane. "I'll distribute the men around the gorge. Your hunting companions won't be long."

He drew away, and the young man, increasingly oppressed, leaned on a tree absent-mindedly. From the top of his hill he overlooked the densest part of the jungle, and a small clearing where a torrent ran that seemed to him to have roseate waves shrouded in vapors.

He bent down. The soil was warm; hundreds of reptiles were slithering rapidly in the same direction, as if fleeing before an enemy.

He raised his head, and saw a veil of black smoke descending the mountain, hanging like hair. *A storm*, he said to himself, and called to his guide in order to seek a refuge; but no voice responded to his own. He was still dazed, his head increasingly tightened in a hard circle, his eyes blind and his ears buzzing. It appeared to him that his being was duplicated, escaping outside himself.

Slowly, he collapsed in the elastic reeds, which protected him from the heat of the ground. Then he perceived that rain was falling, a singular rain made of droplets of fire, sparse at first and indecisive, and then closer together and heavy, extending a flamboyant cloak between the horizon and him, the base of which was fringed with crimson. At times, however, the downpour slowed, only throwing light hailstones, which burst as they fell into fine sprays of seeds.

Then birds of prey flew in all directions, enormous vultures deploying smoky wings, which tore into branches, letting black flakes fall, and red crepes of torn paper.

Thunder was barking incessantly, a lugubrious subterranean thunder, and Stéphane, who was semi-conscious, thought he was hearing the furious howling of an imprisoned dog-pack.

A tiger with green eyes appeared beside him without being moved by his presence. The man and the wild beast considered one another calmly; then the latter, with two bounds, disappeared in a crackle of dry leaves. Black monkeys were galloping in the lianas, calling from one tree to another, making their jaws click like castanets.

It was a mad race, a crawling, a swarming, a haste of everything alive toward deliverance.

Stéphane was thinking as if in an opium torpor, and what surrounded him had the indecisiveness of dreams. He thought that he was at the Opéra, under the electric lights, in the blast of brass instruments. The stage was ablaze with red light, the chorus was clamoring in a discordant fashion, while a bacchanal of golden-helmeted demons agitated madly, their hair flying like flames. The galleries were spinning, carrying strange masks with fixed gesture of lust; women tipped backwards were offering themselves to grunting satyrs covered in bizarre clothes, ineptly disguising their pointed ears and their caprine bodies. There were all the grimaces and all the smiles, all the plaints and all the joys, of a humanity of suffering and debauchery. Painted creatures with excessively bright eyes were fanning themselves near a young man; then one of them leaned over, took his lips in hers, and he lost consciousness in an intense burn.

XII
Fear

Soakia and her anxious sisters interrogate the sky.

"Look at that great cloud!"

"How dark it is!"

"It's covering the mountain."

"The storm will be terrible."

"And Stéphane's gone!"

"Oh, if Mappy hadn't left us, I don't know for what reason, we could send him out here."

"Yes," says Wakiem. "He'd bring back the Beloved, who might not be able to find his own way."

But Soakia shivers. "Never mention Mappy again!"

"Why not?" asks Taminah, astonished.

"I'll explain it to you later . . ."

Sigete and Mana'i have disappeared. A light smoke is still emerging from the perfume-burner in front of the image of Shiva.

Soakia, who knows nothing about the supreme god and his triple incarnation, turns away indifferently and returns her gaze to the horizon.

The storm-cloud, like an immense crocodile, has stopped over the volcano. Its belly is flamboyant, while its spine remains as black as ink and its menacing head looms up in the clouds.

Then the form elongates and undulates slowly; it is a serpent.

The serpent becomes a chimera, an eagle, a vulture, a stream, a lake, an ocean of darkness, and the sky rolls tumultuous waves of hot ash.

Soakia utters a scream and falls to her knees.

Wakiem and Taminah sob, holding one another tightly.

"What should we do?"

"I don't know."

"Let's go out and seek help."

"Yes, yes, let's join Stéphane."

They throw away their heavy necklaces and their ankle bracelets in order to go more rapidly, only covering their heads with a light veil to protect their faces.

At the door, Sigete and Mana'i, posted as sentinels, block their passage.

"Where are you going?"

"We're going to look for the Beloved. Come with us."

Mana'i shakes her head. "Futile. He's doomed."

"Doomed?"

The children look at one another, eyes widened by horror, but Soakia, the most reckless, pushes between the reng'gong.

"You're lying!"

"Listen," says Sigete, trying to drag the dancer away. "You'll never see your lover again. Let us take you to Mappy. He still cherishes you. He'll watch over your future and that of your sisters."

"You'll be our queen, as before," adds Manai.

Soakia, vibrant with hatred and dolor, pushes the perfidious counselors away.

"I understand! I understand! The chief has drawn Stéphane close to the volcano, all of whose anger he knows. He's prepared his frightful vengeance patiently. And you . . . you have the mission of holding us back. Is that true? Is that true?"

The rong'geng lower their heads, moved by the girl's emotion.

"Ah!" the latter continues. "Your silence is a confession. Why do you obey that master who scorns you enough to make you serve the satisfaction of his caprice? Isn't it you that he ought to cherish?"

"That's true," the young women admit, humiliated.

"You're beautiful, you're young, but he neglects you for someone else."

"Alas!"

"And you play the go-between in his vile work, like ugly old women . . ."

"She's right," sighs Sigete.

Soakia takes her sisters by the hand.

"Come on, Wakiem! Come on, Taminah! And may the anger of the gods fall on these culpable women!"

Siegte and Mana'i raise their trembling arms, pointing at the grim sky. "You'll arrive too late."

But the amorous children have already disappeared, into a whirlwind of burning dust, and the crazed running of their bare feet can be heard in the distance.

XIII
The Anger of the Monster

It woke up and roared, the terrible lion of earth tremors; it shook off its temporary lethargy, bounded and crawled, casting its tawny mane to the wind, testing its powerful muscles. Under the ground, other roars responded, and in their sudden convulsions, centenarian trees swayed frenetically, as if seized by vertigo, and then suddenly collapsed, with a heart-rending sob, blocking the path with their gigantic masses.

Houses vacillated and collapsed like houses of cards, all in the same direction, swept by an irresistible wind.

In the darkness, ever more profound, Wakiem murmured: "I'm scared."

Soakia had wings.

"Courage! Don't quit me."

She no longer had any veil, but the two little ones clung on to her long floating hair and ran behind her, thin and light, scarcely touching the fuming ground.

Clouds of soot, mingled with crackling sparks, rolled down the mountain, alternating with a cascade of fire, a golden fall of dazzling brightness under the ebony sky: the sinister sky that resembled the vault of a sepulcher, as immutable as death.

Women and children were fleeing. The men were pressing leather bags to their bosom containing their wealth. Others were taking refuge in buildings that were still standing.

"Hurry!" Soakia repeated.

She headed toward the flaming mountain, knowing that her beloved was there, wanting to save him or to perish with him.

"Faster! Faster still!"

Wakiem and Taminah were suspended from her tresses of living silk, weeping softly.

"We can't do any more."

"Leave me, then . . . I'll go alone."

But the frail lovers were reanimated, and made a supreme effort.

"No, no, we'll follow you anyway."

However, they were obliged to stop. Taminah had fallen, and gashed her knee.

There was a light shining in an abandoned house. The girls went in, thinking that they might find a little water for the injured girl. In front of them, reptiles were fleeing, a stampede of crawling, sticky forms. Without disgust, they drank from an earthenware jar from which the filthy beasts had drunk, to which viscous bodies were still adhering.

Taminah bathed her wound, and declared that she was capable of following her sisters.

As they reached the door, a shadow was framed therein, hiding the conflagration of the forest

"Mappy!"

"Yes Mappy, who forbids you to go any further!"

"You forbid us!"

Soakia uttered a loud laugh, which sounded like a fanfare challenging the growling of the elements.

"Little queen," moaned the chief, "don't you know that the moment is terrible?"

"I know that."

"You'll doom yourself, without saving the one you love."

"At least I'll have attempted the impossible. Let me pass."

"You don't know the path."

"I'll go straight ahead, toward the brightest light."

"I know all the paths that lead to death; I also know the one that leads to salvation."

"Stéphane!" cried Soakia, resplendent with amour. "Stéphane! Lead us to him!"

"Never. In any case, you'd only find his corpse."

"Who knows?"

Mappy shrugged his shoulders. "No living thing remains up there. Look . . ."

Tigers, panthers and lions were fleeing recklessly under the beating wings of birds of prey, whose heavy flight was displacing clouds of ash.

The darkness thickened further, striped at moments by volcanic lightning flashes lashing the clouds like steel thongs. Rivers of lava were flowing, boiling, snaking between the trees, half-uprooted, forming lakes of silvery mud in the hollows. The mouth of the volcano launched, by turns, a rain of boiling water or a sheaf of crimson rockets, which burst at a great height and fell back in sheets of rubies. The ardent river rolled impetuously, entering into houses, drowning people and things.

"Come!" repeated Mappy, quivering with impatience; and he put his arm around Soakia's waist brutally, attempting to draw her away.

The naked, sweat-soaked body of the girl slipped through his hands.

As she ran into the room, where her sisters were motionless, still weeping, she shouted: "I hate you! I hate you!"

He did not become angry, but more humble. "Little queen, I beg you! I love you so much!"

"Stéphane!"

"Nothing can bring him back, I swear. His very ash will be dispersed by the wind."

Soakia was still running around the narrow space, looking for a weapon. Not finding one, she picked up the heavy earthenware jar and, with a supreme effort, hurled it at the chief's head.

While he was still blind, stunned by the shock, she called to Wakiem and Taminah, and recommenced her mad run under the burning rain.

XIV
Supreme Devotion

They went up toward the volcano, amid the ash, the lava flows, the devouring mud, the thunder, the flames and the lightning. They went, martyrs of amour, in a heroic intoxication, a fever, a supernatural delirium, their hair burned, their limbs exhausted, and their flesh palpitating. They went higher, and ever higher, toward the glorious, formidable pyre; they shouted, dominating the angry and profound voices of the sky and the earth, the name of the beloved:

"Stéphane! Stéphane!"

Their feet were bleeding, their knees were buckling, their sides aching under their trident breath. It seemed to them that trains launched at full steam were bounding around them; there were tumultuous sounds of smelting, catastrophic impacts, howls of pain and fear, a torture of the damned struggling beneath the black sky, but the light of a furnace.

Now the bites of the fire became more avid, penetrating the delicate skin of the girls profoundly; the monster's kisses became mortal, and the air, charged with vapors, was no longer sufficient for the work of the lungs.

"Stéphane! Stéphane!"

The appeals weakened, no longer anything but the plaintive wail of infants, the sobbing of turtle-doves.

"Stéphane! Stéphane!"

The sound died away, becoming more tenuous than the vibration of a harp, a distant echo of the breeze, a thread of spidersilk suspended from the pistil of a lily.

"Stéphane! Stéphane!"

This time, only their hearts heard it . . .

XV
The End of a Great Amour

The beloved, however, was not dead. By virtue of a providential hazard, a mysterious decree from On High, he had only been touched lightly by the flames. The man sent by Mappy to draw him to his doom, having reflected that he was certain to receive a nice reward for his good deed, had retraced his steps and had saved him, with the aid of the beaters—intrepid bandits raised in the mountains.

The healing process was long, indecisive and unconscious, Stéphane's mental shock having been far stronger than his physical pain. Finally, when he was out of danger, he enquired about the fate of his little lovers; but all research was in vain.

The light souls had followed the vagabond aromas of the forest, perfumes of women, perfumes of evaporated flowers, like an incense of amour, at the foot of the giant tabernacle ablaze in the night . . .

Amid the other corollas, the three corollas of sensuality had faded and dispersed in impalpable ash.

The King of Siam's Amazon

PART ONE

I
Funeral

Young women clad in saffron yellow veils that fall from a sapphire star fixed to the ear and cover the left side of the body are lighting sticks of incense before the remains of Nai-Rafutt, which will be burned shortly.

The dead girl is one of the wives of Phaja-Tak,[1] who mounted the throne in the year 1129 of the Era of Siam; she reposes on a bed of lotuses and roses, at the summit of an immense catafalque, shaded by a parasol with seven tiers, and already seems partly mummified, having been steeped in balms and aromatics for a long time. Nothing remains of her former beauty; her arms, hands and torso, beneath barbaric jewelry only emphasize any longer the puerile attachment of the bones, and the extended head, with the exception of a clownish hank of hair that rises up vertically, seems carved out of a box-tree root.

The funeral is being celebrated, in great pomp, of the little wife who counted scarcely ten Aprils, and all the notabilities of Bangkok are gathered around the august pyre protected by a scarlet flag adorned with a white elephant.

Mourners, of whom nothing can be seen but the immeasurably enlarged eyes, under linen headbands, are uttering long

---

1 "Phaja-Tak" is better known as Taksin the Great (so called because of his liberation of the realm from Burmese domination, and the other conquests credited to him in the story), who was the king of the Thai realm from 1767-1782. Although the events of the story are wholly fictitious, Taksin was suspected during the final year of his reign of being insane, largely because of his increasing religious fanaticism.

ululations, punctuated by the ironic trills of little flutes and the hoarse hiccups of tambourines.

The priestesses of Buddha are prostrating themselves on the ground as a sign of mourning. Each one is holding one of the cordons of roses that fall from the catafalque in all directions like the threads of a giant spider-web.

In Thai belief, those light links carry good wishes and prayers to the dead woman. Thus, Rafutt knows that she is still beautiful and cherished, that desires and adorations are rising toward her like the perfume of tuberoses, and that one smile from her lips effaces the moon's rays.

Soon, the Chao-Klein-Balat,[1] or high priest of the talapoins, will light the pyre, and the little body of Rafutt will catch fire like a desiccated yam-stock. She will not offer the terrifying spectacle of certain corpses, whose muscles and sinews contact and whose entire quivering being rears up in a sort of macabre dance under the first kisses of the flames. It will be consumed suddenly, a poor yellow floret fallen from the royal herbarium, and her ashes will not fill the golden urn that is awaiting them.

The women of the harem are contemplating the ceremony from the height of the terraces, but the princesses surround the pyre, faces and shoulders dissimulated under a kind of white hood. By contrast, their breasts, loins and legs are only ornamented by a profusion of precious stones, which seem to move over the skin like fulgurant scarabs.

"Kali-Yana, you've just scratched my ear with the pole of your banner!"

"So why aren't you in your rank, Xali?"

"I'm tired, and these weapons are so heavy."

"What would you say, then, if we were fighting the enemy?"

---

1 This title, many of the details of the funeral, and various other details of the Siamese capital are taken from an account first published in Ludovic de Beauvoir's 1867 *Voyage autour le monde*, Some other details appear to be derived from "Voyage dans les royaumes de Siam" in *Le Tour du monde* (1863) by Édouard Charton.

"In battle, courage would come to me, but I hate these fatiguing parades. It's so often necessary for us to assist the king's dead wives!"

"He takes them so young that the first wound afflicts them too profoundly."

"Yes, Rafutt only resisted the sacred rape for two months; she was very pretty, although thinner than one of the cats of the pagoda of Xetuphon."

"She loved to see us file past every morning, and she always had a kind word for Kali-Yana."

"Oh, how my wisdom weighs upon me," sighed Xali, tightening the buckle of her belt at her supple waist. "Let me lean on your shoulder a little, Yana."

Kali-Yana, the prettiest of the royal amazons, was carrying the standard of the white elephant. Her short, thick and shiny hair was traversed by a circlet of stones that sustained a long white plume over her forehead. Her disengaged neck remained bare, but from the shoulders to the thighs a narrow tunic hugged her body, sharpening the curt points of her breasts under its gaudy ornamentations, and emphasizing the supple retreat of her waist, gripped by a curved golden strip. Her slender, harmonious legs were designed beneath a mesh of silk fastened with coral beads. Rings with glaucous cabochons circled her ankles and her red-nailed toes. She was almost boyish under the warrior harness of precious weapons that beat her flanks, but her childlike lips, rounded in the shape of a heart, retained an exceedingly soft smile, and her eyes had the mysterious profundity of sacred lakes.

Behind the amazons stood the king's dancing girls. Upright now in their langoutis beaded with multicolored flames, steeped in balms reeking of cedrat and oliban, they were assisting, weary and nostalgic, in the preliminary ceremonies of the incineration. The tambourines hiccuped more loudly and the perfume burners, intoxicated and almost swooning, lit more incense-sticks with tremulous hands.

From the bosom of the crowd a cry departed: "The King!"

Protected by a squadron of mandarins, he did, in fact, appear, on a palanquin encrusted with ivory and nacre, supported by sixteen bearers clad in violet silk. Young women threw mali petals and golden powder under their feet, while gongs thundered, accompanying the shrill stridulations of klues and kong-vongs, metal and bamboo flutes, and dulcimers of stretched snakeskin. Curved trumpets, bronze and ivory renats, laio organs and rakhes alternated at the height of platforms with the barbaric instruments of the cortege.

After the royal palanquin came a hundred domesticated lions, held on leashes by young boys clad only in loincloths of feathers, and sparkling cavaliers, armored and helmed in gold, agitating pikes or sculpted bronze krises, javelins and lances. The infantry followed in good order, composed of a cohort of six hundred men specially attached to the palace.

Majestic under his hammered gold pectorals constellated with stars, badges and suns, his head covered with a turriculated miter, the King gave his people a benevolent sign, while the brass instruments were unleashed in furious trepidations. Behind the royal cortege, elephants armed for war were ranged in their turn, wearing crocodile carapaces, displaying bracelets of rubies and peridots on their long tusks. They arrived in such great quantity that soon, nothing could any longer be seen but the monotonous swell of their enormous swaying bodies.

The people remained silent; no joyful demonstration had saluted the arrival of Phaja-Tak, the glorious King, the supreme Master in the year 1144 of the Thai Era. However, that monarch had shown himself, in the first years of his reign, to be obliging and liberal. The soldiers had received, and were still receiving, a wage three or four times larger than they had under his predecessors. But he treated the rich and the mandarins harshly, who were spreading slanderous rumors about him. Certain important individuals among those close to him, it was said, were making him take maleficent drugs that were troubling his reason. The king, possessed of criminal desires, was buying for his seraglio wives that were too young, almost all of whom died after a few months, as Nai-Rafutt had died, a little victim of amour.

Families often refused, at first, to sell their daughters, but the fear of reprisals or the lure of gain generally triumphed over resistance.

In less than a year, fifty frail spouses had offered their bruised flesh, steeped in balms, to the pyre. Sometimes, two or three of them were burned on the same day, and the people, stirred up by the families in mourning, were beginning to murmur, no longer recognizing in the eccentric satyr that he had become, the good king of old.

No emotion was visible on the features of the monarch; upright beneath his pectorals decorated with flames, his lips taut and his gaze vague, he seemed to be following some distant dream and to be disinterested in what surrounded him, calm before enthusiasm as before hatred.

But the talapoin, or Buddhist priest, has set fire to Nai-Rafutt's catafalque, and the fragile idol has disappeared in swirls of black smoke. It is the signal for rejoicing and dances.

Kali-Yana lifts the scarlet standard higher, and the amazons rattle their weapons, circling around the pyre and uttering their war cry. Then the sacred dancers allow scarves spangled with silver to float behind them for the game of "the rose and the dragonfly," gliding smoothly and embracing one another, seeming to collect pollen from flowers. Children with gilded skin throw jade amulets to the crowd, burning essences and coconut oil in lachrymatories of red clay. Others offer minuscule statuettes of Buddha, elephants and coral tigers to the avid lips of women. Everywhere, there are lotuses, yams, rose-apples and lychees, elegantly arranged on the ground on brightly colored cloths, which the merchants are hawking in shrill voices.

Again, Xali is leaning on Kali-Yana's shoulder.

"Yana," she said, "this smoke is suffocating me. Let's go away for a while."

"You know full well, Xali, that it's forbidden. Amazons can't quit their posts."

"Oh, people will think that we're obeying a royal order, and no one will worry about our absence. Galanick will carry the standard for an hour or two. Come on, come quickly."

The young woman responding to the name of Galanick meekly took hold of the pole of the scarlet flag in which the white elephant was designed in silk and white pearls, and Xali dragged her companion away.

The crowd parted as the amazons passed, believing that they were carrying a message, and they traversed the square of august funerals, went under the portal of the Green Pagoda, followed the pathways full of talapoins at prayer, and stopped in front of a perforated kiosk in which three cadavers were lying in open coffins, awaiting the pleasure of the vultures.

They were three galley-slaves destined for the final scouring—which is to say, the beaks of the birds of prey—and there was a satisfying contrast between the sumptuous and painted incineration of the royal square and the hideous butchery of the public charnel-house.

Xali and Yana trampled the fleshless skulls that obstructed their passage with a sure tread, scattering the sinister birds grouped around a few bloody shreds, while holding an amethyst bottle of vehement scent to their nostrils in order to combat the frightful stench of putrefaction.

After having passed through the midst of the partly dismantled rib-cages gaping on all sides, long crimson ribbons of intestines and brains displayed like jellyfish on porcelain slabs, having scratched their bare feet on scattered bones, the young women found themselves in a charming place where coconut palms and other palm trees, planted at intervals, allowed the slender steeples and minarets of the city to be seen. The banks of the Me-Nam[1]—the mother of waters—formed by rows of floating houses, extended into the distance in a glorious radi-

---

1 The Me-Nam is nowadays better known as the Chao Phrya. The city founded on the river by Taksin to serve as his capital was Thonburi, which eventually merged with Bangkok, of which it is now a district.

156

ance, setting the roofs ablaze with pink and blue hues. On the firm ground, which loomed over that initial amphibious city, the royal residence appeared, with its crenellated walls, its white towers, its multiple domes with gold ornaments, its colonnettes of porphyry, porcelain and glass, and its galleries of juxtaposed mirrors ornamented with silver, bonze and ivory.

It is a magical vision, reminiscent of a hashish dream, which only Siamese eyes can contemplate without blinking. The firework display of turrets, minarets and obelisks rises high into the sky, punctuated by the rockets of bell-towers and steeples of infinite delicacy. The palaces, lower down, display accumulations of domes covered with scales, paved porphyry esplanades, pagodas with slender pillars flecked with precious stones and porticoes encased with gold, like mounted gems. Other columns rise in spirals, like snakes with ocher and cinnabar patches, sustaining fantastic animals of jade and crystal.

It is a vineyard of precious stones in which the buildings resemble immense clusters of olivines, crimson and golden fruits, and bright amber and topaz gum. Shoots are climbing everywhere, outlined in the rare minarets, and a brazier of incombustible gems is ablaze under the furnace of a delirious sun.

II
The Talapoin of the Dead

After having contemplated the fantastic landscape for a few moments, however, and recovered from the morbid exhalations of the carrion, the young women went back into the pagoda in order to interrogate the talapoin of the dead, who knew how to read in the stars and to seek among funeral ashes the explanation for the mysteries of joy and pain.

Gamakul was asleep amid the vultures when Xali opened the door of his dwelling.

Kali-Yana, however, did not want to go in. "You're crazy, Xali! I assure you that something bad will happen to us."

"No, dear Yana. No one suspects our absence. It was, in any case, necessary to find an opportunity like this to escape the surveillance of which we're the object. I'm so glad to be alone with you!"

"See how strange this dwelling is!"

"I find it charming, and I wouldn't want any other if I were the talapoin of the dead, an astrologer and chiromancer."

On the teak-wood walls, in fact, there were singular rose-patterns of femurs and tibias, arabesques of ribs and clavicles, delicate stars of phalanges: an entire cemetery of flora, whiter than a wedding bouquet.

A few skulls on the tables contained a pink liquid flecked with gold.

"I thought the bonzes never drank wine," said Kali-Yana. "Isn't it written in the holy books: *Only drink water, and do not eat meat, even crocodile or dog?*"

"Oh, the bonzes know how to give themselves the most delicate morsels in their morning tours. The women care for them better than their husbands. For them, the best shrimp paste, and the pickled crayfish spawn the color of amethyst that horrifies us. For them, the plump singing rays and the finest pieces of boa. For them, the yams, rose-apples and fondant lychees."

"Most of all they like wasps' nests and little rats preserved in rose honey."

"If Gamakul heard you . . . !"

"He's fast asleep."

"That doesn't mean anything, since he's a sorcerer."

The talapoin of the dead had a cranium like an egg, and piercing eyes slanting over a shiny nose ornamented with little blackheads like a cinnamon-apples. The cordlets of his hair descended over his slack cheeks; a white langouti enveloped his torso.

In accordance with the sacred books, the servants of Buddha do not submit to any labor. They do not till the soil, "for the life of an earthworm is worth as much as that of a man." They do not cook rice "which contains a vital germ." They do not travel on mares or female elephants, and the frequentation of women is forbidden to them.

All the sons of a family enter into the religious order at about their twentieth year, but do not pronounce eternal vows, and the husband of Nai-Rafutt, whose little body was being consumed in the midst of songs and dances, passed from the most rigorous celibacy to a harem of eight hundred women.

Meanwhile, Xali had woken the bonze.

"Right hand of Buddha, Parcel of Infinity, Ray of the King-Star," she said, prostrating herself, "deign to listen to two little amazons whose virginity will be agreeable to you."

Gamakul got up hastily. "Two amazons! What do you desire, White Lotuses of the Sacred Pool?"

"To know the future. Would you like to read my hand and that of Kali-Yana? Would you care to interrogate the ash of pyres while invoking the beneficent spirits?"

"And you'll make a present to Phra Rodon, the porcelain god of the Green Pagoda, in order that he will be favorable to you?"

"We promise," said Xali, taking a few bahts—silver beads—out of her pocket.[1]

Gamakul caressed an enormous vulture, which was twisting its hideously bare goitered neck nearby and took a pinch of ash from a golden urn.

"It's the ash of a tortured man," he said. "He had his tongue torn out and his eyes punctured before dying. He agonized for two hours at the foot of his pyre because, as he had expiated his crimes, he was not delivered to the vultures. That will be twenty baht."

"I'll be generous," Xali affirmed.

The talapoin smiled as he studied the young woman's hand.

"You're in love," he said, "and you've lost your reason, like a bee drunk on perfumes."

---

1 The original text has *ticaux*, the plural of the French term for the baht (15 grams of silver). Flat coins did not replace round pellets as standard currency in Thailand until 1825.

"Will I be loved?"

Without responding, Gamakul took Kali-Yana's hand and absorbed himself in grave meditations.

"Kali-Yana," he pronounced, finally, "I see great and sad things in the future. You might be happy, but . . ."

"But?" interrogated the young woman, shivering.

"You will follow your whim and disdain the happiness that is offered to you."

Xali had taken off a takrut, a small talisman suspended from her arm in order to offer it to her companion.

"Perhaps this gold leaf, on which I've written my desire, will deflect the maleficent phi away from you. Will the august master help me?"

But Gamakul shook his head. "All your prayers, Xali, will be futile, and even if you went to the King of Fire's forest, the Dong P'aya P'ai, and cut your wrists and your ears, your friend's destiny would be accomplished. Let's see, now, what the ashes of the dead say."

He extended a few pinches of the gray powder on an ivory tray and blew on them three times in order to scatter them in accordance with the will of the gods. Then he agitated a luk-pat, a chaplet of a hundred and eight pearls, which, in Thai belief, represents the number of symbols on the Buddha's soul.[1]

"Ah! I also see misfortune over our country."

"What do you see?"

"Revolt everywhere and the death of a madman!"

"You aren't talking about the Supreme Master?"

"I haven't named the victim. But blood will stream over the steps of the palace; weeping women will be dragged to the feet of executioners, and those who survive the torture will have their throats cut."

"Why that massacre?"

---

1 I have retained *luk-pat* as it is given in the original, although its origin is obscure and Buddhist chaplets of 108 beads are usually knows as malas.

"Because all those who have belonged to a demented individual are accursed and must be exterminated."

Xali and Yana uttered a cry of fright.

"What! It's in these ashes that you see such terrible things! Might a fortunate hazard not change the course of events?"

"The oracle is formal; the signs of death are clearly marked; destiny will be accomplished."

The vulture, its neck extended, agitated its wings feverishly, and Xali now contemplated with horror the interlaced bones on the somber walls. The grimacing heads of torture victims, which Gamakul had grouped in savant rose-shapes, stood out like macabre flowers growing in a cemetery of ribs, and the phalanges emerging like stamens from gaping skulls, crowned the game of ulnas and radii, femurs and tibias.

As the birds of prey took flight heavily, a fine dust fell on the sinister trophies, and mobile rays of light illuminated, here and here, the rictus of a jaw, the crests of an orbit or a chaplet of vertebrae.

"Tell us about the future," Xali demanded. "Will I be happy?"

"Your destiny is linked to that of your companion. But the ashes have been disturbed . . ."

"Look, look hard . . ."

"I see . . ."

At that moment, an adorable child with long, soft and sad eyes brought a spray of lan-tam, the sacred flower with the perverse perfume, of which the phi are fond, and deposited it at the talapoin's feet.

"Thank you, Suk," said the latter, caressing the little boy's cheek. "Thus, the malefic bats will fly out of the window."

The young women, their lips tight and their hands trembling, gazed at the dust of the dead that was scattered in fateful signs.

"Speak!" said Xami, in a low voice.

Gamakul hesitated, his eyes filled with alarm.

"What is the point of spoiling, with somber predictions, the peaceful days that you still have to live? Human knowledge only serves to render people more unhappy. The joys of existence are tarnished by the idea of the end, and perhaps we would be better off if we were simpler."

The vulture flapped its wings again, and dropped a gelatinous ball that it was holding in its beak,

"A bad, bad presage," sighed the bonze.

"What is it, then?" Xali demanded.

The child picked up the little white ball, which had slid into the flowers.

"It's the eye of a dead man. Ket always commences with the choice morsels."

"Oh!" said Xali, fearfully. "But speak, speak quickly; we need to get back there."

"Yes, go back there, and do not seek any other future than the one from which you departed. Let the little amazons of the King serve the King faithfully, and not be ambitious for any other glory. Kali-Yana is too pretty to run around the streets, and her imprudence might cost her dear!"

Xali put her arm around her companion's waist and, squeezing her tenderly, as if to protect her against the malign spirits, tried to draw her away. But Kali-Yana, who had only been paying a vague attention to the talapoin's words until then, cried impatiently: "I want to know!"

"Oh, you want to know! Well, the evil presages concern you particularly. You will suffer and you will cause suffering, you will scorn veritable amour for temporary follies, you will be imprudent and criminal, and if destiny seems to smile upon you, it will only be to crush you more surely. I see tears and blood. I see . . ."

"Come! Come!" sobbed Xali.

The talapoin shrugged his shoulders, and drew pretty Suk toward him, while the young women drew away.

III
Xali's Amour

Xali is now at Kali-Yana's knees. She is caressing the young woman's bare feet with tuberoses, and she is speaking in a curt tone.

"Since you can't divine anything, I'll explain myself without mincing words. I've been hesitating for a long time and my heart is trembling as if a hand were gripping it in my breasts. You've never been in love?"

"No," said Yana, after a momentary hesitation. "We ought not to love, since we can't have husbands."

"Is there only that brutal and deceptive tenderness? Man isn't worthy of us, but amour is everywhere. Don't you feel the emotion of your young flesh?"

"Perhaps. I don't know what I feel. I'm anxious and weary; my days go by in a fever of expectation of an unknown joy and my nights trail by in insomnia. My solitude weighs upon me so much that yesterday, I lay here on my couchette with Mira-Mira, the domesticated panther of the garden of the princesses. I kissed her like a little friend, and she seemed to understand me."

"Felines possess the gift of divination. They're intelligent and gentle with those who love them. But the affection of a panther isn't worth as much as that of a woman. Why don't you take me next to you as you've taken Mira-Mira?"

"You know full well that we're watched, Xali, and that the Great Lady is severe for us."

"When the Great Lady is asleep, I'll come to find you, Kali-Yana, little flower of heaven! In the meantime, take my takrut, which will bring you good luck. On the golden leaf I've had these words engraved:

"*May Kali-Yana keep my tears as the lotus keeps the dew.*
"*And if my tears are tasteless, I will shed my blood for her.*"

Still on her knees before her companion, Xali looked at her avidly. She was older than Kali-Yana, and more vigorous in appearance. Her large somber velvet eyes expressed energy and tenderness; her thick lips allowed a glimpse of little teeth that had not been dishonored by the betel and areca nuts dear to the Thais.

Yana leaned toward her little friend and rubbed her cheek against hers

"Thank you, Xali. I'll 'mention you to my heart.'"

"It doesn't know me yet, then?"

"I don't know, but it will surely make me its confidences."

"Tell me this evening, then, what it has responded to you."

"I'll tell you."

Xali stood up, almost joyful. "Quickly, let's return to Rafutt now, who must now be nothing more than a little heap of blackened bone."

"As long as Galanick hasn't denounced us!"

"No, I gave her a luh-sakhot that she's desired for a long time. Galanick isn't malevolent."

"Oh! Look how those crows are following us! The phra of the dead would tell us that that's yet another bad omen."

"Yes," said Xali, in a low voice, "and hungry dogs are howling behind us."

The young women started running, carried away by a foolish fear. Their weapons rattled in their belts, and the black birds, obstinate in following them, made them a kind of cloak of darkness under the ardent sun.

IV
Last Fumes

Around Rafutt's pyre the rejoicing was continuing. The Flai, the sacred dancers, were executing warrior figures and lascivious steps, in order to celebrate the deliverance of the little wife and her entry into Nirvana.

Mimes were twirling in yellow gauze veils under the threat of pikes and abruptly crossed lances. Children only adorned with a small leaf of precious stones suspended from a belt of golden cord, were throwing garlands of lan-tam at the dancers' legs, and they ran away laughing, avoiding the chains of amour. But when one of them was caught, they all surrounded her, uttering a triumphant clamor.

On the platforms there were players of the khong-vong, the ranat and the takhe. The latter had ornamented themselves with long artificial fingernails in order to be better able to make the metallic strings of the Thai guitar vibrate. Sacred singers gradually inflated their voices like the murmurs of the wind. They sobbed and bellowed, imitating the play of the breeze in the foliage and the frenetic clamors of the tempest. Taking one another by the hand they swayed, at first with a slow movement and then, gradually, faster and faster, and ended up by falling, stunned, intoxicated by perfumes and cries.

There was also the game of sabers or the voluptuous dance of virgins, whose naked bodies folded in a slow spasm on a prolonged chord of kayabs and sos, straightened up again, took off, pirouetting and spinning in an unleashment of boa-skin tambours, and finally abandoned themselves as in a desire or caresses, and lay down, breathless and dazed, on the strewn roses.

While the flames crackled softly round what remained of Rafutt—a few bone fragments, necklaces and rings—pink wine powdered with gold circulated among the groups of high dignitaries and mandarins. The princesses, daughters of the King, and the little dancers ate pralines of lan-tam flowers, mouthfuls of mengdana and hoi-kong—beetles and freshwater mussels—wasps'-nest cakes and tender and delicate insect larvae rolled in almond paste, from baskets filigreed with silver.

Laughter rang out like the little bells of khong-vong, and the talapoins, in the general intoxication, sold their chaplets of the hundred and eight pearls of Buddha's sole and prayer-wheels more dearly.

Kali-Yana and Xali had resumed their places among the amazons, who, from time to time, punctuated the dances with their war cry.

Galanick had returned the standard embroidered with gems to the hands of her companion, and the crimson and gold fabric floated proudly above the Thai flags with scales imbricated by barbaric and audacious artists. Under the fires of the setting sun, the sparks of the stones sizzled oddly, and formidable blue and green furnaces stirred on the saddle-cloths of the elephants whose huge bodies barred the horizon.

Stronger now, Xali leaned on Kali-Yana's shoulder. "What if the phra of the dead was telling the truth, though?"

"Destiny will be somber for me, Xali."

"Because you'll scorn the affection I'm offering you."

"I'm not scorning anything, I'm suffering. It's necessary to pity me, friend."

"Think of my tenderness, then and tell yourself, dear Perfume, that it will render you happy."

"Perhaps . . ."

Kali-Yana closed her eyes on a vision of mysterious joy that her lips did not betray. Xali's caresses scarcely troubled her; she only liked to rub herself against her like a lascivious cat whose unconscious body seeks sensuality. The satisfaction she felt did not lead to desire, For her, Xali was a tender companion, a friend of whom one would like to make a confidante, but who was not a dispenser of joys and pains, the ungraspable and invincible tormenter who makes one think of death while giving life. She was not the amorous chimera who reveals the tortures of hell in the intoxication of paradise. Kali-Yana inclined toward other kisses, and her young flesh quivered at the evocation of forbidden embraces.

Now the tom-toms and the gongs were announcing the end of the ceremony. The Chao-Klein-Balat, the high priest of the talapoins, had received Rafutt's ashes in a golden urn, and the cortege formed for the return to the palace.

166

The Great Lady, or first wife of the harem, held the vase enriched by sardonyxes and peridots, which, combined on high shelves with other vases enriched with rare gems, represented the defunct amours of the King. The perfume burners, under their yellow veils, agitated cassolettes with subtle effluences, and the mourners hid their smoky eyelids under garlands of lan-tam whose petals fluttered behind them.

For the little dancers, their torsoes glittering with a fine sweat under amulets, clasps and plaques, the klues—light bamboo flutes blown through the nose—produced crystalline sighs, trills and the pizzicati of mockingbirds. They danced backwards, their breasts rigid in the battle of amour, their loins vibrant under chains of roses, and their agile feet stirring olivines and topazes, like jumping insects in the dust of the road.

In their wake came the charming troop of children with large eyes of blue enamel, the clownish tufts surrounded by flowers, and little bronze bodies of which a leaf of rubies or emeralds, attached by a golden chain, specified the sex. They gamboled, laughing, and extending their little hands to the crowd, which threw them musky balls and ginger pralines.

The talapoins in white robes, their foreheads ringed by three cordlets, carried statues of Buddha, represented in gold, silver, jade and porphyry in all his transformations, for Buddha only became the Great Doctor of the universe after having been a serpent, the king of the white elephants, a stork, a lion and a venerated master of the simian tribe. A man one day, a demon the next, an archangel in the ten circles of glory that lead to the havens, a dispenser of joys and pains, he showed himself under all forms before concluding in the supreme felicity of Nirvana.

Cakyamouni emerges from pagodas for the incantations and nuptial feasts; the faithful cover him with jewels and flowers, transport him beneath a scintillating awning made of little mirrors combined in diamond shapes and arabesques, and the bonzes agitate great pink flabella around him. There are Buddhas fifteen or twenty meters tall; they have crossed legs, a pointed crown ornamented with little tinkling bells on the head and immense opal or hydrophane eyes, which are moistened with perfumed oil in order to render them alive. Incense burns around them in precious cups, drowning in russet smoke a quintuple row of onyx statuettes grouped at the feet of the initial divinity.

Laotian weapons shine in the hands of the phaya—mandarins—whose bald craniums shelter beneath a parasol of four, five or six stages, depending on the rank of the dignitary. Other bonzes, clad in orange, bear porcelain monsters on their shoulders, encrusted with cabochons of gems representing children on ruby cock-crests, tigers with golden pigtails ridden by women, flying serpents with lions' heads, chimeras and dragons coupled bizarrely with human beings.

As for the Buddha of the pagoda of Xetuphon, which measures fifty meters from the shoulder to the soles of the feet, it is necessary to leave him in his sanctuary of teakwood, where he smiles with his lips of pink enamel at the virgins who bring him flowers every morning.

The little idols leap on the shoulders of the talapoins around the palanquins in which the king's daughters are somnolent. Habituated to these sumptuous incinerations, the princesses no longer obtain any great pleasure from them, and their nostrils inhale the peppery and heady vapors of the cassolettes idly. Clad in gauze spangled with silver, their red-tipped breasts surrounded by a triple row of pearls, the warp their virgin loins, which will never know the shocks of amour, in bright scarves. A sapphire clasp, whose sparks glint over a cold and limpid azure, marks the place of their inviolate sex. Those royal daughters have bruised eyes and dry lips; their smile is as melancholy as moonlight, and they do not feel the kisses of the sun.

Sayameda, the most accomplished of them all, dominates them on a crystal throne.

She seems to irradiate light, so covered is she with scintillating gems. On her head, a sort of pointed crown maintains quite straight the locks of her hair that emerge in a hundred little tresses florid with droplets of sapphires; blue and white stars leap lightly from the tips of her breasts, amid the necklaces and the plaques; a belt of diamonds descends very low over the abdomen, more polished than the petals of the sacred lotus. Sayameda, whose legs and feet are wrapped in pearly gauze, which terminates in a comet's tail on the steps of her throne, is a radiant beauty. Her black eyelashes form a frieze over her cheeks, and her small mouth, open in a puerile heart-shape, is underlined by a golden stripe. Violet streaks elongate her eyes, recoiling toward the temples, where two tufts of champa are quivering.

But the little princess has shivered. A bouquet of phul, with the odor of white roses, has fallen in front of her like a snow-ball. She does not bend down to pick it up, but her lips form an imperceptible smile and the blue stars have trembled more forcefully on the double cup of her breasts.

Whose is the audacious hand that has thrown flowers to the prettiest of the royal daughters? Somber gazes interrogate the crowd, and a murmur of anger departs from the august group. But Samayeda's eyes remain lowered, revealing nothing of her disturbance. Furtively, she has placed her bare foot on the white bouquet, and it seems to her that a delicious caress rises along her legs and her thighs, and penetrates everything. A sigh swells her bosom, her hands, placed on her knees, clench feverishly,

Behind the princess march the amazons, with Kali-Yana at the head, carrying the crimson and gold banner indurated with gems. The young woman's slim figure, under her red tunic, straightens proudly; her somber eyes flash. Xali follows her gaze jealously, seeking to distinguish, in the crowd of spectators, the dear presence that has produced that metamorphosis. Kali-Yana does not have the right to love! Virgin, like the princesses, the amazons must consecrate themselves to the glory of the King, who is the Supreme Master.

V
Return to the Palace

Here is the public square on to which the great portico of the palace opens. From the façade, groups of columns launch forward, stuck like organ-pipes to the body of the principal building. A capital of nine superimposed crowns is terminated by an audacious needle that seems to plunge into the azure ball of the sky. Cabochons of faience, ablaze in the setting sun, distribute a symphony of multicolored notes everywhere; the colors sing more loudly than the bizarre instruments.

On either side of the palace, pink marble balconies advance, which serve to hoist people up on to an elephant's back. It is His Supreme Majesty's footstep, either when he mounts his enormous chargers or when he lets himself relax to the gentle sway of his palanquin.

Kali-Yana has resumed her languid and nostalgic expression; her head no longer turns; she only has eyes for the strange décor, of such an intensity of splendor that it seems as fantastic as an opium dream.

In the background, the spurred roofs of petty palaces appear, whose red blades allow blood to flow over the sandalwood edges of balconies cut out like necklaces of precious guipure. And there are rose windows carved in crystal and porcelain, massive corollas with golden pistils, a fabulous basket that is punctuated by the mineral firebrands of leaves wrapped in all the flames of green, from yellowish zircon to the cerulean gleam of beryl. They are the fruits of olivines and chrysoprases, reflected in the mirrors superimposed on the walls; they are espaliers of pink copper mingled with prodigious clusters of topazes and rubies: a celestial firework display slashing the earth with a shower of stars!

The talapoins have taken the idols back to their respective pagodas, and the princesses have slowly resumed the route to their apartments. In their turn, the amazons return to the halls hung with pennants, ornamented with trophies, masks and the figures of warriors where they live in common when they are not performing in sacred pantomimes or training with weapons in the courtyards of the palace.

Xali helps Kali-Yana to take off her gold-embroidered tunic, which makes her young breasts stick out and shapes her young figure adorably. Semi-naked, the amazon lies down on the cushions of her bed and lifts to her lips the little golden pipe whose tobacco mixed with opium will ease her melancholy. Her faithful friend lies down at her feet, places her forehead on her knees, and softly murmurs a prayer of love and death:

> *Phitthang saranang, khaxami*
> *Thammang saranang khaxami.*
> (Like Buddha, you are my refuge.
> Like nature, you are my refuge.)

Then she adds, varying the sacred text:

> *And I only want your caress,*
> *And I only want your bite,*
> *And I only want your kiss!*

That goes on for a long time. At the final couplet, Xali puts her lips on Kali-Yana's, who closes her eyes, insensible to the precise caress, however, and as warm as her desire for amour.

"Forgive me," she says, in the slightly halting but nevertheless Thai language, reminiscent of the rippling of a stream over dead branches.

"Why?" asks the indolent.

"I have something to tell you."

"Talk about amour!"

"More beautiful than the sun and the moon, Kali-Yana, let yourself go."

Galanick, Mi, Kromalat and Ramesuen, four little amazons with large eyes of onyx and enamel, are gambling on a scarlet mat with the silver balls that represent the country's money. Mun-Si, the oldest of the dainty warriors, fulfils the office of croupier. Ten times a minute she throws a handful of small shells on to the carpet, while her companions' eyes converge upon her anxiously. There are also pieces of nacre and ivory for the smaller stakes, and light Venus shells, a thousand of which are worth five sous.

The girls launch their fortune with full hands, as a sower spreads seed, without worrying about bad days. Are they not nourished at the King's expense? What do they have to fear? The winnings of those passionate games pay for heavy jewelry with cabochons of turquoises and coral, golden takruts, luk-sakhots that protect against bad luck and luk-pats with the hundred and eight symbols of Buddha's sole.

The most indifferent chew betel slowly or use ivory rods to stir bowls of shrimp paste with vehement effluences.

Very young rada, apprentice amazons, roll over the paving stones like goat-kids, hugging marionettes to their chests that represent warriors with the heads of dogs and monkeys. Other bellicose dolls swing on silken threads, which it is necessary to knock down with pellets of bran. A few girls are playing at that game, and when they win they go to deposit their victims in front of the White Elephant flag. The most expert receive a little money of shells or silver pellets.

Kali-Yana closes her eyes now in order to calm the cajoling ardor of Xali, whose constant adoration is importuning her.

"I'm tired, little friend; let me sleep."

"Oh, you don't sleep . . . As soon as I stay tranquil I see your eyelids open again, and I sense that you're anxious, that a thought that you don't want to tell me is haunting you cruelly."

"What secret thought could I have? You're not unaware of anything in my life."

"You're thinking about the caresses of a lover. For weeks, a fantasy has been awakening in you. Malevolent spirits populate your nights, the sin of amour is as resplendent in the shadows as the poisonous corollas of the Forest of Fire that the Vithi illuminate for the death of humans. Beware of succumbing to that dangerous temptation—or, better, let's pluck the flame flower together; you won't have to regret the brutal enterprises of a master, and the velvet of your flesh won't be crumpled by unskillful hands . . ."

Kali-Yana shook her little head with the short curls, impatiently; but her lips remained mute, as if swollen by kisses.

"Yes," Xali went on, her voice more vibrant, her entire body quivering with contained desires, "I haven't been able to find the road to your heart, and nothing can take you away from the vision you cherish. But listen, again, and since my amour doesn't touch you, remember the words of the talapoin of death . . ."

"Oh, Xali," the young woman murmured, "you're giving yourself needless trouble. I assure you that I'm only thinking about repose, and that it will be pleasant for me to sleep beside you."

"What! You'd like that . . . ?"

Satisfied with the result of her ruse, Kali-Yana drew away slightly, and put her arm seductively around her friend's neck, who nestled against her.

VI
Princess Sayameda

When Xali let her brunette head fall back in the cushions, Kali-Yana slid her naked feet gently on to the floor and, having assured herself that her friend was finally asleep, lifted the curtain that masked the doorway. The little companions that she brushed in passing did not wake up, slightly intoxicated by betel and gambling.

Nothing budged in the marble gallery that went around the amazons' pavilion. The young woman guided herself through the rhododendron and rose bushes of the garden, took a faience stairway bordered by red granite monsters and went into the King's Pagoda, her heart fluttering.

On the pavement made entirely of bronze bricks, her frail silhouette was reflected. She was careful not to walk on the silver mats, expertly woven like coats of mail, on which only royal toes could tread.

By the light of jade lamps hanging from the mosaic ceiling, hundreds of idols gleamed under parasols with seven tiers, which seem to fill the nave with a strange flora of luminous corollas. The marvel of Siam, the great solid gold Buddha, reigned in the center of the court of gods and goddesses, defended by the chimeras and dragons of the Mountain of Fire. Standing on his crystal lotus, he overlooked all the idols with his head, made of a single emerald surmounted by a sapphire helmet, and darted fabulous clusters of flashes. The rays of light fused in flight, caressing the summits of phallic columns springing forth all around.

That inconceivable group illuminated itself; incrusted specular stones refracted and dispersed the gleam of gems, which, reverberated by the red bronze paving-stones, sowed a shower of fireflies beneath Kali-Yana's bare feet.

The young woman prostrated herself, struck her forehead on the ground three times and murmured a prayer to the god of wisdom; then she hid herself behind the pedestal of a monster of pink granite, and waited.

The talapoins renewed the provisions of aromatic herbs for the cassolettes, lit sticks of incense in the precious lachrymatories, and erected around the central Buddha a forest of candles enveloped in light gold leaves, on which were inscribed the prayers of the royal spouses and the princesses. In large baskets, yellow and white lan-tam flowers with musky perfume were expiring.

In the morning the amazons had crossed two palm-leaves over the head of the supreme god to affirm their ever-alert vigilance and to drive away the maleficent vithi that wander around Pagodas. Having terminated the preparations for the night, the phra, before returning to their cells, kissed the thumb and toe of the great Buddha, dragged themselves over the bronze paving stones as a sign of submission, and appealed one last time for the benediction of Cakyamouni upon the King, the princes, the princesses and the eight hundred and sixty-five women of the harem.

When all the noise had ceased, a little door opened in the depths of the temple and Sayameda appeared with her gallant. He was an envoy of the King of France, a mariner with bright blue eyes, long blond moustaches whose golden reflection softened over the sun-tanned skin. His tall and supple stature loomed over the frail Sayameda, who resembled, in her robe patterned with pink flames, a little magicienne from the Mountain of Fire.

Her boyish head with short hair, only ornamented by a flowery tuft of jasmines, inclined on the man's breast with languor and passion. Her small breasts supported two stars of diamonds whose thin chains, passed under the arms and crossed over in front, were maintained in arrest over the fragile nipples. A panung of white gauze, ocellated by sapphires and sardonyxes, left visible the charming legs, amber and delicate, with heavy rings of gemstones, whose plates and little bells tinkled at every step.

"My heart is in yours," she said, in a crystalline voice, raising her eyes, immense with amour and dream, to gaze at the young man.

But his understanding of the Thai language was poor, and his only response was to put his lips to Sayameda's, causing her a long frisson.

"I'm running the greatest danger," she murmured then, glad to offer her life to her lover, the man who triumphed over all dreads and all obstacles.

He led her to the silver mat reserved for the King. Such was her voluptuous intoxication that she did not recoil before that profanation, and remained standing, smiling, while he ripped the light fabric that veiled her beauty.

She sprang forth, completely naked, as polished and delicate as a Tanagra statuette, her knees gilded, her loins creased and also gilded, like the lotuses of the temple.

The young man knelt before her, but Kali-Yana, incapable of mastering her jealous anger any longer, made a movement, as if to launch herself toward them, and a perfume-burner fell heavily on to the bronze pavement.

"We're doomed!" murmured the princess, enveloping the young man with her supple arms, in order to defend him.

"Go away!" he said. "If a talapoin has lain in wait for us, I'll be able to buy his silence."

"O dear Smile, don't abandon me!"

"Tomorrow," he said, "I'll come to see you at the same time . . . I swear it to you."

He took her back to the little door, pushed her to the shadow of a hall, and headed toward the pink granite monster that sheltered Kali-Yana.

Seeing that she was discovered, the amazon emerged from her hiding place.

"I won't denounce you," she said. "That would be death for Sayameda; but I demand that you renounce this adventure. The daughters of the King have made a vow of chastity. There's no shortage of courtesans in the city; why tempt the wrath of the gods?"

"Who are you?" he demanded, with a slight irony and a curious gaze that examined the proud loveliness of the young woman.

"An amazon."

"Ah!" he said, with increasing interest. "And why this fine zeal?"

"I'm a guardian of the Pagoda. I would have the right to kill you, if I had the courage . . ."

"Would it be permitted for me to defend myself?" he asked, laughing. And he took Kali-Yana's soft hands in his muscular ones.

She lowered her eyes; tears rolled down her cheeks.

"Yes, you're the stronger, and I'm unarmed."

"You can see that you wouldn't be able to fight me."

"The talapoins are asleep all around the temple. At the slightest cry they would come to lend me assistance."

176

"Oh," he said, disdainfully, "call them, then, and doubtless the Master will be grateful for your fine zeal. No one would dare to attack me, but they'd avenge themselves cruelly on the culpable princess. Is that what you desire?"

"No, I don't want Sayameda's death, I told you that; I'm only ordering you not to see her again . . ."

Maxime de Sainty shrugged his shoulders.

"So be it; I won't see her again. Only, little guardian of the temple, I demand a recompense."

"What?" asked Kali-Yana, her heart fluttering.

"Kiss me."

"The amazons, too, have made a vow of sagacity," she said, in a low voice.

"Bah! Just for once!"

Already he had imprisoned her lips in his, and slowly savored that exquisite caress, as happy as a hornet in the heart of a rose. He felt the young woman gradually abandon herself, quivering in his embrace, and he would undoubtedly have plucked the secret flower of her charming body if a sound of footsteps had not recalled her abruptly to reality.

"That's the phra on watch who has just made his round," she said. "Run away, and don't forget your promise."

Maxime de Sainty enveloped himself in a talapoin's robe, which had protected his nocturnal escapades before, and disappeared into the darkness.

VII
The Magical Garden

Her lips dry and her hands burning, Kali-Yana resumed her place beside Xali, whose placid young breasts were rising and falling rhythmically in sound slumber. The amazon murmured a few vague amorous words. She opened her arms, as if to embrace her friend, and a smile illuminated her features when the other's flesh brushed her own, unconsciously.

Kali-Yana did not sleep. Always present, the image of Maxime continued for her the obsession of other days, with, in addition, the memory of the kiss of flame that they had exchanged. The young woman shivered madly at that troubling vision; a spasm ran through her body, she raised herself up in a reckless desire for caresses, a voluptuous ecstasy of which she savored the unknown charm, and then fell back, exhausted by the futile effort, enervated by expectation and disappointment.

For a long time she had been watching out for the young foreigner, whom she had seen at parades and royal receptions, whom she had acclaimed in the secrecy of her heart, with the power of divination that only belongs to lovers and mothers.

He had the male beauty of distant countries that cradled her vague reverie; he was proud and strong, far superior, she thought, to the men of her race, and a far more elevated soul. She had loved him tenderly and without desire until the day when chance had enabled her to discover the amorous mystery of the Royal Pagoda.

Sayameda, the prettiest and most adulated of the princesses, received Maxime every evening, and if she had not yet fallen, it was because the young man, by virtue of a voluptuous refinement, was in no hurry to complete his triumph, ever avid for pure joys, stammers and delightful fears on the threshold of the vermilion temple. Doubtless he feared the disillusionment that follows possession, the ennui that results from satiety, and was lingering over meager caresses, like a virtuoso sure of himself and others. Sayameda swooned over savant cajoleries, perverse frictions, everything that constitutes the intoxication of amour and the poetry of the carnal act. A docile pupil, she had learned the science of the kiss and the secret of giving everything before the supreme fall. A little animal of sensuality, she repeated the phrase and the gesture with the innate artistry of great lovers, and Maxime teased her like an amorous cat with supple and velvety movements, lascivious frolics and harmonious purring.

178

She taught him, in addition, the Thai language, and he already knew enough to understand her chant of amour. Several times Kali-Yana had discovered the lovers in the temple, and tumultuous sensations had awakened in her. At the sight of their embraces and their kisses a sharp dolor traversed her breast; she was obliged to lean on a wall in order not to fall, so much did anger and desire divide her soul. In love without knowing it, and cruelly jealous too, she suffered incessantly, her mind dominated by an obsession and her entire being extended toward mysterious joys of which she had an adorable prescience.

Kali-Yana got up in the morning burning with fever, exhausted by fatigue as if after a long run under an ardent sun. It was necessary for her to mount guard on the terraces of the royal building and to hoist the scarlet flag adorned with the white elephant three times.

In the first two enclosures of the palace, slaves circulated, along with the masters of the royal stables directing the little princes in their exercises in equitation. The delightful children, crowned with jasmine and roses, without any other garment than a light loincloth of foliage, rode ponies caparisoned with silver, ornamented with pompoms and little bells. In order to excite the animals and the riders, khong-vongs and klues were played at full tilt, while the great lords, pinching their langoutis between thumb and forefinger, circled eccentrically, smiling at the young highnesses, risking entrechats in order to amuse them.

Governesses in severe panungs of black muslin striped with silver circulated among the groups, a hard rod between the fingers, with which to punish the unruly slaves whose troop accumulated in the background.

In the third enclosure, closed to the profane, there was an admirable garden containing in miniature everything that the world offers of the gracious, the grandiose or the savage. Artificial mountains, woods and rivers could be seen there, along with a lake with islets and rocks; frail boats and toy ships, a bazaar full of precious fabrics, coffers, balms and precious stones; pagodas, pavilions, belvederes, statues of divinities and maleficent powers, monsters of jade and porcelain crouched in every bush, green bronze reptiles showing glaucous eyes of peridots and emeralds, and forked tongues with ruby papilli.

It was there that the little princesses, in order to console them for their sequestration, took baths of milky water perfumed with Takeoka flowers and Hovenia balms from Japan. Slaves caressed their fragile breasts, and all the delicate parts of their bodies, with odiferous leaves rolled into a ball, depilated them, massaged them, and poured composites of lemon, cloves and neroli over their hair in order to render it supple and shiny.

The princesses, condemned to eternal virginity, had nostalgic poses and plaintive expressions that contrasted with their voluptuous lips and the somber fire of their eyes. Only the very small amused themselves frankly, chasing one another through the thickets, chirping like warblers, catching enameled beetles and horned butterflies, flying flowers of crimson and gold.

From the height of the terraces, Kali-Yana watched the frolics of the royal daughters, and her heart was constricted by jealous hatred.

VIII
A Thai Guignol

The recluses, sitting on their heels, gambled at dice with their money of meager shells and silver pellets, prestigious pills for the use of children large and small. For the seeresses and chiromancers there were Chinese cards ornamented with chimeras, dragons and fateful kites whose tails lit up like Roman candles, presages of joy or ill-fortune.

Cockfights were reserved for the pleasure of males, but the princesses were passionate about the mortal combats of ant-lions, yellow crickets and grasshoppers. Red and blue fish with human faces battled in jars, and the victor never failed to eat the eyes of the vanquished first, which was the definitive sign of triumph.

180

After the bath, the massage, the cricket-fights and the treats of almond and sesame paste, the princesses savored the emotions of the Siamese guignol. On a stage draped with sparkling fabrics, actors and actresses tattooed in bright colors, coiffed in enormous pointed bonnets, with donkeys' ears and crimson half-masks, moved around furiously. There were almost always scenes of murder and carnage, fabulous stories, and then simulacra of funerals, the bodies of the elect being taken away by the dava-dung angels under the guidance of their king Phra-In.[1]

All voluptuous ideas and lascivious mimes, which might have troubled the innocent souls of the little princesses, were retrenched from those spectacles. Terrifying images of the suffering and tortures of the Thai hell were, by contrast, abundant there, for the sacred books said: *Those who have committed in life, by the body or the spirit, any condemnable action will go after their death into the region of monsters and phantoms, or human larvae.*

There are eight great Thai hells, surrounded by sixteen other hells that are enclosed themselves within forty primary hells. The eight great hells are prisons of red-hot metal in which the damned writhe in a state of eternal roasting. Nothing is heard there except blasphemies, supplications and screams, in a frenetic *danse macabre*. To either side of those hells there is a door guarded by the Phaja-jom, the kings of fire.

But the sanxip, or wind of resurrection, reanimates the dead for more frightful punishments. Those who have killed animals, thieves, rapists and kings who undertake unjust wars will be submitted to that proof. Demons armed with pincers, crampons and hatchets will tear away shreds of flesh, dissect them and scrape them all the way to the bone. Then the sanxip, blowing over them, will resuscitate them for further tortures and a new

---

1 An account of the Davadung angels and their king Phra-In (Indra) is included in *Description du royaume Thai ou Siam* (1854) by Jean-Baptiste Palle-goix, where descriptions of the Buddhist hells, the Phaja-jom and the sanxip can also be found.

death, until the reincarnation in the region of monsters, leprous, deformed or demented men. One day in that hell is equivalent to a hundred thousand terrestrial years.

At these hallucinatory images, the little princesses sensed their reason tottering, and the dread of chastisements preserves them from the temptations of amour.

Other, more terrifying visions passed over the boards of the little theater: the damned, their faces covered with a swollen and purulent mask, played with their eyes and their tongues, which they threw, howling, and a red dew streamed from their trepanned, eroded skulls.

The most impressive spectacles were kept for the evening; a green glow bathed the torture-victims in the midst of surrounding darkness. Reptiles, stags and gigantic, emaciated, starving dogs passed through a décor of dream. Human monsters hung from trees by their fingernails, like bats. Their membranous wings were bleeding at the shoulders, partly torn away, devoured by other hairy beasts, crawling like cobras or as agile as tarantulas.

Finally, came the kruts or garudas, which are enormous birds with the body of a man and the beak of an eagle. They nourish themselves on the hearts and livers of the tortured in the final hells.

"Bravo!" cried the spectators.

The presentations lasted until the appearance of the fireflies, whose prestigious swarm illuminated the atmosphere. The branches of rose-apple trees with pink flowers and maprangs with golden plums parted the insects of flame, crossing their pyrotechnical fantasia in all directions, sowing the garden with a galactic dust.

The little princesses, who had only followed the sacred pantomimes with an indifferent gaze, preferred running through the shady pathways, and then coming together again, their arms full of clusters of mali, champa with the odor of tuberoses, and kadanga with the odor of roses. They fainted a little under the warm gusts of perfume, and then took their clothes off in order to dress themselves in flowers, and nothing was as pretty as the contrast between their brown skin and the white corollas.

The governesses, crouching here, there and everywhere, were chewing betel leaves, reddened by turmeric and areca nuts. Already intoxicated, they closed their eyes and leaned their wrinkled faces over their shoulder, droll beneath the tufts of fluffed-up hair that surmounted their heads.

At the end of the day, Sayameda, covered in mali flowers, with a peppery fragrance of spices and amour, went away in search of other flowers, to pick pale lotuses with golden pistils on the edge of the sacred pool: the male flower that allows the dust to float round it, fecundating for the voluptuous stamens that desire extends into the darkness. The little princess, kneeling in the grass, picked one of the immense corollas and, with one of her hairpins, engraved a few words in the velvet pulp of a petal; then she stood up again and looked toward the wall of the enclosure. The extremely high porcelain barrier did not permit any indiscretion from outside, but an ear stuck against the sonorous wall could hear the sounds of the garden.

Sayameda modulated the plaint of a wounded turtle-dove softly, and the guttural cry of a bird of prey replied to her immediately.

Kali-Yani, who had missed none of those movements from the height of the terrace, then saw the lotus that she had plucked abandoned to the current of a stream that passed under the wall. Borne by the rapid current, the immense flower oscillated from one edge to the other, and then sped with a regular movement, scarcely interrupted by the passage of a swimming spider or the hooked tip of a reed.

"Quickly, Xali," the amazon cried, "Leave the palace, run behind the chakrarasi wall and bring me back that nymphea that is following the current of the stream down there."

Xali, who was somnolent, rubbed her eyes in astonishment.

"What do you want with that flower, Kali-Yana?"

"I'll explain it to you later. Go! Be diligent, and if a stranger blocks your path, tell him that you're Sayameda's confidante."

"All right, dear Smile, I'll obey you."

And the young woman, as light as a gazelle, went down the brilliant steps of the terrace, ran behind the enclosing wall and arrived at the watercourse at the precise moment when Maxime picked up the lotus, which emerged from a little subterranean bridge. As she stopped before the stranger he asked, anxiously: "What do you want?"

"I've been sent by the princess . . ."

He did not let her finish. "You've come in search of the response, no doubt?"

"Yes," Xali murmured, mechanically.

"Well, go tell our mistress that whatever happens, I'll be exact at the rendezvous this evening."

"Don't you want to give me the flower?"

"It's more precious to me than my life; I want to respire its troubling perfume for a long time yet. Go, little messenger, and keep our amorous secret."

IX
The Amazons

"The stranger didn't want to give me the lotus, Kali-Yana. I could see that there was something written on the leaves, but I couldn't read it . . ."

"Oh!" said the amazon. "He's forgotten his oath already!"

"What oath? He only said that he'd be exact at the rendezvous."

"That man is a traitor who has designs on the life of the King."

"Really? Well, tonight we'll mount good guard, Kali-Yana. Don't you want to warn our companions?"

"Yes, when the moment comes."

But Xali reflected. "We're no longer at war with the distant countries. Why would that pharang have anything against our Master Phaja-Tak?"

"Oh," said Yana, who feared letting Xali into the secret of her amour, "you know very well that the nations are anxious about our victories and are trying to reduce Phaja to impotence. Our valorous King has already retaken Ligor, Phitanulok and Xieng-Mai, in spite of the Birmans, whom he has reduced to slavery."

"That's true," murmured the amazon, proudly.

"He has taken the Lao realm of Vieng Chan and has brought back, marvel of marvels, the prodigious gold idol larger than nature with the emerald head."

"That's a unique treasure."

"Phaja-Tak, I tell you, has made many people envious, and we ought to mistrust all these strangers who come from foggy lands to spy on us, and perhaps betray us . . ."

"The pharang is tall and handsome. Not one of our soldiers can be compared to him."

Kali-Yana shivered delightfully. "His race is proud. We'll try to capture him without doing him any harm."

"You think that he'll enter the palace?"

"Yes, tonight, and we'll wait for him at the door of the Royal Pagoda."

"Why not warn the King?"

"Our master has been suffering for some time, and it's necessary not to alarm him."

"He's suffering and becoming cruel. The people are murmuring; don't you think, Kali-Yana, that the mob is menacing us and that it will soon be necessary to fight in the city to suppress the mutiny?"

The young woman shrugged her shoulders indifferently.

"We'll fight, Xali, if the security of the state requires it. Anyway, this continuous inaction weighs upon me. I'd doubtless find in battle the satisfaction of the passions that are torturing me . . ."

"Oh, little friend, we could be happy without shedding the blood of the humble, without being unjust and barbaric. It isn't the love of battles that's tormenting you, it's another very tender amour that you misunderstand. We have to remain virgins, it's true, but there are compensations for that severe law. Isn't the tenderness of a woman a thousand times better than that of a man? You desire to give yourself a master, poor darling. Don't you know that the more you love him, the more he'll despise you? A man only has vulgar instincts. He is only susceptible to desire, and his beautiful flame of amour is extinguished as soon as it's satisfied, like the joyful fires that children light with old papers. A man loves women, but he's incapable of loving one woman. He follows his destiny of a primordial male, without worrying about his divine essence, and his pride only desires the variety of the pleasure. He's superficial and banal, and his stupidity equals his conceit. Oh, how much better and closer to the divine ideal our tenderness is!"

"Undoubtedly," said Kali-Yana, "but that isn't the desire of nature."

"It's necessary for us to purify the shameful mud! Don't you want, dear Caress, to raise yourself above humanity and know the delights of an amour without failings?"

Kali-Yana thought about the handsome foreigner whose embrace was powerful and sweet, whose mouth knew such profound kisses! At that voluptuous evocation, a more impetuous blood beat in her arteries, and it seemed to her that a mysterious hand was gripping her heart.

The golden flies were still flying above the terrace, to which the amazons had hoisted large palm branches, as they did every evening, in order to drive away the demons of the Kala-Sut, the second hell, which torment the sleep of kings.

A network of the flames of flying insects shivered over the sky, punctuated here and there by the cabochon of a star. The mesh overlapped and became entangled, and suddenly, the magical décor was extinguished, as if by the passage of a wind of death.

186

When the luminous flies stopped shining three times in succession, it was because a maleficent influence was hovering over the palace, and all those who observed the phenomenon prostrated themselves and struck the ground with their foreheads.

"The golden wings are favorable to us," remarked Xali, on seeing a fiery image form around the white elephant flag.

"Yes, we'll succeed in our enterprise."

"The moment's approaching. Let's alert our companions."

"Oh, one lone man! Three of us can subdue him. Go and fetch Galanick."

X
The Danger of Caresses

Galanick, who was fast asleep on her narrow couchette, got up, rapidly donned her red embroidered tunic, and followed the little amazons into the Royal Pagoda.

As on the previous evening, the talapoins were renewing the provision of coconut oil in the lachrymatories and putting fresh herbs into the perfume-burners. Thick garlands of champa and kadanga adorned the knees of the great golden Buddha and climbed loosely around the seven-tier parasol, almost all the way to the mosaics of the vault. On the ground there was a heap of cut flowers, a true lovers' bed, as if everything had been foreseen for the embrace of the pharang and the little princess.

Frowning, her lips trembling, Kali-Yana trampled the amorous petals furiously, reddening her feet with the blood of roses.

"The Buddha will avenge himself!" murmured Xali, terrified. "No one has the right to touch the presents of Cakyamouni. You've walked over the King's pavement and you've mutilated the sacred corollas!"

"Yes, and let the punishment attain me, if that is the will of the gods."

"What are you daring to say?"

"I'm saying that the odor of those flowers importunes me, and that it's an irony to decorate a temple that sin is about to soil."

"I don't understand, dear Smile."

"You don't need to understand. Stay here, and mount good guard. I'm going to cast an eye over the terraces."

"At the slightest danger, call me."

"Agreed."

But Xali, as if warned by a jealous presentiment, was unable to let go of her companion. Her arms around her waist, she hugged her passionately and sought her lips.

"Let me go," said Kali-Yana, impatiently, and, disengaging herself from the importunate caress, she went out of the pagoda.

The faience monsters with glaucous eyes watched her pass along the terraces; a domesticated panther rubbed itself against her legs, but she disdained to stroke it, as she did habitually.

The day before, the Frenchman had left via the gardens; perhaps he would follow the same route to enter the palace. Just in case, she traversed the enclosure reserved for the games of the princes and went into the sector reserved for the daughters of the King.

The rose-apple trees were spreading heavier odors, the Chinese figs with golden fruit were allowing their flavorsome fruits to fall into the deserted pathways. At every step Kali-Yana crushed pink takhob plums and trod on dwarf tufts of mali, the musky aroma of which dominated all the other perfumes.

The high porcelain walls presented a serious obstacle to a thief of amour, but there was the little subterranean bridge through which the overflow of the lakes poured out. The water was low, and by crawling, a thin man might try that route in the present season without any other risk than a slightly disagreeable bath.

The young woman wandered nonchalantly alongside the florid waters, picking rosy nenuphar, which Sayameda liked to use for her amorous correspondence. Time was passing, however, and the gallant did not show himself. Perhaps he was waiting for a new signal, which the little princess, detained in the pagoda, could not give him.

With the tip of a stylet, Kali-Yana traced a few words on the petals of a large flower, which she abandoned to the current, and waited . . .

Her heart was beating forcefully; a nervous contraction tightened her throat. She had never experienced a similar emotion.

The babble of the stream seemed to her to be drawing faint laughter through the reeds; horned bats with gaudy wings, like gigantic hairy moths, collided with the faience walls, as if trying to seize their image in a mirror.

The panther returned, familiarly, in a desire for a caress, and rubbed her phosphorescent back against the young woman. Her metallic eyes were fiery, and, yawning nervously, she stretched herself, rolled over, and got up again, alternately cajoling and anxious

"Leave me alone, Mira-Mira. I'm not in a mood for tenderness."

But the beast came back insistently, a jealous gleam in her yellow eyes.

"Oh, yes, you'd like wasps' nests? I have nothing to give you this evening. Catch nocturnal birds, if you like. They nourished themselves on the flesh of a slave yesterday, and ought to be delicate . . ."

There was a rustle in the grass and the blond head of Maxime de Sainty appeared. Mita-Mira bounded, furiously, but the young woman calmed her with a word . . . and then, tragically, put her hand on the young man's shoulder.

"You're my prisoner," she said.

He contemplated her, laughing.

"Your prisoner, child? And what do you want to do with me?"

"Listen: you're doubly culpable, for you've introduced yourself treacherously into this enclosure forbidden to the profane, and you've broken your word."

"That's true—I won't try to disculpate myself. But amorous adventures are so rare in your wretched country."

"There's no shortage of courtesans."

"Fie! Greedy Chinawomen or graceless Cambodians. Only the King's daughters are lovable."

"The King's daughters!" sighed Kali-Yana, dolorously.

"You too—you're charming in spite of your warrior accoutrement. Didn't I tell you so last night?"

"You told me so, and you were wrong to do it . . . for I think about you incessantly . . ."

Before that candid confession, Maxime shuddered with pleasure.

"Be mine, then, since you love me. Isn't thinking about a man loving him?"

Kali-Yana shook her head sadly.

"The princesses and the amazons don't have the right to give themselves. I beg you not to trouble our repose any further. You'll find other women in the city who will be glad of your caresses. By searching a little you'll find others as seductive as us, who will cherish you without danger. You can even buy a little wife for a few bahts, and you'd thus have a devoted companion who would make you a pleasant home, prepare flower preserves for you and look after your garments. It must be so pleasant to encounter the smile of a beloved mouth at every return to one's dwelling, and when one has a creature of one's own, the soul is not alone . . ."

With some bitterness, the young woman thought that such happiness would never be accorded to her; however, she continued, hoping to convince the foreigner.

"Go away, I won't betray you. My companions are watching in the pagoda; they won't ever know that you've come if you consent to follow my advice. I've already forgiven you once . . . I won't forgive you again . . ."

"I don't want your forgiveness . . . danger amuses me, it's the only thing that gives some pleasure to the monotony of my sojourn here. Look, let me pass, Sayameda's waiting for me . . . and I'll recompense you . . ."

A cry of rage sprang from the young woman's lips. "Money! Money! You dare to propose to pay me for my silence!"

He sensed that he had offended her cruelly, and, in order to console her, he drew her toward him and placed his lips on her moist eyelids.

Kali-Yana was as beautiful as the little princess and Maxime, at that moment, desired her madly, forgetful of past oaths.

"Darling," he said, "I'd like nothing better than to obey you, but it's necessary to facilitate the task . . ."

Again his lips imprisoned those of the young woman, who tottered under his embrace. He was about to triumph over her last resistance when Mira-Mira uttered a dull growl and, as if by magic, the luminous flies lit up again, imprisoning the stars in a golden mesh.

"We can be seen from the terraces—go away!" moaned Kali-Yana. But he drew her into a clump of flowering hibiscus, which closed upon them, and, kneeling before her, he implored her mercy in such a seductive voice that she forgot even the memory of her resentment.

Under the violently perfumed corollas that masked the sky, she felt her head growing heavy. Squat trees reigned round them, covered with creepers and hectic vegetation, the smallest fissure in the bark giving shelter to seeds that sprouted there, bursting forth in light rockets, plumes, smoke and dusts of flowers of infinite delicacy. Four or five hundred stems, covered in multicolored leaflets overlapped one another, incessantly shedding petals scented with almond and vanilla, the persistent wetness of which exasperated the nerves. Mira-Mira watched them with metallic and mysterious eyes without budging, lying curled up in the flowers, also slightly intoxicated by perfumes and amour.

"Oh," said Kali-Yana, "if you love the royal daughter, you must find me very ugly and disgraceful."

He did not reply, sniffing with delight the voluptuous effluvia of her young body, brushing the pure cups of her breasts with his avid lips.

"The little princess is accomplished," the amazon went on, bitterly. "The duennas have rendered her limbs supple and impregnated her skin with vehement balms. She has nacreous hands and opaline fingernails that have never been bruised by handling weapons. She sings the sacred airs of the Maha-xat, accompanying herself on the takhe and the kayab. She dances in front of the idols at the command of the talapoins, and her only work is nourishing bees on jasmine and roses. Have you seen her, with her sisters, throwing stones into the water in order to make ripples, and chasing dragonflies? Nothing is as pretty as her gauze scarf under the somber foliage, and the King is prouder of her than the great idol of the Green Pagoda and all the Hindu gods that warm their two thousand years in the sunlight of his gardens!"

"Shut up," said Maxime. "No other woman exists any longer for me. You are the Adored, the Unique . . . give me your lips!"

His mouth has taken Kali-Yana's mouth. At close range he sees the young woman's pupils, which dilate, vacillate momentarily, and are then veiled by almost dolorous ecstasy, while her eyebrows, ebony darts, draw closer together in lascivious effort. Slyly, expertly, he darts the supple and ingenious sensuality that animates all his desire and his passionate fantasy . . .

He is about to make her his when Xali's voice rises, tearfully.

"Kali-Yana! Where are you? Kali-Yana!"

With a bound, the young woman is on her feet. "Someone's calling me. Let me go . . ."

But he hangs on to her.

"Tomorrow, if you wish? Tomorrow, at the same time?"

And devoid of strength, she consents. "Yes, tomorrow, but I'll get out of the palace and I'll come to join you . . ."

"Tomorrow . . ."

XI
The Lie of Lust

Palpitating, the amazon has quit the hibiscus bush, her hair full of pink petals.

"Here I am," she says to Xali, who is searching for her anxiously.

"And the foreigner?"

"I haven't seen anyone?"

"No one?"

"No, I swear to you."

"What were you doing so far away from us?"

"Nothing; I fell asleep."

"Is that possible? You, who put so much ardor into your pursuit? Why, then, have you imposed that sentry duty in the pagoda on us?"

Without replying to her friend's embarrassing question, Kali-Yana, her soul suddenly traversed by a surge of jealousy, demanded in her turn:

"Has Princess Sayameda not come to adore the golden Buddha?"

"Certainly," said Xali, "and our presence surprised her greatly. I can assure you that she seemed very annoyed."

A smile crossed Kali-Yana's burning lips at the idea of her rival's disappointment. She drew Xali away irresistibly, in order to permit the foreigner to escape, and it was with a voluptuous frisson that she nestled into her narrow couchette, closed her eyes and pursued her beautiful dream of amour . . .

※

"Xali, I'm happy this morning!"

Aurified by light, the immense hall of the amazons filled with the buzz of a beehive at the first caress of the dawn.

The young women were polishing their weapons, and brushing their scarlet tunics with fine embroidery carefully. Soon, the King, accompanied by the high dignitaries, would traverse the courtyard of the palace, and his amazons would form a hedge for his passage.

Once a week, His Majesty visited the white elephant in order to present his respects to it, for, according to Thai belief, the souls of princes and kings pass into the bodies of immaculate pachyderms, and those animals are venerated as much as, or perhaps more than, images of Cakyamouni.

In the wars of Pegu, a white elephant cost the lives of more than six hundred thousand men. The one that Phaja-Tak had come to visit was huge, bad-tempered and more covered in jewels than Queen Mahirat, the current favorite. Four mandarins clad in yellow langoutis, agitated talapats of ostrich flabella in order to chase away the flies, and a seven-tier parasol sheltered its august head. The water it drank was at least six months old, and it was offered in golden vases, mingled with lan-tam and phut flowers.

"I'm happy," Kali-Yana repeated, twirling a long dagger with a jade hilt around her head.

Unconsciously tormented, Xali yielded to the bitter pleasure of spoiling that joy slightly.

"Remember the prediction of the talapoin of the dead: you will suffer and you will cause suffering; you will scorn true love for temporary follies. There are tears and blood in your destiny. Your smile frightens me."

Kali-Yana shrugged her shoulders, and, with a very particular care, added luster to her short hair, enlarged her eyes by means of a mixture of antimony, gum, musk and ebony, and touched her lips and nostrils with a little brush steeped in carmine.

"What are you doing?" asked Xali. "You're not a harem doll, to make yourself up in that fashion!"

"Is it forbidden for the King's guardians to care for their beauty?"

194

"Your beauty can surpass those vile retouches. Who do you want to seduce, then?"

"You, little Xali."

And the liar, laughing, rubbed her cheek against that of her little friend, put her arm around her waist and, in spite of her resistance, twirled madly around the room, to the rattle of the weapons beating her flanks. But silence fell. Two superior rada, gaudily decorated with gold, had come to inspect the company of amazons.

XII
The White Elephant

Between the double hedge of prostrate mandarins, followed by the foremost dignitaries of his realm, Phaja-Tak traverses the court of honor and goes to visit the living god whom all his people worship in a similar fashion to Cakyamouni

His Majesty is preceded by twenty little princes, his children, whose grave and meditative expressions contrast with their delicately candid features. Their heads are shaven, with the exception of the summit, which is crowned by a bouffant lock, florid with mali and traversed by a diamond pin. Their upper bodies do not seem to buckle under the weight of necklaces, amulets, fetishes and luk-sakhots of every color.

One is carrying a carob box in which there is betel and areca nuts, another the King's great dagger, this one an emerald scepter and that one a spittoon enriched with amethysts.

Around the elephant-king are the stalls of slave elephants. Each one has a hangar ten meters square, to which it is attached by the foot. Some are armed for war, ready to depart at the slightest alert. Their immense tusks are circled with gold, a crocodile carapace is displayed on the occiput in order to protect it from enemy thrusts, and an entire panoply of lances, pikes, javelins and maces shines at their sides. There are more than eight hundred elephants in the palace, which accompany the King on his voyages. When Phaja-Tak recaptured Ligor, Phitanulok and Xieng-Mai, six thousand elephants fought in the two camps, and the generalissimo put the Birmans to flight by surprising them at night with four hundred elephants to whose tails flaming torches had been attached. It was a fine debacle, the crazed pachyderms running in all directions, knocking things over, falling down and agonizing in the midst of a gigantic firework display.

As he passed through the courtyards, the King asked the young cornacs whether any new captures had been made in the depths of the virgin forests. Domesticated males had been taken, a week before, to impenetrable jungles where passionate females were wandering in pursuit of a mate, and they had come back with a troop of amorous cows. Each female, subjugated, had similarly brought back a good number of affectionate and impetuous cavaliers, whose eyes were still glittering with resentment at deceptive amours.

Phaja-Tak examined the wild beasts, solidly attached, which a strict diet was beginning to discipline. He even deigned to present them with a few armfuls of tender grass, which were greatly welcome.

A young white elephant captured in Laos was awaiting the death of the old one in order to succeed him. A caravan had brought him back recently in great pomp, and he was being educated slowly, in the midst of perfumes, flowers and the prayers of talapoins.

In their superstition, the Siamese imagine that the souls of kings and princes pass into the bodies of white animals; there were also large monkeys with long, fine, snowy hair in the depths of sumptuous niches, which priestesses crowned with roses and intoxicated with betel.

However, Phaja-Tak arrived in front of the palace of the idol venerated by all. The two battens of a gigantic door incrusted with ivory and nacre opened under the concentric colonnades of a kind of pagoda, garnished with a hundred silver, bronze and porphyry statuettes. It was there that the white elephant, the ancestor adorned with sparkling fabrics indurated with precious stones, received the homages of the faithful, his foot retained by golden chains. Laotian panoplies were fixed to the walls, and at intervals, a seven-tiered parasol was supported there like a gigantic lotus.

Before the pachyderm with the wrinkled eyelids, in the weary attitude of a valetudinarian old bonze, the King put both hands to his forehead in a sign of veneration, and the mandarins, lying face down, kissed the ground with humility, while trumpets, drums and gongs resounded three times. The amazons formed a hedge within range of the idol, which was now grazing aromatic herbs, fruits and sacred flowers.

Phaja-Tak swung a perfume-burner before the august trunk and caressed it gently, while reciting the list of the thirty-two parts of the human body and deploring the instability of terrestrial things. Then he described the adorable qualities of the Buddha, whose divine essence penetrated the substance of white elephants.

The talapoins resumed the incantation to the Supreme Master, on a shrill note that was punctuated by the strokes of the gong and accompanied by the cooing of little bamboo flutes.

Buddhists do not recognize and first creative cause, but suppose that everything is created by a sort of inexplicable magic. They then attribute to the special virtues of animals the reconstitution of worlds the skies and all gods in general. By "animals" one ought to understand all creatures endowed with life. Beauty, nobility, honors, wealth and health originate from virtues that each individual has possessed in his anterior lives; in the same way, deformity, poverty, grief and suffering flow from the demerits of each individual in times past.

When someone dies, the good and the evil are immediately presented to him. If the good triumphs, the defunct individual is reincarnated in a better condition or, if he has traveled through all the terrestrial cycles, rises to some order of the heavens. But if the evil actions prevail, he is reborn in a despicable condition in the region of monsters, madmen or some other degree of the hells. The enjoyment of happiness uses up merit, in the same way that demerit is effaced by suffering and calamity. These numerable transmigrations are called vien-kot vien-tai, or continual successions of births and deaths.[1]

Except for Buddha and the saints of the first order, everyone forgets their past lives, the memory of which is effaced by the tempest that blows after death. Souls must necessarily undergo transmigrations until, having gradually risen through the eight degrees of sanctity, they are delivered from all corruption. Having then traversed the stormy sea of terrestrial passions, they land on the blessed shore, the shore of eternal bliss that is called Muang-Keo-amatha-maha-neruphan, the immortal and precious realm of the great extinction, or annihilation.

XIII
The People Murmur

Phaja-Tak had rendered his customary homages to the White Elephant. Then he bowed to the enormous beast, which that veneration scarcely troubled, and the mandarins prostrated themselves and kissed the ground three times, as they had done at the beginning of the ceremony.

Taking the emerald scepter from the hands of one of his sons, the King then went on to one of the highest terraces in order to show himself to his people and collect, in his turn, the homages that were due to him.

The square in front of the palace was full of a multicolored, agitated, noisy crowd, perhaps even more hostile than it had been on the day of Nai-Rafutt's funeral.

Orators had succeeded one another, uttering furious proposals. Paid by the rich and the Chinese, whom Phaja-Tak had of-

---

1 This passage is paraphrased from Pallegoix's 1854 volume.

fended particularly, they were trying to whip up a spirit of revolt in the people. Heads emptied by famine were seeing red; dreams of fire and blood were whirling in brains.

The silky ribbon of the Me-Nam circled that howling multitude with a broad blue line. Royal pirogues were bobbing on the tranquil river, carved from the single trunk of a giant tree. The poop and the prow, delicately gilded, rose in gracious curves, displaying ornaments of sculpted wood: dragons and chimeras, dolphins and sirens of original workmanship. In the center, the awning fringed with precious stones awaited His Majesty's pleasure. But the King, his eyes bleak and his lip disdainful, raised the glaucous flash of his emerald scepter over his people in vain.

In the bright sunlight there was a fury of brown faces with somber eyes and thick mouths open in order to insult; an entire rut of hungry men and women eager for just reprisals, for there were many country folk there. The villages had been abandoned long ago, the houses and enclosures falling into ruins, and grass covering once-fecund land everywhere. The mandarins, exceeding the master's orders, held the cultivators in a slavery and oppression so extreme that they were attempting, like the others, to shake off their yoke. Deprived of their instruments of fishing and agriculture, with no money, with no food, their poverty was even more frightful than that of the city-dwellers, and many had already succumbed.

The amazons, however, raised the scarlet flag on the terraces, and crossed over the pole the two palm branches, the symbol of peace.

Kali-Yana was searching in the pressed ranks of the crowd for a beloved presence. Her ardent gaze went from one to another, and standing upright, almost next to the King, she held herself almost in evidence, in spite of the etiquette that prescribed a humbler attitude for her.

Phaja-Tak was immobilized in a kind of stupor. It was generally believed that the phi and the astrologers had cast a spell on him, so different did he seem from what he had been at the beginning of his reign.

Once, acclaimed by a people in delirium, considered everywhere as the liberator of the country, he had defeated the Birmans who, during the preceding reigns, had brought pillage and conflagration into Siam, burning villages, robbing houses and decapitating the inhabitants in the public square. For two months, the Me-Nam had ferried cadavers and its putrefied waves poisoned those who had not perished under the axes of the executioners. The red work lasted for a long time, and then, Ajuthia no longer being anything but a smoking ruin, all the Thai territory fell into anarchy, at the mercy of the victors and the vanquished, who took pleasure in completing the drama of death. The forests and the deserts, even the most inaccessible, had ceased to be a shelter for the fugitives and had been changed into lairs of bandits who cut one another's throats in order to steal their booty.

Siam was therefore close to its end when Pin-Tak, Chinese in origin, the governor of Tak, his native city, had taken, on his own initiative, the title of Phaja. Courageous, full of determination and audacity, he had gathered ten thousand men in Chanthaboun in order to treat with the leaders of Cambodia and Annam. Sometimes using cunning and sometimes force, he had taken possession of the northern districts, after having killed Phaja-Nackong, the Birman governor. Finally, installed in Bangkok, he had established his capital there and built a palace on the occidental bank of the river.

He had always emerged victorious from his battles with the Birmans, and the people, calling him their savior, had offered him the crown.

Continuing his regenerative work, he repopulated the land in its southern part and in the oriental province bathed by the gulf. He reconquered the region of Korat, and at the end of three years the powerful enemies recognized him as the absolute master of Siam. Not satisfied with that result, the following year he led an expedition against the Malay peninsula with the intention of taking possession of Ligor. Triumphant, as always, he had captured

200

for his harem the daughter of the governor, named Ajutana, who charmed him with her great beauty.

Thus had the monarch shown himself, whom destiny abruptly inflicted with a thousand evils. Somber, melancholy, hateful, cruel and perverse, no one could any longer recognize in him the liberator of old.

Still immobile in his crimson robe, his forehead inclined beneath the turriculated miter that coiffed him, Phaja-Tak now presented to his people a face of the earthen grey of lava, bony cheekbones projecting beneath hollow orbits, and lips drawn back by cruelty and passion.

Insensible to insults, he gazed into the distance, lost in sinister thoughts, perhaps weary of the futility of all power and the unrealizable desires to which it gave birth. Perhaps his vitreous pupils were seeing once again the agony of children that he had tortured and mutilated in his curiosity for rare sensualities and morbid sensations. No one knew what happened in the secrecy of his harem, but muffled plaints sometimes pierced the walls, and the little corpses that were steeped in essence and incinerated in balms all had the dolorous faces of martyrs.

That, above all, made the crowd indignant, and the families in mourning for the dead made cries of revolt heard on the terraces.

In his gaze, as ominous as a low sky, Phaja-Tak allowed nothing to be divined of his secret sentiments. One only sensed in him the abolition of all enthusiasm, all contentment and all pain, the exhaustion of thought itself, which, too long directed inwards, no longer had any impetus, and remained as inert as the monarch's body.

Finally, he seemed to wake up. A large bouquet of lan-tam, thrown by a sure hand, had slapped him in the midst of the dignitaries, who were talking about decapitating the guilty party. But Phaja-Tak, shrugging his shoulders, adjusted the golden pleats of his mantle and slowly quit the terrace.

XIV
Kali-Yana's Toilette

"Xali, make up my brown beauty as if I were a lover rather than a warrior."

Kali-Yana stretches herself nonchalantly before her couchette, while Xali mixes essences of different colors, passes a brush steeped in carmine over her companion's breasts and fingernails, and softens her skin with sesame balm and coriander oil.

"Am I not as pretty as Sayameda, the king's daughter?"

"Prettier, certainly, but why these complicated cares? Do amazons doll themselves up like courtesans?"

The young woman smiles without replying, fixes a tuft of mali with a peppery scent in her short hair, and, naked beneath the takruts and gold luk-sakhots that were given to her to protect her from evil spirits, she trembles like a little dancer of the royal pagodas.

Sonorous balls tinkle on her breast, dotting pale flashes in the pale bronze of her flesh. She is exquisite, with her slim hips, the harmonious curve of her breasts and the entire serpentine line of her inviolate body.

The other amazons, without paying any heed to her, are talking anxiously about recent events, the madness of the King, mystical and perverse by turns, his severe penitences after the orgies of the harem, and the bizarre tortures imposed on the companions of Nai-Rafutt, the latest victim, whose ashes now repose at the feet of the great golden Buddha

"Personally," said Kromalat, "I heard a voice imploring and sobbing while I was on sentry duty at the door of the harem."

"Without making any noise," said Ramesuen, "I went into the apartment of Kanha, who, as you know, has succeeded Nai-Rafutt; she was dragging herself at the King's knees and her panung, ripped away, was full of blood. I also saw that she had a wound between the breasts and red foam was coming out of her mouth."

"He'll kill her as he killed the other," sighed Mi, pouring herself a cup of syrup of meng-lak—basil seeds.

"Fortunately, we have nothing to fear; the amazons are sacred."

"Our chastity is devoid of charm, alas. Better the cruelty of a demanding master than the monotony of a life without amour!"

"Speak for yourself," said Kromalat. "I don't wish for anything but the pleasure of war!"

"You'll get your wish before long, then," said Galanick, laughing. "The revolution is rumbling. Phaja-Tak has exhausted the patience of his people."

"Oh, the people aren't very terrible," murmured Mi, yawning. "Only the mandarins and the rich are to be feared; they're only waiting for an opportunity to seize power . . ."

Kromalat clapped her hands. "We're going to fight to save our King!" she said. "There'll be blood elsewhere than in the harem."

The rada now played dice, inundating the carpet with a rain of silver pellets and small shells. It was no longer a question of revolt and the monarch, nor of combat; all the faculties of the little warriors were absorbed in the contemplation of ivory cubes, which impatient hands caused to roll by turns.

Even the evening meal did not disturb the gamblers, who, crouched on the cushions, passed one another the jade and amber trays containing the makkau. There was a soup of freshwater mussels and coconut milk, stews of gray turtles with soft carapaces that were eaten whole, mengdama in turmeric, mashed leeches, and the inevitable kapi, or marinated crayfish spawn, which is the repast of every good Siamese. Wasps' nests and Chinese figs, Lychees and Lamu-Sida plums disappeared with no more ceremony, and the young women, no longer being hungry, took the pink chalk from saurit vases that one chews while smoking. They rolled up dried betel leaves in the form of cigars, cut an areca nut into four, and sucked the fragments with the betel.

Kali-Yana, steeped in perfumes that were evaporating from her flesh in heavy gusts, continued to ornament herself with gems and flowers, trying on fabrics, necklaces and girdles of precious cabochons. Standing thus in her veils patterned with flames, aureoled with effluvia, she abandoned herself to the caresses of Xali, who was rejoicing, believing her to be entirely hers.

"It's for me, then," interrogated the rada, "that you want to be so pretty?"

"It's for you."

"You'll permit me to love you, then?"

"Yes, Xali, and we're going to drink this lotus wine, speckled with gold, in order to be one another's more completely . . ."

"Let's drink, Kali-Yana, in order that our intoxication might be confounded, and cradle us until tomorrow!"

They sought forgetfulness in the same cup, solely in order to absorb themselves in one another, but Xali, already drunk and more ardent in the game than her companion, soon got carried away, slid her arm around Kali-Yana's waist, and drew her to her couchette.

XV
The Rendezvous

In the huge room illuminated by the moon, the amazons were asleep, and only their light breath animated the night.

After having assured herself that her friend, weary of ardent words, protestations and caresses, was finally asleep, Kali-Yana slipped out of the room and traversed the garden at a run. Clad in a simple silk langouti, she threw herself into the shallow water, crawled under the subterranean bridge and found herself on the other side of the porcelain wall in Maxime's arms.

"You know that I've been waiting for you for an hour," he said, kissing her eyes.

"Xali didn't want to go to sleep, but here I am, and I'm all yours for the rest of the night."

"Come, then."

"Where are you taking me?"

"You'll see. Only it's necessary for us to go along the river; we're going to the poorer quarter, but the dwelling is nice."

He drew her into a pirogue, which the oscillating paddle enabled to glide like a nutshell. Soon, they abandoned the mandarins' quarter and passed before innumerable floating houses surrounded by narrow terraces, on which a few lamps illuminated idols. The richest had altars of sculpted wood garnished with festoons of golden paper. Sticks of incense were being burned there as well as coconut oil in red clay lachrymatories. Tubs of pink lime alternated with fruits amassed in baskets, tiger skins and multicolored mats.

Kali-Yana no longer knew what was real in that décor, so far did her emotion transport her beyond human vision. Leaning on the pharang's shoulder, she no longer pulled away from the kisses that ran over her face, seeking the savor of her lips. Had she been more experienced she would have mistrusted that lover, who forgot his past oaths so easily in order to indulge himself in a new amour. And the words that another had taught him served at present for a passion born the night before, illuminating it with the same seductive phrases, whispered in the ear in a growing desire.

"Dear Perfume! I love you!"

"Oh," she sighed, "I want to forget the evil presages, and take my part of happiness, since happiness is offered. You can't know how sad the days are that don't sustain any tenderness."

"Women, dear Smile, are only made to give themselves. Chastity is an anomaly, and religions go against the wishes of nature in demanding virgins for celebration of their worship. Nothing exists but the kiss!"

"The kiss! Why am I so troubled in your arms? My being seems to be duplicated and my soul is entirely in you. If you quit me, I would no longer be able to live!"

The boat glided more swiftly, borne by the current. Aquatic plants clung on to the terraces of the floating houses, whose roots were under the water. During the passage of the rowers, who were maneuvering their short oars artfully, moths took flight heavily from the branches, shaking the blue powder of their wings; luminous flies woke up the heart of lotuses and described illusory rainbows from one bank to the other. There were also golden insects on the surface of the water, which scattered in all directions, moved by lustful desire. Only the females displayed phosphorescent carapaces, fleeing before the hastening males, eager to link their ephemeral existence to that of a companion, at least for a few minutes of amour.

Very softly, the oarsmen intoned a monotonous and sad song, which lulled the lovers. The young woman had never even had the vision of such a felicity. Brought up from a very young age to serve in the royal guard of amazons, she had not wished for any other goal, and her senses were ardent although her reason remained calm, ignorant of the joy of loving. It had required the confidences and caresses of Xali, and then the encounter with the handsome stranger, for the scales to fall from her eyes and to inform her of her own state of mind.

Maxime had been prowling around the palace incessantly; she had watched out for him with a jealous prescience, and had soon discovered his rendezvous with Sayameda and the mystery of the Great Pagoda while the talapoins slept. Now, clasped against the young man's breast, she told him how she had suffered in seeing him with another, and how her vehement passion would henceforth reject any idea of sharing.

Smoothly, he reassured her, punctuating every phrase with a kiss, and the chaplet of kisses extended indefinitely, having long surpassed the hundred and eight symbolic pearls of Buddha's sole.

She closed her eyelids over the extraordinary dream, wishing to die thus in the glory of her amour.

The "great royal city of the angels, the admirable and in-vincible city" was no longer anything but a labyrinth of canals bordered by strange huts in which a famished and feverish people were swarming. Children lay on the terraces, sleeping under the stars; rolled up in a mat, lovers embraced one another freely, not ceasing their caresses as the pirogue passed by.

They were naked, without even the little leaf of metal that the little boys wore, and their bodies, thin but harmonious and polished, gleamed like fine marble. Old women crouching on the thresholds of floating houses were slowly chewing betel mixed with pink lime and displaying long black teeth from which the gums had retreated.

There were also gambling dens, glimpsed by the glimmer of oiled paper lanterns. The Cambodians and Annamites play bacouan and "twelve beasts" with trays and bags filled with dice. The Chinese prefer to intoxicate themselves with opium, and could be seen heating long needles in the flame of lamps in order to introduce the poisonous pellet into their bamboo pipe. Lying on their backs, hands open, a few of the hallucinated were talking in quavering voices; others were sleeping feverishly, agitated by abrupt spasms, or remained motionless in a death-like rigidity.

Young women, standing on the terraces, parted their langoutis as boats went by, appealing softly to seekers of amour. They leaned over, showing their slender forms, agitating their necklaces of coral and shells.

There were tea-houses where the strings of takhes and sos vibrated from dusk to dawn, and where minuscule Thai dancers, on the threshold of temples of lust, made the little bells on their ankles and arms tinkle.

Chinese, Malays, Annamites, Cambodians, Laotians, Hindus, Parsis, Peguans and Birmans lived in the floating city, but the Chinese element was dominant, and little shops with peppery odors could be seen everywhere, in which were displayed, by day, the sparkling fabrics, boxes of ivory and nacre, precious stones, dried fish, preserves and ginger pastilles of the Sons of Heaven. At the present hour, a simple drawn curtain hid the magnificence of the display, but the merchant, lying behind the counter, was sleeping with one eye open, ready to pounce upon any imprudent individual who attempted to rob him.

"I have something to say to you," repeated the brown dolls to every belated passer-by whose boat passed over the balconies. But the men often preferred the gambling dens to the sellers of sensuality, so attractive is gambling to the Thai people.

The lovers had arrived in front of a small house fresher and more florid than the others, the entrance of which was defended by two women asleep on mats. A chalet of lamps and painted lanterns ornamented the façade.

"Is this where you live?" asked Kali-Yana.

"Live, no; I reside near the palace, and I'm under surveillance, but we're in a hospitable lodging, and everything is ready to receive you."

The young woman's face darkened.

"But you said . . ."

"I didn't want to frighten you, dear Smile. Perhaps you would have refused to accompany me to a strange dwelling, so I let you believe that we were going to my home. In any case, I am at home here . . . come."

He helped her to go up the three narrow steps that ended at the terrace, the remainder of the stairway disappearing under the water.

"Wanida, Chem," he said, "light up for us."

The two women stood up and, after having put their hands to their foreheads as a sign of respect and obedience, introducing the young couple into a small room garnished with rare flowers, fresh mats and broad divans. On lacquer side-tables, baskets full of delicacies were displayed: honey and sesame cakes, clusters of lychees tasting of Muscat and bottles of wine the color of amethyst.

Anxiously, Kali-Yana hid her face behind a flap of her veil, and made a sign to Maxime to dismiss the servants.

"Don't worry," he said, "Wanida and Chem are accustomed to amorous visits; they're discreet and faithful."

Laughter burst forth behind the partition walls; sighs and kisses were also audible.

"You have company this evening?" the young man asked.

"Yes," said Chem, "a Frenchman like you, who's amusing himself with a Chinese woman. As for the English officer, he prefers an Annamite."

"It's necessary to allow for all tastes, isn't it?" Wanida concluded.

Laughing, the two women withdrew, and it seemed to the amazon that they were mocking her slightly.

Already, however, Maxime had clasped her to his heart, kissed her hair, her forehead, her somber gold-flecked eyes and her small ears, slowly, as one savors a long-coveted treat. She let him do it, already forgetting the bad first impression. She thought she was loved in a different fashion from the servants of lust of whose facile suppleness and humor, consenting to all of a master's whims, she was scornful. Maxime, certainly, was the grave and passionate lover that all priestesses of amour desire, the lover skillful enough never to make the disdainful pride of his triumph felt.

He gripped her more feverishly, felt the tremor of her shoulders and her entire charming body rubbed with aromatics. The warmth of her skin exasperated his desire, and he lifted off her amulets, tore away the langouti that veiled her loins, his fingers trembling madly, irritated by the obstacles.

Docile, she obeyed his movements, and followed him on to the divan, where he initiated all the small caresses that intoxicate as much as a perfumed wine.

Certainly, she was as beautiful as the little princes Samayeda, with a certain androgynous charm that he had not yet encountered anywhere. She did not yield like another woman, with fears, sighs and supplications; she gave herself generously now that the decision had been made, and all her ambition consisted of showing herself to be as brave in amour as she would have shown herself to be in death.

And the hours passed in that exquisite and dolorous initiation, which the little amazon had desired so much. She was as instructed as the most famous lovers, and, knowing everything, convinced that there was no other science to acquire in life, she wanted to die of the excess of her intoxication, for, as the Thai song says, in translation:

> *If love flowers again for faithful lovers*
> *In the land of the elect, let me die*
> *On your lips in flower, to pluck from the kiss*
>   *Eternal roses!*

PART TWO

I
The Warning

It was necessary to quit one another. The sun was shining in sumptuous floods in the little white room, where the flowers were dying in the jade vases, into which the cushions thrown at hazard put all the disarray of a voluptuous night.

The boat that had brought them was waiting, with the oarsmen asleep over the oars. Silent and weary, temples beating furiously, the lovers sat down on the banquette covered in cotton, and resumed the route of the troubled water in the inverse direction.

Flying from one pagoda to another, the crows were cawing more loudly, and a bald-headed adjutant stork in quest of some scrap of meat was inspecting the banks.

Women were going to market, skillfully steering their light boats filled with bananas, mangoes, durians and mangosteens with penetrating scents. They only wore a panung of striped cloth wound round their loins, and their firm breasts jutted out at every thrust of the paddle. Luk-sakhots rattled their metallic pellets, sometimes on their chest and sometimes on their back, fluttering at excessively abrupt movements.

Little boys, charming in their vivacity and grace, offered mengdanas or aquatic beetles whose blue carapaces were agitating in death-throes in the bottom of baskets. They also proffered green leeches and freshwater mussels, along with tails of "Aaron's rod," a kind of exceedingly spicy amorphophallus. Pink soft-shelled turtles reposed in nets, along with singing rays, delicate little snakes and crocodile eggs.

On the roofs of houses, tuk-hai, a sort of iguana covered in red pustules, known as "living clocks," were uttering strident cries announcing the hour of awakening. In response to its voice, housewives pulled the curtains of their huts, and shook out the mats, while old people installed on the terraces wove straw, while chewing the betel mixed with pink lime that causes the gums to bleed and withdraw from the teeth.

Kali-Yana clung to Maxime tightly, chilly in spite of the warmth of the day, enfevered by too many exquisite memories.

"This evening," he said, "you'll come back, won't you?"

"Yes, this evening."

"How can I do without your kisses now?"

"Oh," she sighed, "I sense that I'm going to suffer . . ."

"Why?"

"Because I'm too happy."

"Don't think about the future. All wisdom, you know, consists of taking advantage of the present moment, without creating chimerical torments."

"Perhaps, but we're not free to drive away the black swarm of evil presages . . . they come back like bees to flowers."

"Last night you weren't thinking about anything. Weren't you happy?"

Maxime smiled with a little pride in reminding his mistress about the hour of prestigious sensualities. Certainly, no one else would have been able, with such an enveloping seductiveness, to educate the little savage woman of distant countries in all the mysteries of amour.

But she shook her head, still sad.

Impatiently, he asked, in a slightly hoarse voice that she had not heard before: "In sum, what do you want?"

"What I want . . ."

She closed her eyes, sensing instinctively that she was about to displease him, to irritate a confused sentiment in him, temporarily buried by recent intoxications.

"Answer," he said, in the same harsh voice.

"Well, I want you never, ever, to go back to the Royal Pagoda."

He shrugged his shoulders. "Why should I go back, since it's you that I love? But that jealousy seems strange to me in this land of sharing, where every man, even in the poorest class, can have several wives."

"I'm not a woman like any other."

"Undoubtedly, but you've been brought up with the customary ideas of Thai women. Your supreme master, Phaja-Tak, possesses a harem of more than eight hundred wives. They're only playthings in his hands; he disposes of their life and their death. None of them is jealous."

"Certainly, but I'm an amazon of the royal guard, not a harem doll. For you I've compromised my reputation, I've risked the most terrible of punishments, for my peers have made a vow of chastity. It's only just that you recognize my sacrifice, at least by your fidelity."

"Reproaches and demands already, Kali-Yana? I thought your soul more generous."

He pushed her away gently, a bitter crease at the corners of his lips and a cold gleam in his pale eyes.

"Oh, that's because you don't know," she murmured. "You can't know . . ."

"Indeed . . ."

"The talapoin, the talapoin of the dead . . ."

But she uttered a cry.

Gamakul, standing on a pink granite lion, was haranguing the crowd. Hundreds of women in loose rags, holding children in their arms, were uttering ululations of revolt from time to time. Others, still child-like, but with the inflated breasts of warriors, were brandishing branches and red clay vases from which water was dripping on to their shoulders. Old women, more frightful than the vultures of the Green Pagoda, were howling so loudly that the fibers of their neck were stretched to breaking point, as vibrant as the strings of a takhe.

The men, calmer, were listening attentively to the guttural speech of the phra, but their eyes were burning and the black holes of their mouths were visible, corroded by betel and areca nuts, open for confused murmurs of reprisals.

Above their heads, pikes and krises glistened, agitated by the vengeful hands of the most turbulent.

Anger, hunger, long months of suffering and, above all, the interested rancor of the mandarins and the talapoins had elongated into the jaws of wild beasts the habitually resigned faces of the subjects of Phaja-Tak, the infallible King and Supreme Master. Kali-Yana could not hear what Gamakul was saying, but she divined by means of the play of the physiognomies that the revolution was rumbling around her, and that the peril, which she had only glimpsed thus far, was looming up, menacing.

"Adieu," she said to Maxime. "I love you!"

"Until this evening, isn't it?"

"Yes, this evening."

She had leapt on to the bank, and had frayed a passage through the turbulent crowd. The young man soon lost sight of her, and, having lain down in the bottom of the boat, ordered the oarsmen to continue their excursion, to rock his dream gently with the rhythmic beat of their paddles.

II
The Necessity of Killing Suk

"Where have you been?" demanded Xali, in a curt voice, when her irritated gaze fixed upon Kali-Yana's, seeking to penetrate the speckled surface of her irises.

"I've been . . ."

"Your breasts are bruised; I can see bites, marks of love or hatred all over your body! And then, do amazons go out naked now? Even your panung is in tatters, and you've lost the takrut that I gave you!"

Fearfully, Kali-Yana put her hand to her breast, where a link in the golden chain retaining the talisman had broken.

"That's true," she said. "Forgive me."

"The luk-sakhot was to preserve you from evil; it was your safeguard against the black vithi of the King of Fire. What will become of you now?"

"Forgive me!" stammered the culpable again, bowing her head.

"Not before knowing what you've done and why your flesh is more bruised than the Buddha's lotus after the sacrifice!"

Kali-Yana remained silent, trembling under her friend's burning gaze. Suddenly, however, an inspiration came to her.

"Don't scold me," she said. "I've acted in accordance with my conscience and for the good of all."

"What are you saying?"

"I'm saying that while you were asleep, I heard the clamors of the crowd under the walls of the palace, and that I wanted to know the danger that the Master was running, without awakening suspicions. So I went out like this, and I saw . . ."

"What did you see?" Xali, still suspicious, had seized her companion's wrist and was squeezing it madly, her lips dry and her nostrils quivering.

"Let me go, or you won't know anything. These injuries were inflicted on me by the irritated people. There's fighting near here."

"Fighting!"

"You can judge for yourself."

The amazons, who had been listening curiously to the argument of the two friends, picked up their weapons and went out on to the terraces. But they did not show themselves at first, desirous of studying the attitude of the demonstrators in order to take account of their hostile dispositions and prepare the defense in case of danger.

The tremor that was agitating the people was spreading beyond the canals into the outlying districts and the entire surrounding area.

Gamakul was becoming more heated on his granite lion, launching forceful invective against the unworthy monarch and his complaisant ministers. People were listening to him as if to an oracle, for it was said that he had commerce with the phi and must certainly know the future. Did he not know the vithi, the arcana of magical mystery and the hou, the secrets of astrology, and did he not occupy himself actively with prethat, or alchemy?

Ket, the great vulture of the Green Pagoda, was circling around his head, and Suk, the beautiful child with the velvet eyes, sitting tranquilly against the pedestal, was weaving garlands of lan-tam, singing in a high-pitched voice covered by the cries of the multitude.

Gamakul was now demanding a human sacrifice in order to assure the future prosperity of the Thai people. In accordance with custom, he proposed that a ditch should be dug at the entrance to the Green Pagoda. A horizontal beam would be placed there at a certain height, and on the day marked for the general uprising of the nation, three victims would be taken in great pomp to the place of torture; they would be charged, after being intoxicated by opium, with precious recommendations for the spirits of air, water and fire; then the heavy mass would be allowed to fall upon them, which would crush them.

"Well then," said a talapoin of the Pagoda of Samonakodom, "sacrifice little Suk, whom you seem to cherish so particularly! That magnificent offering will surely be agreeable to the phi."

"Sacrifice Suk!" moaned Gamakul. "A child! You can't think so!"

"The blood of an innocent is more agreeable to the powers of air and fire than the most splendid offerings!"

"But Suk charms my solitude! In the midst of the smoke of pyres and the filthy feasting of vultures on decomposing bodies, Suk is the divine flower who perfumes my abode. Suk is the angel of my desert hearth, the blue cricket who sings in the shadow of the charnel-houses, in the stink of the abattoirs. Kill Suk! Rather take my life!"

The insouciant child continued weaving white and yellow garlands, singing softly. Sometimes, his somber velvet eyes widened with curiosity, fixing pensively on the gold of a takrut or the crystal pearls of a luk-pat whose bright reflection charmed him, He extended his hands toward the coveted object, and sketched a smile of resignation if the jewel with the prestigious gleam was refused to him.

"Kill Suk!" sobbed Gamakul, again. "It's the evil spirits at are inspiring you!"

"If you accomplish that sacrifice," said a man of the people, supportively, "we'll believe that you really are the envoy of the gods, and your determination will be ours."

But the talapoin, shrugging his shoulders, quit his pedestal of pink granite, and, taking the child by the hand, went away, in the midst of jeers.

III
A Fortunate Diversion

"Come on," said Kali-Yana. "The time has come to show ourselves."

At the sight of the young women, whose red tunics cut through the whiteness of the marble colonnades, there was an undulation in the crowd, and all heads turned toward the palace.

Xali, very brave, hoisted the flag of the White Elephant and brought down the palm branches that, freshly-cut every morning, were crossed on the flagpole. That was a challenge that gave rise to a long clamor of astonishment.

But Gamakul had disappeared, and only Ket, the sinister vulture of the Green Pagoda, was still circling over the crowd. The women calmed down, very proud of their royal guard.

"You can see," said Kromalat, "that they aren't so malevolent. Without the rich and the mandarins who want to bring him down, Phaja-Tak could remain tranquil."

"Those people are ingrate," affirmed Ramesuen, "for after all, what would remain of our country if the King hadn't saved it from the Birman invasion?"

"Siam would no longer exist, and the entire nation would be reduced to slavery."

"Certainly, the Master's present eccentricities ought to be pardoned in favor of his past conquests," sighed Mi.

"He isn't responsible, since the talapoins have cast a spell on him," concluded Kali-Yana. "Let's shout: 'Long Live the King!'"

In sonorous voices, the little ones launched the glorious appeal, and the people, surprised at first, soon smiled at the virgin warriors, and united their own enthusiasm with theirs in a formidable acclamation.

IV
Voluptuous Nights

For some time, peace seemed to have returned. Kali-Yana, under the pretext of surveillance and espionage, was able to escape the palace every night without awakening the jealous suspicions of her companion. The latter merely begged her to take her with her, to allow her to share the danger of those expeditions.

"With two, one is full of audacity. I want to go with you, dear Smile."

Kali-Yana shuddered at the thought that Xali might one day discover her amorous secret.

"No, no," she begged. "There can't be too many amazons in the palace to defend the King. You mustn't abandon your post. And then, one woman can slip in anywhere without attracting attention, whereas if there were two of us . . ."

Xali did not insist, but she was desolate in seeing her friend's feverish eyelids close in an invincible exhaustion, and her pure breasts, arms and thighs florid with blue stigmata.

"Have you been beaten, then?"

"Yes, a little."

"Oh, if I were there!"

"You couldn't have prevented anything," said Kali-Yana, smiling. "These marks are dear to me. I'm happy to suffer."

"A strange taste!"

And, in fact, in the house of pleasure to which Maxime took his mistress, there were sometimes brawls that continued on the terraces between clients drunk on opium and black wine. The Chinese mewled like cats, rolled on the floor, scratching, knocking over the paper partitions and screens. Kali-Yani did not always have time to get out of the way, and received a few blows in passing.

"Why don't you take me to your home?" she asked her lover. "We'd be so comfortable!"

But his expression darkened and he replied, in a dry voice: "That's impossible; your chiefs would find out, and you'd be severely punished. For your sake, little darling, it's necessary not to commit that imprudence."

"Perhaps you're right, but this neighborhood is frightful!"

"Bah! A warrior ought not to fear encounters of this sort. . ."

"I'm no longer anything but a lover . . ."

"A lover ought to learn to brave danger. It's always useful."

Maxime laughed, but Kali-Yana had tears in her eyes, for it is usual that the most infatuated are also the most unhappy.

The prostitutes of the low quarters knew her now, and did not hesitate to treat her as an equal. Displaying their nudity on the edges of terraces, they asked her whether her lover knew savant sensualities and rendered her happier than those of the yellow race.

She did not reply, always fearful of betraying her secret. What would people say in the city and the palace if they learned that an amazon of the Royal Guard went in search of adventure every night to the low quarters of the capital and forgot herself until morning in strange amours? It would be shame and death: ignominious death in the depths of the river, to which she would be abandoned, stitched in a donkey-skin with a stone around her neck.

The sellers of pleasure were astonished by her silence and irritated by it. One night, she found herself in the midst of twenty of those prostitutes, who took her into their hovel, forced her to drink arak with them and subjected her to a multitude of little refined tortures that caused her days of fever and strange malaise.

The worst thing was that Maxime sometimes seemed to weary of her tenderness, made her wait, and sometimes did not come, leaving her in anguish for hours, more dead than alive, in the equivocal house where he always arranged to meet her—for she came alone now in the light craft that paraded her melancholy along the canals in the midst of the ironic propositions of men and the insults of cruel and voluptuous women.

To those long stations in the empty room she preferred the anger of her lover, his rebuffs and his injustices. To suffer at his will was still a joy for which she showed herself avid, fearing nothing except the absence that left her devoid of strength, bruised in heart and soul, mutilated in the entirety of her amorous being.

V
The Flagellation

One night, when she had remained waiting thus, crucified by dread and jealousy, a woman who was watching her through a rip in the paper partition told her that she was foolish to weep for so little and that she knew a remedy for all ills. Then she took her into the depths of an obscure back street where prostitutes were laughing in front of a stone lingam, which each of them adored in her turn. Perfumes were burning in bronze cassolettes, and at the foot of the ancient symbol of eternal fecundation there was such a profusion of flowers that the knees of the participants sank into it and they seemed to be borne away by a flood of roses.

220

Kali-Yana wanted to flee, but her companions, putting their hands on her shoulders, forced her to prostrate herself like the others in an equivocal prayer.

Bloodstains marbled the stone, seemingly indicating that there had been a recent immolation here, but the young woman searched in vain for the bodies of victims—goat-kids or doves that were sometimes offered to the gods.

The women nudged one another while looking at her. They wanted to make her kiss the obscene image, and when she refused, they attached her to a block of granite, took off her panung, and thorny branches played over her breasts, her loins and her legs, from which droplets trickled, increasingly rapid, enveloping her in a crimson network.

Around her, other prostitutes, newly arrived, had taken one another by the hand and were whirling madly, trampling the roses. They were all naked beneath their belt-clasps and their necklaces of barbaric gems, but their flesh exhaled violent perfumes, their fingernails were red, and they wore turquoise studs in their ears and nostrils.

The Thai women recognized one another by their clownish hanks of hair twisted in clumps of champa, but they were in the minority, rarely practicing the cult of the lingam. The milder expression of their physiognomy was sometimes nuanced with pity, and they implored Kali-Yana's forgiveness, recognizing one of their own.

The young woman had been made to undergo the tortures of the "offering," the "consecration," and the "accomplishment," in accordance with the sacred rites of the worshipers of the emblem of amour. The idol was still red with the victim's blood; while she veiled her face, moaning, the lubricious dances were exasperated under the flight of luminous flies attracted by the flowers. Then, two candles of yellow wax were placed in Kali-Yana's hands, and she was obliged to hold them up above her head, singing a canticle of adoration, while thorns were plunged into her breasts and thighs.

The young woman's eyes clouded, she begged for mercy in a faint voice. It was then necessary to dance in her turn under the burning wax, which ran in tears over her skin, mingling with the red droplets. Finally, she fell to her knees and refused to obey. Then the rods fell upon her shoulders again, and the angry prostitutes, after having taken her jewels and amulets, coupled with one another in the roses, drunk on arak, cries and insults. Kali-Yana, still attached to the granite lingam, could no longer hear anything but sighs and the friction of kisses . . .

In the morning, the anxious oarsmen came to liberate her, carried her away, and laid her down in the boat, where she remained motionless for several hours, incapable of moving her agonized limbs.

Xali dressed her wounds with sesame balms and meng-lak compresses, scolded her tenderly for her imprudence, but never knew that the amorous woman had expiated the folly of her tenderness, and that the wounds in her heart were causing her to suffer even more cruelly than the wounds in her flesh.

VI
The Burning of Allah-Kanha

Another of the King's wives was dead, and the pyre, as for Nai-Rafutt, had been built in the public square. The workmen were finishing arranging everything for the games, festivities, dances and open-air performances. Artistes were cutting out wooden ornaments and covering them with leaves of pure gold, around the mountain of cardboard, prestigiously painted and decorated, at the summit of which Allah-Kanha, the latest favorite of Phaja-Tak, was to repose. A little more robust than Nai-Rafutt, she had resisted the fantasies of her royal lover for six months, and had died without too much suffering thanks to the infusions of narcotic herbs that her companions had made her take, on the advice of a talapoin.

The little body, steeped in balms and ornamented by lan-tam corollas, reposed on a golden sheet in the midst of prostrate phras. A luk-sakhot of precious stones had been placed in the mouth of the corpse, and two young talapoins were waving ostrich flabella over her head in order to drive away the bees attracted by the musky odor of aromatics.

Soon, the phaya, the royal guard and the high dignitaries arranged themselves around the catafalque, and the remains of Allah-Kanha were hoisted up to the cardboard mountain. The Chao-Klein-Balat lit the pyre in the midst of cries of delight and lascivious dances. Three hundred sacred mimes struck poses of amour and lust, shaking their breasts and buttocks, and falling back in a swoon in voluptuous simulation. Over their pale amber skin barbaric cameos and the metallic pellets of talismans rattled; pubes florid with roses were offered to the liveliest chords of khong-vongs, flutes and kayabs, punctuated by the hoarse sighs of gongs.

Gradually, the smoke dissipated, the furnace crackled, and the cadaver appeared on the blackened catafalque. Perhaps Allah-Kanha had not been sufficiently steeped in perfumes, for her muscles were contracting under the action of the fire, her arms were writhing, her phalanges were stirring in a game of knucklebones, and the legs, abruptly distended, were throwing themselves sideways as if to flee.

The audience was untroubled, because the effect was often produced for the dead who had not waited long enough for the supreme combustion. The royal spouse, who was shaking her limbs frenetically and still seemed to be swooning in sensual pleasure or pain on her bed of embers, excited the joy of the spectators, who threw her fruits and flowers, urging her to keep struggling in that frightful agony of the afterlife.

Gamakul's great vulture, Ket, circling above the pyre, seemed to be regretting the prey that was escaping him, and Gamakul himself, was proffering his death-threats in the tightly-packed ranks of the crowd.

"When, then, people, will you put a stop to these atrocities? The ashes of Nai-Rafutt are not yet cold, and here is a new victim of your King's senile debauchery! All the daughters of quality will pass this way, and you can hear the plaints and sobs of frail victims under the walls of the harem! This one was not twelve years old, and she was fresher than a lotus bud of the sacred rivers! In her veins ran the generous blood of young races; she was made to live on many years of amour, and she would have given the Master superb and glorious children! People, revolt!"

Murmurs were heard; women, in particular, were showing their fists to Phaja-Tak, who had just appeared, surrounded by the Guard of Honor of his amazons, his halberdiers, his infantry regiments and his mandarins clad in silver silk. He was carried on a palanquin of nacre and ivory by sixteen men, and two large white seven-tier parasols sheltered him with a vacillating shadow. His sons followed him on ponies caparisoned with precious stones, and the princesses, his daughters, were radiant in golden butsa-baks.

As always, Sayameda, the beauty of beauties, occupied the central throne under an awning of flowers, and from time to time, Kali-Yana turned toward her, trying to discover a tender preoccupation, an anxiety or a jealousy in her gaze. But the little princess seemed joyful, a smile wandered over her painted lips, and her long smoky eyebrows were lowered over the ecstasy of a mysterious dream.

The rada, whose bruised shoulder was having difficulty sustaining the crimson flag, nudged Xali's elbow.

"What do you want?"

"Come on, let's slip into the crowd. I want, as at the funeral of Nai-Rafutt, to interrogate the talapoin of the dead, since his science can only be exercised during funeral ceremonies."

"He won't tell you any more than he's already told you."

"How do you know? Anyway, I have no need of his aid."

Kali-Yana's brows were furrowed, and her hands were trembling. Xali, who feared displeasing her, consented to that new caprice.

It was Kromalat who, in exchange for a few golden pellets, took charge of the scarlet banner, while the two friends, seemingly bearing a royal message, slipped between the mandarins, the swooning dancers and the troop of praying talapoins and finally reached the clump of rose-apple trees where Gamakul, hoisted up on a branch dusted with pink flowers, was exhorting the crowd to revolt.

"Vile slaves, rise up! Never has theft been practiced as it is today by an unworthy prince! Only the ministers and mandarins profit from the country's wealth, while you crouch in poverty, counting for no more than the rough stones of Mount Koh-Sabap! For the forty provinces of the realm, the endless series of governors and deputy governors is a cause of ruinaton. The title of Sarevinal, which they award themselves, means 'devourer of the people.' They are all embezzlers, pirates and traitors. The king knows that, and closes his eyes. What does the distress of the poor matter to him as long as he can kill his wives at his leisure in the closed harem and intoxicate himself with culpable delights? Here, you are divided into slaves, forced laborers and people paying tribute. If the mandarins want to build a house, the manual labor costs them nothing; they require the people to work relentlessly, and flagellation and the cangue can chastise the recalcitrant! The provinces and the capital furnish the materials, and if the building next door is an obstacle, they will demolish it. The rich desire your daughters for their harems or your sons for their troupes of actors? You have to consent to their caprices under penalty of fines, and sometimes death. Nothing is yours and you are nothing! People, stand up, show that you are a force and an intelligence!"

After having listened for a few minutes, Kali-Yana could not retain her indignation.

"People," she said, "the phra is toying with you, and his speech is culpable."

"Chung! Chung!" cried the women. "The King your master is a murderer! Let him return to us all those he has sent to the Dong P'aya P'at!"

"May the Koh-Sabap crush you if I'm not telling the truth!" shouted the rada, with a vehement movement that swelled her young warrior breasts, her slender nostrils quivering.

"You don't know what you're talking about," riposted a brown girl with long hateful eyes.

"Phaja-Tak has saved you all from slavery! He's a skillful and valorous leader! He took possession of the northern provinces, killed Phaja-Nackong and built your capital. Continuing his work with perseverance, he was victorious in all his encounters with the Birmans and liberated the country from its oppressors. Then the people were grateful and called him their benefactor. If he has changed, it's on the perfidious advice of the mandarins and talapoins who conspire in the shadows!"

The amazon raised her voice, very brave now that she was wearing the costume of the royal guard, and the crowd was not astonished to hear the young woman taking the defense of her Master, to the scorn of all discipline. But the rada were not considered as part of the regular troops, and scarcely anything was required of them than that they be pretty, virginal and intrepid.

From his tree, Gamakul looked at Kali-Yana, and his thin lips sketched a smile.

"You speak well," he said, "but that proves nothing, since another could have accomplished what Phaja-Tak did."

"No," replied the young woman, becoming increasingly animated, "another could not have struggled against China and reconquered Korat with insufficient troops and an unknown name. Our King has made his own, and three years after his accession, still victorious, he reestablished order and peace, subjugated Ligor and enriched the country with all the spoils of the enemy. Once you had nothing but actions of grace and protestations of amour to offer him in exchange for such benefits."

"Yes, the Master has been great, but you're passing over in silence the recent years of his reign, his injustices and his cruelties, his murders, his crimes against defenseless children!"

226

As Kali-Yana was about to reply, Gamakul leapt down from his branch and, taking her by the hand, snapped at her with furious laughter: "Instead of supporting such a sad cause, you'd do better, little rada, to keep watch on your lover."

Xali, who had heard that, started to tremble.

"What are you saying, wretched sorcerer?"

"I'm affirming that Sayameda is prettier than the prettiest of the amazons, and that the young foreigner knows it, since he's already unfaithful. Isn't that what you desired to know, Kali-Yana, in quitting your post in spite of the orders you were given?"

The amazon could scarcely sustain herself. Xali put an arm around her waist and drew her away, while Gamakul, triumphant, climbed back into his tree and resumed his harangue at the point where he had left it. But the people were incredulous; already groups were protesting, and women, won over by the rada's vibrant words, were insulting the talapoin. One of them, who had seen him embrace little Suk, demanded the sacrifice of the child.

"Yes, yes!" howled the crowd. "We need a victim, and if you want the death of the King, begin by turning the anger of the evil spirits away from us by immolating what you love most in all the world!"

Gamakul sobbed, and pink rose-apple flowers shaken by his convulsions rained down upon his bald head.

Suddenly, he appeared to make a resolution.

"So be it," he said, in a quavering voice. "To show you how just my cause is. I consent to that offering; Suk will perish for the triumph of the truth, and his torture will attract upon us the indulgence and the favor of the spirits of air, water and fire!"

"Ham!" cried the crowd, enthusiastically.

Gamakul, whose flaccid cheeks were trembling, wiped his bloodshot eyelids.

"Tomorrow," he said, "I invite you to the sacrifice. Suk, adorned with white lam-tan corollas, will be immolated for the good of the nation and the satisfaction of the gods. Before dying, he will listen to precious recommendations in order to transmit them to the supreme powers, and you will be able to dip your fingers in the blood of his mutilated body. I am thus giving you the greatest proof of tenderness that a man can give!"

"Ham!" roared the crowd. And vigorous arms snatched the talapoin from his flowery retreat and carried him in triumph, while the bones of Allah-Kanha finished being consumed in the distance, no longer forming anything but a little heap of gray ash on the completely black pyre.

VIII
The Most Beautiful

Xali and Kali-Yana resumed their places in the royal cortege behind the butsa-baks of the princesses, and the rada's black gaze, charged with storms, never quit the golden throne where her rival seemed to be asleep, weary of perfumes and ardent visions.

Sayameda, in her veils patterned with blue flames, beneath clasps, cabochons, necklaces and plaques that stirred like scarabs over her gleaming skin, seemed happy, in spite of fatigue, and when her brown eyelids with curly lashes were raised, they allowed a glimpse of ecstatic pupils lost in the infinity of a dream.

Xali, whose tumultuous soul wanted an explanation, interrogated Kali-Yana. "What did the phra of the dead say to you?"

The young woman, who did not want to reveal her secret, remained silent, a new frisson agitating her hands and lifting her bosom dolorously.

"Are you in pain, Kali-Yana?"

"Yes, the wounds I received in my nocturnal expedition . . ."

"There's something else. Your thought is fleeing me. I can no longer read your joys and troubles there, as before, and your tenderness, which I thought I had conquered, has shed its petals without even having flowered. What, then, is the malaise that is curbing you like an old woman, desiccating your loins and your lips and rendering you insensible to everything that surrounds you?"

"I'm trembling for the King, you know that."

"Of course . . . but at your age, such a preoccupation cannot suffice. Like you, I shall do my duty if the Master is in peril; however, I prefer you to him, and nothing that exists is comparable for me to the sweetness of your affection."

Kali-Yana shuddered again, so violently that Xali had to sustain her.

That was because Sayameda had turned round on her chariot and her painted lips were smiling at a man lost in the crowd, but whom the rada must have seen, as she had.

Surprised by the movement of the princess, Xali's thick eyebrows furrowed.

"What the talapoin of the dead said to you is true, then? You're jealous, your heart is twisted by anguish and hatred? You're like a wounded panther gathering its strength to tear its prey apart!"

"No, the phra was lying!"

"Why this emotion, this agonized gaze, this shuddering of your entire being? Oh, dear Perfume, don't hide anything from me! I have enough tenderness in me to forgive you and cherish you even more. My amour isn't exclusive and cruel, like that of men, it's generous and mild; it would be capable of crucifying itself to spare you a tear! Tell me, little Flower, what is troubling you and making you faint."

Softened, Kali-Yana squeezed her friend's hand, and leaned more forcefully on her shoulder, but her mouth remained mute; her amorous secret could have crushed her heart without her betraying it, so infatuated was she by her dolorous chimera and ready for the worst follies in order to keep it forever . . . like the fakir who conserves until death the cobra that is biting his bosom.

"Don't interrogate me any more," she murmured. "I'm so tired!"

"Well, I'll respect your dementia, and if, one day, you find me worthy of hearing you, you'll tell me what's torturing you so cruelly. Come on, little Flower, no amour is worth as much as mine, and you'll realize that at the moment of awakening, which won't be long delayed. Your dreams are already stained by the crimson of your heart. The moment is imminent when you'll no longer be able to support the horror of the torture, and you'll open your eyes to the reality, drive away the empusas and lamias of the shadows, the vampires of the lie that has been living within you for too long!"

"The princess is beautiful," sighed the young woman.

Xali enveloped Sayameda with her black gaze, charged with passion and terror.

"Certainly, no woman is as accomplished."

Kali-Yana revolted. "Didn't you tell me that I was better still, that no corolla was worth the corolla of my mouth, that my eyes had the profundity of the sacred lakes and that my figure, as slender and flexible as a lotus stem, wasn't comparable to any other?"

"That proves," Xali declared, "that for me, you're the most beautiful. Others, however, might judge differently. Perfection is conventional and everyone bears within themselves a secret ideal that suits their particular nature. Nothing exists and everything exists. Evil is in good, everything created responds to the needs of nature. There cannot, in consequence, be any perfect ugliness or beauty."

After having caressed the beloved lost in the crowd with her velvet gaze, Sayameda had resumed her indifferent and weary pose. The veils constellated with sapphires that fell around her sizzled with lunar flames; a serpent of aquamarines and chrysoberyls that she wore around her waist was rutilant upon her skin, its head lost between her legs, as if to defend against violation the corolla of election that no mortal ought to pluck.

VIII
Xali Resigns Herself

"Let me alone!"

"No."

"Xali, I want to go out."

Kali-Yana, sitting up on her couchette, rejected her friend's embrace, and slid her slender leg, which rings kissed with a tawny light in the half-light of jade lamps, out of the cushions.

"Something bad will happen to you again! What's the point of these distant excursions from which you come back bruised and fainting?"

"The revolution is rumbling, you know that. Here, we don't know what's happening in the maritime city."

"We'll learn soon enough; better to remain at our post. At the moment of danger, all courage will be useful."

"At the moment of danger, I'll be among you."

"Unless you're subjected again to the humiliating flagellation of which your flesh still bears the traces. I beg you, little Flower, stay with me!"

"Oh, your resistance is annoying me. Certainly, you're stronger and you can oppose my design, but I can also kill myself in front of you, and that's what I'll do if you don't let me go."

Kali-Yana had stood up, in a supreme effort, and, putting the sharp point of a dagger to her breast, she stood up to her friend with all the force of her exasperated desire.

Xali was weeping now, and sobs lifted her shoulders.

"I want to go out," the rada repeated.

"Well, then go—and may Samonakodom protect you!"

IX
Calvary

Before going to the house on the water's edge, Kali-Yana explored the terraces, the gardens and all the shadowy corners propitious to voluptuous embraces.

The luminous insects cast their magical canvas over the sky, which the cabochons of the stars dotted with golden nails. The horned moths, in a fever of looting, were tearing their wings on the pistils of lilies; everywhere, love and death were mingled in a haste of fecundation and destruction, as if, in that earth of fire, the cruel labor of lust and suffering, of resurrection in corruption, ought never to be interrupted: a symbol of the futility of any solitary effort in the eternal struggle of nature for the egotistical triumph of her splendor.

Mira-Mira, the domesticated panther, caressed the amazon's legs and rubbed her whiskers against her thigh, her metallic eyes filled with a cajoling softness.

Kali-Yana spoke to her as to an indulgent companion, who understood her and consoled her better than Xali and her jealous remonstrations.

"You, at least," she said, "only want my hand on the velvet of your fur, and when I forget myself against your flanks full of stars, it seems to me that a calmer blood flows in my veins; I'm appeased by your tenderness."

Mira-Mira seemed to understand, and her throat emitted tender gasps, a sort of soothing throb.

"You see," the rada went on, "I ought to hide myself here from everyone, and from Xali as from everyone else, because Xali only loves me with a suspicious and quarrelsome passion, whereas with you, there's no treason to fear. Your large amber eyes read my heart, and understand it, because you're something of a sorceress. You've passed through the Kala-Suta-narok, the second hell of transformations, which has given you a mysterious

232

soul, after having been cut into a thousand little pieces. Oh, how well you've done to take that superb and voluptuous form! How I love your tawny coat with splashes of ink,[1] the marvelous coat that is almost as phosphorescent as the flight of golden flies over the infinity of the sky!"

Mira-Mira was still rubbing her spine against the young woman's legs, more supply and more lasciviously, and the tip of her pink tongue seemed ardent for more delicate sensualities—but Kali-Yana suddenly pushed her away and started running, traveling the garden in all directions, recommencing her search with a greater determination and an ever-increasing feverish haste.

A heavy desolation was weighing upon the young woman. Skillful in striking the most sensitive parts of her amour, she imagined Maxime's treasons, the mocking artfulness that he had deployed in order better to deceive her, and the malevolent triumph of his pride after each humiliation to which he had subjected her.

Certainly, she was only a little savage of distant shores, which the pharang did not know, but she was worth as much as many of the pale-eyed women of the lands of mist! Her body and soul had the beauty that retains men, and puts a little of the divine into carnal felicities.

She had therefore given everything, braving the death that threatens the immodest rada, exposing herself to the gibes and insults of the populace in undignified rendezvous—for she was no longer ignorant now of the infamy of the brothel to which her lover had taken her, and she had often wept with rage and disgust during her long waits in the chamber with the equivocal reeks. The paper walls there did not protect her against indiscreet gazes, and the women passing through, prostitutes with heavy breasts, after revealing to her the shame of their couplings and

---

1 This is odd, implying that the "black panther" is not melanic, but simply resembles other leopards, with darker spots. Symbolic black panthers occur frequently in La Vaudère's work, however, and most, if not all, of the others are definitely entirely black.

their complaisances, insulted her, sending her the bronze pellets of their amulets through holes that their fingernails excavated.

Huddled in a corner of the narrow room like a hunted beast, she brought her panung up over her head, constraining herself to immobility in order not to reveal her presence, and only the flowers, which were never changed, troubled the silence with the light fall of their shed petals.

Maxime had not come for six days, and Kali-Yana, before going to the infamous house, searched the gardens of the palace and the mysterious hiding places where two lovers might have been able to embrace.

She climbed the porcelain steps bordered with monsters with glaucous eyes, fantastic animals of jade and porphyry, which led to the Royal Pagoda. There too, all was calm. The talapoins had renewed the oil in the lamps that burned beside the golden Buddha; perfumed candles were melting over the heads of divinities, and feverish perfumes of Takeoka and Rondeletia escaped from cassolettes.

Phras, their eyelids ringed and their fingers trembling, were distributing in onyx vases essences of lemon, frangipane, clove and neroli, which stimulated the carnal appetite. Furtively, they dipped the ends of their yellow scarves in the mixture before pouring it into the perfume-burners, and went out two by two, holding hands.

Kali-Yana heard the cells closing on a soft whispering and, alone in the pagoda, she waited. With her ear stuck to the little door that led to the apartment of the princesses, she immobilized herself in an anguishing surveillance, believing continually that she could hear the friction of silky fabric, the rattle of gems lifted up by kisses, or the whisper of a confession of ardent sensuality.

But nothing appeared to be alive in the royal halls. Around the Pagoda, the monsters with glaucous eyes were charged with more terror; the dragons, the vultures, the cobras with forked tongues, recovered all the horror of forests of Himaphan resembling the Pretas that, according to legend, suffered an eternal thirst, and only drank the blood of virgins, whom they visited at certain moments in monstrous nightmares, from which they emerged exhausted and morbid.

Kali-Yana thanked Cakyamouni for having spared her the ordeal that she feared more than death, and, in a surge of gratitude, she kissed the paving stones at the foot of the great golden idol three times.

Behind the walls of the palace, the boat that took her to the house of ill-repute every evening was swaying on the wavelets of the cabal; she took her place within it, and the oarsmen, beating the water in cadence, sang softly in order to animate the journey.

Their song was as passionate and sad as the night. They recounted the adventure of the Indian hero and the young Himalayan woman:

"Prince Axa, next to a Himalayan woman, respired the enchanting lotus; but he was involved in a distant war, fought for three years and died on the battlefield. Prince Axa loved a Himalayan woman.

"In purgatory, his superhuman dolor touched the archangel that watches over the heavens. 'Go,' said the archangel, 'your tenderness is faithful; find the one who has captured your heart. Go and respire the enchanting lotus, Prince Axa, next to the Himalayan woman.

"But afterwards, your sojourn in hell will be augmented by ten thousand years of pain. On earth, Axa searched for the Himalayan woman. Another lover was pressing her to his heart.

"Then, mad with rage, he related his dolor to the great archangel who watches over the heavens. 'Angel,' he said, 'I prefer my chain and your hell to the hell of earth.'

"'Go,' said the archangel, 'enter the divine abode; you have gained by losing our amour. Such a martyrdom is worth ten thousand years of hell!'"

X
The Immolation

In the vicinity of the Green Pagoda, one could not have dropped the pearl of a luk-sakhot, so tightly packed is the crowd.

The hour of the sacrifice is approaching; the bells are ringing; young women are hanging garlands of lan-tam and champa from the murderous beam that will soon crush Suk's frail body.

Young boys adorned with the sacred signs of Cakyamouni are selling prayer-mills and takruts ornamented with hydrophane that the tears of virgins, at the sight of the child martyr, are causing to radiate multicolored flames. Lingam fetishes carved in uvarovites, olivines, milky cymophanes and ash-gray fossil turquoises, are passing from hand to hand in order to be attached to the necklace of some Hindu woman who has made the acquisition of them. The yoni-lingam, or complete symbol, is preferentially purchased by men, who wear it on the arm or attached to a panung by a slender chain.

All the Buddhas of the Pagoda have been brought out and arranged in front of the door, where the torture will take place after the preparatory invocations. Trenches ending in a little marble vessel have been hollowed out in order to collect the precious blood of Suk, and the talapoins will dip lan-tam flowers into it, which they will distribute to the audience. Ribbons of odorous corollas indicate the route that the child will follow; cassolettes are burning at intervals, emitting thin jets of blond smoke that scarcely scatter, so calm is the atmosphere.

Gamakul has swept the sinister field where, only yesterday, chaplets of vertebrae and necklaces of phalanges trailed, and the games of bowls played with abandoned skulls. Nobody will be burned today, and the vultures are describing anxious parabolas over the place of torture, demanding their prey.

"Ham!" said an old woman with lips reddened by betel and areca nuts. "The stork with the bald head has perched on the Pagoda, which announces that the sacrifice is agreeable to the powers of the Maha-roruva . . ."

"Last night," said a young woman who was wearing a beryl lingam between her breasts, "I saw monsters with human heads hanging by the fingernails from the walls of the palace. They had the long wings of bats, which hung down behind them like black veils, and with abrupt jumps they were still climbing, moaning like little children."

"Yes," said the old woman, "they're the lamias and the empusas of the Lokanta-narok, and their appearance is a presage of death."

"Is it true that the revolution is rumbling all the way to the mouth of the Me-Nam?"

"Certainly, the people are only waiting for a signal to take possession of the King."

"Alas, what will we gain from the revolution? There will be new massacres, as in the times of the Birman domination; famine and disease will desolate our countryside."

"Pillage and conflagration will destroy cities, as in the reign of the Peguan Phaya-Nackong, and our capital will perish, as Ajuthia perished after four hundred and seventeen years of existence."

"The entire Thai country will fall into anarchy. The forest and deserts, even the most inaccessible, will cease to be a refuge for the oppressed, who will run with the lions and tigers in order to escape men."

"Ham!" roared the old woman. "The ferocious beasts are not in the distant savannahs but in the cities where parents and children are tearing one another apart for a little gold, where nothing exists except interest, and where the man who is poor dies like a leper for the great joy of the vultures!"

At that moment, a young woman of great beauty, but whose face was wet with tears, pushed between the tightly packed ranks of the crowd. Everyone stood aside before her dolor; the men merely advanced their hands to touch her charming body, in order to conserve, in a brief caress, the pure contour of her breasts and her hips.

She did not seem to pay any heed to the whispers or to the touches, marching as if in a dream, guided by a sort of instinct more powerful than her will.

"Kali-Yana," murmured the old woman who had already spoken, "your place is not here."

The rada shivered and seemed to wake up from her somnambulistic state.

"You know my name?"

"Yes, you're one of the little amazons of the King. Yesterday, you spoke to defend your Master, and in spite of your disguise, I recognize you. Go, return to your post. In a little while, the red dew will pearl on these lan-tam flowers and the howls of the multitude will drown out the agonized screams of the child martyr. Then there will be blood, and more blood, the flood of which will rise all the way to the steps of the throne."

"I'm suffering," said Kali-Yana. "Let me savor my pain for a moment. Afterwards, I'll leave and I'll do my duty. In the meantime, let me weep."

"Weep on my shoulder, then," said the old woman; "the tears that moisten my flesh will do you less harm than those that fall into the void. The tortures of oblivion, shadow and silence are the most frightful."

The rada, huddled in the infamous chamber, had waited for the pharang in vain, and slowly, her heart had been crucified, emptied of all the blood of amour that hope had caused to seethe during the journey.

Maxime, capricious, weary or delayed in other rendezvous, had avoided the habitual caress, and had neglected, carelessly, to calm or numb the torment of his mistress.

He was not wicked, but he was unable to bend himself to long fidelities; in any case, for him, these brown dolls were not women, but living playthings destined to charm the hours of exile, to enable him to forget, momentarily, the distant objects of adoration with white skin and savant and artificial prettiness. And then, he did not believe that he was loved.

Almost everywhere in his travels he had plucked a few blooms of amour, and had got himself out of it with a few jewels, silky fabrics, perfumes and promises. None of those adventures had concluded tragically, for those women, in countries of slavery, are only considered as voluptuous flowers that one plucks and shreds at the whim of one's caprice. Resigned to caresses with no tomorrow, and humiliating sharing, they are ignorant of jealousies and revolts, submissive, with an almost joyful complaisance, to the fantasies of the master and his ephemeral desires. Better still, they serve on their knees, according him the right of life or death over them, even able to resolve themselves to sacrifice, to the mutilation of their beauty, if such is the pleasure of the temporary lover.

Maxime had collected pollen from the elect corolla, curious about that warrior virginity that he had encountered for the first time. Then, after a sincere passion of a few days, he had wearied of that fearful submission, which resembled that of all women.

The rada, truly, had nothing grim but their name; they were slaves of sensuality like the others, prostrated by amour, whom one gained with a caress, led with a smile, and sent away with a present.

The pharang resumed his desire for Sayameda, whom he had not yet possessed, and who united with her pure charm the prestige of rank. The little princess could not leave the palace, and the danger of those clandestine rendezvous had a savor that was very appreciable for the blasé voyager.

The rada understood her humiliation vaguely, and a thousand sentiments of hatred, jealousy, indignation and vengeance divided her soul.

Leaning on the shoulder of the old Thai woman she let her tears flow slowly, biting until she drew blood the thick lips that Maxime, in his first transports, had pressed so ardently between his own.

In a mist, she saw talapoins covered in amulets passing by, the chariot of Cakyamouni Phra Chao Xang Phuok, master of the seven white elephants, and an infinity of idols and monsters borne on the shoulders of the faithful. Apprentice phra, children of the Pagoda choirs, were dancing backwards in front of the Butsa-bak in which Suk, naked and gilded from head to foot, was reposing on cushions. The child's eyes were closed and his immobility was such that one could not even see his chest rising. Two other small boys standing to either side of him were holding a yellow veil above his forehead to hide it from the curiosity of the crowd or to protect him from the glare of the sun.

Klue and so players terminated the march, and the talapoins were singing the praises of Nirvana in a minor key. Suk was deposited on the threshold of the pagoda, and two phra, having made grave recommendations in his ear, put a gold takrut between his lips in order to prevent him from betraying his secret. Then Gamakul laid him down on a bed of lan-tam, kissed him tenderly, and the cords sustaining the enormous beam were cut . . .

But the red stream did not flow into the bowl, and the audience accused the talapoin of only having sacrificed a cadaver to the spirits of the air, water and fire.

While the nearest spectators seized Gamakul and suspended him head down, in order to bleed him instead of the child, the spectators in the rear, who had not understood the fraud, turned toward the palace uttering a frenetic clamor.

"Death to Phaja-Tak! To death! The gods want it!"

XI
The Mob

Before the palace there was now a frightful confusion of men, women and children, encumbering the area all the way to the river, where the boats were also grouped in a bellicose flotilla.

And that furious crowd was about to be crushed against the porcelain walls of the harem and the perforated balustrades of the galleries.

On both banks, the most determined were hanging on to the branches of sycamores and palm trees, hurling fruits and stones on to the terraces. The talapoins of the Pagoda of Xetuphon were ringing the alarm bell to implore the good spirits while the troops of the royal guard assembled in the courtyards.

An enormous accumulation of the populace was waiting on the far side of the Me-Nam, the men only being able to pass over the narrow footbridge that linked the banks two by two; soon, however, the joists having given way, the variegated, bare-limbed crowd seemed to be swarming on the water like clusters of reptiles.

However, Kali-Yana, slipping through the groups, her panung in tatters and new wounds on her bruised limbs, had regained the rada's terrace. All the amazons, at their posts, were only waiting for a signal to commence the attack, but an order from the Kromluang instructed them to hoist the scarlet flag three times as a sign of peace, Phaja-Tak not wanting to exasperate his people.

Kali-Yana, therefore, raised above her head the crimson banner adorned with the silver emblem, and, upright beneath the rays of sunlight that caressed her brown and supple body of a young warrior, she waited.

The crowd did not calm down; a more violent pressure threw the first ranks against the walls, and a thousand cries erupted from black lips twisted by rage and pain. A few fanatics hung on to the rose-patterns on the balconies and the towers, attempting to haul themselves up as far as the rada.

An amazon struck by a stone fell, her forehead gashed, and Xali, drawing a knife from her belt, slashed the wrist of the first assailant who presented himself. The man uttered a scream of pain, fell backwards and smashed his skull on a granite boundary-marker. A hail of projectiles immediately fell on the rada, several of whom were wounded.

Troops emerging from the palace attempted to drive the rebels back; there was a general melee. The red tunics of the soldiers were flamboyant in the midst of naked torsos shiny with sweat.

The clamor became deafening, compounded of plaints, gasps and cries of death. But the royal infantry weakened, and the reserve troops, stopped by the Me-Nam, all of the bridges having been invaded, massed in the narrow streets of the outlying districts, were reduced to a distant resistance.

Kali-Yana, struck cruelly by a stone, was only able to sustain the sacred flag with one hand and Xali, by her side, exhorted her gently, begging her not to expose herself further.

There was a diversion: women advanced, agitating something at the tip of a pike, howling insults and imprecations. There was a mad dance around the bloody trophy, Gamakul's head, which the fanatics had severed after crucifying him on Suk's beam while the talapoin was in his death-throes. Thin bloody ribbons were hanging down beneath the yellow mask, which was grimacing its last smile, one eye hideously open, almost projected out of its orbit, and the other closed on the sinister vision.

A prostitute, still drunk after her night of debauchery, suggested that the phra must be thirsty, and two sepoys who had stolen a bottle of arak poured the contents into the dead mouth of the victim. The eau-de-vie, tinted red, passed through the gaping wound of the throat and ran along the pike, and the women, extending their hands, collected it, saying that it was much better, having two souls, the soul of the alcohol and the soul of the talapoin.

Excited by the sight of blood, other furies struck the soldiers with their own weapons, attacking them furiously, finding unknown tortures and bizarre refinements of cruelty that brought long groans from the martyrs; and the women laughed, saying that Phaja-Tak had killed enough women for those revenges to be just and agreeable to the gods.

But the doors of the palace opened wide and the elephants emerged, armed for war, with golden rings on their long tusks. The conductors, perched on the pavilions, maneuvered a whole series of lances, pikes, javelins, clubs and maces. The cornacs, on the rump of the enormous beasts, excited them with shrill voices.

The first twenty trampled the people, crushing those who did not draw back quickly enough; those in the rear were still pushing, and there was a horrible confusion. Then the eight hundred royal elephants emerged from the enclosures in their turn, trampling the crowd, clearing a passage invincibly, overturning obstacles like a victorious torrent.

The cries of the wounded and dying rose higher, while the fugitives threw themselves into the Me-Nam in order to escape the terrible pressure, preferring drowning to being crushed.

The pachyderms were still advancing, and their conductors, with thrusts of lances and pikes, repelled those who tried to cling on to the straps of the howdahs.

The ground was now shaking, as if by an earthquake; pools of blood were expanding everywhere, cadavers fallen in all directions, in frightful postures, their chests caved in, their arms twisted, howled their silent howls of death with wide-open mouths, the teeth blackened by betel. Women's amulets were wrapped in viscous ribbons of entrails; the rings of their ankles and arms were driven into the flesh; and broken bones overlapped over cabochons of glass.

Kali-Yana, who was still gazing from the height of the terrace, the scarlet banner leaning on her bloody shoulder, uttered a faint sigh, extended her arms, and collapsed.

PART THREE

I
Kali-Yana's Vision

"How are you feeling, dear Delight?"

"Better, Xali, your warm caress has done me good. The red fog has dissipated. How many are there down there, the dead and the dying?"

"How should I know? A thousand, perhaps."

"Alas."

"Don't mourn them. It required nothing less than the formidable charge of the elephants to defeat the people in delirium."

"They're hungry, Xali, their misery is great."

"Will you absolve them, after what they've done to you?"

"They haven't done anything to me. In my dolor, last night, I found sympathetic souls . . ."

"And these wounds, dear Perfume?"

Kali-Yana smiled mysteriously; then her eyes clouded, and a tear pearled on the ends of her eyelashes.

"I went where I should never have gone. Don't accuse anyone, Xali; I'm bearing the punishment of my imprudence . . ."

"Oh yes, the secret that you keep so carefully . . ."

"The Thais are not as wicked as the Pharang. The evil comes from further away!"

With a nonchalant hand, the rada, lying on her couchette, caressed the cheek of her friend, who was kneeling beside her, gazing at her passionately. In the vast hall, still full of the communicative joyful twittering of young women the day before, was now only vibrant with the intermittent plaints of the wounded. Almost all of them had been hit by some projectile, and strips of delicate cloth were wrapped around the bruised limbs or pressed against dolorous foreheads, through which red droplets filtered anyway, making hair sticky and descending in ruby threads over feverish cheeks.

Kromalat, one of whose nipples was gashed, was hiding the delicately rounded cup of her breast in a lotus corolla, for the stamens of pink nympheas are particularly beneficent. Ramesuen was pouring the essence of the male kadanga, drop by drop, over her swollen arm, and Mi was making compresses of Meng-lak and aquatic bindweed, the bitter-tasting leaves of which she sometimes chewed in order to distract herself from her pain.

Only the youngest rada, who had not taken part in the combat, retained their turbulent gaiety. Sourinam. A child of ten years, with a topknot traversed by coral darts, was rolling stark naked on the back of Mira-Mira, the domesticated panther. Kroumil, another apprentice amazon with the slender limbs of a Thai statuette, was gravely cutting a bamboo stem in order to make a klue, a chirping flute whose songs are sweeter than that of the skylark.

Kali-Yana, raising herself up on her couch, uttered the long cry of a wounded animal, and Xali, terrified, sent for the chao-luang, the palace physician.

All the rada, their eyes turned toward the young woman, upright and quivering, wondered whether she might be prey to a sudden fit of madness. And, in fact, troubled by so much suffering and emotion, Kali-Yana felt her reason buckling like a reed in a storm wind; sinister shadows floated before her, and the ground seemed more unstable than the sand of the sea-bed.

Unconscious, and shaken by furious sobs, she talked now, about her long journeys on the Me-Nam to go meet Maxime in the brothel, her furious kisses, her invincible passion and the ingratitude of the too-beloved. Her voice swelled and growled, like the roar of a wild beast, or was ripped into the moans of a little girl. Her delirium retraced the vain afflictions behind the thin partition that separated her joys from other joys more shameful still. Oh, she was no longer ignorant of vile bargains, filthy offers, the traffic in human flesh that was conducted there in the laughter and hiccups of lovers of passage already drunk on arak or opium.

The perverse prostitutes boasted brazenly, recounting their voluptuous science; horrible old women, dragging some trembling starveling by the hand, snatched away the panung that covered her loins, praising her fragile prettiness, and retired after having collected the price of the rape. Kali-Yana recalled the cries of the tortured children, their supplications, accompanied by the hoarse breath of satyrs obstinate in their cruel task. One little girl, who had been tied up as if crucified in the doorway, and martyrized all night long had died the following morning, and the rada imitated her last plaint of a disemboweled beast.

"Shut up! Shut up!" implored Xali, putting her hand over her friend's mouth. "It's the fever, you don't know what you're saying!"

"Yes, I know, I've seen, I've heard! Oh, if you could imagine the terrible impression of those nightmares of vice, the vision of those frightful scenes! And I've given myself to that shame, I've savored morbid delights in that house of crime! It's there that I loved . . . loved . . . !"

Kali-Yana laughed and fell backwards on the cushions, and that laughter was more anguishing than her tears, more heart-rending than her sobs . . .

"Don't talk any more!" Xali was still begging. "Close your eyes and go to sleep in my arms, affectionately, as before. What does the ugliness of life matter, when the dream is so sweet? Sleep, Kali-Yana, and slumber will calm your fever."

But the rada was still delirious; bell-clappers were hammering her temples; a convulsive shudder was shaking her shoulders. With an abrupt movement, she pushed Xali away, tore away the dressings covering her wounds and started dancing, bathed in the crimson of her blood. The movement of her loins accelerated, her

246

bare feet slid over the porcelain tiles; she resembled a red lotus swaying over the mirror of the pools of Xetuphon.

"Look! Look, Xali! This is how I danced before the stone lingam, and my blood, under the flagellation of the prostitutes, ran is the same way . . . I was no longer a woman but a scarlet rag spinning at the whim of Lum! Then they threw me on to the icy idol, and my blood ran again, from another wound, the most painful of all . . . Look! Look!"

She was breathless, her hands clenched above her head, her eyes revulsed in hatred or ecstasy, the irises raised above the blue-tinted cornea, her lips parted over the sparkling double row of her teeth.

"Look! Look!"

She crossed her arms over her breasts to defend herself, crawled on her knees, and fell backwards, her entire body agitated by crazy shocks, as if snakes were crawling under her skin, and her fingernails, enlarging her wounds, dug more profoundly into the living flesh . . .

"Look . . ."

But the rada threw themselves upon her, and, in order to prevent her from injuring herself further, they bound her to her couchette with the torn strips of their langoutis.

II
The King's Dementia

For a week the rada struggled in the delirium of an intense fever, rediscovering the torments that she had endured, reliving the hours of lust and hatred. Xali thus knew every detail of her passionate calvary, and her generous soul forgave her friend, the victim of the dream of amour thrown back palpitating into the reality of life.

The mob was still growling, but more dully, in spite of the exhortations of the talapoins. Fearful of further reprisals, the people listened weakly to words of revolt, falling back into their habitual apathy.

In the meantime, Phaja-Tak, having retired into his harem, did not seem to see anything, and his morose humor was only dissipated by voluptuous pleasures, which he stimulated every day with new fantasies. The latest favorite, Ajutana, charmed him with her perverse precocity; she was said to be adroit and wily, capable of standing up to her royal lover and finally mastering him in amorous games.

One of the generals, Chakri,[1] who was in command in Cambodia, spread the most malevolent rumors about the King, only awaiting an opportunity to seize power. It was known that the governor of Ligor had sought refuge with the chief of Patawi, another city of the Malay peninsula, and that Phaja-Tak, after having seized his treasures and had the members of his family killed, had only accorded mercy of Ajutana in order to take her into his harem. But the little favorite knew charms that triumph over all lusts, philters that throw a maddened male lover at the feet of the invincible female lover, always unassuaged.

By means of savant mixtures of tuberose, spikenard and mitcham, she awakened the senses of the Master, infatuated with her singular beauty, her eyes speckled with rust, and her hair tinted with sapan and wild jô. She excited his carnal appetite by means of precise extracts of ayapana, champak and sarcanthus, with scents of human and feline fur; then, combining the poisonous juices of the accursed forests where the vampire flowers, sylvan gouges with leech-like corollas, were radiant, she threw him on the cushions, palpitating, and by means of expert caresses dug

---

1 The general in question, who founded the Chakri dynasty that continued to rule Thailand into the twentieth century, was also known by several other names, including Rama I. The depiction of him in the present story is entirely false; Taksin's leading supporter, he became King after putting down the rebellion that had deposed his predecessor, having returned from Cambodia in order to do so.

into his cranium, emptied the marrow of his bones, and shook his nerves with frenetic and galvanic spasms.

On emerging from those embraces, her lover's gaze remained dazed, his limbs unsteady and his will abolished in a morbid stupor. Thus Ajutana avenged herself, serving the projects of Chakri in order to liberate her father, captive in Patawi.

III
The Vigil of Love or Death

"How do you feel, dear Delight?"

Xali repeated the phrase incessantly, anxiously, leaning over Kali-Yana's weakness maternally.

The amazon seemed to be emerging from a long opium dream, and her thoughts, still clouded by phantoms of hallucination, were floating uncertainly and deceptively.

"Answer me, little Flower . . ."

With furtive but precise gestures, Xali plumped up a cushion, refreshed the little invalid's temples, brought her floral tisanes, and spread around her the peppery perfumes that stimulate the senses, renewing the desire to live.

After ten days without saying a word, however, Kali-Yana felt stronger, and ceasing to follow the chimeras of the dream, began to ripen a new project. In the darkness, her eyes gleamed like lightning-flashes in a stormy sky, her lips agitated silently in mysterious invocations to the malevolent phi of air and fire.

She had suffered too much, sobbed too much in amour and humiliation; she would make the worth of her anger known, and, even if she had to pay with her existence for the ephemeral satisfaction of a vengeance, she would go straight to her goal.

In order to lull the anxious surveillance of Xali, who, with her tender perspicacity, seemed to be able to read her heart, she simulated a complete prostration, her eyes closed, annihilating herself in an immobility of stone.

It was the day of the theater; the princesses, after the fatigue of the performance, the game of Chinese tarot, the combats of cocks, peacocks and gray crows, retired to their apartments earlier. Similarly early, the talapoins renewed the oil of the lamps and the perfumes of the cassolettes in the Royal Pagoda, which became propitious for culpable rendezvous. Sayameda and Maxime ought to be able to meet more easily if, as Kali-Yana thought, the pharang and the little princess had resumed their barely-interrupted amorous duet.

At that idea, the amazon clenched her fists feverishly, and the emotion of her hatred was so vehement that she felt faint.

That evening, as Xali, wearied by so many cares, was asleep against her heart, she gently moved her friend's head aside, posed her burning lips in her hair in a kiss lighter than the flight of a bee, and went out. She walked with a velvet tread, supporting herself on the walls, for an icy chill was rising under her skin, and the little lamps seemed to her to be whirling over the sleeping rada like Gamakul's vultures over the field of the dead.

The night was calm, solely traversed by the swarm of luminous flies tracing fantastic parabolas on the blue mantle of the sky. They were like other little stars of the Milky Way en route for infinity, the incessant rise of terrestrial souls toward an abode of repose and glory.

In her infantile belief in all the monsters of the Buddhist hells of the roruwa and the maha-dapha-narok, Kali-Yana thought that her wounded soul might soon be going thus into the azure abyss, not to be annihilated in the Nirvana of amour but to pass through the ordeals of the eight purgatories of the sassada, master of angels and humans, doctor of animals, who leads everyone, in accordance with their merits, toward the domain of his splendor.

She knew that she was about to commit a frightful action, which would soil the astral essence of her being for thousands of centuries, but she went on, impelled by an invincible force, a desire for murder stronger than her will and the eight hells of the Phakhava.

IV
Voluptuous Artifices

In the chamber of porcelain, nacre and ivory, Sayameda was delivering herself to the urgent cares of her women.

Entirely naked, she had just bathed her charming body in the milky water of a bath, and, still damp beneath the convergent rays of lamps, she was smiling at her image.

Phu, a negress whose nostrils were traversed by two turquoise studs, was opening little pots and bottles. With a silk tampon she spread a pale ocher cream over her mistress' cheeks, which, under the influence of heat, took on delightful lunar tones. She chose, on a thin brush, a little Japanese gold and cantharide green, which, extended over her lips and her nipples, became blood-red. She elongated the profound eyes, half-veiled by the expectation of the night of amour, moistened the eyelashes with Indian ink, made precious mixtures of the serkis of the harem, carthame and benzoin, rubbed, depilated, perfumed, and, finally content with her work, fell at Sayameda's feet.

"Now you are more adorable than the lotus of the pool of Xetuphon! You have no more to do than receive the pharang, little princess!"

"I lack my large necklace of aquamarines, the one that winds around my neck ten times and suspends between my breasts the luk-sakhot with the diamond pellets. The beloved has never seen such jewels, and my father Phaja-Tak gave them to me because I am the most beautiful."

"You know, dear Felicity, that that necklace brings bad luck? It would be better to throw it in the Me-Nam than to adorn your divine flesh with it!"

"Oh, I'm not superstitious. Such splendid adornments can't be maleficent. Gems give joy and constancy, and green stones are twice as agreeable to the gods. Go fetch me the luk-sakhot with the hundred and eight glaucous pearls and the seven diamonds."

The negress touched her forehead in a sign of obedience.

"Very well, Royal Star; let it be done as you desire."

The item of jewelry that Sayameda had demanded was truly unique in the world, with its aquamarines falling like lunar tears around seven diamonds of an improbable size. Sayameda let the necklace flow slowly through her fingers, enjoying the contact of the cold gems on her feverish skin; then she completed her costume of an exotic little lover with tufts of champak pinned over her ears, and a girdle of Mali flowers whose light clusters hung down to her knees.

"The pharang ought to be there . . ."

"Yes—go on tiptoe in order not to wake the talapoins," Phu recommended.

"As long as the new favorite Ajutana doesn't come to burn candles in golden takruts as she did the other night! We waited for an hour behind the jade Khatephra, under the great talapat."

"Oh, dear Delight what a risk you're taking, and for a foreigner too!"

"Certainly, Phu, but I love him. He knows such lovely things, and he murmurs them in such a sweet voice! No man here can be compared to him. And then, he has the seduction and the science of distant lands, in which woman is worshiped night and day like the lingam-yoni of Brahmanism. Accompany me as far as the little door to the Pagoda."

Gliding like an angel of death over the crystal surface of the sky, which, according to legend, extends all the way to the walls of the world, supported by the wind, Sayameda traversed the Mahaprasat, in which defunct kings were placed in golden urns, the great hall with gigantic granite statues in which the King gave his audiences in the presence of more than a hundred prostrate mandarins with their faces on the floor, and reached the secret entrance to the Pagoda.

Phu stopped on the sacred threshold, and Sayameda, having taken a few steps under the luminous vaults, fell into her lover's arms.

"Maxime!"

"Sayameda!"

The poor little amazon, huddled behind one of the terrible Buddhas on the pagoda, felt a red-hot iron claw in her breast. It seemed to her that her heart, gripped by pincers, contracted in an extraordinary dolor, in a mortal spasm. Her lover, her dear lover, was there with another, and saying to her, in the same soft lying voice, the tender words with which he had so often soothed her.

"Sayameda, let my lips linger on yours! Your mouth is perfumed like the golden fruit of the Chinese fig, your eyes are Kadanga flowers, you are as intoxicating as soran or the delicious juice of the homa. No woman has that slender and soft body . . . Oh, give me your lips . . ."

And the kisses extended, running in ardent pearls over the shoulders, the arms and the wrists of the living idol, half-swooning, unconscious of what was happening within her and around her.

The pharang lingered over the hiding places of sensuality, turning the brown doll over like a great child, curious and a little cruel. She was not more beautiful than Kali-Yana, but different, with mischievous gestures, ingenuous smiles, recoils and abandonments that the rada, more passionate, did not know. This one changed into the other, and in the arms of the princess, he thought nevertheless about the amorous warrior, thus deceiving them both, mutually, without malevolence, but with the unconsciousness of a handsome fellow accustomed to playing with women.

"Tell me again that you only love me! Tell me, in order that my sin should seem less heavy!"

And Maxime, who was searching in the kisses of his royal lover for the taste of Kali-Yana's kisses, repeated with a smile: "I love no one but you!"

"Swear it by the Samonakodom!"

"I swear it!"

"And put your lips on the luk-pat with the seven diamonds that shines between my breasts, in order never to forget your oath."

"What's the point, dear Delight? Our beliefs aren't the same. It's unnecessary to tempt rival gods."

"Only my belief is good."

But Maxime gave other proofs of his amour, and Kali-Yana, crawling on her hands and knees, drew nearer to the enlaced couple . . .

V
The Murder

A flash, a hoarse scream, and Sayameda's body rolled over the silver mats, soon changed into a crimson carpet. And while Maxime looked on, bewildered, the rada, bending down, seized the necklace of aquamarines and diamond pellets, and squeezed it with all her strength around the frail neck of the royal daughter.

The little princess was writhing in furious spasms, her eyes bulging, her hands clenched over her throat, trying, in a supreme effort, to break the necklace that was digging into her flesh. But when Maxime, recovered from his stupor, finally threw himself on the amazon, the glaucous gems scattered beneath his fingers, with the last gasp of his mistress.

The talapoins came running from all directions, frightened by the cries of agony. They seized the pharang and the amazon, took them to the hall of the Mahaprasat and sent for the Chao-Klein-balat, who, declaring himself incompetent, announced in his turn, with a thousand precautions, to Phaja-Tak that his daughter of election had just been murdered.

The King, enervated by the erudite hysterias of Ajutana, her complicated and corrosive philters, and her vehement caresses, nevertheless arrived in the presence of the guilty parties.

Maxime bowed his head, but the rada, shaken by a great frisson, sustained the Master's gaze.

"Yes," she said, "it was me, it was me who killed her."

"You!"

"Punish me, I deserve it."

Phaja-Tak, emerging from his sadistic dream, did not understand. His eyes troubled, his ideas confused, he said, in a soft voice: "Why have you committed this crime?"

But Kali-Yana, moved by a generous sentiment, did not want to betray the secret of the little princess. She replied, with a vague shake of the head: "I don't know . . ."

"And this one, what has he done?" The King pointed at Maxime.

The rada, still devoted, said: "He hasn't done anything."

"Why was he in the pagoda in the middle of the night?"

"He was doubtless locked in; he's a foreigner who doesn't know the customs of the land. Don't seek other guilty parties, Master; I struck in a moment of madness, a fit of fever, but my crime must be punished, and I'm ready for the expiation."

The talapoins, interrogated, could not furnish any further details of the crime. They had found the amazon leaning over Sayameda's body, still clutching the necklace of aquamarines, which the pharang was trying to tear away from her. The dagger that had served initially for the murder was similar to those that all the rada possessed.

Phaja-Tak, anxious, considered the guilty party, whom he found strangely desirable with her large passionate eyes and her erect breasts, florid with two golden corollas, of which the disturbed panung permitted the perception.

"You know," he said, "that you have merited death?"

"I know."

"The phras will choose the genre of torture that it is appropriate to inflict on you, for you have committed the most frightful of all crimes in killing my beloved daughter."

"I know."

Phaja-Tak gradually became animated as he spoke. A real indignation caused his voice to vibrate. He was no longer thinking about the rada's beauty, her luminous pale amber skin, and all the efflorescence of her charming body of a young warrior, apt for exercises of strength and suppleness.

"Take her away," he said to the talapoins. "Put a cangue on her, after giving her a hundred strokes of the lath. As for the pharang, since he hasn't done anything, you can let him go."

With a firm tread, Kali-Yana drew away, conducted by the Chao-Klein-balat, who wanted to recommend her to the executioners personally, in order that the accomplishment of the punishment would leave nothing to be desired.

Indecisively, Maxime followed her with an emotional gaze, and decided to beg for mercy, to attempt the impossible in order to soften the royal wrath. He prostrated himself before the Master, raised his hands above his head, and murmured a few words of pardon, but Phaja-Tak turned his back on him.

VI
The Embalming

The little princess is lying in the hall of the Mahaprasat, between the funereal urns of the ancient kings of Siam. For a few days she will be steeped in balms and perfumes. She will be passed through seven different emanations, until she is a state of complete immunity to putrescence. After the neroli, the myrrh and the oliban, the discreet and austere mystical fragrances, she will know the effluvia of the Takeoka, the Japanese Hovenia, the fragrant Olea and, finally, will delight in a precise effusion of balm of tuberose and Tonkin musk, with terrible and powerful odors. She will then become the color of a ripe lemon, and her flesh, in a perfect state of maceration, will adhere to her bones. She will be deposited, her knees having been drawn up to her chin and bound three times by a cord of wild jô, in a crystal urn, in which the little princesses, her sisters, will come to see her every morning, offering her lan-tam flowers while singing her praises to the accompaniment of the takhe, long guitars with metallic strings that are plucked with golden fingernails.

But the event is so singular that a sort of stupor still reigns over the court. Sayameda, in her tunic strung with sapphires and opals, is even prettier dead than alive. The strangulation only altered her delicate and voluptuous features momentarily. Phu, uttering the cries of a wounded beast, has repainted her lips, still swollen by amour, has touched up her carmine nostrils and the adorable shell of her ears with her carmine brush. A little crimson also animates the tips of her breasts, which seem still to be quivering with pleasure, swooning under the crepitant gems of necklaces. A serpent of sapphires is knotted tightly round her bruised neck, hiding the marks of death, and a takrut composed of forty-three leaves of gold hangs over her bosom.

Each of the princesses, in the presence of Phaja-Tak and all the prostrate mandarins, detaches one of the leaves of the takrut and passes it over the tongue of the dead woman, whose mouth is still open. Each one must say a prayer silently, which will be engraved on the precious leaf, and formulate three wishes, which will be realized between the day of the death and that of the funeral.

The eldest comes first, touches the ground before Sayameda's remains three times with her forehead, and then, delicately, slides the leaf of gold between the teeth of the corpse, seeking the tongue. A little blood foams at the edge of the lips, and runs down both sides of the chin. Ramada recoils, frightened, but the high priest of the talapoins wipes the scarlet foam away with a silk tampon, and Pudjalia, the second great princess, also comes to request the blessing of the deceased. The prayer-mills turn in the hands of the prostrate phra, the mourners sway gently, moaning, and the embalmers bustle around the flowers of the catafalque like bees around a hive.

Phaja-Tak, last of all, inclines his emerald scepter toward the murder victim, pronouncing the sacred words of the Traiphum. As is customary, there is the listing of the thirty-two parts of the human body, by which one reminds oneself of the instability of terrestrial things and the ultimate end . . .

The Chao-Klein-balat, who will later light the pyre of the royal deceased, replies to the Master with the enumeration of the divine qualities of the Buddha, who governs alone, in accordance with his will, the heavens, the earth and the eight principal hells, the lokanta-narok, the twenty orders of corporeal phrom, or mystics, and the souls of defunct little princesses.

VII
The Pagoda of Tortures

In front of the bamboo cage in which Kali-Yana has been imprisoned, Maxime is wandering sadly, having slipped past the executioners. The rada lost consciousness under the first blows of the lath, and has been thrown into her prison like a human rag, without any further attention being paid to her. Soon, when she opens her eyes again, she will be taken to the Red Pagoda, where the instruments of torture for use on the condemned are arranged.

Around the terrible idol of black granite there are pincers for tearing out the fingernails and the eyes, irons with which to frill the flesh like the collars of clowns, scissors that cut out the frayed petals of orchids and tuberoses on the abdomen and thighs, combs with twenty razor-sharp teeth with which to rake the skin, carving out shallow grooves into which boiling oil will be poured, drop by drop. There are wooden sticks that are slid between the phalanges of the fingers and toes in order to disarticulate them and rip them away; cangues furnished with nails that only allow the head to pass through; enormous spikes for fixing the hands and feet to planks that are violently separated;

boxes equipped with a few holes in which the condemned individual, folded up, dies of hunger without being able to stand up or turn round; impaling spikes on which men whirl like gigantic vertiginous tops.

There are more than a hundred complicated and bizarre items of apparatus, to which muscles and bodily fluids are still adhering; as in the charnel-house of the vultures, a sickening odor of death reigns in the Red Pagoda.

The condemned await the final torture in narrow bamboo cages. They suffer from hunger and thirst; their limbs sink into fetid mud; naked, shivering and fleshless, the healthiest rub their ulcers against the bars, imploring the charity of passers-by in a moaning voice.

The tormentors are incessantly occupied in some new torture, sharpening their instruments and pouring coconut-oil over their muscular arms, numbed by effort. A few victims are swinging, suspended by one foot or one hand, others are rotating at the end of a rope whose iron crampons harpoon their kidneys. Women astride spikes, which are tearing them profoundly, no longer make any sound but an intermittent plaint, tipping back their exsanguinated heads with revulsed pupils. The executioners are amusing themselves sticking flowers in the flesh of a young woman, and the blood, mingling with the corollas, tints the white petals of champak and mali pink.

Here, an accused has been forced into a box whose upper part, composed of two planks, is equipped with sharp spikes that only let the head pass through, the man is not suspended if he can remain on tiptoe, but if he relaxes, the spikes enter into his throat.

Over all of that, the martyrs of impalement spin, whom the tormentors activate with their iron rod. From a distance they seem to be turning at the whim of the wind, like the light paper windmills of which children are fond. Captive balloons, brightly-colored kites, painted talapats of courtesans, fireworks and floating banners, at a certain distance from the field of anguish the impaled resemble the site of a fairground.

Phaja-Tak is not cruel, but the talapoins, on the advice of Chakri, avid to reign in his turn, have poured him the philter of dementia, and his sadism finishes in tears and blood. These tortures, once unknown to the Thais, come from the Celestial Empire, where twisted souls take pleasure in the games of lust and death.

Having given a few silver beads to the guards of the Red Pagoda, Maxime has been able to slip next to Kali-Yana. He contemplates her, very frail in her filthy prison, and he would sacrifice the best years of his life in order to open that door of infamy. His pride is delectably flattered by the rada's crime, which only a fit of amorous folly could have provoked. His skepticism capitulates before that supreme proof of amour; he is certain now that the amazon loved him recklessly, and he compares that sublime passion with the pale marks of interest that his other mistresses have given him. His admiration for this one is so complete that he almost forgets the death of Sayameda, the royal lover whose august virginity he plundered.

"Kali-Yana!" he sighs, caressing the naked shoulder of the rada with a trembling hand.

At that cherished voice, she opens her eyes.

"Maxime!"

She has raised herself up in that cry of amour, and, of all the sufferings she has endured, she no longer feels any except her jealous dread. Her large gold-flecked red onyx eyes open immeasurably, as if to fill themselves with the adorable vision.

"Maxime!" she repeats, in a sob. "Can you ever forgive me for my crime?"

"I've forgotten it, and I love you."

"You still love me?"

"I love you more than in the past, dear Delight! I love you as I have never loved, for in the creature of amour I discover more than a lover, a soul!"

"Is that possible?"

She extends her chained arms toward him, passing her little bruised hands through the bars, which he covers in kisses.

"Kali-Yana, for me you were only a doll like the others, a charming and fragile plaything, which I caressed with a distracted hand. I only supposed you to have the feeble and vainglorious intelligence of a pretty amorous girl, and I thought that after me you'd cajole others with the same velvet gestures and the same attractive voice."

"You thought that?"

"Yes, I thought that you were only a delightful flower whose corolla would open for anyone, and that after the butterfly from a distant land, other butterflies would come to drink the nectar of your beauty."

"You were wicked!"

"I have been wicked, because I did not understand your heart. If you knew, dear Smile, how light, unconscious and cruel women are! They all think of nothing but the pleasure of adorning themselves in order to be desirable. The quality of the incense that is distributed to them matters little, provided that it is abundant!"

"Truly, are they all like that?"

"Yes, all of them; and I thought that, like them, you were frivolous, forgetful and coquettish. I no longer loved you, because I thought I knew you, and my imbecilic pride floated above your delicate suffering . . ."

"Oh, my love . . . !"

"Kali-Yana, nothing henceforth will be able to expel you from my life. You are my wealth, my wife, my treasure, the only being I adore!"

As the anxious guards drew closer to them, the rada murmured, in a tremulous voice: "It's necessary for us to part, my cherished lover. I shall die joyful, since you have forgiven me and that your heart has returned to me."

"I don't want you to die."

"Only a miracle can save me."

"I shall accomplish that miracle."

"After the crime that I have committed, even the most frightful tortures will appear too lenient."

"I'll cover your executioners with gold."

"The King is richer than you."

"I'll dethrone the King!"

"No, no, he's my venerated Master, and I shall serve him meekly until the end."

"What! In spite of our amour!"

"My amour is above suffering and death. It will be sweet for me to expire for you, for it is uniquely my immense tenderness that led me to murder. It is only just, you see, that every sin ought to be expiated. I have dipped my hands in the blood of an innocent, and I merit the punishment."

"I will surrender myself in your place, for I am more culpable than you! My treachery has killed Sayameda, and I provoked your jealous indignation. Without me, you would not have known evil . . ."

"Perhaps . . ."

"You see that it is necessary that I expiate in your stead, since the veritable murderer is me."

With her feverish little hands, Kali-Yana seized her lover's hands, and bore them delightfully to her lips.

"Oh, how much good you're doing me! I'm happy, Maxime, very happy, and I couldn't wish for a more adorable agony! My sole desire, now, is to go into that extraordinary dream, to reach the celestial Nirvana on the wings of this incomparable felicity! You see, the claws can only tear my flesh and even if the pincers delve all the way to my heart, they will do me no more harm than the stem of a wild flower. The martyrdom of amour metamorphoses dolor into a voluptuous spasm."

"Dear Kali-Yana!"

"Have no fear for me; I love you too much to suffer!"

VIII
The Tortured

Executioners who were taking away a woman whose skin, carved all the way to the loins, was swollen into a girdle of bloody ribbons, told Maxime to leave; but the latter, having no more money, offered them his watch and a gold chain.

The tormentors smiled, and, to thank the pharang, obliged the torture victim to dance in her crimson tunic of living flesh. As she howled incessantly, in furious convulsions, they struck her with their laths and she fell down on her knees, extended her arms in one last gesture of defense, and rendered her soul.

Kali-Yana recognized then the old woman who had sustained her on the day of the death of Suk and Gamakul. Doubtless she had been found among the rebels and had been condemned to torture, like the others, in order to oblige her to reveal the names of the ringleaders.

The rada's strength was exhausted.

"Don't worry," she said to Maxime. "I sense that I shall die before the expiation. If only I could kiss you again!"

"I'll come back tonight!"

"They won't let you in."

"Bah! With gold one can do anything."

"But I won't be able to quit my prison."

"You'll quit it, and you'll flee before daybreak."

"I'll flee?"

"Yes, you'll depart for distant shores where I have relatives and friends. You'll take refuge with them, and await my return."

"Alas," she said, "I won't have the strength to flee. Look, my limbs have profound wounds, and I've been undermined by fever for a week."

"You'll think about the happy existence that awaits us, and you'll draw from the hope of that blessed moment the energy necessary for your escape. My ship will soon be returning to France; I've accomplished my mission, and we won't be separated again."

"Oh, my adored!"

So much emotion had exhausted the young woman; her stiffened fingers, which were gripping Maxime's hand, suddenly opened, and she fell backwards, unconscious again.

"A little water!" implored the pharang. "It's necessary to help this child!"

The tormentor who was passing by shrugged his shoulders. "She'll see many others. Better if she dies in her faint."

"You intend, then, to subject her to all the tortures of this hell?"

The man sniggered. "Perhaps she won't have the strength to get through the first ordeal. It's a dying woman that they've delivered to us."

"Spare her, then."

"We've received precise orders in her regard. She's committed the greatest of crimes."

"She acted in a fit of fever, under the influence of delirium; she isn't guilty, but unconscious."

"Try to obtain mercy for her then. We can only obey, for we're the servants of the law."

"All right," said Maxime. "I'll see what I can do." And, darting a last glance at the young woman, he left the Pagoda of tortures.

IX
The Golden Candles

Meanwhile, the rada had received the frightful news, and they were desolate at the idea that one of their own was about to be subjected to infamous punishment. Xali had already slipped out of the palace wearing a panung of dark wool and a thick serki, a flap of which hid her face. But it was difficult for women to enter the Red Pagoda without special authorization, and she did not want to betray her presence.

A merchant of candles and takruts, who was passing by, furnished her with the opportunity that she was seeking.

"Woman," said the young woman, "will you cede me your fetishes and amulets in order that I can sell them in the pagoda?"

The merchant's eyes glinted. "That depends on the price, child. I have silver luk-sakhots and coral luk-pats, not to mention my candles, which are covered in the thin metal sheets of the Phra Chao Xang Phuok."

"I'll buy your golden candles and everything you possess." And the rada gave the woman her weapons, the rings from her arms and legs, and her necklaces.

The woman laughed, in satisfaction. "You can say, child, that you're my niece and that you're replacing me because I'm ill."

Xali has installed herself at the foot of a terrible idol, whose eight arms are extended in a gesture of eternal malediction, and she has ranged all her fateful objects on a mat in front of her.

Already, the relatives of torture-victims have bought candles, agreeable to the phi and all the spirits of the Mountain of Fire who watch over those condemned to death.

Odorous candles, the tears of which run over the flowers and precious mats, are burning next to the divinities. Hundreds of disparate objects are suspended from the cords that go from one column to another. There are crude dolls clad in scraps of silk, metal statuettes, delicately embroidered fabrics, girdles and pectorals with cabochons of glaucous gems, hanks of the hair of torture-victims woven with pearls, rosaries of human phalanges, and figurines fabricated with the agglomerated ashes of pyres. On amber and jade trays, there are also fruits, flower preserves, dried fish and bottles of eau-de-vie, of arak, meng-lak, cumin and palm, sesame cakes, virgin lotuses and turmeric, and then, in saurit jars, the pink lime that is mixed with betel.

The Pagoda of Tortures contains on the one hand, the instruments of death, and on the other, everything that ought to calm the anger of malevolent spirits whose claws, by night, bloody the walls of prisons; for the powers of air and fire suspend themselves by the fingernails in accursed places and hang motionless like enormous vampires.

Intoxicated by anxiety, perfumes and fatigue, Xali sensed that her reason was evaporating like the light smoke of cassolettes; her hand extended in an unconscious gesture to receive the price of fetishes and shiny candles. She was waiting for nightfall in order to search the court of tortures for the bamboo cage in which her friend was agonizing.

Every time the door of the pagoda opened she put all her heart into the anguished gaze that searched the sunlit area. The cries of the victims arrived more distinctly then, along with the click of laths on lacerated backs and the grating of pulleys making the lamentable human rags twirl like leaves in the wind.

In one profound groan she seemed to recognize the voice of Kali-Yana, and it required an extraordinary courage for her not to throw herself forward to help her beloved, or to offer to share her martyrdom.

More feverishly, she murmured to a young woman who was passing: "Adunaduang, buy my beautiful golden candles, and you'll be saved by amour!"

She did not know what she was saying, but the sale of the poor objects generated activity around the idol with the eight menacing arms; the entire pagoda scintillated under the flames of the candles, the tears of which fell incessantly, like a dolorous and burning dew.

X
Escape Attempt

"Give me incense and betel, young seller."

That is Maxime, who has been multiplying himself since morning, imploring mercy for the rada, and, without being discouraged, using all his influences. But Kali-Yana's crime is without excuse; nothing can absolve her, and Thai justice will follow its course.

"Young seller, give me arak and opium; I want to intoxicate myself until death!"

Xali turns her troubled gaze toward the pharang.

"Do you have a friend who is about to perish?" she asks, in a bland voice. "You're enfevered and you want to forget?"

"Yes, the torment of my soul makes me desire to be clawed by the executioners. Those who suffer in their flesh are perhaps less unhappy than those who suffer in their tenderness."

"Is it a brother, a father of a wife for whom you're weeping?"

"It's the most adorable of mistresses, the one for whom amour alone put a weapon in her hand, the one who killed the royal daughter."

Xali utters a cry and seizes the pharang's arm. "You've come for Kali-Yana?"

A sudden anger makes the rada tremble; she raises her quivering fists in order to punish the perfidious lover, but another thought soon calms her features.

"Listen," she said. "All the evil has come about by your fault, and no chastisement would be cruel enough to punish you."

"I know that," Maxime replied, lowering his eyes.

"In her delirium, Kali-Yana talked. I was beside her, and I know your hypocrisies, your lies and the insulting ingratitude with which you repaid her!"

"I confess my sins."

"It isn't my companion who killed Samayeda, it's you. It isn't the executioner who will kill Kali-Yana, it's you again."

"I'm ready to do anything to redeem my crimes. What can I do?"

"I don't know. Let's wait, and search together. When night falls, we'll act."

"Yes, we'll join forces to save the rada."

"I have philters, liquors of soran and opium."

"I have gold."

The door of the pagoda opened under an abrupt push, and a rain of blood spurted on to the steps, splashing Maxime and Xali.

Men with lacerated flesh, muscles laid bare, hurtled out, seeking a refuge behind the idols. The tormentors, red thongs in hand, followed them, vociferating. There was a furious melee; the gods rolled from their pedestals, the candles, overturned, set fire to the mats and the precious fabrics.

In the furnace, the combatants sought one another, seized one another, dug their fingernails into one another's flesh; under the red light, the lake of blood spread among the flowers, the perfumes and the sputtering candles.

"Come on! Come on!"

And Xali, taking Maxime by the hand, dragged him into the courtyard of the condemned, where the bamboo cages had opened. Many cadavers had been extracted from their prison and the vultures of the neighboring pagoda were circling over the dead and dying, sometimes taking the risk of carrying away a scrap of flesh, a woman's breast, or digging into an orbit in order to pluck out an eye.

"This is it," said Maxime, stopping in front of Kali-Yana's cage. The amazon, curled up, seemed to be asleep, but new wounds attested that blows of the lath had not been spared; a bloody dew was falling around her, and a continuous tremor was agitating her limbs.

"Kali-Yana! Dear Smile!"

She did not seem to hear; her eyelids remained closed.

"Speak to her in your turn, she'll respond to you."

"My Beloved!" murmured Maxime.

Immediately, the rada stiffened more forcefully, and a gleam of joy opened her eyes slightly.

"You see," said Xali, "amour is stronger than friendship; your voice has accomplished the miracle. Stay with her; I'll inspect the surroundings."

Night was falling rapidly; the luminous flies were extending their golden network over the sky, still punctured by the somber flight of the vultures.

On the steps of the pagoda in flames, the executioners were jostling one another, trying to save the treasures of the interior: the precious statuettes, the silver mats, the fabrics embroidered with fine pearls. The moment might be favorable for an escape. Xali returned to the two lovers.

"Quickly, quickly, we have to flee! Let's unite our efforts to free Kali-Yana!"

They shook the wooden bars, and succeeded in wrenching away two of them, uncovering a space wide enough to draw the amazon's slender body through. She was soon in their arms, laughing and weeping, but so weak that she would have fallen without the aid of her friends.

"Here, take my panung, hide your face with this thick veil."

They drew her away, under the avid gaze of prisoners who implored them, weeping.

"Come on! Come on!"

They paddled through blood, driving away the birds that barred their passage. But a heap of bodies stopped them. The tormentors, surprised by the fire, had not finished their task, and the torture-victims, mouths open in a last scream, limbs torn away, abdomens excavated by iron instruments, were lying pell-mell.

Maxime tried to push the bodies away, but they were too numerous, falling upon one another like dislocated puppets, sometimes losing an arm or a leg, or letting intestines flow out of their ruptured bellies.

The young man then took Kali-Yana on his shoulders, scaled the wall of flesh, and recommenced his course between the little cages where the misery and agony of more than a thousand victims were sobbing. In his emotion, he went astray, unable to find a liberating door in the midst of the sinister corridors, and Xali, who was running out of breath behind him, also lost her head.

Finally, he stopped.

"We'll never get out!"

"Perhaps it's necessary to go through the pagoda," Xali groaned. "I don't think there's another exit."

"The pagoda's in flames!"

"What shall we do?"

"Well, child, search, keep searching. There must be a door at the end of this wall. Go, I'll wait for you here. Go! Hurry up, the moments are counted!"

Xali drew away, slipping in the sticky pools, holding on to bodies, and the horrible breath of the starving, passing over her face, made her feel faint. Cries, insults, mad laughter and anguished gasps rose up around her. Large red disks passed before her eyes, widened by fear, and her temples were throbbing with a feverish tocsin.

Women extended clenched hands with menacing fingernails toward her; some, picking up the noxious litter of their jail, threw it in her face with the convulsions of she-wolves.

And the howling cages succeeded one another; the hell had no issue, it seemed.

Only the furnace of the pagoda opened its formidable mouth in the night.

Xali went back, and sobbed: "I haven't found anything!"

"Let's go into the flames, then."

"Oh, yes! Anything rather than this frightful vision!"

The fever of the danger had given some strength to Kali-Yana. Maxime and Xali put her between them and, each putting an arm around her waist, drew her toward the pagoda.

There was now the region of impalements, where the forgotten dead, fixed to their sinister poles, resembled torn flags after a battle. In a flamboyant apotheosis, the human rags were magnified, reaching the sky, and the obstinate vultures made them quivering wings of darkness.

Men with red arms emerged from the fire, carrying figurines of crystal and jade, delicate objects that they placed on the ground in order to try to save other riches. They did not pay any attention to the fugitives, who were able to emerge under the crackling vaults; but the heat was so frightful that they were obliged to recoil, also suffocated by the thick smoke. Three times they renewed their attempt, with no more success. Only the tormentors, accustomed to the acrid emanations of pyres, were able to confront the bite of the flames.

But the walls were cracking; an entire sheet of the roof collapsed, and tongues of fire sprang toward the sky with such impetuosity that the entire night was illuminated by them.

"Let's wait," said Xali. "We'll pass over the debris; before daylight the walls will have collapsed."

"Yes, we'll see."

"Let's hide in the alleyways."

The howls redoubled; a furious madness pressed the condemned against the bars, which their feeble hands tried in vain to break.

Suddenly, a guard went past the fugitives.

"The rada has escaped!" he shouted.

Other men came running.

"A prisoner has gone?"

"The one who killed the royal daughter?"

"Yes, her cage is empty. But the bird can't have flown very far."

Kali-Yana uttered a sigh and fainted, while the executioners pushed Maxime away.

Xali had an inspiration then.

"I'm the one you're searching for!" she said.

"You're the rada of the palace guard?"

"Yes, I killed Sayameda, Phaja-Tak's beloved daughter."

The emotional pharang had clasped Kali-Yana to his heart again.

"And these?"

"I don't know them."

"What are they doing in the Pagoda of Tortures? No one can get into it by night."

As Maxime remained silent, Xali murmured: "Visitors gone astray, no doubt—the fire took hold so suddenly."

Already, two of the guards had bound the young woman's wrists, and were shoving her brutally toward a vacant cage with solid bars. They passed her head into a cangue and attached her by the ankle, in such a way that any escape became impossible.

In spite of the resistance and supplications of Maxime, Kali-Yana was also imprisoned, but in a more spacious jail, and as she remained inert, the executioners, sniggering, authorized the pharang to share her captivity in order to recall her to life with warm caresses.

XI
The King

Maxime, however, was liberated the next day, the government being apprehensive of discontenting a friendly power. The officer was now traveling through the popular quarters where sedition against the King had been whispered in the miserable huts for a long time. He was gliding along the canals in the boat that had so often conducted him to his amours; as before, he glimpsed the glittering dome of the pagoda of Borovanivet and the spires of the temples of Xetuphon, where the great golden Buddha reposed, which no one could contemplate without shuddering, and, dominating the river, the gibbosity of the royal palace, covered with towers, terraces, perforated arcades like precious guipures, and columns with a cladding of fulgurant gems.

But the magical vision vanished at times. He slid between narrow and dirty banks, crowded with a ragged, leprous population. Over the tangled canals there were projecting balconies in planks painted ocher and cinnabar, with a perspective of rickety staircases leading up to unequal openings of doors and windows, obscure passages sometimes putting holes in luminous distances.

The open-air merchants were offering, in high-pitched voices, dried fish and reeking crayfish spawn, iridescent mengdana, freshwater hoi-khong, golden and silver sua woven by women, honey of mali and phut—for bees can be trained only to take nectar from one kind of flower—wasps' nests, water-chestnuts with spiny shells, meng-lak, sesame pomades and coriander oil.

But the turbulent population was scarcely buying, gained by a new fever, and orators hoisted on the pedestals of idols and granite monsters were continuing Gamakul's work. Maxime had put his last hope in the toppling of Phaja-Tak, and he wanted to take account for himself of the state of minds. If the King were dethroned the prisons would be opened, and Xali and Kali-Yana would be saved.

In the morning, when he was set at liberty, he had requested an audience with the Master and had implored him at length. When he received him, Phaja-Tak had emerged from the gynaeceum, divined by the cooing of women in the depths of mysterious galleries. His Majesty had gone through large halls with gigantic frescoes on sheets of enamel tiles, and had abruptly presented himself before the pharang in his garments of precious stones, disturbed by the impetuosity of Ajutana's recent embraces.

"What do you want with me?"

"I've come to implore mercy for the rada."

And, suppressing his pride, Maxime had touched the ground three times with his forehead.

"You know very well that I can do nothing for you. In any case, what does the life of a little amazon matter to you?"

"She's innocent. It was me who struck the royal daughter."

"You? Get away! For what motive would you have committed that crime?"

"I loved Samayeda, and, not being able to possess her, I killed her in a moment of amorous folly."

"You're lying. The weapon that was used belonged to the amazon."

"I had stolen it from her."

Motionless, Phaja-Take appeared to reflect.

"Listen," he said. "I can't grant the killer mercy, but I'll spare her the torture. She'll be decapitated in the royal square, before the people, to set an example. As for you, I know full well that you didn't commit that abominable murder. In any case, as a Frenchman, you're sacred to me. Go away!"

XII
The People

And Maxime had gone. At hazard, he had roamed the city, knowing that Chakri, supported by the mandarins, was stirring up the poor quarters. Since the famous sortie of the elephants, which had claimed a thousand victims, the mob, seemingly calmed, had been growling dully. As the pharang passed by, before the idols and granite lingams at the street corners, menacing fists were waved at him; there was every reason to fear of a further revolt. Country dwellers with hollow cheeks and bloodshot gazes, fired up by famine and ill-treatment, were arriving in wretched junks; drunkards were rolling into the Me-Nam, chased by naked women who had recognized them as soldiers of the king; and takhe players, as they strummed the metal strings with their long golden fingernails, were singing obscene songs that insulted the ruling power.

All of them who had weapons, krises dipped in cobra venom, pikes or javelins, gathered at crossroads around orators whose words rose up wildly. What enraged them, above all, was the oppression they had suffered, the injustice of the laws, excessive taxes augmenting from one week to the next without any reason. And the cup of indignation had overflowed during the funerals of the latest favorites, immolated during a night of lust and blood. They knew that the entire Thai nation would support them, weary of a reign so contrary to its traditions of justice and mildness, and the opulent families whose children Phaja-Tak was murdering were finally in revolt.

For it was not only the people who were insurgent, but the rich and the powerful, coming from all the provinces, led by Chakri, who was ambitious for the scepter. Former warriors had armed their elephants, hung their javelins and their daggers from the howdahs, mounted banners on their lances, and were traveling the banks of the Me-Nam with menaces.

Maxime advanced with difficulties in the midst of junks that were ever more crowded, shouting encouragements to the oarsmen, haranguing the crowd, and the women laughed at the pharang, whose handsome face charmed them. A few proposed to set him at the head of the rebels, offering to carry him in triumph on their shoulders with necklaces of amber and coral . . .

Alongside the Pagoda of Tortures, other houses had caught fire; the air reeked of burned things and flames were still running in capricious crests along bamboo constructions that no one was trying to preserve.

Maxime continued advancing through the poor quarters, where a swarming population drunk on arak and opium was vociferating.

The savage blood of the Lao and the Birmans reawakened. The Lao-Phugdam—"black bellies"—took off their langoutis to display the warrior tattoos on their thighs. There were inhabitants of Xieng-Mai there who wore amulets depicting tigers and lions, children of Laphun and Lakhon the color of sapan or ayu sumac, others from Muang-Phre and Muang-Snan, who were known as "white bellies" because they did not tattoo themselves. Inhabitants of Muang-Lakhon were joined by aboriginal tribes that lived in the impenetrable forests and on the shores of crocodile-infested lakes. From Tringanu, Kalantan, Patani and Quedah, yellow men with hooded eyes, big noses and wide mouths disfigured by black teeth were also arriving. Their long, straight, coarse hair was retained on the summit of the head by a silver or copper dart. They were playing dice on the thresholds of houses and sometimes showing oval coins of impure metal or a few small round coins.

Talapoins were circulating, almost all favorable to the mob. A few were offering lan leaves on which they had written revolutionary maxims with a golden stylet. The most zealous were striking rattles of sonorous wood in cadence and proclaiming the will of the Kha te phra.

And the junks were depositing along the quays, continuously, men from Xieng-Mai, Laphun, Lakhon, Phre, Nan, Luang-Phra-Bang and Muang-Lom.

Sometimes, quarrels burst out; the strongest struck old women and impotent phra with blows of pikes and clubs; the lamentations of the wounded rose up along the river under the huge red sun, consuming the vegetation with an indelible rust of chrome and cinnabar. Bodies were swarming on the steps of terraces; thin trickles of blood were sliding into the muddy water. Everywhere, the people were being drawn to the revolt.

Slightly less anxious, Maxime returned to the Pagoda of Tortures, hoping that he would be allowed to go in for the price of a few gold baht; but the wall, reduced to ashes, had been replaced by a high balustrade of bamboo, and guards were on watch every ten paces.

All day long the pharang wandered around the garden of tortures, in the midst of the plaints of the agonizing. Nearby, sometimes, brains splashed the walls, heads rolled, the eyes filled with a supreme terror.

A few women, their hands bound, came to rub their backs against the bars of the enclosure in order to cause the darts that pierced their flesh to fall out; others agitated their fingers from which the fingernails had been torn out, or shook scalped heads from which the blood, falling in warm cascades, blinded them.

At dusk, Maxime, drunk with horror, went away. He had only learned that the rada's execution would take place the following day, in the royal square.

XIII
The Execution

Xali had not been able to see Kali-Yana again, but her torture had been sweet for her, for she thought that her companion, thanks to her devotion, might have been able to escape and follow Maxime to some peaceful retreat.

Kali-Yana, for her part, was unaware of Xali's sacrifice; in any case, her weakness was so great that she was living in a kind of morbid dream. At moments of fever, however, a furious tremor agitated all her limbs, delirium succeeded prostration and her unconscious dolor was exhaled in incoherent phrases, passing from tenderness to hatred, and from prayer to rage.

On the morning of the third day, the bells and gongs announced the public execution. Xali was taken out of her bamboo cage in order to dress her in a black panung and conduct her in great pomp to the royal square, for her crime was not one of those that was expiated in darkness,

Again, Xali offered that martyrdom to the one that she had not ceased to cherish, and wished, with all the force of her poor crucified heart, that her friend would be happy next to the pale face.

As she had not been put to the torture her march was firm; she emerged between the executioners, six in number, clad in scarlet. Her head was placed in a cangue, and her hands were bound.

There was a precipitate gallop, soldiers overflowed from the palace, with the amazons at the head, and the entire cortege traversed the city before heading for the place of execution where Kali-Yana's frightful crime was inscribed in red letters on a high platform.

The procession of mandarins gathered, facing that of the talapoins crowned with foliage, who were waving lan-tam flowers on the end of long golden reeds.

The princesses had not wanted to watch the execution, preferring to remain at prayer next to Sayameda's remains, which had been deposited in the crystal urn, where she would be soaked in balms.

At the place of execution, Xali finally perceived Maxime, who, at the cost of a thousand efforts, had pierced the crowd to arrive close to her.

"Xali! Xali!" he murmured.

She made a movement of her lips, which signified: "Shh! For you I'm Kali-Yana!"

Then, her large tender eyes interrogated those of the young man, and he understood, too, that she was recommending him to be good to the person that she loved more than anything, and that she wanted him never to abandon her.

"Where is she?"

And he, in order to give her that supreme satisfaction, said the single word for which she was waiting, trembling with anguish.

"Safe."

Immediately, she seemed reassured and joyful; she knelt down in order that the cangue could be removed and allowed her hair to be cut.

The Chao-Klein-balat kneaded clay, blocked her ears and nostrils with it, and put a golden takrut on her tongue. The six executioners came forward, armed with sabers, and the first severed her head with a single blow.

But the ceremony was not concluded; it was a matter of butchering the body for the vultures, for incineration was not carried out on criminals.

Talapoins appeared, armed with sharp instruments, and while the Chao-Klein-balat threw Xali's head to the people, ten arms fell upon her virginal body, cutting, carving and sawing with a feverish activity.

At that moment there was a bristling of pikes and javelins, a reckless revolt of wild beasts, which the soldiers, not having received orders, repelled brutally. The ground shook under the feet of combatants who were traversing the Me-Nam, ever more numerous.

One man fixed Xali's bloody head, whose wide-open eyes seemed to be demanding vengeance, to the end of a pike, and then a terrible cry resounded:

"To the palace! To the palace!"

XIV
The Massacre

Maddened by blood, the rebels broke the idols, the lingams of onyx and jade, and in spite of the resistance of the soldiers, the amazons and the talapoins of the Royal Pagoda, they penetrated into the courtyards and the gardens. All the slaves they encountered were killed, as well as the huge domesticated lions, astonished by that wild invasion. Men were lying on the ground face down, the napes of their necks slashed; some were begging for mercy, others retaining their entrails, which were spilling out of their gashed bellies, grinding their teeth and making futile efforts to stand up.

The elephants, as tall as towers, emerged from their stables, but their cornacs had been massacred, with the consequence that they were wandering at random, inoffensive henceforth. They were employed in demplishing light constructions, the kiosks of the magical garden which was now sticky with blood everywhere. In an ever-increasing vertigo, the rebels climbed up to the terraces where the faces of women appeared; sobs emerged from the gynaeceum, for it was said that Phja-Tak had locked himself in with Ajutana, his latest favorite.

The King, affirmed a slave, who was being prompted with saber thrusts, was weakened and maddened by nights of lust, and the cries of revolt had reached him as in a dream, without precise significance. They would capture him easily with the aid of the mandarins; it was sufficient to want to do it.

There was a stampede; the heads of amazons emerged in the courtyards; the young women threw themselves on the assailants, and fought like lionesses, but their number was insufficient, and, in spite of their courage, they were obliged to capitulate. They were torn from their saddles and the people, laughing, undressed them and raped them, living or dead. Then a Laotian took possession of the scarlet flag, fixed Xali's head to it, from which blood was still trickling feebly, and, as the rada's eyes had a terrifying expression, he gouged them out, in order that there would be two red holes instead of the tragic pupils.

"To the palace! To the palace!"

The crowd jostled along the porcelain stairways, tipping over the monsters that garnished them from top to bottom. In the great Pagoda, the golden Buddhas were plucked from their lotus leaves, and the silver mats were swept away as if by a tempest.

The first besiegers reached the Mahaprasat, whose four facades, covered in mirrors, were sparkling in the red sunlight. In the great silent hall where the princesses were weeping next to their dead sister, the Thai women recoiled, but Patanians drunk on arak smashed the crystal urn and took out Sayameda's body, which they waved above their heads like a precious trophy.

Thus, they traversed the galleries bordered by gigantic granite statues brought from China, the hall of the throne, which, with its seven-tier awning, presented the form of an altar, and, after having disemboweled a few slaves who opposed their passage, they forced the doors of the royal apartment.

But the sumptuous rooms were empty. Without difficulty, the most avid took possession of treasures of silver, gold and precious stones; young women draped themselves in spangled and gem-studded silks, threw velvet copes indurated with cabochons of amethysts and topazes over their shoulders, and passed heavy strings of scintillating stones around their necks.

The King's children appeared, with fearful gestures, but the women caressed them, finding them pretty under their crowns of mali, their golden rings and the little sapphire diadems surrounding the curly tufts on their heads.

Bronze Buddhas and perfume-burners depicting dragons and chimeras were gleaming everywhere; crimson cushions fell on to carpets with designs of fantastic beasts, and on the porcelain walls gigantic painted vegetations attained skies of lapis lazuli and turquoise. Veils spangled with silver falling over the doorways stirred in the breath of that invasion, and the first to arrive, with cries of delight, unhooked Asiatic weapons whose blades expanded like comets' tails.

A door opened to a sumptuous redoubt with a ceiling in a cupola, terminated by an oval aperture, into which the sky put an azure eye. On a golden altar, constellated with sardonyxes, chrysoberyls and unvarovites, a diamond pedestal brighter than the sun supported a giant lingam crowned with flowers. All around, low divans awaited the Master's pleasure, for it was there that Phaja-Tak passed the most voluptuous hours of his nights, listening to the distant sound of takhes and gazing through glass partitions at the lascivious gestures of his two hundred dancers.

The chapel of amour was empty, but women showed one another indignantly the bloody stains on the silver mats, and singular instruments encrusted with rare gems in golden cases.

"Where is he? Where is he?" cried the men, brandishing the weapons snatched from the trophies.

"In the harem!" gurgled an old woman with black teeth. "Let's break down the partitions!"

With the blows of clubs they shattered the glass walls, precipitated into an apartment where girls between eight and thirteen years of age, almost naked, were fleeing in all directions, taking refuge on spiral staircases, behind columns and in perforated niches of nacre and ivory.

"The King! The King!" howled the crowd.

A curtain drew aside and, resplendent with jewels, with a headband of pearls over her thick hair, raised up in a volute, Ajutana appeared.

Slowly, her head held high, she advanced, and, fixing her eyes of a female wild beast on the rebels, she demanded: "If I deliver the King to you, what will you give me?"

She confronted them all, arrogant and disdainful.

"What will you give me?" she repeated, in the astonished silence that followed her advent.

"What do you want from us?" demanded a Laotian, sniggering. "We can only offer you our amour, for we have no money."

She shrugged her shoulders. "You can demand from Chakri, who already governs you, the liberty of my father, whom the King has taken prisoner."

"Certainly, your demand is just."

She smiled mysteriously. "Chakri has promised, like you, but I know what the word of the powerful of this world is worth. You, at least, will remember, for your interest is not at stake."

"We'll remember, Ajutana," said a talapoin from the Pagoda of Xetuphon. "Deliver your royal husband to us."

"My father," she said, "sought refuge with the governor of Patawi, but he was denounced and thrown in a dungeon, while my brothers and my sisters were murdered. I hate Phaja-Tak, who was our executioner, and I abandon him to you."

She lifted the curtain again, and showed them the King, who was sprawled on cushions, drunk on soran and opium, fast asleep.

A sword was brandished; the body, after a few somersaults, remained motionless, the head only attached to the body by a strip of flesh.

Soon, the body of the King, under his diamond clasps and his emerald pectorals, was dragged through the palace and thrown down to the square from the height of the grand terrace, with the embalmed body of Sayameda, his cherished daughter. An entire howling people was waiting for that prey, lifting arms still red with the blood of slaves, soldiers and amazons, killed in the courtyards or tied up two by two in the path of elephants, which crushed their skulls.

The bodies spun, rebounding from the projections of glass and jade of the lower floors, and then flattened on the ground like rags, while the detached head of the King bounced in a red flood. But the talapoins surrounded the cadavers, threw a somber veil over them, declaring that they belonged to the pyre, and that a splendid funeral would be accorded to them after an eight-month sojourn in the urns of the Mahaprasat.

Chakri, who was only waiting for that moment to show himself to the people, appeared on the terrace in his turn, and a formidable acclamation saluted the dawn of his reign.

XV
The Last Vision

"To the prisons! To the prisons!"

Maxime had uttered that cry with all his might, and the human livestock, turning away from the ransacked palace, galloped toward the Pagoda of Tortures.

The torturers had fled; the populace rushed, toppled the enclosures raised on the site of the burned buildings and opened the cages. But all the condemned had suffered frightful tortures, and very few were able to follow their liberators.

Some, with efforts that drew cries of anguish from them, tried in vain to stand on their disarticulated feet. Many dragged themselves on her hands, crawling like larvae in the fetid mud; a few, extenuated by hunger, expired in shock. Bones pierced flesh, gangrene burst out everywhere in livid pustules; an insupportable charnel-house odor caused even the bravest to recoil.

The pharang finally found Kali-Yana, whose swollen eyelids were still closed in spite of the agitation in the alleyways. Backed up against the bars of her jail, she seemed to be asleep, and it was in vain that the young man pronounced her name several times. However, as her breast was rising slightly, he carried her away on his shoulders, laid her down in the grass on the river bank, and washed her wounds. The caress of the cold water appeared to reanimate her; a more profound sigh inflated her bosom and, recognizing Maxime, she raised her arms toward him.

"You've come! You've come! I thought I'd never see you again!"

"We won't be separated again, little Adored!"

She shivered. "Oh, dear lover, let's go away! Take me to your beautiful country; people must be so happy there!"

"I'll take you away."

"Right away."

She tried to get up, and fell back on her lover's heart.

"Tomorrow," he said, "we'll go; today, you're too weak."

"It's really true, then—you still want me? You swear to me?"

"I swear to you."

"Here, you see, men are too wicked. You've been subject to the malefic contagion yourself, and you've made me suffer greatly! I too have been criminal . . . oh, it's horrible!"

"Be quiet; all is forgiven."

"It's over, then—we'll love one another until death?"

"Until death."

In a voice softer than the murmur of the wind in the rushes, she made a thousand plans for the future, convinced that there was, somewhere in the world, a city of bounty and justice where they would live happily. And in the phantasmagoria of her amorous desire, she imagined the house in which they would live, out there, in the marvelous city of pale people, the cares with which she would surround him, being, simultaneously, a slave, a friend and a lover. Oh, he would not regret anything, and he would be proud of her, for she would adorn her beauty in order to charm him forever . . .

Maxime allowed her to soothe herself with that soft speech, and he held the body of his mistress tenderly, whose mouth was babbling at the height of his kiss.

For a long time she remained in that ecstasy, her gaze distant, filled with magical visions, her little hands around her friend's neck; then, suddenly, her pupils revulsed and her lips turned blue on a final word of amour.

In a boat full of roses and tuberoses, in the darkness of the night, the pharang took away the little corpse in order to bury it in a nest of verdure that he alone knew, not wanting that charming body to be abandoned to the vultures.

A PARTIAL LIST OF SNUGGLY BOOKS

G. ALBERT AURIER *Elsewhere and Other Stories*
S. HENRY BERTHOUD *Misanthropic Tales*
LÉON BLOY *The Tarantulas' Parlor and Other Unkind Tales*
ÉLÉMIR BOURGES *The Twilight of the Gods*
JAMES CHAMPAGNE *Harlem Smoke*
FÉLICIEN CHAMPSAUR *The Latin Orgy*
FÉLICIEN CHAMPSAUR *The Emerald Princess and Other Decadent Fantasies*
BRENDAN CONNELL *Clark*
BRENDAN CONNELL *Unofficial History of Pi Wei*
RAFAELA CONTRERAS *The Turquoise Ring and Other Stories*
ADOLFO COUVE *When I Think of My Missing Head*
QUENTIN S. CRISP *Aiaigasa*
QUENTIN S. CRISP *Graves*
QUENTIN S. CRISP *Rule Dementia!*
LADY DILKE *The Outcast Spirit and Other Stories*
CATHERINE DOUSTEYSSIER-KHOZE *The Beauty of the Death Cap*
BERIT ELLINGSEN *Now We Can See the Moon*
BERIT ELLINGSEN *Vessel and Solsvart*
ENRIQUE GÓMEZ CARRILLO *Sentimental Stories*
EDMOND AND JULES DE GONCOURT *Manette Salomon*
REMY DE GOURMONT *From a Faraway Land*
GUIDO GOZZANO *Alcina and Other Stories*
RHYS HUGHES *Cloud Farming in Wales*
J.-K. HUYSMANS *Knapsacks*
COLIN INSOLE *Valerie and Other Stories*
JUSTIN ISIS *Pleasant Tales II*
JUSTIN ISIS AND DANIEL CORRICK (editors)
    Drowning in Beauty: The Neo-Decadent Anthology
VICTOR JOLY *The Unknown Collaborator and Other Legendary Tales*
BERNARD LAZARE *The Mirror of Legends*
BERNARD LAZARE *The Torch-Bearers*
MAURICE LEVEL *The Shadow*
JEAN LORRAIN *Errant Vice*
JEAN LORRAIN *Masks in the Tapestry*
JEAN LORRAIN *Nightmares of an Ether-Drinker*
JEAN LORRAIN *The Soul-Drinker and Other Decadent Fantasies*

ARTHUR MACHEN *N*

ARTHUR MACHEN *Ornaments in Jade*

CAMILLE MAUCLAIR *The Frail Soul and Other Stories*

CATULLE MENDÈS *Bluebirds*

CATULLE MENDÈS *For Reading in the Bath*

ÉPHRAÏM MIKHAËL *Halyartes and Other Poems in Prose*

LUIS DE MIRANDA *Who Killed the Poet?*

OCTAVE MIRBEAU *The Death of Balzac*

TERESA WILMS MONTT *In the Stillness of Marble*

CHARLES MORICE *Babels, Balloons and Innocent Eyes*

DAMIAN MURPHY *Daughters of Apostasy*

DAMIAN MURPHY *The Star of Gnosia*

KRISTINE ONG MUSLIM *Butterfly Dream*

PHILOTHÉE O'NEDDY *The Enchanted Ring*

YARROW PAISLEY *Mendicant City*

URSULA PFLUG *Down From*

ADOLPHE RETTÉ *Misty Thule*

JEAN RICHEPIN *The Bull-Man and the Grasshopper*

DAVID RIX *A Suite in Four Windows*

FREDERICK ROLFE (Baron Corvo) *Amico di Sandro*

FREDERICK ROLFE (Baron Corvo)
   An Ossuary of the North Lagoon and Other Stories

JASON ROLFE *An Archive of Human Nonsense*

BRIAN STABLEFORD (editor)
   Decadence and Symbolism: A Showcase Anthology

BRIAN STABLEFORD *The Insubstantial Pageant*

BRIAN STABLEFORD *Spirits of the Vasty Deep*

COUNT ERIC STENBOCK *Studies of Death*

COUNT ERIC STENBOCK *Myrtle, Rue and Cypress*

MONTAGUE SUMMERS *Six Ghost Stories*

DOUGLAS THOMPSON *The Fallen West*

TOADHOUSE *Gone Fishing with Samy Rosenstock*

JANE DE LA VAUDÈRE *The Demi-Sexes and The Androgynes*

JANE DE LA VAUDÈRE *The Double Star and Other Occult Fantasies*

AUGUSTE VILLIERS DE L'ISLE-ADAM *Isis*

RENÉE VIVIEN *Lilith's Legacy*

RENÉE VIVIEN *A Woman Appeared to Me*

KAREL VAN DE WOESTIJNE *The Dying Peasant*

www.ingramcontent.com/pod-product-compliance
Lightning Source LLC
Chambersburg PA
CBHW031645100726
47898CB00006B/1980